Welcome to thi[...] [...]
Presents! You'll [...] [...] feel by our
gorgeous heroes and their seductive ways.

First of all, be sure not to miss out on the next
installment of THE ROYAL HOUSE OF NIROLI,
Bought by the Billionaire Prince by Carol Marinelli.
Ruthless rogue and rebel Luca Fierezza knows a scandal
will end his chance to be king, but he can't stay away
from supposed thief Megan Donovan. Sandra Marton's
glamorous trilogy THE BILLIONAIRES' BRIDES also
continues this month with *The Greek Prince's
Chosen Wife.* Prince Damian Aristedes is shocked
when he discovers Ivy is pregnant with his baby—
and now he's not going to let her go. Next we have
two sexy Italians to get your hearts pumping! In
Blackmailed into the Italian's Bed by Miranda Lee,
Gino Bortelli is back, and determined to have Jordan
in his bed once again. In Kim Lawrence's *Claiming His
Pregnant Wife,* Erin's marriage to Francesco quickly fell
apart but she'll never be free of him—she's pregnant
with his child! Meanwhile, in Carole Mortimer's
The Billionaire's Marriage Bargain, Kenzie Masters
is in a fix and needs the help of her estranged
husband, Dominick—but it will come at a price....
In *The Brazilian Boss's Innocent Mistress* by
Sarah Morgan, innocent Grace has to decide whether
to settle her debts in Rafael Cordeiro's bed! And in
The Rich Man's Bride by Catherine George, wealthy
Ryder Wyndham is determined that career-minded Anna
be his lady-of-the-manor bride! Finally, in *Bedded at His
Convenience* by Margaret Mayo, Keisha believes Hunter
has a strictly business offer, but soon discovers he has
other ideas.... Happy reading!

BILLIONAIRES' BRIDES
Pregnant by their princes...
by Sandra Marton

Take three incredibly wealthy European
princes and match them with three beautiful,
spirited women. Add large helpings of intense
emotion and passionate attraction. Result: three
unexpected pregnancies—and three possible
princesses, if those princes have their way.

THE ITALIAN PRINCE'S PREGNANT BRIDE
Available in August

THE GREEK PRINCE'S CHOSEN WIFE
Available in September

THE SPANISH PRINCE'S VIRGIN BRIDE
Available in October

Sandra Marton

THE GREEK PRINCE'S CHOSEN WIFE

BILLI🌸NAIRES' BRIDES
Pregnant by their princes...

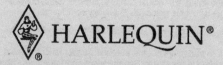

HARLEQUIN®

TORONTO • NEW YORK • LONDON
AMSTERDAM • PARIS • SYDNEY • HAMBURG
STOCKHOLM • ATHENS • TOKYO • MILAN • MADRID
PRAGUE • WARSAW • BUDAPEST • AUCKLAND

ISBN-13: 978-0-373-12660-6
ISBN-10:   0-373-12660-3

THE GREEK PRINCE'S CHOSEN WIFE

First North American Publication 2007.

www.eHarlequin.com

Printed in U.S.A.

All about the author...
Sandra Marton

SANDRA MARTON wrote her first novel while she was still in elementary school. Her doting parents told her she'd be a writer someday and Sandra believed them. In high school and college, she wrote dark poetry nobody but her boyfriend understood, though looking back, she suspects he was just being kind. As a wife and mother, she wrote murky short stories in what little spare time she could manage, but not even her boyfriend-turned-husband could pretend to understand those. Sandra tried her hand at other things, among them teaching and serving on the board of education in her hometown, but the dream of becoming a writer was always in her heart.

At last Sandra realized she wanted to write books about what all women hope to find: love with that one special man, love that's rich with fire and passion, love that lasts forever. She wrote a novel, her very first, and sold it to the Harlequin Presents Line. Since then, she's written more than sixty books, all of them featuring sexy, gorgeous, larger-than-life heroes. A four-time RITA® Award finalist, she's also received five *Romantic Times BOOKreviews* awards for Best Harlequin Presents of the Year, and has been honored with a *Romantic Times BOOKreviews* Career Achievement Award for Series Romance.

Sandra lives with her very own sexy, gorgeous, larger-than-life hero in a sun-filled house on a quiet country lane in the northeastern United States.

My special thanks to Nadia-Anastasia Fahmi
for her generous help with Greek idioms.
Any errors are, of course, entirely mine!

Sandra

CHAPTER ONE

DAMIAN was getting out of a taxi the first time he saw her.

He was in a black mood, something he'd grown accustomed to the last three months, a mood so dark he'd stopped noticing anything that even hinted at beauty.

But a man would have to be dead not to notice this woman.

Stunning, was his first thought. What he could see of her, anyway. Black wraparound sunglasses covered much of her face but her mouth was lusciously full with enough sexual promise to make a monk think of quitting the cloister.

Her hair was long. Silky-looking. A dichromatic mix of chestnut and gold that fell over her shoulders in a careless tumble.

And she was tall. Five-nine, five-ten with a model's bearing. A model's way of wearing her clothes, too, so that the expensive butterscotch leather blazer, slim-cut black trousers and high-heeled black boots made her look like she'd stepped straight out of the pages of *Vogue*.

A few short months ago, he'd have done more than

look. He'd have walked up to her, smiled, asked if she, too, were lunching at Portofino's…

But not today.

Not for the foreseeable future, he thought, his mouth thinning.

No matter what she looked like behind those dark glasses, he wasn't interested.

He swung away, handed the taxi driver a couple of bills. A driver behind his cab bleated his horn; Damian shot a look at the car, edged past it, stepped onto the curb…

And saw that the woman had taken off her sunglasses. She was looking straight at him, her gaze focused and steady.

She wasn't stunning.

She was spectacular.

Her face was a perfect oval, her cheekbones sharp as blades, her nose straight and aristocratic. Her eyes were incredible. Wide-set. Deep green. Heavily lashed.

And then there was that mouth. The things that mouth might do…

Hell!

Damian turned hard so quickly he couldn't believe it but then, he'd gone three months without a woman.

It was the longest he'd gone without sex since he'd been introduced to its mysteries the Christmas he was sixteen, when one of his father's many mistresses had seduced him.

The difference was that he'd been a boy then.

He was a man now. A man with cold hatred in his heart and no wish for a woman in his life, not yet, not even one **this** beautiful, this desirable…

"Hey, dude, this is New York! You think you own the sidewalk?"

Damian swung around, ready and eager for a fight, saw the speaker…and felt his tension drain away.

"Reyes," he said, smiling.

Lucas Reyes smiled in return. "In the flesh."

Damian's smile became a grin. He held out his hand, said, "Oh, what the hell," and pulled his old friend into a bear hug.

"It's good to see you."

"The same here." Lucas pulled back, his smile tilting. "Ready for lunch?"

"Aren't I always ready for a meal at Portofino's?"

"Yeah. Sure. I just—I meant…" Lucas cleared his throat. "You okay?"

"I'm fine."

"You should have called. By the time I read about the, ah, the accident…"

Damian stiffened. "Forget it."

"That was one hell of a thing, man. To lose your fiancée…"

"I said, forget it."

"I didn't know her, but—"

"Lucas. I don't want to talk about it."

"If that's how you want it—"

"It's exactly how I want it," Damian said, with such cold surety that Lucas knew enough to back off.

"Okay," he said, forcing a smile. "In that case… I told Antonio to give us the back booth."

Damian forced a smile of his own. "Fine. Maybe they'll even have *Trippa alla Savoiarda* on the menu today."

Lucas shuddered. "What's the problem, Aristedes? Pasta's not good enough for you?"

"Tripe's delicious," Damian said and just that easily,

they fell into the banter that comes with old friendships.

"Just like old times," Lucas said.

Nothing would ever be like old times again, Damian thought, but he grinned, too, and let it go at that.

The back booth was as comfortable as ever and the tripe was on the menu. Damian didn't order it; he never had. Tripe made him shudder the same as Lucas.

The teasing was just part of their relationship.

Still, after they'd ordered, after his double vodka on the rocks and Lucas's whiskey, straight up, had arrived, he and Lucas both fell silent.

"So," Lucas finally said, "what's new?"

Damian shrugged. "Nothing much. How about you?"

"Oh, you know. I was in Tahiti last week, checking out a property on the beach…"

"A tough life," Damian said, and smiled.

"Yeah, well, somebody has to do it."

More silence. Lucas cleared his throat.

"I saw Nicolo and Aimee over the weekend. At that dinner party. Everyone was sorry you didn't come."

"How are they?" Damian said, deliberately ignoring the comment.

"Great. The baby's great, too."

Silence again. Lucas took a sip of his whiskey.

"Nicolo said he'd tried to call you but—"

"Yes. I got his messages."

"I tried, too. For weeks. I'm glad you finally picked up the phone yesterday."

"Right," Damian said as if he meant it, but he didn't. Ten minutes in and he already regretted taking Lucas's call and agreeing to meet him.

At least mistakes like this one could be remedied, he thought, and glanced at his watch.

"The only thing is," he said, "something's come up. I'm not sure I can stay for lunch. I'll try, but—"

"Bull."

Damian looked up. "What?"

"You heard me, Aristedes. I said, 'bull.' Nothing's come up. You just want a way to get out of what's coming."

"And that would be…?"

"A question."

"Ask it, then."

"Why didn't you tell Nicolo or me when it happened? Why let us hear about it through those damned scandal sheets?"

"That's two questions," Damian said evenly.

"Yeah, well, here's a third. Why didn't you lean on us? There wasn't a damned reason for you to go through all of that alone."

"All of what?"

"Give me a break, Damian. You know all of what. Hell, man, losing the woman you love…"

"You make it sound as if I misplaced her," Damian said, his voice flat and cold.

"You know I didn't mean it that way. It's just that Nicolo and I talked about it and—"

"Is that all you and Barbieri have to keep you busy? Gossip like a pair of old women?"

He saw Lucas's eyes narrow. Why wouldn't they? Damian knew he was tossing Lucas's concern in his teeth but to hell with that. The last thing he wanted was sympathy.

"We care about you," Lucas said quietly. "We just want to help."

Damian gave a mirthless laugh. He saw Lucas blink and he leaned toward him across the table.

"Help me through my sorrow, you mean?"

"Yes, damn it. Why not?"

"The only way you could help me," Damian said, very softly, "would be by bringing Kay back."

"I know. I understand. I—"

"No," he said coldly, "you do not know. You do not understand. I don't want her back to ease my sorrow, Lucas."

"Then, what—"

"I want her back so I can tell her I know exactly what she was. That she was a—"

The men fell silent as the waiter appeared with Damian's second double vodka. He put it down and looked at Lucas, who took less than a second to nod in assent.

"Another whiskey," he said. "Make it a double."

They waited until the drink had been served. Then Lucas leaned forward.

"Look," he said softly, "I know you're bitter. Who wouldn't be? Your fiancée, pregnant. A drunk driver, a narrow road…" He lifted his glass, took a long swallow. "It's got to be rough. I mean, I didn't know Kay, but—"

"That's the second time you said that. And you're right, you didn't know her."

"Well, you fell in love, proposed to her in a hurry. And—"

"Love had nothing to do with it."

Lucas stared at him. "No?"

Damian stared back. Maybe it was the vodka. Maybe it was the way his old friend was looking at him. Maybe it was the sudden, unbidden memory of the woman outside the restaurant, how there'd been a time he'd have wanted her and not despised himself for it.

Who knew the reason? All he was sure of was that he was tired of keeping the truth buried inside.

"I didn't propose. She moved in with me, here in New York."

"Yeah, well—"

"She was pregnant," Damian said flatly. "Then she lost the baby. Or so she said."

"What do you mean?"

"She'd never been pregnant." Damian's jaw tightened. "The baby was a lie."

Lucas's face paled. "Hell, man. She scammed you!"

If there'd been one touch of pity in those words, Damian would have gotten to his feet and walked out. But there wasn't. All he heard in Lucas's voice was shock, indignation and a welcome hint of anger.

Suddenly the muted sounds of voices and laughter, the delicate clink of glasses and cutlery were almost painfully obtrusive. Damian stood, dropped several bills on the table and looked at Lucas.

"I bought a condo. It's just a few blocks from here."

Lucas was on his feet before Damian finished speaking.

"Let's go."

And right then, right there, for the first time since it had all started, Damian began to think he'd be okay.

A couple of hours later, the men sat facing each other in the living room of Damian's fifteen-room duplex. Vodka and whiskey had given way to a pot of strong black coffee.

The view through three surrounding walls of glass was magnificent but neither man paid it any attention. The only view that mattered was the one Damian was providing into the soul of a scheming woman.

"So," Lucas said quietly, "you'd been with her for some time."

Damian nodded. "Whenever I was in New York."

"And then you tried to break things off."

"Yes. She was beautiful. Sexy as hell. But the longer I knew her… I suppose it sounds crazy but it was as if she'd been wearing a mask and now she was letting it slip."

"That's not crazy at all," Lucas said grimly. "There are women out there who'll do anything to land a man with money."

"She began to show a side I hadn't seen before. She cared only for possessions, treated people as if they were dirt. Cabbies, waitresses…" Damian drank some of his coffee. "I wanted out."

"Who wouldn't?"

"I thought about just not calling her anymore, but I knew that would be wrong. Telling her things were over seemed the decent thing to do. So I called, asked her to dinner." His face turned grim and he rose to his feet, walked to one of the glass walls and stared out over the city. "I got one sentence out and she began to cry. And she told me she was pregnant with my baby."

"You believed her?"

Damian swung around and looked at Lucas. "She'd been my mistress for a couple of months, Lucas. You'd have done the same."

Lucas sighed and got to his feet. "You're right." He paused. "So, what did you do?"

"I said I'd support her and the baby. *She* said if I really cared about the baby in her womb, I would ask her to move in with me."

"Dear God, man—"

"Yes. I know. But she was carrying my child. At least, that's what I believed."

Lucas sighed again. "Of course."

"It was a nightmare," Damian said, shuddering. "I guess she thought it was safe to drop the last of her act. She treated my staff like slaves, ran up a six figure charge at Tiffany…" His jaw knotted. "I didn't want anything to do with her."

"No sex?" Lucas asked bluntly.

"None. I couldn't imagine why I'd slept with her in the first place. She thought I'd lost interest because she was pregnant." He grimaced. "She began talking about how different things would be, if she weren't…" Damian started toward the table that held the coffee service. Halfway there, he muttered something in Greek, veered past it and went instead to a teak cabinet on the wall. "What are you drinking?"

"Whatever you're pouring."

The answer brought a semblance of a smile to Damian's lips. He poured healthy amounts of Courvoisier into a pair of crystal brandy snifters and held one out. The men drank. Then Damian spoke again.

"A couple of weeks later, she told me she'd miscarried. I felt—I don't know what I felt. Upset, at the loss of the baby. I mean, by then I'd come to think of it as a baby, you know? Not a collection of cells." He shook his head. "Once I got past that, what I felt, to be honest, was relief. Now we could end the relationship."

"Except, she didn't want to end it."

Damian gave a bitter laugh. "You're smarter than I was. She became hysterical. She said I'd made promises, begged her to spend her life with me."

"But you hadn't."

"Damned right, I hadn't. The only thing that had drawn us together was the baby. Right?"

"Right," Lucas said, although he was starting to realize he didn't have to say anything. The flood gates had opened.

"She seemed to plummet into depression. Stayed in bed all day. Wouldn't eat. Went to her obstetrician—at least she said she'd gone to her obstetrician—and told me he'd advised her to get pregnant again."

"But—"

"Exactly. I didn't want a child, not with her. I wanted out." Damian took another swallow of brandy. "She begged me to reconsider. She'd come into my room in the middle of the night—"

"You had separate rooms?"

A cold light flared in Damian's eyes. "From the start."

"Sure, sure. Sorry. You were saying—"

"She was good at what she did. I have to give her that. Most nights, I turned her away but once…" A muscle knotted in his jaw. "I'm not proud of it."

"Man, don't beat yourself up. If she seduced you—"

"I used a condom. It made her crazy. 'I want your baby,' she said. "And then—"

Damian fell silent. Lucas leaned forward. "And then?"

"And then," Damian said, after a deep breath and a

long exhalation, "then she told me she'd conceived. That her doctor had confirmed it."

"But the condom—"

"It broke, she said, when she—when she took it off me—" He cleared his throat. "Hell, why would I question it? The damned things do break. We all know that."

"So—so she was pregnant again."

"No," Damian said flatly. "She wasn't pregnant. Oh, she went through all the motions. Morning sickness, ice cream and pickles in the middle of the night. But she wasn't pregnant." His voice roughened. "She never had been. Not then, not ever."

"Damian. You can't be sure of—"

"She wanted my name. My money." Damian gave a choked laugh. "Even my title, the 'Prince' thing you and I both know is nothing but outdated crap. She wanted everything." He drew a deep breath, then blew it out. "And she lied about carrying my child to get it."

"When did you find out?"

"When she died," Damian said flatly. He drained his glass and refilled it. "I was in Athens on business. I phoned her every night to see how the pregnancy was going. Later, I found out she'd taken a lover and she'd been with him all the time I was gone."

"Hell," Lucas said softly.

"They were on Long Island. A narrow, twisting road on the Sound along the North Shore. He was driving, both of them high on booze and cocaine. The car went over a guardrail. Neither of them survived." Damian looked up from his glass, his eyes bleak. "You talked about grief before, Lucas. Well, I *did* grieve then, not for her but for my unborn child…until I was going through Kay's papers, tying up loose ends, and found an article she'd clipped from some magazine, all about the symptoms of pregnancy."

"That still doesn't mean—"

"I went to see her doctor. He confirmed it. She had never been pregnant. Not the first time. Not the second. It was all a fraud."

The two friends sat in silence while the sun dipped below the horizon. Finally Lucas cleared his throat.

"I wish I could think of something clever to say."

Damian smiled. "You got me to talk. You can't imagine how much good that's done. I'd been keeping everything bottled inside."

"I have an idea. That club of mine. Remember? I'm meeting there with someone interested in buying me out."

"So soon?"

"You know how it is in New York. Today's hotspot is tomorrow's trash." Lucas glanced at his watch. "Come downtown with me, have a drink while I talk a little business and then we'll go out." He grinned. "Dinner at that place on Spring Street. A pair of bachelors on the town, like the old days."

"Thank you, my friend, but I wouldn't be very good company tonight."

"Of course you would. And we won't be alone for long." Another quick grin. "Before you know it, there'll be a couple of beautiful women hovering over us."

"I've sworn off women for a while."

"I can understand that but—"

"It's what I need to do right now."

"You sure?"

Inexplicably an image of the woman with green eyes

and sun-streaked hair flashed before Damian's eyes. He hadn't wanted to notice her, certainly didn't want to remember her…

"Yes," he said briskly, "I'm positive."

"You know what they say about getting back on the horse that threw you," Lucas said with a little smile.

"I told Nicolo almost the same thing a year ago, the night he met Aimee."

"And?"

"And," Damian said, "it was good advice for him, but not for me. This is different."

Lucas's smile faded. "You're right. Well, let me just call this guy I'm supposed to meet—"

"No, don't do that. I'd like to be alone tonight. Just do a little thinking, start putting this thing behind me."

Lucas cocked his head. "It's no big deal, Damian. I can meet him tomorrow."

"I appreciate it but, honestly, I feel a lot better now that we talked." Damian held out his hand. "Go have your meeting. And, Lucas— Thank you."

"*Para nada,*" Lucas said, smiling. "I'll call you tomorrow, yes? Maybe we can have dinner together."

"I wish I could but I'm flying back to Minos in the morning." Damian gripped Lucas's shoulder. "Take care of yourself, *filos mou.*"

"You do the same." Lucas frowned. Damian looked better than he had a few hours ago but there was still a haunted look in his eyes. "I wish you'd change your mind about tonight. Forget what I said about women. We could go to the gym. Lift some weights. Run the track."

"You really think it would make me feel better to beat you again?"

"You beat me once, a thousand years ago at Yale."

"A triviality."

The men chuckled. Damian slung his arm around Lucas's neck as they walked slowly to the door. "Don't worry about me, Reyes. I'm going to take a long shower, pour myself another brandy and then, thanks to you, I'm going to have the first real night's sleep I've had in months."

The friends shook hands. Then Damian closed the door after Lucas, leaned back against it and let his smile slip away.

He'd told Lucas the truth. He did feel better. For three months, ever since Kay's death, he'd avoided his friends, his acquaintances; he'd dedicated every waking minute to business in hopes he could rid himself of his anger.

What was the point in being angry at a dead woman?

Or in being angry at himself, for having let her scam him?

"No point," Damian muttered as he climbed the stairs to his bedroom. "No point at all."

Kay had made a fool of him. So what? Men survived worse. And if, in the deepest recesses of his soul he somehow mourned the loss of a child that had never existed, a child he'd never known he even wanted, well, that could be dealt with, too.

He was thirty-one years old. Maybe it was time to settle down. Marry. Have a family.

Thee mou, was he insane?

You couldn't marry, have kids without a wife. And there wasn't a way in hell he was going to take a wife anytime soon. What he needed was just the opposite of settling down.

Lucas had it right.

The best cure for what ailed him would be losing himself in a woman. A soft, willing body. An eager mouth. A woman without a hidden agenda, without any plans beyond pleasure...

There it was. That same image again. The green-eyed woman with the sun-streaked hair. Hell, what a chance he'd missed! She'd looked right at him and even then, trapped in a black mood, he'd known what that look meant.

The lady had been interested.

The flat truth was, women generally were.

He'd been interested, too—or he would have been, if he hadn't been so damned busy wallowing in self-pity. Because, hell, that's what this was. Anger, sure, but with a healthy dollop of Poor Me mixed in.

He'd had enough of it to last a lifetime.

He'd call Lucas. Tell him his plans for the night sounded good after all. Dinner, drinks, a couple of beautiful women and so what if they didn't have green eyes, sun-streaked hair...

The doorbell rang.

Damian's brows lifted. A private elevator was the sole access to his apartment. Nobody could enter it without the doorman's approval and that approval had to come straight from Damian himself.

Unless...

He grinned. "Lucas," he said, as he went quickly down the stairs. His friend had reached the lobby, turned around and come right back.

Damian reached the double doors. "Reyes," he said happily as he flung them open, "when did you take up mind-reading? I was just going to call you—"

But it wasn't Lucas in the marble foyer.

It was the woman. The one he'd seen outside Portofino's.

The green-eyed beauty he hadn't been able to get out of his head.

CHAPTER TWO

OH, WHAT a joy to see!

Damian Aristedes's handsome jaw dropped halfway to the ground. Seeing that was the first really good thing that had happened to Ivy in a while.

Obviously his highness wasn't accustomed to having his life disrupted by unwanted surprises.

Damian's unflappable, Kay had said.

Well, okay. She hadn't said it exactly that way. Nobody can get to him, was probably more accurate.

Not true, Ivy thought. Just look at the man now.

"Who are you? What are you doing here?"

She didn't answer. The pleasure of catching him off guard was wearing off. She'd prepared for this moment but the reality was terrifying. Her heart was hammering so hard she was half afraid he could hear it.

"You were outside Portofino's today."

He was gaining control of himself. His voice had taken on authority; his pale gray eyes had narrowed.

"Are you a reporter for one of those damned tabloids? I don't give interviews."

He really didn't know who she was. She'd wondered about that, whether Kay had ever shown him a photo or pointed out her picture in a magazine, but she'd pretty much squelched that possibility at the restaurant, where she'd followed him from his Fifty-Seventh Street office.

He'd looked at her, but only the way most men looked at her. With interest, avarice—the kind of hunger she despised, the kind that said she was a plaything and they wanted a new toy.

Although, when this man had looked at her today, just for a second, surely no more than that, she'd felt— she'd felt—

What?

She'd seemed to lose her equilibrium. She was glad someone had joined him because she knew better than to confront him with another person around.

This discussion had to be private.

As for that loss of equilibrium or whatever it was, it only proved how dangerous Damian Aristedes was.

That he'd been able to mesmerize Kay was easy to understand. Kay had always been a fool for men.

That he'd had an effect on Ivy, even for a heartbeat, only convinced her she'd figured him right.

The prince of all he surveyed was a sleek jungle cat, constantly on the prowl. A beautiful predator. Too bad he had no soul, no heart, no—

"Are you deaf, woman? Who are you? What do you want? And how in hell did you get up here?"

He'd taken a couple of steps forward, just enough to invade her space. No question it was a subtle form of intimidation. It might have worked, too—despite her height, he was big enough so that she had to tilt her head back to meet his eyes—but Ivy was not a stranger to intimidation.

Growing up, she'd been bullied by experts. It could only hurt if you gave in to it.

"Three questions," she said briskly. "Did you want them answered in order, or am I free to pick and choose?"

He moved quickly, grasped her wrist and forced her arm behind her back. It hurt; his grip was strong, his hands hard. She hadn't expected a show of physical strength from a pampered aristocrat but she didn't flinch.

"Take your hand off me."

"It'll take me one second to phone for the police and tell them there's an intruder in my home. Is that what you want?"

"You're the one who won't want the police involved in this, Your Highness."

His gray eyes focused on hers. "Because?"

Now, Ivy thought, and took a steadying breath.

"My name is Ivy."

Nothing. Not even a flicker of interest.

"Ivy Madison," she added, as if that would make the difference.

He didn't even blink. He was either a damned good actor or— A tingle of alarm danced over her skin.

"You are—you are Damian Aristedes?"

He smiled thinly. "A little late to ask but yes, that's who I am."

"Then—then surely, you recognize my name…"

"I do not."

"I'm Kay's sister. Her stepsister."

That got a reaction. His eyes turned cold. He let go of her wrist, or maybe it made more sense to say he dropped it. She half expected him to wipe his hand on his trousers. Instead he stepped back.

"Here to pay a condolence call three months late?"

"I'd have thought you'd have been the one to call me."

He laughed, although the sound he made had no mirth to it.

"Now, why in hell would I do that? For starters, I never knew Kay had a sister." He paused. "That is, if you really are her sister."

"What are you talking about? Certainly I'm her sister. And, of course you know about me."

The woman who claimed to be Kay's sister spoke with authority. Not that Damian believed she really was who she claimed to be.

At the very least she was up to no good. Why approach him this way instead of phoning or e-mailing? What the hell was going on here?

Only one way to find out, Damian thought, and reached for his cell phone, lying on the marble-topped table beside the door.

"What are you doing?"

"Calling your bluff. You won't answer my questions? Fine. You can tell your story to the cops."

"You'd better think twice before you pick up that phone, Mr. Aristedes."

His intruder had started out full of conviction, like a poker player sure of a winning hand, but that had changed. Her voice had gone from strong to shaken; those green eyes—so green he wondered if she were wearing contact lenses—had gone wide.

A scam, he thought coldly. She was trying to set him up for something. The only question was, what?

"Prince," he said, surprising himself with the use of his title. Generally he asked people to call him by his first or last name, not by his honorific, but if it took royal arrogance to shake his intruder's self-control, he'd use it. "It's Prince Damian. And I'll give you one second to start talking. How did you get up here?"

"You mean, how did I bypass the lobby stormtroopers?"

She was trying to regain control. Damned if he'd let it happen. Damian put down the phone, angled toward her and invaded her space again so that she not only stepped back, she stepped into the corner.

No way out, except past him.

"Don't play with me, lady. I want straight answers."

She caught a bit of her lower lip between her teeth, worried it for a second before releasing it and quickly touching the tip of her tongue to the flesh she'd gnawed.

Damian's belly clenched. Lucas had it right. He'd been too long without a woman.

"A delivery boy at the service entrance held the door for me." She smiled thinly. "He was very courteous. Then I used the fire stairs."

"If you're Kay's sister, why didn't you simply ask the doorman to announce you?"

"I waited all this time to hear from you but nothing happened. Telling your doorman I wanted to see you didn't strike me as useful."

"Let me see some ID."

"What?"

"Identification. Something that says you're who you claim to be."

"I don't know why Kay loved you," Ivy said bitterly.

Damian decided it was the better part of valor not to answer that. Instead he watched in silence as she dug through the bag slung over one shoulder, took out a wallet and opened it.

"Here. My driver's license. Satisfied?"

Not satisfied, just more puzzled. The license said she was Ivy Madison, age twenty-seven, with an address in Chelsea. And the photo checked out. It was the woman standing before him. Not even the bored Motor Vehicle clerks and their soulless machines had been able to snap a picture that dimmed her looks.

Damian looked up.

"This doesn't make you Kay's sister."

Without a word, she dug into her purse again, took out a business-card size folder and flipped it open. The photo inside was obviously years old but there was no mistaking the faces of the two women looking at the camera.

"All right. What if you are Kay's sister. Why are you here?"

Ivy stared at him. "You can't be serious!"

He was…and then, with breathtaking speed, things started to fall into place.

The sisters didn't resemble each other, but that didn't mean the apple had fallen far from the tree.

"Let me save you some time," Damian said coolly. "Your sister didn't leave any money."

Those bright green eyes flashed with defiance. "I'm not here for money."

"There's no jewelry, either. No spoils of war. I donated everything I'd given her to charity."

"I don't care about that, either."

"Really?" He folded his arms. "You mean, I haven't ruined your hopes for a big score?"

Her eyes filled with tears.

Indeed, Damian thought grimly, that was exactly what he'd done.

"You—you egotistical, self-aggrandizing, aristocratic pig," she hissed, her voice shaking. "You haven't spoiled anything except for yourself. And believe me, Prince or Mr. or whatever name you want, you'll never, ever know what you missed!"

It was an emotional little speech and he could see she was determined to end it on a high note by shoving past him and striding to the door.

There was every reason to let her go.

If she was willing to give up so easily and disappear from his life as quickly as she'd entered it, who was he to stop her?

Logic told him to move aside.

To hell with logic.

Damian shifted his weight to keep her trapped in the corner. She called him another name, not nearly as creative as the last, put her arms out straight and tried to push him away.

He laughed, caught both her wrists and trapped her hands against the hard wall of his chest. Anger and defiance stained her cheeks with crimson.

"Damn it, let go!"

"Why, sweetheart," he purred, "I don't understand. How come you're so eager to leave when you were so eager to see me?"

She kicked him in the shin with one of her high heeled boots. It hurt, but he'd be damned if he let her know that. Instead he dragged her closer until she was pressed against him.

He told himself it was only to keep her from gouging his shin to the bone.

And that there was no reason, either, for the hot fist of lust that knotted in his groin as he looked down into her flushed face.

Her eyes were wild. Her hair was a torrent of spun gold. Her lips were trembling. Trembling, and full, and delicately parted, and all at once, all at once, Damian understood why she was here.

What a thickheaded idiot he was!

Kay had obviously told Ivy about him. That he had money, a title, an eye for beautiful women.

And now Kay was gone but Ivy—Ivy was very much alive.

Incredibly alive.

His gaze dropped to her mouth again. "What a fool you must think me," he said softly. "Of course I know why you're here."

Her eyes lit. Her mouth curved in a smile. "Thank God," she said shakily. "For a while there, I thought—"

Damian silenced her in midsentence. He thrust his hands into her hair, lifted her face to his and kissed her.

She cried out against his mouth. Slammed her fists against his chest. A nice touch, he thought with a coldness that belied his rising libido. She'd come to audition as her sister's replacement. Well, he'd give her a tryout, all right. Kiss her, show her she had no effect on him and then send her packing.

Except, it wasn't happening that way.

Maybe he really had been without a woman for too long.

Maybe his emotions were out of control.

Sex, desire—neither asks for reason, only satiation and completion. He wanted this. The heat building inside him like a flash-fire in dry brush. The deep, hungry kiss.

The woman struggling for freedom in his arms.

She was pretending. He knew that. It was all part of the act. He nipped at her bottom lip; she gave a little cry and he slid his tongue into her mouth, tasted her sweetness, caught the little sound she made and kissed her again and again until she whimpered, lifted herself to him, flattened her hands against his chest...

Thee mou!

Damian jerked away. The woman stumbled back. Her eyes flew open, the pupils so enormous they'd all but consumed the green of her irises.

What the hell was he doing? She was just like Kay. A siren, luring a man with sex—

Her hand flew through the air and slammed against his jaw.

"You bastard," she said in a hoarse whisper. "You evil, horrible son of a bitch!"

"Don't bother with the theatrics," he snarled. "Or I'll call you some names of my own."

"I don't understand why Kay loved you!"

"Your sister never loved anything that didn't have a price tag on it. Now, go on. Get the hell out before I change my mind and call the police."

"She loved you enough to let you talk her into having this baby!"

Damian had swung away. Now he turned around and faced Ivy Madison.

"What are you talking about?"

"You know damned well what I'm talking about! She lost the first baby and instead of offering her any comfort and compassion, you told her to get out because she couldn't give you an heir."

Could a woman's lies actually leave a man speechless? Damian opened his mouth, then shut it again while he tried to make sense of what Ivy Madison had just said.

"You would have tossed away the woman who loved

you, who adored you, just because she couldn't give you
a child. So my sister said she'd give you a baby, no
matter what it took, even after the doctors said she
couldn't run the risk of pregnancy!"

"Wait a minute. Just wait one damned minute—"

Ivy stared at him, emerald eyes bright against the
pallor of her skin.

"You used her love for you to try to get your own
way and you didn't care what it did to her, what
happened to her—"

Damian was on her in two strides, hands gripping her
shoulders, fingers biting into her flesh, lifting her to her
toes so that their faces were inches apart.

"Get out," he said in a low, dangerous voice. "Do you
hear me? Get out of my home and my life or I'll have
you arrested. And if you think you'll walk away after a
couple of hours in jail, think again. My attorneys will see
to it that you stay in prison for the next hundred years."

It was an empty threat. What could he charge her
with besides being a world-class liar? He knew that.
What counted was that she didn't.

But it didn't stop her.

"Kay was in love with you."

"I just told you what Kay loved. You have five
seconds, Miss Madison. One. Two—"

"She found a way to have your child. You were
happy to go along with it but now, you refuse to acknowledge that—"

"Goodbye, Miss Madison."

Damian spun Ivy toward the door. He put his hand
in the small of her back, gave her a little push and she
stumbled toward the elevator.

"I'm going to call down to the lobby. If the doorman

doesn't see you stepping out of this car in the next couple of minutes, the cops will be waiting."

"You can't do this!"

"Just watch me."

The elevator door opened. Damian curled his fingers around her elbow and quick-marched her inside.

Tears were streaming down her face.

She was as good at crying on demand as Kay had been, he thought dispassionately, though Kay had never quite mastered the art. Her face would get red, her skin blotchy but despite all that, her nose never ran.

Ivy's eyes were cloudy with tears. Her skin was the color of cream. And her nose—damn it, her nose was leaking.

A nice touch of authenticity, Damian told himself as he stepped from the car and the door began to close.

"I was a fool to come here."

Damian grabbed the door. Her words were slurred. Another nice touch, he thought, and offered a wicked smile.

"Didn't work out quite the way you'd planned it, did it?"

"I should have known. All these months, no call from you…"

"I'm every bit the son of a bitch you imagined I'd be," he said, smiling again.

"I tried to tell Kay it was a bad idea, but she wouldn't listen."

"I'll bet. Two con artists discussing how to handle a sucker. Must have been one hell of a conversation."

She brushed the back of her hand over her eyes but, more credit to her acting skills, the tears kept coming.

"Just be sure of one thing, Prince Aristedes."

"It's Prince Damian," he said coolly. "If you're going to try to work royalty, you should use the proper form of address."

"Don't think you can change your mind after the baby's born."

"I wouldn't dream of…" He jerked back. "What baby?"

"Because I won't let you near this child. I don't give a damn how many lawyers you turn loose on me!"

Damian stared at her. He'd let go of the elevator door and it was starting to close again. He moved fast and forced it open.

"What baby?" he demanded.

"You know damned well what baby! Mine. I mean, Kay's." Ivy's chin lifted. "Kay's—and yours."

The earth gave a sickening tilt under his feet. There was a baby? No. There couldn't be. Kay had never really been pregnant. Her doctor had told him so…

"You're a vicious little liar!"

"Fine. Stay with that idea. I told you, I won't let my baby—Kay's baby—near a son of a bitch like—"

She let out a shriek as he dragged her from the elevator, marched her into his apartment and all but threw her into a chair.

"What the hell are you talking about?" He stood over her, feet apart, arms folded, eyes blazing with anger. "Start talking, and it better be the truth."

She began sobbing. He didn't give a damn.

"I'm waiting," he growled. "What baby are you talking about? Whose is it? And where?"

Ivy sprang to her feet. "Get out of my way."

He grabbed her again, hauled her to her toes.

"Answer me, goddamn it!"

Ivy looked up at him while the seconds seemed to turn to hours. Then she wrenched free of his hands.

This baby," she said, laying a hand over her belly. "The one in my womb. I'm pregnant, Prince Damian. Pregnant—with your child."

CHAPTER THREE

PREGNANT?

Pregnant, with his child?

Damian's brain reeled.

Thee mou, a man didn't want to hear that accusation from a woman he didn't love once in a lifetime, let alone twice...

And then his sanity returned.

This woman, Ivy, might well be pregnant but it didn't have a damned thing to do with him. Not unless science had come up with a way a man could have sex with a woman without ever seeing her or touching her.

She was looking at him, defiance stamped in every feature. What was she waiting for? Was he supposed to blink, fall down, clap his hand to his forehead?

The only thing he felt like doing was tossing her over his shoulder and throwing her out. But first—but first—

Damian snorted. Snorted again and then, to hell with it, burst out laughing.

Ivy Madison gave him a killing look.

"How can you laugh at this?" she demanded.

That only made him laugh harder.

He'd heard some really creative tall tales in his life. His father had been especially adept at telling them as he took his company to the edge of ruin but nothing, *nothing* topped this one.

It was funny.

It was infuriating.

Did she take him for a complete fool? Her sister had. Yes, but at least he'd had sex with the sister. There'd been a basis—shaky, but a basis—for Kay claiming she was pregnant.

Hell, the hours the two women must have spent talking about what a sucker he was, how easily he could be taken in by a beautiful face.

"Perhaps you'd like to share what's so damned amusing, Prince Damian?"

Amusing? Damian's laughter faded. "Actually," he said, "I'm insulted."

She blinked. "Insulted?"

"That you'd come up with such a pathetic lie." He tucked his hands in his trouser pockets and sighed dramatically. "You have to have sex with a man before he can impregnate you, Miss Madison, and you and I…"

Suddenly he knew where this was heading. He'd heard of scams like it before.

A beautiful woman chooses a man who's rich. Well-known. A man whose name would garner space in the tabloids.

When the time is right, she confronts him, tells him they met at a party, on a yacht—there were dozens of places they could have stumbled across each other.

That established, she drops the bomb.

She's pregnant. He's responsible. When he says *That's impossible, I never saw you before in my life,* she starts to cry. He was drinking that night, she says. He seduced her, she says. Doesn't he remember?

Because she does.

Every touch. Every sigh. Every nuance of their encounter is seared in her memory, and if he doesn't want it all over the scandal sheets, he'll Do The Right Thing.

He'll give her a fat sum of money to help her. Nothing like a bribe, of course. Just money to get her through a bad time.

Some men would give in without much of a fight, even if they could disprove the story. They'd do whatever it took just to avoid publicity.

Damian's jaw tightened.

Oh, yes. That was how this was supposed to go down... Except, it wouldn't. His beautiful scam artist was about to learn she couldn't draw him into that kind of trap.

He'd already been the victim of one Madison sister. He'd be damned if he'd be the victim of the second sister, too.

Damian looked up. The woman had not moved. She stood her ground, shoulders squared, head up, eyes glittering with defiance.

God, she was magnificent! Anyone walking in and seeing her would be sure she was a brave Amazon, overmatched but prepared to fight to her last breath.

Too bad there wasn't an audience. There was only him, and he wasn't buying the act.

Damian smiled. Slowly he brought his hands together in mocking applause.

"Excellent," he said softly. "An outstanding performance." His smile disappeared. "Just one problem, *kardia mou*. I'm on to you."

"What?"

"You heard me. I know your game. And I'm not going to play it."

"Game? Is that what you think this is? I come to you after my sister's death because you didn't have enough concern to come to me and you think—you think it's a game?"

"Perhaps I used the wrong word. It's more like a melodrama. You're the innocent little flower, I'm the cruel villain."

"I don't know what you're talking about!"

Damian started slowly toward her. He saw her stiffen. She wanted to back away or maybe even turn and run. Good, he thought coldly. She was afraid of him, and she damned well ought to be.

"Don't you want to tell me the rest? The details of our passionate encounter?"

She looked at him as if he were crazy. "What passionate encounter?"

"Come now, darling. Have you forgotten your lines? You're supposed to remind me of what we did when I was drunk." He stopped inches from her, a chill smile curling across his lips. "Well, I'm waiting. Where did it happen? Here? Athens? A party on my yacht at the Côte d'Azur? Not that it matters. The story's the same no matter where we met."

"I didn't say—"

"No. You didn't, and that's my fault. I never gave you the chance to tell your heartbreaking little tale, but why waste time when it's so trite? I was drunk. I seduced you. Now, it's—it's— How many months later, did you say?"

"Three months. You know that, just as you know the rest of what you said isn't true!"

"Did I get the facts wrong?" His eyes narrowed; his voice turned hard. "Frankly I don't give a damn. All I care about is seeing the last of you, lady. You understand?"

Ivy understood, all right.

This man her sister had worshipped, this—this Adonis whose face and body were enough to quicken the beat of a woman's heart...

This man Kay had been willing to do anything for, was looking at her and lying through his teeth.

How could Kay have loved him?

"Shall I be more direct, Miss Madison?" Damian clamped his hands on her shoulders. "Get out of here before I lose my temper."

His voice was low, his grasp painful. He was furious and, Ivy was sure, capable of violence.

That wasn't half as important as being certain she understood exactly what he was telling her.

He didn't want the child she was carrying.

She'd figured as much, when she hadn't heard from him after the accident. She'd waited and waited, caught up first in shock at losing Kay, then in growing awareness of her own desperation until, finally, she'd realized the prince's silence was a message.

Still, it wasn't enough.

He had to put his denial of his rights to his child in writing. She needed a document that said he didn't want the baby, that he'd rather believe her story was a lie than acknowledge he'd fathered a child.

Even that was no guarantee.

Damian Aristedes was powerful. He could hire all the lawyers in Manhattan and have money left over. He could not only make his own rules, he could change them when he had to.

But if she had something on paper, something that might give her a legal edge if he ever changed his mind—

"I can almost see you thinking, Miss Madison."

Ivy blinked. The prince was standing with his arms folded over his chest, narrowed eyes locked on her face.

It was disconcerting.

She was accustomed to having men look at her. It went with the territory.

When you had done hundreds of photo shoots, when your own face looked back at you from magazine covers, you expected it. It was part of the price you paid for success in the world of modeling.

Men noticed you. They looked at you.

But not like this.

The expression on Damian Aristedes's face spoke of contempt, not desire. How dare he be disdainful of her? She'd made a devil's bargain—she knew that, had known it almost from the beginning—but she'd been prepared to stand by that bargain even if it tore out her heart.

Not him.

He was the man who'd started this. Now, he was pretending he didn't know what she was talking about.

That was fine. It was perfect. It meant she'd kept her promise and now she was free to put the past behind her and concentrate on the future. On the child she'd soon have.

Her child, not his.

It was just infuriating to have him look at her as if she were a liar and a cheat.

Except, there'd been a moment, more than one, when she'd caught him watching her in a different way, his eyes glinting not with disdain but with hunger.

Hunger only she could ease.

And when that had happened, she'd felt—she'd felt—

"You're as transparent as glass, Miss Madison."

Years of letting the camera steal her face but never her thoughts kept Ivy from showing any reaction.

"How interesting. Do you read minds when you're not busy evading responsibility, Your Highness?"

"You're trying to come up with a way to capitalize on that moment of shock I showed when you told me I was your baby's father." He smiled thinly. "Trust me. You can't."

He was partly right. She was trying to come up with a way to capitalize on something, but not that.

Ivy took a steadying breath.

"I'll be happy to leave, happier still never to see you again, Prince Damian. But first—"

"Ah. But first, you want a check for... How much? A hundred thousand? Five hundred thousand? A million? Don't shake your head, Miss Madison. We both know you have a price in mind."

Another steadying breath. "Not a check."

"Cash, then. It doesn't matter."

The icy little smile slipped from his lips and she repressed a shudder. The prince would be a formidable enemy.

"I don't want money. I want a letter. A document that makes it clear you're giving up all rights to the child in my womb."

He laughed. Laughed, damn him!

"*Thee mou,* lady. Don't you know when to quit?"

"Sign it, date it and I'll be out of your life forever."

His laughter stopped with the speed of a faucet

turning off. "Enough," he said through his teeth. "Get out of my home before I do something we'll both regret."

"Just a letter," she said. "A few lines—"

He said something in what she assumed was Greek. She didn't understand the words but she didn't have to as he gripped her by the shoulders, spun her around, put a hand in the small of her back and shoved her forward.

"And if you're foolish enough to tell your ridiculous story to anyone—"

The thing to do was hire a lawyer. Except, he'd hire a dozen for every one she could afford. He had power. Money. Status. Still, there had to be a way. There had to be!

"And if you really are knocked up, if some man was stupid enough to let your face blind him to the scheming bitch you really are—"

Ivy spun around, swung her fist and caught him in the jaw. He was big and strong and hard as nails but she caught him off guard. He blinked and staggered back. It took him all of a second to recover but it was enough to send a warm rush of pleasure through her blood.

"You—you pompous ass," she hissed. She marched forward, index finger aimed at his chest, and jabbed it right into the center of his starched white shirt, her fear gone, everything forgotten but his impossible arrogance. "This isn't about you and who you are and how much money you have. It isn't about you at all! I don't want anything from you, Prince Damian. I never—"

She gasped as he caught her by the elbows and lifted her to her toes.

"You don't want anything from me, huh?" Damian's lips drew back from his teeth as he bent his head toward hers. "That's why you came here? Because you don't want anything from me?"

"I came because I thought I owed it to you but I was wrong. I don't. And I warn you, letter or no letter, if you should change your mind a month from now, a decade from now, and try and claim my baby—"

"Damn you," he roared, "there is no baby!"

"Whatever you say."

"The truth at last!"

"Truth?" Ivy laughed in his face. "You wouldn't know it if it bit you in the tail!"

"I know that I never took you to bed."

"Let go!"

"How come you didn't factor that into your little scheme?" Damian yanked her wrist, dragged it behind her back. She flinched but she'd sooner have eaten nails than let him know he was hurting her. "You made several mistakes, Miss Madison. One, I don't drink to excess. Two, I never forget a woman I've been with." His gaze swept over her with slow deliberation before returning to her face. "Believe me, lady, if I'd had you, I'd remember."

"I'm done talking about that."

"But I'm not." He drew her closer, until they were a breath apart. "Why should I be? You said we were intimate. I said we weren't. Why not settle the question?"

"It isn't worth settling. And I never said we'd been intimate."

His lips drew back from his teeth. "Ah, Ivy, Ivy, you disappoint me. Backing down already?" His smile vanished; his eyes turned cold. "Come on, *glyka mou*. Here's your chance. Convince me we slept together. Remind me of what it was like."

"Stop it. Stop it! I'm warning you, let me—"

She gasped as Damian slipped one hand lightly around her throat.

"A woman can only taunt a man for so long before he retaliates. Surely someone with your skills should have learned that by now."

"You're wrong! You know the truth, that we never—"

Damian kissed her.

Her mouth was cool and soft, and she made a little sound of terrified protest.

That was how she made it sound, anyway.

It was all part of the act. Part of a performance. Part of who she was and why she was here and...

And she tasted sweet, sweeter than the first time he'd kissed her, maybe because he knew the shape of her mouth now. The fullness of it.

The sexy silkiness.

She cried out again, jammed her hand against his chest and Damian told himself it was time to let go of her.

He'd accomplished what he wanted, met her challenge, showed her that she had no power over him...

His arousal was swift. He put one hand at the base of her spine and pressed hard enough so she had no choice but to tilt her hips against his and feel it.

God, he was on fire.

Another little sound whispered from her mouth to his and then, same as before, he felt the change in her. Her mouth softened. Warmed. The stiffness went out of her body and she leaned toward him.

He reminded himself that nothing she did was real. It was all part of her overall plan.

And it didn't matter.

He knew only that he wanted this. The taste of her.

The feel of her. He was entitled to that. Hell, he'd been accused of something he had not done.

Why not do it now?

Lift Ivy into his arms. Carry her up the stairs to his bedroom. Take everything she wanted him to believe he'd taken before, again and again and again…

"Please," she whispered, "please—"

Her voice was soft. Dazed. It made him want her even more.

Deliberately he slid his hand inside her jacket and cupped the delicate weight of one breast.

"Please, what?" he growled. "Touch you? Take you?"

His fingers swept over her breast, blood thundering in his ears when he felt the thrust of her nipple through the silk that covered it. She moaned against his mouth.

A wave of lust rolled through him, shocking him with its intensity.

She moaned again and he gathered her closer. Slid his hands under the waistband of her black jeans. Felt the coolness of her buttocks, the silk of her flesh.

Primal desire flooded his senses. He wanted her, no matter what she was. And she wanted him. Wanted him. Wanted him…

Panagia mou! Damian flung her from him and stepped back. Tears were streaming down her face. If he hadn't known better, he'd have honestly thought she was weeping.

"I can't believe Kay loved you, that she wanted to give you a child!"

"Your story's getting old. And confused. You're the one who's pregnant. Who I took to bed, remember?"

"That's not true! Why do you keep saying it? You know we didn't go to bed!"

"Right," he said, his voice cold with contempt and sarcasm. "I keep forgetting that. We didn't. We did it standing up. Or sitting in a chair. Or on a sofa—"

"There was no chair. No sofa. You know that. There was just—just your sperm. A syringe. And—and me."

"Yeah. Sure. You, my sperm, a syringe..." Damian jerked back. "What?"

"You damned well know what! And you didn't even have the—the decency to let Kay be artificially inseminated by a physician. Oh, no. You wanted to protect your precious privacy! So you—you used a—a condom to—to—" Her voice turned bitter. "I knew what you were when you didn't ask to meet me in advance. When you didn't care enough to come with Kay the day she— the day I—the day it took place."

Damian wanted to say something but he couldn't. He felt as if his head were in a vise.

Her story was fantastic. Far more interesting than the usual *He made me pregnant* tale.

And the media loved fantasy.

They'd fall on this like hyenas on a wounded antelope. By the time a different scandal knocked the story off the front pages, the damage would have been done. To his name, to Aristedes Shipping, the company he'd spent his adult life rebuilding.

"Nothing to say, Your Highness?" Ivy put her hands on her hips and eyed him with derision. "Or have you finally figured out that denial will only take you so far?"

Tossing this woman out on her backside was no longer a viable option. She was too clever for such easy dismissal.

"You're right about that," he said calmly. "Denial only goes so far and then it's time to take appropriate action." He closed the distance between them, relishing the way she stumbled back. "You will take a pregnancy test. Then, if you're really pregnant, a paternity test."

Ivy stared at him. She couldn't think of a reason he'd want her to take such tests... Unless he was telling the truth. Unless he really hadn't known about the baby.

And if he hadn't... What would happen once he did?

"I don't want to take any tests," she said quickly. "You said you didn't want the baby. That's fine. You only have to give me a document—"

"No, *glyka mou*. It is you who will provide *me* with a document that legally establishes that you and I and a syringe never met, except inside your scheming little brain."

"But—"

Damian took her arm, marched her to the elevator and pushed her inside it. Seconds later, the doors slid shut in her face.

CHAPTER FOUR

IT TROUBLED her all the way back to her apartment.

If Kay's lover had known about the baby, if he'd orchestrated it as Kay claimed, why would the details of the baby's conception have shaken him?

And he had been shaken.

He'd recovered fast but not fast enough to hide his initial shock.

And why would he want these tests? Unless, Ivy thought as she unlocked the door to her apartment, unless he'd just been getting rid of her...

But the light on her telephone was blinking. A man identifying himself as the prince's attorney had left a message on her voice mail.

She was to be at one of the city's most prestigious hospitals at eight the next morning.

Someone would meet her in the reception area.

Ivy sank into a chair. The day had finally caught up to her. She was worn-out and close to tears, wondering why she'd ever thought that seeking out Damian Aristedes was the right thing to do...

But she'd done it.

Now, she could only put one foot ahead of the other and see where this path led.

* * *

A tall, dark-haired man, his back to her, was standing in the main lobby of the hospital when she arrived there the next day.

Her heart leaped. Was it Damian?

The man turned. He was balding and he wore glasses. It wasn't the prince. Of course not. Why would she want him here? And why would he be here when he hadn't shown up with Kay for the procedure he'd demanded?

The procedure that had taken a drastic turn at the last minute.

The memory struck hard. Ivy wrapped her arms around herself. She should never have agreed to it.

Or to this.

This was another mistake.

But it was too late to run. The tall man had seen her. He came toward her, her name a question on his lips. From the look on his face, he was as uncomfortable with this whole thing as she was.

He introduced himself. He was, he said, holding out his hand, the prince's attorney, here to offer whatever assistance she might require.

"You mean," Ivy said, deliberately ignoring his out-stretched hand, "you're here to make sure I don't try to phony-up the test results."

He had the good grace not to try to contradict her as he escorted her to a small office where a briskly efficient technician took over.

"Come with me, please, Miss Madison. The gentle-man can wait outside."

"Oh, he's not a gentleman," Ivy said politely. "He's a lawyer."

Even the attorney laughed.

Then Ivy blanked her mind to everything but what had to be done.

The results, they said, would take up to two weeks.

She said that was fine, though two centuries would have been more to her liking.

They told her to take it easy for a couple of days and she did, even though it gave her more time to think than she wanted.

Day three, she organized the drawers and closets of her apartment. They didn't need it: she'd always been neat, something you learned quickly when you spent part of your growing-up years in foster care, but straightening things was a good way to kill time.

Day four, her agent called with a job. The cover of *La Belle* magazine. It was a plum but Ivy turned it down. She was tired all the time, her back ached and besides, she'd never much liked modeling. But she needed the money. She'd given most of what she'd saved to Kay.

Kay, who had come to her in tears.

She lived, she'd said, with Damian Aristedes. Ivy had heard of him before. You couldn't read *People* or *Vanity Fair* without seeing his name. The magazines said he was incredibly good-looking and incredibly wealthy. Kay said yes, he was both, but he was tight with a dollar and he'd refused to pay the money she still owed on her condo even though he demanded she not work.

He wanted her available to him at all times.

Ivy had given her the money. It was an enormous amount, but how could she have said no? She owed Kay so much... Money could never begin to repay that debt.

A few weeks later, Kay came to her again and

confided the rest of her story. How she'd miscarried. How Damian now demanded proof she could give him an heir before he'd marry her.

Ivy thought the man sounded like a brute but Kay adored him. She'd wept, talked about how much she wanted his baby, how much she wished she could give him such a gift.

She'd reminded Ivy of the years they'd shared as teenagers, of memories Ivy was still doing her best to forget.

"Do you remember how desperate you were then?" Kay had said through her tears. "That's how desperate I am now! Please, please, you have to help me."

In the end, Ivy had agreed to something she'd convinced herself was good even if it might prove emotionally difficult, but she'd never expected it to go as far as it had. To turn into something she'd regretted almost immediately, something she wept over night after night—

Something she might well end up fighting in court, and how would she pay those legal fees?

Ivy picked up the phone, called her agent and told him she'd do the *La Belle* cover after all.

It was excellent money and it was a head shot; nobody would see that she was pregnant.

Still, head shot or not, the photographer insisted she be styled right down to her toes. She spent the day in heavy makeup and endless outfits matched by spectacular sky-high Manolos on her feet.

When she finally reached her Chelsea brownstone, it was after five. She was exhausted and headachy, her face felt like a mask under all the expensive makeup she hadn't taken time to remove and her feet…

Her feet were two blobs of pain.

She was still wearing the last pair of Manolos from the final set of photos. Actually she was swollen into them.

"Poor darling," the stylist cooed. "Keep them as a gift."

So she'd limped into a taxi, limped out of it. Now, if she could just get up the three flights of steps to her apartment…

Three flights of steps. They never even made her breathe hard. Now, they loomed ahead like Mount McKinley.

Ivy took a deep breath and started climbing.

She was shaking with fatigue when she finally reached her landing, and wincing at the pain in her feet. She waited a minute, then took out her key and fumbled it into the lock.

Soon. Oh, yes, soon. Off with the shoes. Into the shower, then into a loose T-shirt and an even looser pair of fleece sweatpants. After that, she'd put together a peanut butter and honey sandwich on the kind of soft, yummy white bread that the health gurus hated…

Ivy shut the door behind her, automatically slid home the chain lock, turned around…

And screamed.

A man—dark hair, broad shoulders, long legs, leather jacket and pale blue jeans—was seated in a chair in her living room.

"Easy," he said, rising quickly to his feet, but it was too late. The floor had already rushed up to meet her.

"Thee mou," a voice said gruffly.

Strong arms closed around her.

After that, there was only darkness.

* * *

Damian had never moved faster in his life.

A damned good thing he had, he thought grimly, though the woman he held in his arms was as limp as the proverbial dishrag.

A man might joke about wanting a woman to fall at his feet, but this was surely not the way it should happen.

Especially if the woman was pregnant.

He cursed ripely in his native tongue and shoved that thought aside. He had come here to deal with that fact and he would. Right now, what mattered was that Ivy had passed out cold.

She felt warm and soft in his arms, but her face was frighteningly pale. Her breathing seemed shallow. What was he supposed to do now? Call 9-1-1? Wait until she stirred? Did he search her apartment for spirits of ammonia?

Ivy solved the problem by raising her lashes. She looked at him and he saw confusion in her deep green eyes.

"Damian?"

It was the first time she'd called him that.

"Damian, what—what happened?"

"You fainted, *glyka mou*. My fault. I apologize."

She closed her eyes, then opened them again. This time, the confusion was gone.

Anger had taken its place.

"I remember now. I unlocked the door and—"

"You saw me."

"How did you get in here? I never leave the door unlocked!"

"The super let me in." His mouth twisted. "A story

about being your long-lost brother and a hundred-dollar bill melted his heart."

"You had no right—"

"Unfortunately you don't have a back entrance and a flight of service steps," he said dryly.

"It's hardly the same thing."

"It's exactly the same thing."

Ivy stiffened in his arms. "Please put me down."

"Would you prefer the bedroom or the sofa?"

"I would prefer my feet on the floor."

He almost laughed. She was still pale but there was no mistaking the indignation in her voice.

"You will lie down while I phone for a doctor."

Ivy shook her head. "I don't need a doctor. I fainted, that's all."

She was right. He decided not to argue. They'd have enough to argue over in a little while.

"You're a stubborn woman, Miss Madison."

"Not half as stubborn as you, Your Highness."

Damian carried her to a small, brocade-covered sofa and sat her on it.

"Amazing, how you manage to make 'Your Highness' sound like a four-letter word. No. Do not even try to stand up. I'm going to get a cold compress."

"I told you—"

"And I'm telling you, sit there and behave yourself."

He strode off, found a towel in the kitchen, filled it with ice and returned to the living room, surprised to find she'd heeded his warning.

It was, he thought, a bad sign.

Almost as bad as the feverish color that was replacing the pallor in her skin. He wanted to take her in his arms, hold her close, tell her he was sorry he'd frightened her...

Hell.

"Here," he said brusquely, thrusting the ice-filled towel into her hands.

"I don't need that," she snapped, but she took the towel anyway and pressed it to her wrists.

He took the time to take a long look at her.

She looked worn out. Dark shadows were visible under her eyes despite a layer of heavy makeup. She hadn't worn makeup the other day. Why would she, when her natural beauty was so breathtaking?

His gaze swept over her.

She had on a loose-fitting, heavy sweater. A matching skirt. And, *Thee mou*, what was she doing, wearing those shoes? They were the kind that would normally make his blood pressure rise but that wasn't going to happen when he could see the straps denting her flesh.

Damian looked up. "Your feet are swollen."

"How clever of you to notice."

"Are you so vain you'd wear shoes that hurt?"

"I am not vain—what are you doing?"

"Taking off these ridiculous shoes."

"Stop it!" Ivy tried slapping his hands away as he lifted one of her feet to his lap. "I said—"

"I heard you."

His fingers moved swiftly, undoing straps and tiny jeweled buckles. The shoe fell off. Gently he lowered her leg, then removed the second shoe. When he'd finished, Ivy planted both her bare feet on the floor.

It was all she could do to keep from groaning with relief.

"Better?"

She didn't answer. *Thee mou*, he had never known such an intractable female.

Damian muttered something under his breath and lifted her feet to his lap again.

"Of course they're better," he said, answering his own question. His tone was brusque but his hands were gentle as he massaged her ankles, her toes, her insteps. "Why a woman would put herself through such torture—"

"I just came from a cover shoot. The stylist gave me the shoes as a gift. They do that kind of thing sometimes," she said, wondering why on earth she was explaining herself to this arrogant man.

"And you were so thrilled you decided to wear them home even though they were killing you."

Ivy's eyes narrowed. "Yes," she said coldly, "that's right." She tugged her feet from his hands and sat up. "Now that you've told me what you think of my decisions, try telling me something that matters, like what you're doing here."

A muscle knotted in his jaw. Then he took an envelope from his pocket and tossed it on the coffee table.

Ivy caught her breath.

"Are those the test results?"

He nodded.

"They were supposed to send them to me."

"And to me."

"Well, that's wrong. That's an invasion of privacy. The results of *my* test are *my* business—"

Ivy knew she was babbling. She stopped, reached for the envelope but she couldn't bring herself to touch it. They'd tested for pregnancy. For paternity. For the first time, she realized they could also have tested for maternity…

Her hands began to shake. She sat back.

"Tell me," she said softly.

"You already know." His voice was without intonation, though she sensed a restrained violence in his words. "I am the father of the child in your womb. The child that would have been Kay's."

Ivy swallowed hard. "And the sex?" she whispered.

"It is a boy."

A little sound broke from her throat and she put her hand over her mouth. It was, Damian thought coldly, one hell of an act.

"I tried to tell you I was pregnant. That you were the father. You wouldn't listen."

"I am listening now." Damian sat back and folded his arms. "Tell me again, from the beginning. I want to hear everything."

She did, from the moment Kay proposed the idea until the moment she'd confronted him in his apartment, though there were some parts—all right, one part—she left out.

She didn't dare tell him that. Not yet.

Maybe not ever.

But she went through all the facts, pausing to answer his questions, biting her lip each time he shook his head in disbelief because, in her heart, she still shared that disbelief.

What Kay had asked of her, what she'd agreed to do, was insane.

"Why?" he said, when she'd finished the tale. "Why would Kay ask you to be a— What did you call it?"

"A gestational surrogate. Her egg. Your—your sperm." She knew she was blushing, and wasn't that ridiculous? The procedure Kay had planned, even the one they'd actually ended up doing, was about as intimate as a flu shot. "And I told you why. You wanted a child. She knew she couldn't carry one."

Damian shot to his feet. "Lies! I never said anything about a child. And she didn't know if she could carry one or not."

"You asked me to tell you everything. That's what I'm doing."

She gasped as he hauled her to her feet.

"The hell you are," he snarled. "What did she pay you for your role in this?"

"Pay me?" Ivy laughed. "Not a penny. You kept Kay on a tight allowance."

"Another lie!"

"Even if you hadn't, I'd never have done this for money."

"No," he said grimly. "You did it out of love."

"I know you can't understand something like that but—"

"I understand, all right. You hatched out a plot between you. You'd have a baby Kay didn't want to have, she'd use it to force me into marriage. And when she divorced me, the two of you would split whatever huge settlement a shyster lawyer could bleed out of me."

Ivy jerked free of his hands. "Do you have any idea how much I earn in a day? How much I'll lose by not modeling for the next five or six months? Hell, for the next couple of years?"

"Is that why you took an assignment today?" he said, sneering. "Because you have so much money you don't need any more?"

"That's none of your business!"

"You're wrong," he said coldly. "From now on, everything about you is my business."

"No, it isn't."

"What did I just say? Starting now, everything about you is also about me."

"The hell it is!"

Ivy glared at him. Damian glared back. Her chin was raised. Her eyes were cold. Her hands were knotted on her hips.

She looked like one of the Furies, ready and determined to take on the world.

He wanted to cover the distance between them, grab her and shake her. Or grab her, haul her into his arms and kiss her until she trembled.

He hated the effect she had on him, hated himself for bending to it… And it was time to put all that aside.

He knew what he had to do.

It was time she knew it, too.

"We're getting sidetracked," he said.

"I agree, Your Highness."

That drove him crazy, too. The way she said "Your Highness." He hadn't been joking when he'd told her she made it sound like a four-letter word.

"Under the circumstances," he said brusquely, "I think you should call me Damian."

She got his meaning; he knew because he saw her cheeks flame. Good, he thought grimly. He wanted her a little uncertain. Why should he be the only one who was balancing on a tightrope?

"This is a pointless conversation. Why should it matter what I call you? Once we determine what happens after my—after the baby's born, we don't have to see each other again."

"Is that what you would you like to happen?"

Was he really asking? Ivy could hardly believe it but she was ready with an answer. This was all she'd thought about since the day she'd gone to his apartment.

"I'd like a simple solution," she said carefully, "one that would please us both."

"And that is?"

She could hear her heart pounding. Could he hear it, too?

"You—you've fathered a baby you say you didn't want."

"More correctly, I fathered a baby I didn't know about."

If that was true—and she had to believe it was—it worried her. The way he'd just stated the situation worried her, too. Fathering a baby he didn't want wasn't the same as fathering a baby he hadn't known about.

She wanted to call him on it but that wouldn't help her case, and that was the last thing she wanted to do.

"A baby you didn't know about," she said, trying to sound as if she really believed it. "A baby my sister wanted."

"But?" He smiled thinly. "I could hear the word, even if it was unspoken."

She drew a breath, then let it out. "But, everything's changed. Kay is gone and I—I want this baby. I didn't know I'd feel this way. That I'd love the baby without ever seeing it. That I wouldn't want to give it away or—"

"Very nice," he said coldly. "But please, spare me the performance. How much?"

She looked puzzled. "I just told you. I want the baby with all my heart."

Damian came toward her, shaking his head and

smiling. "You have it wrong. I'm not asking about your heart, I'm asking about your wallet. How much must I pay you to give up this child you carry?"

"This has nothing to do with money."

"You are Kay's sister. Everything has to do with money." His mouth twisted. "How much?"

"I want my baby, Damian! You don't want it. You said so."

"You don't listen, *glyka mou*. I said, I didn't know about the child." Slowly he reached out and slid his hand beneath Ivy's sweater. She grabbed his wrist and tried to move it but it was like trying to move an oak.

His fingers spread over her belly.

"That's my son," he said softly. "In your womb. He carries my genes. My blood."

"And mine," she said quickly.

"You mean, Kay's."

She flushed. "Yes. Of course that's what I mean."

"A baby you meant to give up."

The words hurt her heart.

"Yes," she whispered, so softly he could hardly hear her. "I thought I could. But—but just as you said, this baby is in my womb—"

Damian caught her face in his hands.

"My seed," he said. "Your womb. In other words, our child." His gaze, like a caress, fell to her lips. "Via a syringe, Ivy. Not you in my arms, in my bed, the way it should have been."

"But it wasn't." Was that high, breathless voice really hers? "Besides, that has nothing to do with the facts."

She was right.

But he'd given up trying to be logical. Nothing about

this was logical, he thought, and he bent to her and kissed her.

The kiss was long. Deep. And when she made a soft, sweet sound that could only have been a sigh of desire, Damian took the kiss deeper still. His tongue slipped into her mouth; he tasted her sweetness, God, her innocence...

Except, she wasn't innocent.

She'd entered into an unholy bargain with her sister and he didn't for a minute believe she'd done it as some great humanitarian gesture...

And then he stopped thinking, gathered her tightly in his arms and kissed her again and again until she was gripping his shoulders, until she was parting her lips to his, until she rose to him, pressed against him, sighed into his mouth.

She swayed when he let go of her. Her eyes flew open; she looked as shaken as he felt.

He hated her for it.

For the act, the drama...the effect it had on him.

"So," he said, his tone calm despite the pounding surge of his blood, "we have a dilemma. How do I claim a child that's mine when it's still in your womb?"

"You don't. I just told you, I want—"

"Frankly I don't give a damn what you want. Neither will a judge. You entered into a devil's bargain with your sister. Now you'll pay the price."

Her green eyes went black with fear. At least, it looked like fear. He knew it was greed.

"No court is going to take a child from its mother."

"You're not his mother, *glyka mou*. But I am its father."

"Still—"

"There is no 'still,' Ivy. No if, no but, no maybe. I've spoken with my attorney."

"Your attorney isn't God."

Damian laughed. "Try telling him that." His laughter faded. "Do you have any idea how much I pay him each year?"

"No, and I don't give a damn! Your money doesn't impress me."

"I pay him a million dollars. And that's only a retainer." He reached for her. She stepped back but he caught her with insolent ease and pulled her into his arms again. "He's worth every penny. And I promise, he will take my son from you."

"No." Tears rose in Ivy's eyes. "You can't do this. You wouldn't do this!"

"But I'm not heartless," Damian said softly. "I'm even willing to believe there's some truth to what you say about not wanting to give up my child." He bent his head to hers; she tried to twist her face away but he slid his hands into her hair and held her fast. "So I've decided to make you an offer." He smiled. "An offer, as they say, you cannot refuse."

The world, the room, everything seemed to stop.

"What?" Ivy whispered.

Damian took her mouth with his. Kissed her as she struggled. As she wept. As she tried to break free until, at last, she went still in his arms and let the kiss happen.

It wasn't what he wanted, damn it.

He wanted her to kiss him back, as she had before. To melt against him, to moan, to show him that she wanted him, wanted him…

Even if it was a lie.

He drew back. She stood motionless.

"I return to Greece tomorrow."

"You can return to Hades for all I care. I want to know what you're offering me."

What he'd come up with was surprisingly simple. He'd worked it out late last night, on the impossible chance her story about her pregnancy turned out to be true.

This morning, after the test results had proved that it was, he'd run the idea past his attorney who'd said yes, okay, with just a couple of touch-ups, it would work.

Ivy would put herself into the hands of a physician of his choosing. She would stop working—he would support her through the pregnancy. He'd move her into a place nearer his condo. And when she gave birth, he would give her a one time payment of ten million dollars and she would give him his son.

He'd even permit her to visit the child four times a year, if she was really as emotionally committed to him as she made it seem.

More than generous, his attorney had agreed.

"Damn you," Ivy demanded, "what offer?"

Damian cleared his throat. "Ten million dollars on the birth of my child."

She laughed. Damn her, she laughed!

"Until then, I will move you to a place of my choosing. And, of course, I will support you."

Another peal of laughter burst from her throat. He could feel every muscle in his body tensing.

"You find this amusing?"

"I find it amazing! Do you really think you can buy my baby? That you can take over my life?"

"The child is not yours. You seem to keep forgetting

that. As for your so-called life…" His eyes darkened. "Your sister had a life, too, one that was inappropriate."

"And you are a candidate for sainthood?"

Damian could feel his control slipping. Who was she, this woman who thought she could defy him? Who had entered into a conspiracy that would change his life?

"I know who I am," he said coldly. "More to the point, I know who you are." His eyes flickered over her in dismissal. "You are a woman who agreed to bear a child for money."

"I'm tired of defending myself, tired of explaining, tired of being bullied." Ivy's voice trembled with emotion. "I don't want your money or your support, and I'm certainly not moving to an apartment where you can keep me prisoner!"

She kept talking. He stopped listening. All he could see was her face, tearstained and determined.

Did she think he was a complete fool? That this show of rebelliousness would convince him to up the ante?

"I am not some—some meek little lamb," she said, "eager to do your bidding." She folded her arms and glared at him. "Do you understand, Your Highness? My answer to your offer is no!"

She gasped as he captured her face in his hands.

"It wasn't an offer," he growled. "It is what you will do—but I'm changing the terms. Forget the apartment near mine. I am taking you to Greece with me."

She stared at him as if he'd lost his mind. He hadn't. He'd simply begun to see things more clearly.

He was in New York once a month at best. What would she be doing while he was away? He had the right to know.

She slung an obscenity at him that almost made him laugh, coming as it did from that perfect mouth.

"I will not go anywhere with you. There are laws—"

"What laws?" His mouth thinned. "I am Prince Damian Aristedes. Do you think your laws have any meaning to me?"

Ivy couldn't speak. There was no word to describe what she felt for this man. Hatred didn't even come close—but he was a prince. He could trace his lineage back through the centuries. She was nobody. She could trace her lineage back to a foster home where—where—

No. She wasn't going there.

Damian's hands tightened. He raised her face until their eyes met.

"Do you understand what I've told you? Or are you going to be foolish enough to try to fight me?"

"I despise you!"

"Ah, *glyka mou,* you're breaking my heart."

"You're a monster. I can't stand having you touch me."

"A decision, Ivy. And quickly."

Tears spilled down her face. "You know my decision! You haven't left me a choice."

Damian felt a swell of triumph but it was poisoned by the hatred in Ivy's eyes. With a growl of rage, he captured her mouth, kissing her without mercy, without tenderness, nipping her bottom lip when she refused the thrust of his tongue.

"A reminder," he said coldly. "Until my son is born, you belong to me."

Even in his anger, he knew a good line when he heard it.

He turned around and walked out.

CHAPTER FIVE

DAMIAN went down the stairs with fury clouding his eyes, went out the door to the street the same way.

His driver had brought him to Ivy's apartment. The Mercedes was at the curb and Damian started toward it. Charles must have been watching for him; he sprang from behind the wheel, rushed around to the rear door and swung it open.

Charles had only been with him a couple of months but surely Damian had told him he was capable of opening a car door himself a hundred times.

A thousand times, he thought, as his temper super-heated.

Then he saw the way Charles was looking at him.

"My apologies, Your Highness. I keep forgetting. It's just that you are the first employer I've had who doesn't want me getting out to open or close the door. I promise, it won't—"

"No, that's all right," Damian said. "Don't worry about it." He paused beside the car. He had a meeting later in the day. There was just time for him to go to his office and do some work.

But work wasn't what he needed right now. What he needed was a drink.

"I won't be needing the car," he said briskly, and slapped the top of the Mercedes.

"Very well, sir. I'll wait until you—"

"I won't need the car at all." He forced a smile. After all, none of this was his driver's fault. "Take it back to the garage and call it a day."

Charles looked surprised but he was too well-trained to ask questions. A good thing, Damian thought as he walked away, because he sure as hell didn't have any answers. Not logical ones, anyway.

Logic had nothing to do with the mess he was in.

At the corner, he took out his cell phone, called his assistant and told her to cancel his appointment. Then he called Lucas.

"Are you busy?"

He tried to make the question sound casual but his old friend's response told him he hadn't succeeded.

"What's wrong?" Lucas said sharply.

"Nothing. Why should anything be…" Damian cleared his throat. "I don't want to discuss it over the phone, but if you're busy—"

"I am not busy," Lucas said.

A lie, Damian was certain, but one he readily accepted.

Forty minutes later, the two men were pounding along the running track at the Eastside Club. At this hour of the day, they pretty much had the place to themselves.

Despite the privacy, they hadn't exchanged more than a dozen words. Damian knew Lucas was giving him the chance to start the conversation but he'd been content just to work up a sweat, first with the weights, then on the track.

There was nothing like a hard workout for getting rid of anger.

He'd learned that in the days when he'd been rebuilding Aristedes Shipping. There'd been times back then he'd deliberately gone from a meeting with the money men who held his destiny in their greedy hands to unloading cargo from a barge on the Aristedes docks.

Right now, he thought grimly, right now, he could use a ton of cargo.

"Damian."

More than that. Two tons of—

"Damian! Man, what're we doing? Working out, or trying for heart attacks?"

Damian blinked, slowed, looked around and saw Lucas standing in the middle of the track, head bent, hands on his thighs, dripping with sweat and panting.

And, *Thee mou,* so was he. How many miles had they run? How fast? Neither of them got like this doing their usual six-minute mile.

He stepped off the track, grabbed a couple of towels from a cart and tossed one to Lucas.

"Sorry, man."

"You should be," Lucas said, rubbing his face with the towel. He grinned. "Actually I didn't think an old man like you could move that fast."

Damian grinned back at him. "I'm two months older than you are, Reyes."

"Every day counts when you're pushing thirty-two."

Damian smiled. He draped the towel around his shoulders and he and Lucas strolled toward the locker room.

"Thank you," he said, after a minute.

Lucas shot his friend a look, thought about pretending he didn't know what he meant and decided honesty was the best policy.

"Para nada," he said softly. "The way you sounded,

I'd have canceled a meeting with the president." He pushed open the locker room door, then followed Damian inside. "You want to tell me what's going on?"

Damian hesitated. "Let's shower, change and stop for a drink."

"Here?"

He laughed at the horror in Lucas's voice. The Eastside Club had a bar. A juice bar.

"No. Not here. I'm old but not that old."

Lucas grinned. "I'm relieved to hear it. How about that place a couple of blocks over? The one with the mahogany booths?"

"Sounds good."

It was good.

The bar was dark, the way bars should be. The booths were deep and comfortable. The bartender was efficient and the Gray Goose on the rocks both men ordered was crisp and cold.

They were mostly quiet at first, Lucas talking about some land he was thinking of adding to his enormous ranch in Spain, Damian listening, nodding every now and then, saying "yes" and "really" when it seemed appropriate.

Then they fell silent.

Lucas finally cleared his throat. "So," he said quietly, "you okay?"

"I'm fine."

"Because, you know, you didn't sound—"

"Kay's sister turned up."

Lucas lifted his eyebrows. "I didn't know she had a—"

"Neither did I."

"Well. Her sister, huh? What's she want?"

"I think they were actually stepsisters. That's what Ivy—"

"The sister."

"Yes. That's what she said."

"Same mother?"

"Same father. I think. Same last name, anyway. Maybe he adopted one of them…" Damian huffed out a breath. "It doesn't matter."

"What does?"

"The rest of what this woman—Ivy—told me."

Damian lifted his glass and took a long swallow of vodka. Lucas waited a while before he spoke again.

"You want to explain what that means?"

"The rest?" Damian shrugged. He took another mouthful of vodka. Took a handful of cashews from the dish on the table. Looked around the room, then at Lucas. "The rest is that she's pregnant with my child."

If Lucas's jaw dropped any further, Damian figured it would have hit the table.

"Excuse me?"

"Yeah." Damian gave a choked laugh. "Impossible, right?"

Lucas snorted. "How about, insane?"

"I told her that. And—"

"And?"

"And, you're right. *I'm* right. It's impossible. Insane. There's just one problem." Damian took a deep breath and expelled it as his eyes met Lucas's. "She's telling the truth."

Damian explained everything.

Then, at Lucas's request, he explained it all over

again, starting with Ivy's unexpected visit to his apartment and finishing with his impossible dilemma.

Lucas listened, made an occasional comment in Spanish. Damian didn't always understand the words but he didn't have to.

The other man's reaction was just what his had been.

Finally Damian fell silent. Lucas started to speak, took a drink of vodka instead, then cleared his throat.

"I don't understand. Your mistress convinced Ivy to have a baby for her but didn't tell you about it. What was she going to do when the child was born? Bundle him up, carry him through the door and say, 'Damian, this is our son'?"

Damian nodded. "I don't get it, either, but Kay wasn't big on logic. For all I know, she never got that far in laying out her plan."

"And Ivy…" Lucas's eyes narrowed. "What sort of woman is she?"

A beautiful woman, Damian thought, tall and lithe as a tigress with eyes as green as new spring grass, hair shot with gold…

"She's attractive."

"I didn't mean that. What I'm asking is, what kind of woman would agree to be part of a scheme like that?"

Damian lifted his glass to his lips. "Another excellent question."

"A model, you say. So she must be good-looking."

"You could say that."

"A model's body is her bread and butter. Why would she put herself through a pregnancy?"

"I don't—"

"I do. For money, Damian. You're worth a fortune. She wants to tap into that."

"I offered her ten million dollars to have the baby and give up all rights to it. She said no."

"Ten million," Lucas said impatiently. "That's a fraction of what you're worth and I'd bet you anything the lady researched your worth to the nearest penny." He lifted his glass, found it empty and signaled for another round. "She's good-looking, and she's smart."

"So?"

"So, my friend, if she's smart, good-looking and devious as the devil, give some thought to the entire idea having been hers in the first place."

"No. It was Kay."

"Think about it, Damian. She knew your lover could not carry a child and so she planted this idea in your lover's head—"

"Don't keep calling Kay my lover," Damian said, more sharply than he'd intended. "I mean, technically, she was. But the fact is, we had an affair. A brief one. I was going to end it but she lied and said she was—"

"Yes. I know." Lucas paused until the barman had delivered their fresh drinks. Then he leaned over the table. "Ivy observed it all. She watched you do the right thing when her sister pretended to be pregnant." He sat back, looking grimly certain of his next words. "Absolutely, the more I think about it, the more certain I am that this plan was her idea."

"Ivy's?"

"*Si.* Who else am I talking about? She saw the way to get her hands on a lot of money. She would carry a child. You would not know about it but once it was born, you would once again do the right thing. You would accept it into your life, and you would pay her anything she asked. Billions, not a paltry few million, and she and Kay would be on easy street."

Damian ran the tip of his finger along the chill edge of the glass.

"It sounds," he said, "like it could almost work. The perfect plan." He looked up, his eyes as cold as his voice. "I didn't buy into Ivy's crap about doing this out of love for her sister but I couldn't come up with anything better, especially after she turned down the ten million."

"And so now, what will you do? What did you tell this woman?"

Damian shrugged. "What could I tell her?"

"That you would support her until the child is born. That you would support the child. Pay for his care. Send him to the best boarding schools…" Lucas frowned. "Why are you shaking your head?"

"Is that what you would do with a child of your own blood? Pay to keep him out of your life?"

"Yes, of course…" Lucas sighed and rubbed his hands over his face. "No," he said softly. "I would not. His arrival in the world would be a gift, no matter how it happened."

"Exactly." Damian reached for the fresh drink, changed his mind and signaled for their check. "So," he said, carefully avoiding eye contact, "I did the only thing I could. I told her I'd take her to Greece."

Lucas almost leaped across the table. "You told her what?"

"I can't stay in New York the next six months, Lucas. You know that."

"Yes, but—"

"I need to keep an eye on her. I don't know what

she's like. How she's treating this pregnancy. If she's anything like her sister…"

The barman handed him the leather folder that held the check; Damian opened it, took a quick look and handed the man a bill, indicated he should keep the change and began rising to his feet.

Lucas grabbed his arm.

"Wait a minute! I don't think you've thought this through."

"Believe me, I have."

"Damian. Listen. You take her to Greece, she's in your life. Right in the middle of your life, man! And you don't want that."

"You're right, I don't. But what choice do I have? She needs watching."

"You're playing into her hands."

"No way! She fought me, tooth and nail. I'm forcing her to do something she absolutely doesn't want to do."

"Aristedes, you're not thinking straight. Of course she wants to do it! A model who sold her body for another woman's use? Why would she do such a thing, huh?" Lucas's eyes narrowed. "I'll tell you why. For money. And now, with her sister out of the picture, the stakes are even higher."

Damian wanted to argue but how could he when he held those same convictions? And since that was the case, why did he feel his muscles knotting at Lucas's cold words?

"She's playing you like a Stradivarius, Damian."

"Perhaps," Damian said carefully. "But that doesn't change the facts. She's carrying my—"

"She can carry him here as well as in Greece. You want her watched? Hire a private investigator but for

God's sake, don't play into her hands. She's no good, Damian. The woman is an avaricious, scheming bitch."

"Don't call her that," Damian snapped.

Lucas looked at him as if he'd lost his mind. Hell, maybe he had. Lucas had just given a perfect description of Ivy…

Except for those brief moments she'd softened in his arms, let his mouth taste the sweetness of hers. Those moments when she'd responded to him…

Pretended to respond, he thought coldly, and forced a laugh.

"I'm joking," he said lightly. "You know that American expression? Apple pie, the flag, motherhood? You're supposed to show respect for all three."

Lucas didn't look convinced. "Just as long as it's a joke," he finally said.

Damian nodded. "It was. Thank you for worrying about me but trust me, Lucas. I know what I'm doing."

I know what I'm doing.

The words haunted him the rest of the day. At midnight, after tossing and turning, Damian rose from his bed, made a pot of coffee and took a cup out onto the terrace that wrapped around his apartment.

Did he really know what he was doing? He'd had mistresses and lovers but he'd never taken a woman to live with him.

Not that he proposed to do that with Ivy.

Moving her into one of the suites in his palace was hardly taking her to live with him. Still, was it necessary? He could hire someone to watch her, as Lucas suggested. He could hire a companion to live with her.

He almost laughed.

He could imagine Ivy's reaction to that. She'd confront the private detective, order the companion out the door. She had the beauty of Diana and the courage of Athena. It was one hell of a combination.

Wind tousled his hair. Damian shivered. The night was cold and he was wearing only a pair of black sweatpants. It was time to go inside. Or put on a sweatshirt.

Not just yet, though.

He loved New York, especially at night.

People said the city never slept but at this hour, especially on a weekday night, Central Park West grew quiet. Only a few vehicles moved along the street far below.

Was Lucas right? Had he handled this all wrong?

He could warn Ivy that any tendency she had to behave like her sister would result in severe penalties. A cut in allowance, for a start.

As for the child… Plenty of kids grew up without their fathers. He certainly had. Hell, he'd grown up without either parent, when you thought about it. His mother had been too busy jet-setting to one party after another to pay attention to him; his father had done exactly what *his* father had done, ignored him until he was old enough to send to boarding school.

He had survived, hadn't he?

Damian sipped at his coffee, gone cold and bitter.

As cold and bitter as Ivy Madison's heart?

It was a definite possibility. She might well have plotted and schemed, as Lucas insisted. For all he knew, she was out celebrating, knowing she was on her way to collecting the big prize, that he had demanded she go to Greece with him.

Out celebrating with whom?

Not that he gave a damn. It was just that the mother of his unborn child should not be out drinking or dancing or being with a man.

With a man. A faceless stranger, holding her. Kissing her. Taking her into his bed…

The cup fell from Damian's hand and shattered on the flagstone. He cursed, bent down, started scooping up the pieces…

"Son of a bitch," he snarled, and he opened the French doors and marched to his bedroom.

He dressed quickly. Jeans, a cashmere sweater, mocs and a leather bomber jacket. Then he snatched his keys from the dresser and took the elevator to the basement garage where he kept the big Mercedes as well as a black Porsche Carrera. He'd bought the car because he loved it, even though he rarely had the chance to use it.

The Carrera was a finely honed mass of energy and power.

Right now, so was he.

He'd felt that way since he first laid eyes on Ivy Madison. Who in hell was she to come out of nowhere and turn his existence upside down?

The streets were all but deserted. He made the fifteen-minute drive in half that time, pulled into a space marked No Parking on the corner of her block. The front door to her brownstone was not locked. Even if it had been, that wouldn't have stopped him.

Not tonight.

He took the three flights of steps in seconds, rang her doorbell, banged his fist on the door.

"Ivy!" He pounded the door again, called her name even louder. "Damn you, let me in!"

The door opened the inch the antitheft chain allowed.

Damian saw a sliver of dimly lighted room, a darkly lashed eye, a swath of gold-streaked hair.

"Are you crazy?" she snarled. "You'll wake the entire building!"

"Open the damned door!"

The door closed, locks and chain rattled and then the door swung open. Damian stepped inside and slammed it behind him. Ivy stared at him, hair disheveled, silk robe untied, feet bare.

She looked frightened, sleep-tossed and sexy.

The combination sent his already-racing heart into higher gear.

"Do you know what time it is?"

"The real question," he said roughly, "is, do you?"

He heard the flat challenge in his voice, saw her awareness of it reflected in the sudden catch of her breath.

"Have you been drinking?"

"Not enough."

He took a step forward. She took one back. "Your Highness…"

"I think it's time we stopped being so formal." Another step. His, followed by hers. "My name is Damian."

"Your Highness. Damian." The tip of her tongue swept across her bottom lip. He felt his entire body clench at the sight. "Damian, it's very late. Why don't we—why don't we talk tomorrow?"

One more step. Like that. And then her shoulders hit the wall.

"I'm done talking," he said, reaching for her. "And so are you."

"No! Get out. Damian! Get—"

"Isn't it amazing," he said softly, his eyes hot and locked to hers, "that I've seen a piece of paper that says you're pregnant with my child, I've had my hand on your belly." He caught a fistful of her robe, tugged her closer. "But I've never seen you."

"Of course you—"

"You," he said thickly. "Your body. How your breasts look, how your belly looks as your body readies itself for my son."

"Damian! I swear, I'll scream—"

Slowly he drew the robe open. Her eyes widened. Her lips parted. But she didn't scream. No. Oh, no. She didn't scream as he dropped his gaze and looked down at her.

She was wearing a cream-silk nightgown. Thin straps. Silk cups. Shirring over her midriff, then a long, slender fall of silk that ended just above her toes.

Damian's gaze lifted. His eyes swept her face. Her lips were still parted, her eyes still wide…

"Don't," she whispered.

But he did.

Slowly he hooked his fingers under the thin silk straps, Drew them down her arms.

Bared her breasts. Her beautiful breasts. Small. Round. Tipped with pale pink nipples that were already beading. Praxiteles, who had sculpted Aphrodite's beauty in marble, would have wept.

"Damian…"

"Shh," he whispered and cupped her breasts. Thumbed the delicate nipples. Ivy swayed unsteadily as he bent his head and touched his mouth to her nipples. Licked them. Sucked them. Felt his erection strain against his jeans.

"Damian," she said, the word a sigh. A moan.

A plea.

He lifted his head. Her lashes had drooped against her cheeks. Her breasts rose and fell with her quickened breath.

Her eyes opened, locked on his face as he pulled the gown down, down, down her torso. Her hips. Her legs. Those long, long legs.

The gown was a chrysalis at her feet.

And she—she was more than beautiful. She was Aphrodite rising from the sea. She was every dream a man could have, and more.

And yes, her body was readying for his child.

He could see the delicate swell of her belly. The exquisite rounding. The burgeoning fullness.

Slowly he cupped her belly.

Felt the smoothness of her skin. The heat of it. The perfect arc of it beneath his palms.

He stroked one hand lower. Lower still. Watched her face, heard her moan as he slipped it between her thighs and God, God, she was hot, wet, sweetly swollen with need...

"Don't," she sighed, but her hands were on his chest. On his shoulders. She was on her toes, lifting herself to him, her mouth a breath from his.

She wanted this. Wanted him.

It was all he could do to keep from taking her down to the floor, unzipping his jeans, parting her thighs and burying himself deep inside her warmth...

Except, Lucas was right. It was all an act.

Damian let go of her. Picked up her robe, wrapped it around her shoulders. Trembling, panting, she clutched it to her.

"Do you remember what I told you this afternoon?" The tip of her tongue slid along the seam of her mouth.

"You said—you said you were taking me to Greece."

He nodded, reminded himself of Lucas's advice and stepped back. "I've changed my mind."

"You mean, you'll let me stay here?" Her breath caught. If he hadn't known better, he'd have thought it was with relief.

Of course, that was what he meant. Certainly it was what he meant…

The hell it was, he thought, and pulled her into his arms.

"I mean," he said roughly, "that I'd be a fool to pay for your upkeep without getting anything in return."

"I don't understand."

"You will share my bed. You will give birth to my son. And if, in the intervening months, you have proven yourself sufficiently accomplished as my mistress, I will marry you, give you my name, my title…and permit you to be a mother to this child you claim to want for your own." He drew her closer. "If you haven't pleased me, I will keep my son, send you back to New York and you can fight me in the courts."

Time seemed to stand still. Then Ivy looked unflinchingly into his eyes.

"I hate you," she said, "hate you, hate you—"

Damian kissed her again and again mercilessly, fiercely, until, finally, she gave a little sob and melted against him.

Was that, too, part of the act?

It didn't matter.

"Hate me all you like, *glyka mou*. From this moment on, I own you."

CHAPTER SIX

A WOMAN identifying herself as Damian's personal assistant phoned at six and offered no apology for calling at such an early hour.

"Do you have a passport, Miss Madison?"

Ivy was tempted to say she didn't but what was the point? For all she knew, traveling with royalty meant doing away with passports.

"Yes. I have."

"In that case, please be ready to leave for Greece at eight-thirty. Promptly at eight-thirty," the P.A. said emphatically. "His Highness does not like to be kept waiting."

"Shall I stand at attention until he arrives?" Ivy said, trying to mask a sudden wave of fear with sarcasm.

It was a wasted effort. Ivy could almost see the woman's raised eyebrows.

"His driver will come for you, Miss Madison, not the prince himself."

"Of course he won't," Ivy said, and hung up the phone.

Damian Aristedes was not a man who would sully his hands with work. Not even when it came to making arrangements about a woman.

His assistant probably did this kind of thing all the time. Fly one woman to Greece, fly another to Timbuktu… The prince would expect a mistress to be available on demand.

He was in for a big surprise.

She would never become his mistress. She would never agree to become his anything, much less his wife—although that, obviously, had been a lie. A little bait to lure her into his bed.

Not that he'd need bait for most women.

Put him in a room with a dozen women, all beautiful enough to get any man they wanted, he'd have to fight them off. All that macho. The aura of power. The beautiful, masculine face; the hard-bodied good looks…

The prince would collect lovers with disquieting ease.

But she would not be one of them.

Getting sexually involved with a man was not on the list of things Ivy wanted to do with her life. And if that ever changed—and she couldn't imagine that it would—she would choose someone who was Damian's opposite.

She'd want a lover who was gentle, not authoritative. Caring, not commanding. A man whose touch would be nonthreatening.

The prince's touch was not like that.

Each caress left her shaken. Trembling. Feeling as if she were standing on the edge of a precipice and one more step would send her plunging to the rocks below…

Or soaring into a hot, sun-bleached sky.

Ivy let out a breath. Enough of this. There was more than an hour to go until the prince's driver came for her.

Plenty of time to get ready. Too much time, really. The last thing she wanted was to think about what lay ahead.

Ivy brewed a cup of ginger tea. She sat in a corner of the wide windowsill, shivering a little in the cool dawn hours as she sipped her tea and wondered how long it would be until she sat here again.

Soon, she promised herself. Soon.

At seven, she packed, showered and dressed. She was ready long before Damian's driver rang the bell.

He was polite.

So was she.

The big Mercedes rolled silently through the busy Manhattan streets. Ivy looked out through the dark glass at people going about their everyday lives and wondered why she'd let this happen. She didn't have the money for a good attorney but she knew lots of people in high places. Surely someone could help her...

Then she remembered what had started all this. She had agreed to have this baby and Damian Aristedes was the child's father.

She had no choice but to do as he wished.

It was the right thing, for Kay's memory, for the baby...

"Miss?"

Ivy looked up. The car had stopped; the driver stood beside her open door.

"We're here, miss."

"Here" was a place she'd been before. Kennedy Airport, a part of it that was home to private jets.

She'd been a passenger in private planes going to and

from photo shoots in exotic locations. The planes were often big, but she'd never seen a noncommercial aircraft the size of the one ahead of her.

Sunlight glinted off the shiny aluminum wings, danced on the fuselage and the discreet logo emblazoned there. A shield. A lance. An animal of some kind, bulky and somehow dangerous, even in repose.

"Miss Madison?"

A courteous steward led her to the plane. He had that same logo on the pocket of his dark blue jacket and she realized it was a crest. A royal crest, for the royal house of Aristedes.

What are you doing, Ivy? What in the world are you doing?

She stumbled to a halt. The steward looked at her. So did Damian's driver, who was carrying her suitcase to the plane.

Someone else was looking at her, too, from inside the cabin. She couldn't see him but she knew he was there, watching her through cool eyes, seeing her hesitate, assessing it as a sign of weakness.

She would never show weakness to him!

Ivy took a breath and walked briskly up the steps that led into the plane.

It was cool inside the cabin. Luxurious, too. The walls were pale cream; the seats and small sofas soft-looking tan leather. Thick cream carpet stretched the length of the fuselage to a closed door in the rear.

And, yes, Damian was already there, sitting in one of the leather chairs, not looking at her but, instead, reading a page from the sheaf of papers stacked on the table in front of him.

"Miss Madison, sir," the steward said.

Damian raised his head.

Ivy stood straighter, automatically taking on the cool look she'd made famous in myriad ads and magazine covers.

She had deliberately taken time with her appearance this morning. At first, she'd thought she'd wear jeans and a ratty jacket she kept for solitary walks on chill winter mornings, just to show the prince how little all his wealth and grandeur meant.

She'd known, instinctively, he'd have a private plane. Men like him wouldn't fly in commercial jets.

Then she'd thought, no, far better to make it clear nothing he owned, nothing he was, could intimidate her. So she'd dressed in cashmere and silk under a glove-leather black jacket she'd picked up after a shoot in Milan the prior year.

She needn't have bothered.

Damian barely glanced at her, nodded curtly and went back to work.

It angered her, which was ridiculous. It was good, wasn't it, that he had no intention of pretending this was a social occasion?

She nodded back and started past him. His arm shot out, blocking her way.

"You will sit here," he said.

"Here" was the leather chair next to his.

"I prefer a seat further back."

"I don't recall asking your preference."

His tone was frigid. It made her want to slap his face but she wasn't fool enough to do that again. Far better to save her energy for the battles ahead, instead of wasting it on minor skirmishes.

Ivy sat down. The hovering steward cleared his throat.

"May I bring you something after we reach cruising altitude, madam? Coffee, perhaps, or tea?"

"No coffee," Damian said, without lifting his head. "No tea. No alcohol. Ms. Madison may have mineral water or juice, as she prefers."

Ivy felt her face flame. Why didn't he simply announce her pregnancy to the world? But if he was trying to lure her into all-out war, he was going to be disappointed.

"How nice," she said calmly, "to be given a choice, even if it's a minor one."

Damian looked up. Waited. His mouth gave a perfunctory twitch. "Should Thomas take that to mean you don't want anything?"

"What I want," she said matter-of-factly, "is my freedom, but I doubt if Thomas can provide that."

The steward's eyes widened. Damian's face darkened. For a second, no one moved or spoke. Then Damian broke the silence.

"That will be all, Thomas." He waited until the steward was gone. Then he turned to Ivy. "That is the last time I will tolerate that," he said in a low voice.

"Tolerate what, Your Highness? The truth?"

His hand closed on her wrist, exerting just enough pressure to make her gasp.

"You will show me the proper respect in front of people or—"

"Or what?"

His eyes narrowed. "Try me and find out."

A shudder went through her but she kept her gaze steadily on his until he finally let go of her, turned away and began reading through the papers spread in front of him again.

Ivy drew a deep, almost painful breath.

She would get through this. She'd survived worse. Far worse. Things that had happened long ago, that she wanted to forget but couldn't…

That had made her strong.

The mighty prince didn't know it, but he would learn just how strong she was.

When they were airborne, the steward, brave man, appeared with both juice and water as well as a stack of current magazines. Ivy thanked him, leafed through one and then another, blind to the glossy pages, thinking only about what lay ahead.

And about what Damian had said last night.

She'd refused to dwell on it then but now, after this display of power, his words haunted her.

From now on, he'd said, *I own you.*

She thought—she really thought he might believe it. That he had bought her. That she would go to his bed. That she would do whatever he commanded, become the perfect sex slave.

Let him kiss her breasts, as he had so shockingly done yesterday.

Let him undress her. Stand her, naked, before him.

Let him take her in his arms, gather her tightly against him while his aroused flesh pulsed against her.

Let him do all the things men did to women, things men wanted and women surely despised…except, she hadn't despised what Damian did last night.

When he'd touched her. Held her. Kissed her. Parted her lips with his…

Tasted her, let her taste him.

Ivy turned blindly to the window.

The baby. She had to think about the baby. That was all that mattered.

* * *

It grew dark outside the plane.

The cabin lights dimmed.

She yawned. Yawned again. Tumbled into darkness… And shot awake to see Damian leaning over her.

"What—what are you doing?"

His mouth twitched. She'd seen that little movement of his lips enough to know he was trying not to smile.

"Did you think I was going to ravish you while you slept?" This time, the smile he'd repressed broke through. "I'm not a fool, *glyka mou*. When I make love to you, I want you fully awake in my arms."

She was too tired to think of a clever response. Or maybe he was too close, his fallen angel's face an inch from hers.

"I was going to adjust your seat," he said softly. "So that you could lie back while you were sleeping."

"I wasn't sleeping."

"While you were resting, then," he said, with another of those heart-stopping little smiles. "Here. Let me—"

He leaned closer. All she had to do was turn her face a fraction of an inch and her mouth would find his.

Ivy jerked back. "Don't you ever get tired of giving orders?"

"Don't you ever get tired of ignoring good advice?" He shifted his weight. The little distance she'd put between them disappeared. "We have hours left before we land."

"So?"

"So, you're exhausted."

"And you know this, how? You read cards? Palms? Crystal balls?"

His smile tilted. "Unless I'm mistaken, you slept as little as I did last night."

She wanted to ask him why he hadn't slept. Was it because he was sorry he'd demanded she go with him? Or was it—was it because he'd lain in the dark, imagining what it would be like if they had made love? If, together, they'd made the baby growing inside her?

Did what she'd just thought show on her face? Was that why his eyes had suddenly darkened?

"And," he said, very softly, "you're pregnant."

Amazing. They had discussed her pregnancy in excruciating—if not entirely accurate—detail. Still, the way he said the word now, his husky whisper intimate and sexy, made her heartbeat stumble.

"I see. Now you're an expert on pregnant women." She spoke quickly, saying the first thing that came into her head in a desperate effort to defuse the situation, and knew in an instant she'd made a mistake.

A mask seemed to drop over his face.

"What little I know about pregnancy," he said, drawing away from her, "comes courtesy of Kay. Your sister used endless ploys to convince me she was carrying my child."

"Kay wasn't my real sister," Ivy said, and wondered why it suddenly seemed important he understand that.

"Yes. You said you were stepsisters. The same last name... Then, your mother married her father and he adopted you?"

Why had she brought this up? "Yes."

"How old were you?"

"It's not important."

She turned away from him but he cupped her jaw, his touch firm but light.

"I have the right to know these things."

She supposed he did. And he could learn them easily enough. Anything more than that, she had no intention of sharing.

"I was ten. Kay was fourteen."

"She told me her father died when she was sixteen. Another lie?"

"No." Ivy laced her hands in her lap. "He died two years after my mother married him. They both died, he and my mother. It was a freak accident, a helicopter crash in Hawaii. They were on vacation, on a tour."

"I am sorry, *glyka mou*. That must have been hard for you."

She nodded.

"So, who took care of you then? What happened?"

Everything, Ivy thought, oh God, everything…

"Nothing," she said airily. "Well, Kay and I went into foster care. When she turned eighteen, she got a job and a place of her own."

"And you went with her?"

"No." Ivy bit her lip. "I stayed in foster care."

"And?"

And my world changed, forever.

But she didn't say that. Her life was none of his business, and that was exactly what she told him.

"The only part of my life that concerns you," she said sharply, "is my pregnancy."

Ivy expected one of those cold commands that were his specialty or, at least, an argument. Instead, to her surprise, Damian gave her a long, questioning look. Then he turned away and pressed the call button.

The steward appeared as quickly as if he were conjured up from Aladdin's lamp.

"We would like dinner now, Thomas," Damian said. "Broiled salmon. Green salad with oil and vinegar. Baked potatoes."

"Of course, Your Highness."

He was doing it again. Thinking for her. Speaking about her as if she were incapable of speaking for herself. It made her angry and that was good.

Anger was a safer emotion than whatever Damian had made her feel a little while ago.

"I'm not hungry," Ivy said sharply.

Nobody answered. Nobody even looked at her.

"I'll have a glass of Riesling first, Thomas. And please bring Ms. Madison some Perrier and lemon."

"I do not want—"

"No lemon in the Perrier? Of course. No lemon, Thomas. *Neh?*"

"Certainly, sir."

Ivy smoldered but kept silent until they were alone. Then she swung angrily toward Damian, who was calmly putting the documents he'd been reading into a leather briefcase.

"Do you have a hearing problem? I said I wasn't hungry!"

"You are eating for two."

"That's outmoded nonsense!"

"If you are vain enough to wish to starve yourself—"

"I am not starving myself!"

"*Ŏhi,*" Damian said evenly. "That is correct. You are not. I will not permit it."

"Damn it," Ivy snarled, letting her anger rise, embracing it, reminding herself that she hated this man, that it would be dangerous to let any other emotion come into play where he was concerned, "I don't even understand what you're saying. Since when does 'no' mean 'yes' and 'okay' mean 'no'?"

He looked blank. Then he chuckled. "It's not 'no,' it's *'neh.'* It means 'yes.' And I didn't say 'okay,' I said *ŏhi,* which means 'no.'"

Yes was no. No was yes. Would a white rabbit pop out of the carpet next?

"I shall arrange for a tutor to teach you your new language, *glyka mou.*"

"My language is English," she said, despising the petulance in her own voice.

"Your new home is Greece."

"No. It isn't. My home is the place you took me from. That will always be my home, and I'll never let you forget it." She glared at him, her breath coming quickly, furious at him, at herself, at what was happening, what she had brought down on herself. "And if you really think I'd starve myself and hurt my baby—"

"My baby," he said coldly, all the ease of the last moments gone. "Not yours."

The true answer, the one she longed to give him, feared to give him, danced on the tip of her tongue. He claimed he hadn't loved Kay, but Kay had sworn he had. There were too many lies, too many layers of them to risk the one truth that might tear the whole web asunder.

Far too much risk.

So Ivy bit back what she'd come close to saying. Damian filled the silence with yet another order.

"You will eat properly. And you will not contradict me in front of my people. Is that clear?"

"Do I have to genuflect in your presence, too?"

No telltale twitch of his lips this time, only a cold glare.

"If you feel you must, by all means, do so."

He turned away. So did she. There seemed nothing more to say.

They ate in silence.

Ivy tried to pretend disinterest in her food but she was ravenous. Had she eaten anything since her first confrontation with Damian? She couldn't remember.

The steward cleared their tables and brought dessert. Two crystal flutes filled with fresh strawberries, topped with a dollop of cream. She could, at least, make a stand here.

"I never eat whipped cream," she said with lofty determination.

"I'm happy to hear it because this is crème fraîche."

Hadn't she promised herself she wouldn't try to fight him on little things? Crème fraîche was absolutely a little thing, wasn't it?

Little, and delicious. She ate every berry, every bit of the cream...

And felt Damian's gaze on her.

His eyes—hot, intense, almost black with passion—were riveted to her mouth as she licked the last bit from the spoon.

A wave of heat engulfed her; a choked sound broke from her throat. He heard it, lifted his gaze to hers...

The cabin door slid open. Thomas appeared, looked quickly from his master to Ivy...

Ivy sprang to her feet. "Where's the—where is the lavatory, please?"

"In the back, miss. I can show you..."

"I can find it myself, thank you," she said.

And fled.

* * *

They were flying through a black sky lit by a sliver of ivory moon.

Damian had the light on. There were papers in his lap but he wasn't looking at them. Ivy had a magazine in hers but she wasn't looking at it, either.

She was trying to stay awake. Trying to stay awake...

To her horror, she gave a jaw-creaking yawn.

"If you were tired," Damian said coolly, "which, of course, you are not, you could recline your seat and close your eyes."

She went on ignoring him. And yawned. Yawned again...

Her eyelids drooped. A minute, that was all she needed. Just a minute with her eyes shut...

She jerked upright. Her head was on Damian's shoulder. Flustered, she pulled away.

"You are the most stubborn woman in the world. Damn it, what will you prove by not sleeping?"

"I told you, I'm not—"

"Oh, for heaven's sake..." His arm closed around her shoulders. She protested; he ignored her and drew her to his side. "Close your eyes."

"You can't order someone to—"

"Yes," he said firmly, "I can." His arm tightened around her. "Go to sleep." His tone softened. "I promise, I'll keep you safe."

Safe? How could she feel safe in the embrace of this imperious stranger?

And yet—and yet, she did. Feel safe. Warm. Content to lean her head against his hard shoulder. To feel the soft brush of his lips on her temple.

Strong arms closed around her. Lifted her, carried her

through the dark cabin. Lay her down gently on a wide, soft bed.

Was she dreaming?

"Yes," a husky voice whispered, "you are dreaming. Why not give yourself up to the dream?"

It wasn't a dream. The bed was real. The voice was Damian's. And she was in Damian's arms, her body pressed to the length of his.

"I won't sleep with you," she heard herself whisper.

He gave a soft laugh. "You are sleeping with me right now, *glyka mou*," he whispered back, though that term he used for her, whatever it meant, sounded somehow different. Softer. Sweeter...

Sweet as the whisper of his mouth over hers, again and again until she sighed and let her lips cling to his for one quick, transcendent moment.

"You are killing me, *glyka mou*," he said thickly. "But sleep is all we'll share tonight." Another kiss, another gruff whisper. "I want you wide-awake when we make love."

"Never," Ivy heard herself whisper.

She felt his lips curve against hers in a smile.

"Go to sleep," he said.

After that, there was only darkness.

CHAPTER SEVEN

IN THE earliest hours of the morning, Damian's plane landed on his private airstrip on Minos.

The intercom light blinked on; the machine gave a soft beep. "We have arrived, Your Highness," the steward's voice said politely.

"*Efharisto,* Thomas."

Ivy didn't stir. She'd been asleep in Damian's arms for almost two hours, her head tucked into the curve of his shoulder.

By now, his shoulder ached but he wouldn't have moved her for anything in the world.

How could sleeping with a woman, sleeping with her in the most literal sense of the word, feel so wonderful?

Damian turned his head, breathing in Ivy's scent. Silky strands of her hair brushed against his lips. He closed his eyes and thought about staying here with her, just like this, until she awakened.

Impossible, of course.

They had to return to reality eventually. It might as well be now.

But he could wake her quietly. Show her that every moment they were together didn't have to be a battle.

Gently he rolled her onto her back, bent to her and kissed her.

"*Kalimera*," said softly.

Ivy sighed and he kissed her again.

"Ivy," he whispered. "Wake up. We're home."

Her lashes fluttered open to reveal eyes were dark, still clouded with sleep.

"Damian?"

His name was soft on her lips. She'd never spoken it that way before, as if he and she were alone in the universe.

"Yes, it's me, sweetheart. Did you sleep well?"

"I don't—I don't remember. How did we…?"

Her eyes widened and he knew she'd realized she was not only in his arms but in his bed. He'd watched Lucas taming a mare once; that same wild look had come into the animal's eyes.

"Easy," he said.

"What am I doing in this bed?"

"Sleeping. Nothing more than that."

"But—how did I get here? I don't remember…"

"I carried you. You were exhausted."

She closed her eyes. When she opened them again, they were cool. "Let me up."

"In a minute."

"Damian—"

"Do you see what sleeping in my arms has accomplished?" He smiled. "You've begun calling me Damian."

She started to answer. He kissed her instead. She didn't respond. But he went on kissing her, his mouth moving lightly over hers, and just when he thought it would never happen, she sighed and parted her lips to his.

The joining of their mouths was tender.

The need that swept through him was not.

His erection was instantaneous and he groaned and shifted his weight to accommodate the ache of his hardened flesh. Ivy shifted, too…and he found himself cradled between her parted thighs.

She gasped into his mouth.

His blood thundered.

Now, it said, take her now…

Beep. "Sir? Will you be deplaning, or shall I tell the pilot to leave the electrical system on?"

That was all it took to destroy the fragile moment. Ivy tore her mouth from Damian's. Her face was flushed, her lips full and heated from his kisses. He wanted to cup her face, kiss her into submission…

Instead he rolled away and rose from the bed. She did, too, but as she got to her feet, he scooped her into his arms.

"I can walk."

"It's dark outside."

"I can see."

"I know the terrain. You don't."

A Jeep and driver waited on the side of the runway. His driver was well-trained. Either that, or the arrival of his employer with a woman in his arms was not an unusual event.

Ivy was not as casual. She saw the driver and buried her face in Damian's throat.

The feel of her mouth on his skin, the warmth of her breath… He loved it almost as much as the feel of her in his arms during the short drive to his palace, perched on the ancient, long-dormant volcanic summit of Minos.

The palace was lit softly in anticipation of his arrival. He wondered what Ivy would think of his home when she saw it tomorrow by daylight. He'd learned that most people envisioned a palace as an imposing edifice of stone.

His home, if you could call a palace a home, was built of marble. The oldest part of it dated to the fourth century, another wing to the sixth, and the balance to the early 1600s. It was an enormous, sprawling, overblown place...

But he loved it.

Would Ivy? Not that it mattered, of course, but if she lived here with him, if, after his son's birth, she became his—she became his—

The huge bronze doors swung open, revealing his houseman, Esias. Despite the hour, Esias was formally dressed.

Damian had given up trying to break him of the habit. Esias had served his grandfather, his father and now him. How could you argue with an icon—an icon who was as determined as the Jeep's driver not to show surprise at seeing his master with a woman in his arms.

"Welcome home, Your Highness."

"Esias."

"May I, ah, may I help you with—"

"I am fine, thank you."

"Damian," Ivy snapped. "My God, put me—"

"Soon."

Trailed by Esias, he carried her up a wide, curving marble staircase to the second floor, then down the corridor that led to his rooms.

Esias stepped forward and opened the door.

"Efharisto," Damian said. "That is all, Esias. I'll see you in the morning."

The houseman inclined his head and moved back. Damian carried Ivy through the door and shouldered it shut, and the silence of the room closed around them.

"Who was that?"

He was alone with his mistress and the first words out of her mouth were not the ones a man ached to hear...

But then, Ivy wasn't his mistress.

Not yet.

"Damian. Who was—"

He answered by kissing her. She tried to turn her face away but he was persistent. He kept kissing her, nipped gently at her bottom lip and, at last, she made a little sound and opened her mouth to his.

He slipped the tip of his tongue between her parted lips. She jerked back. Then she made that sweet little whisper again and accepted the intimate caress. Accepted and returned it as he carried her through the sitting room, through the bedroom, to his bed.

Pleasure coursed through him.

What had happened in the darkness of the plane had changed everything. Had she realized she couldn't fight him or herself? That she wanted him as much as he wanted her?

God knew, he wanted her. From the minute she'd turned up at his door, despite everything, his anger, hell, his rage...

No woman had ever stirred such hunger in him.

Gently he lay her down in the silk-covered bed. Moonlight, streaming through the French doors behind it, touched her hair with silver. Her eyes, brighter than the stars, glittered as she looked up at him.

"Ivy," he said softly. He bent to her. Kissed her

temples. Her mouth. Her throat. Whispered in Greek what he would do to her, with her…

What she would feel as he made her his.

"Damian?"

Her whisper was soft. Uncertain. It had an innocence to it that he knew was a lie but it suited the way she was looking at him, the way her hands had come up to press lightly against his chest.

A little game could be exciting, though she excited him enough just as she was. He was almost painfully hard. It would not be easy to go as slowly as he wanted, this first time, but he would try.

Her dress had a row of tiny buttons down the bodice. He undid them slowly, even as her hands caught at his, and he paused to kiss each bit of warm, rosy skin he exposed.

She was breathing fast; the glitter in her eyes had become almost feverish.

"Damian," she whispered. "Please…"

He kissed her, harder this time, deeper, and she moved against him. Yes God, yes. Like that. Just like that…

Her bra opened in the front. He sent up a silent prayer of thanks as he undid the clasp, let the silk cups fall open…

And groaned.

She was exquisite.

She had small, perfect breasts crowned by pale pink nipples. It had almost driven him insane, touching them that one time…

"Damian! Stop."

She was moving against him again. It was too much. If she kept lifting herself to him this way, he would—

"Stop!"

He didn't hear her. Or yes, he heard her voice but her words had no meaning as he drew one nipple deep into his mouth—

Something slammed into his chest. He jerked back. It was Ivy's fist; even as he watched, she swung at him again. Stunned, he grabbed her wrists.

"What the hell are you doing?"

"Get—off—me!"

She was crying. And yes, moving against him, not in passion but in an attempt to free herself of his weight.

He sat up, stunned, disbelieving. She scrambled away from him and shot to her feet, clutching the open bodice of her dress, staring at him as if he were a monster.

"Don't touch me!"

"Don't touch you? But—"

"I told you I didn't want to come here. I told you I would not be your—your sex toy. And now—now, the minute we're alone in this—this kingdom you rule, you start—you start pawing me."

Pawing her? She had clung to him. Kissed him. Looked into his eyes with desire and now...

And now, it was time to up the ante. Make the game more interesting because she knew damned well he could always toss in his cards and walk away from the table.

He wanted to throw her back down on the rumpled bed, pin her arms over her head, force her thighs apart and finish what she had started, but she would not reduce him to that.

For all he knew, that was exactly what she wanted.

He snarled a name at her, one he'd never called any

woman. Then he turned on his heel, strode through the suite, into the hall and slammed the door behind him.

Lucas had called it right. First Kay had played him for a sucker. Now Ivy was doing it. And he, fool that he was, had let it happen.

She was only a woman. A pretty face, a ripe body. God knew, there were plenty of those in his life. Yes, she carried his child but he knew damned well she hadn't done it out of love for her sister.

She'd done it for money. Lots of it, probably. And then fate had intervened, taken Kay out of the picture, and Ivy would have seen that whatever Kay had promised her could be increased a hundredfold, a thousandfold, if she played the game right.

The lock clicked.

Panagia mou! She had locked the door against him. Locked *his* door against him. To hell with that. If she thought he'd put up with such crap, she needed to learn a lesson.

Starting right now.

He took a step back, aimed his foot at the door…

"Sir?"

Damian whirled around. "Get the hell out of here, Esias!"

His houseman stood his ground, no emotion showing on his face as if it were perfectly normal to find his master about to kick down the door of his own sitting room.

"I am sorry to disturb you, Your Highness, but your office in Athens is trying to reach you. They say it is urgent."

Esias held out the telephone. Damian glared at it. What did he give a damn for his office in Athens? Except—except, it was the middle of the night.

The bitch laughing at him behind that door was only one woman. He could deal with her at his leisure. But if there was a problem in Athens, it could affect the hundreds of people who worked for him.

He held out his hand and Esias gave him the phone.

An Aristedes supertanker had run aground on a reef in South America. Oil might begin oozing into the ocean at any moment.

Damian tossed the phone to Esias. "Wake my pilot," he snapped. "Tell him—"

"I have taken the liberty of doing so. The helicopter will be ready when you get there."

"Thank you."

"You are welcome, Your Highness." The houseman paused and looked at the closed door. "Ah, is there anything else, sir?"

"Yes," Damian said coldly. "The lady's name is Ivy Madison. Make her comfortable, but under no circumstances is she to leave this island."

Two days later, the crisis in South America had been resolved and Damian was on his way back to Minos.

It had been a hard, exhausting couple of days but it had given him time to calm down.

If he hadn't been called away…

No, he thought, staring at the ocean swells far below the fast-moving helicopter, no, he wouldn't think about that. Ivy had deliberately taken him to the brink of self-control.

He was certain of it.

But he hadn't let her push him over the edge. And there was no chance it would happen again.

Two days in Athens. Two days away from temptation.

Two days of rational thought and he'd come to a decision.

He'd made a mistake, bringing her to Minos. As for the rest, telling her he'd make her his mistress, that he might marry her...

Damian shook his head. Crazy. Or perhaps crazed was a better way to put it.

Why would he have even considered making her his mistress? All the emotional baggage that went into an arrangement like that? No way. The world was full of beautiful women. He surely didn't need this particular one.

As for marriage... Crazy, for sure. He wasn't marrying anybody. Not for years to come, if at all. And when that time came, assuming it did, *he* would choose his own wife, not let her choose him.

Because that was what had been going on. How come he hadn't seen it right away?

Like her sister, Ivy had been angling for marriage from the start. She was just cleverer about it. An ambush, instead of a head-on attack. That way, the target didn't stand a chance.

Her weapon had been the oldest one in the world. Sex. What could be more powerful in the hands of a beautiful woman, especially if a man was vulnerable?

And he sure as hell was vulnerable. He hadn't had a woman for months. Damian's jaw tightened. But he would, very soon.

Late last night, once he was sure the South American situation was under control, he'd phoned a French actress he'd met a few weeks ago. A couple of minutes of conversation and the upshot was, he'd fly to Paris next weekend.

She was looking forward to it, she'd purred.

So was he.

A long weekend in bed with the actress and Ivy would be forgotten. Hell, he'd forgotten her already…

"Your Highness?"

How long had the pilot's voice been buzzing in his headset? Damian cleared his throat.

"Yes?"

"Touchdown in a couple of minutes, sir."

"Thank you."

They were flying lower now, skimming over a group of small islands that were part of the Cyclades, as was Minos, but these bits of land were uninhabited, as beautiful as they were wild.

Back in the days he'd had time for such things, he'd sailed a Sunfish here and explored them. Sometimes, making his way through the tall pines that clung to them, he'd half expected to come face-to-face with one of the ancient gods his people had once worshipped.

Or one of the goddesses. Aphrodite. Artemis. Helen of Troy. Not a goddess, no, but a woman whose beauty had brought a man to his knees.

Ivy had almost done that to him, but fate had intervened.

A man could come to his senses, given breathing room.

The helicopter settled onto its landing pad. Damian slapped the pilot on the shoulder with his thanks and got out, automatically ducking under the whirring blades as he ran to the Jeep, parked where he'd left it two nights ago. It was six in the morning. He was tired, unshaven and he couldn't recall when he'd showered last. Added to that, he was hungry enough to eat shoe leather.

But all that would wait. Dealing with Ivy was more important. He wanted her off his island, and fast.

Yes, he thought, as the Jeep bounced along the narrow road, she was carrying his child. And yes, she needed watching. He knew that, better than before.

But he didn't have to be the one doing the watching. She'd said that herself. Of course, he knew now that she hadn't said it in hopes he'd listen. Just the opposite: she'd wanted to lure him into doing exactly what he'd done.

The funny thing was, it might have been the one true thing to come out of her mouth.

That soft, beautiful, treacherous mouth.

Damn it, what did that have to do with anything? Who gave a damn about her mouth or any other part of her anatomy except her womb?

He'd contact his lawyers. Have them make arrangements to set her up in a place of her own. Have them organize round-the-clock coverage of her and her apartment.

Until his son was born, he would regulate who she saw, what she did, every breath she took. But not in New York City.

Damian smiled coldly as he took the Jeep through a hairpin turn.

He'd keep a watch on her from a much closer vantage point.

Athens.

She would give birth here, in his country, where his peoples' laws, where his nationality and his considerable leverage, would apply.

She wouldn't like it—and that, he had to admit, was part of the reason the plan gave him so much pleasure.

* * *

He entered the palace through a secret door some ancestor had added in the fifteenth century so he could spy on a cheating wife, or so the story went.

He had no desire to go through the usual polite morning moves— *Good morning, sir. Good morning, Esias.* Or Elena, or Jasper, or Aeneas, or any of the half dozen others on the household staff.

The only person he wanted to see was Ivy. He'd ring for a cup of coffee. Then he'd have her brought to him so he could tell her what would happen next.

She'd moved into one of the guest suites. Esias had phoned to tell him that within an hour of his reaching his office. It had been well before he'd come to his senses and, for a wild moment, he'd imagined returning to Minos, storming into her suite, tumbling her back on the bed and finishing what had started before he'd had to leave for Athens.

Thank God, he hadn't.

He didn't want to carry through on the threat he'd made in New York, either. He didn't want to own her, only to get rid of her. So what if, despite his newfound sanity, he could still remember the smell of her skin? The sweetness of her mouth? The taste of her nipples?

Damian stopped halfway up the stairs. Stop it, he told himself angrily. There was nothing special about Ivy. Another few days and he'd be with a woman who would not play games, who would not stir him to frustration and madness.

Who wouldn't sigh the way Ivy did, when he kissed her. Or whisper his name as if it were music. Or fall asleep in his arms, as if he were keeping her safe…

"Damn it, Aristedes," he said under his breath, and opened the door to his suite…

And saw Ivy, standing with her back to him…

Waiting for him.

His heart turned over, and he knew everything he'd told himself the last two days were lies.

The truth was, he wanted this woman more than he wanted his next breath—and she wanted him, too. Why else would she be here, waiting for his return?

He said her name and she swung to face him. His heart began to race. There was no artifice in her expression. Whatever she told him next would be the truth.

"Damian. You're here."

"Yes," he said softly, "and so are you."

"I—I heard the helicopter. And—and I went downstairs and asked Esias if you were coming and he said—he said yes, you were returning to Minos. And when he told me that, I felt—"

She was hurrying the words, rushing them together and he understood. It wouldn't be easy to admit she'd been teasing him, that the teasing was over.

"You don't have to explain."

"But I do. I owe you that. I know—I know you think what I did the other night—that I did it deliberately, but—"

He closed the distance between them, caught her wrists and brought her hands to his lips.

"It was a game. I understand. But it's over with. No more games, Ivy. From now on, we'll be honest with each other, *neh?*"

She nodded. "Yes. Absolutely honest."

Damian brought her hands to his chest. "Let me shower. Then we'll have some breakfast. And then—"

His voice roughened. "And then, sweetheart, I'll show you how much I want you. How good it will be when we make love."

Ivy jerked her hands from his. "What?"

He grinned. "You're right. No breakfast. Just a quick shower…" His gaze dropped to her mouth, then rose again. "You can shower with me," he whispered. "Would you like that?"

"You have no idea what I'm talking about!"

"I do, *kardia mou*. You want to apologize for—"

"Apologize?" Her voice rose in disbelief. "Apologize? For what?"

"For the other night," he said carefully. "For teasing me—"

"Teasing you?" She stared at him; for a second, he wondered if he were speaking Greek instead of English. "Are you crazy?"

Damian's mouth narrowed. "It would seem that one of us is."

"You—you tried to take advantage of me the other night. And now—now, my God, you're so full of yourself that you think—that you think… Do you really think I waited here to beg you to take me to bed?" Ivy lifted her hand and poked her forefinger into the center of his chest. "I waited here to tell you that I am going home!"

"You came to my rooms, waited for me, all so you could tell me you're leaving Minos?"

Damian's voice was low and ugly. It made Ivy's heart leap.

Nothing was going the way she'd planned.

She'd expected him to be sharp with her. That would be her cue to tell him that it was illogical for them to spend the next six months in lock-step. What had happened the other night was proof they couldn't get along.

Why torture each other when it wasn't necessary?

She would go home. And she would agree to give him visiting rights to his son.

That was what she'd intended to tell him, but Damian had misunderstood everything. She'd waited in his rooms because she wanted this meeting to be private. She'd approached him in a conciliatory fashion because getting him angry would serve no purpose.

It had all backfired, and now he was looking at her the way a spider would look at a fly.

All right. She'd try again.

"Perhaps I should explain why I waited for you here."

"There's no need. I know the reason."

"I did it because—"

"Because you thought, perhaps I overplayed my hand. Perhaps my performance the other night convinced him to get rid of me."

"It wasn't a performance!"

"And then, because you're so very clever, so very good at this, you thought, yes, but if I say it first, if I tell him I want to leave, it will probably make him anxious to keep me."

"You're wrong! I never—"

She cried out as he caught hold of her and lifted her to her toes.

"The stakes are higher now, *neh?* Whatever Kay promised you as payment for your role in this ugly scheme—"

"She didn't promise me anything!"

"Perhaps not. Perhaps you thought to wait until my

son was in my arms before you asked for money." His fingers bit into her flesh. "But fate dealt you a better card."

"Can't you get it through your thick skull that not everything is about you?"

"You're wrong. This is all about me. My fortune. My title." His mouth twisted. "And the sweetener you keep dangling in front of my nose."

Before she could pull away, he kissed her, savaging her mouth, forcing her head back. Ivy stood immobile. Then memory and fear overwhelmed her and she sank her teeth into his lip.

He jerked back, tasting blood.

Slowly, deliberately, he wiped it away with the back of his hand.

"Be careful, *glyka mou*. My patience is wearing thin."

"You can't do this!"

"You are in my country. I can do anything I damned well please."

He let go of her, picked up the nearest telephone and punched a key.

"Esias. I want Ms. Madison's things moved to my rooms. Yes. Immediately."

Damian broke the connection and looked at Ivy. She stood straight and tall, head up, eyes steady on his even though they blazed with rage.

She was magnificent, so beautiful the sight of her made the blood roar in his ears.

He could take her now. Teach her that she belonged to him. Turn all that frost to flame.

But he wouldn't. The longer he waited, the sweeter her submission would be.

Damian strolled into the huge master bath. Turned on the shower, toed off his mocs, unbuckled his belt, pulled his cotton sweater over his head as if he were alone.

A priceless vase whistled past his ear and shattered on the tile a couple of feet away.

He swung around and looked at Ivy. She glared back, head high, hands on hips, her eyes telling him how she despised him...

And then her gaze dropped to his broad shoulders, swept over his muscled chest and hard abs.

"Want to see more?" he said, very softly, and brought his hand to his zipper.

His Ivy was brave but she wasn't stupid. Cheeks blazing, she turned and fled.

CHAPTER EIGHT

TRAPPED.

She was trapped like a fly in amber, Ivy thought furiously, held captive within something that looked beautiful but was really a prison.

The door to the guest suite she'd commandeered in Damian's absence stood open. One of the maids was emptying the dresser drawers; Esias stood by, supervising.

"Leave my clothes alone!"

The maid jumped back. Esias said something and the girl shot a glance at Ivy and reached toward the dresser again.

"Did you hear me? Do—not—touch—my—things!"

Esias barely looked at her. "His Highness said—"

"I don't give a damn what he said." Ivy pointed to the door. "Get out!"

The houseman stiffened but, well-trained robot that he was, he snapped an order at the maid. She scurried away at his heels as he marched from the room.

Ivy slammed the door behind them, locked it and sank down on the edge of the bed.

She would not remain on Minos. That was a given.

What wasn't so clear was how to escape. There were no bars on the windows of Damian's palace, no locks on the doors, but why would there be?

The island was in the middle of the Aegean. You could only leave it by sea or by air.

And yes, there was an airstrip, a helipad, a couple of small boats in a curved harbor, even a yacht the size of a cruise ship anchored just offshore in the dark blue sea.

But all those things, every ounce of white sand beach, dark volcanic rock and thousand-foot-high cliffs belonged to Damian. He owned Minos and ruled it with an iron fist.

She could only leave Minos if he permitted it.

Aside from Esias, who watched her with the intensity of Cerberus, that ancient three-headed dog guarding Hades, the people who lived in Damian's tightly controlled little kingdom were pleasant and polite.

The maids and gardeners, cook and housekeeper all smiled whenever they saw her. The pilot of Damian's jet, poring over charts in a small, whitewashed building at the airstrip, had greeted her pleasantly; down by the sea, an old man scraping barnacles from the bottom-up hull of a small sailboat doffed his cap and offered a gap-toothed grin.

They all spoke English, enough to say oh, yes, it was very hot this time of year and indeed, the sea was a wonderful shade of deepest blue. But as soon as Ivy even hinted at asking if someone would please sail her, fly her, get her the hell off this miserable speck of rock, they scratched their heads and suddenly lost their command of anything other than Greek.

Terrified, all of them, by His Highness, the Prince.

His Horribleness, the Prince.

Ivy shot to her feet and went to the closet. There had to be someone with the courage to help her. Maybe the helicopter pilot. Maybe Damian had neglected to tell him that she was a prisoner. Either way, this was her last chance at freedom.

She had to make it work and the best way to do that was to look and sound like Ivy Madison, woman of the world, instead of Ivy Madison, desperate prisoner.

Quickly she stripped to her bra and panties. Grabbed a pair of white linen trousers from their hanger, stepped into them...

"Oh, for God's sake..."

She inhaled until it felt like her navel was touching her spine. No good. The zipper wouldn't budge.

Ivy kicked the trousers off and turned sideways to the mirror. Her expression softened and she lay her hand gently over her rounded belly.

The baby—her baby—was growing. Her baby... and Damian's.

No. A condom's worth of semen didn't make a man a father. Concern, love, wanting a child were what mattered. Where was Damian's concern, his love, his desire for this baby?

Nowhere that she could see. He wanted her child because he wanted an heir, and because he was the kind of unfeeling SOB who could not imagine giving up that which he believed was his.

A man like that was not going to raise her baby.

Two days out from under his autocratic thumb and Ivy had had time to think logically.

Maybe she couldn't afford a five hundred dollar an hour Manhattan lawyer but she knew people who knew people. It was one of the few benefits of a high-profile career. Surely some acquaintance could fast-talk a hotshot attorney into taking her case on the cheap, maybe even pro bono, if only for the publicity.

Which was really pretty funny, Ivy thought as she tried and discarded another pair of trousers.

She'd always avoided publicity. Sometimes she thought she was the only model who tried to keep her private life under wraps. But if winning the right to raise her child alone meant having her face plastered in the papers, she'd do it.

She'd do whatever it took to get Damian out of her and her baby's lives.

Damian Aristedes was a brute. A monster. A man who went into a rage when he was denied sex, who'd come close to forcing her to yield to him and, instead, had flown to Athens to find a woman who wouldn't stop him from taking what he wanted.

Why else would he have left her and Minos? That was what men did. Even Damian, who looked so civilized.

He hadn't been civilized when he'd taken her in his arms the other night. Neither had she. Just for a moment, she'd felt things threaten to spin out of control... Until she'd come to her senses, realized where things were heading, what he would want to do next...

Ivy blinked, reached for the only remaining pair of trousers, sucked in her tummy and pulled them on.

Okay.

The zipper didn't close but at least it went up halfway. A long silk T, a loose, gauzy shirt over that...

She stuck her feet into a pair of high-heeled slides. Freed her hair from its clip, bent at the waist and ran her hands through it before tossing it back from her face. A little makeup…

Ivy looked at herself in the mirror, gave her reflection her best camera pout and tried to imagine herself facing the helicopter pilot, whoever he was.

"I know you must be awfully busy," she said in a breathy whisper. It made her want to gag when she heard other women talk like that but whatever worked… "I mean, I know you have lots to do…"

And what if the sexy look, the artful smile didn't budge him? If he said sorry, he had to clear it with the prince?

"Oh," she said, "yes, I know, but—but…" Ivy chewed on her lip. "But I have to get to Athens without telling him because—because—"

Because what?

"Because I want to buy him a gift. See, it's a surprise but it won't be if he knows about it…"

Not great but add a smile, fluttering lashes, maybe a light touch on the guy's arm…

Ivy's sexy smile faded.

"Yuck," she said.

Then she propped her sunglasses on top of her head, hung her purse over her shoulder and got moving.

The helicopter was still on its pad.

Better still, a guy wearing a ball cap and dark glasses was squatting alongside it, examining one of the struts.

It had to be the pilot.

Ivy paused, ran her hand through her hair, then down her torso. She was dusty and sweaty, thanks to the long walk to the helipad, plus she'd come close to turning her ankle on the road's gravel surface. There were Jeeps garaged near the palace but you had to get keys from Esias.

Fat chance.

Besides, some men liked sweaty. All those times she'd had to be oiled before a shot…

"Stop stalling," she muttered as she walked past the hangars, placing one foot directly ahead of the other.

Her modeling strut had always been among the best.

She waited until she was a couple of yards away. "Hi."

The guy looked up, gave a very satisfactory double-take and got to his feet.

Ivy held out her hand. "I'm Ivy."

He wiped his hand on his khakis, took her hand and cleared his throat. "Joe," he said, and cleared his throat again.

"Joe." Ivy batted her lashes. "Are you the one who flies this incredible thing?"

He grinned. "You got it, beautiful."

Perfect. He was American. And even with dust on her shoes and sweat beaded above her lip, she'd clearly passed the test.

"Well, Joe, I need a lift to Athens. Are you up for that?"

Joe took off his dark glasses, maybe so she could see the regret in his eyes, and peered past her.

"Are you, uh, are you looking for somebody?"

He nodded. "I'm looking for the prince."

"Oh, we don't need him." Ivy moved closer. "You see," she said, lowering her voice and gazing up at Joe's face, "he doesn't know I'm doing this."

She launched into her story. It sounded so good, she almost believed it. Joe said "uh huh" and "sure" and "cool." And just when she thought she had it made, he shook his head and sighed.

"Wish I could help you, beautiful, but I can't."

Ivy forced a smile. "But you can. I mean, it's just a little trip. And afterward, when the prince knows about the surprise, you know, after I've given it to him, I'll tell him how great you were, how you did this for me—"

"Sorry, babe. This chopper doesn't leave the ground unless His Highness says it's okay. You want to use the phone in the office over there to call him, that's fine. Otherwise—"

"For heaven's sake! Do you need his permission to breathe, too? You're a grown man. He's just a—he's just a pompous, self-serving—"

Joe stared past her, eyes widening.

"Glyka mou," a husky voice purred, "here you are."

Ivy's heart sank. She closed her eyes as a powerful arm wrapped around her shoulders.

"I've been looking everywhere for you. How foolish of me not to have thought to check here first."

Ivy looked up at Damian. He smiled, pleasantly enough so the pilot smiled, too, but Ivy wasn't fooled.

Behind that calm royal smile was hot royal rage.

"You cannot do this," she hissed.

His eyebrows rose. "Do what?"

"You know what. Refuse to let me leave. Make me into your—your—"

He bent his head and kissed her, the curve of his arm anchoring her to him while his mouth moved against hers with slow, possessive deliberation. She heard Joe clear his throat, heard her heart start to pound.

And felt herself tumble into the flood of dark sensation that came whenever his lips touched hers.

"I hate you," she whispered when he finally lifted his head.

His smile was one part sex and one part macho smirk. "Yes," he said. "I can tell. Joe?"

The pilot, who'd walked several feet away, turned to them. "Sir?"

"We are ready to leave," Damian said, and he took Ivy's elbow and all but lifted her into the helicopter.

They flew to Athens.

Even in her anger, Ivy felt a little thrill of excitement as they swooped over a stand of soaring white columns. She'd been to Athens before but it had been on business, four rushed days and nights of being photographed with no time for anything else except a hurried visit to the Parthenon.

Was that the Acropolis below them now? She wanted to ask but not if it meant speaking to Damian.

She didn't have to. He leaned in close, put his lips to her ear and told her what was beneath them.

The whisper of his breath made her tremble. Why? How could she hate him and yet react this way to him? To any man? She knew what they were, what they wanted...

"I should have thought to ask," he said. "Is the flight making you ill?"

Ivy pulled away. "Not the flight," she said coldly, but he didn't hear her, couldn't hear her over the roar of the engine, and that was just as well.

His show of concern was just that. A show, nothing more. She was his captive and that was how he treated her and why in God's name did she respond to his touch?

He must have had the same effect on Kay. Otherwise, she wouldn't have given in to his demands. The bastard! Forcing Kay to do what he wanted, then turning his back

on the situation he'd created once Kay was gone,
unless...

Unless he really hadn't known about the baby.
Unless the story Kay had told her was—unless it was—

"Ivy."

She looked up. Damian was standing over her; the
helicopter had touched down. He reached for her seat
belt. She ignored him, did it herself and walked to the
door. Joe was already on the ground. He held up his
arms and she let him help her down.

"Careful of the rotor wash," he yelled.

And then Damian's arm was around her waist and he
led her to a long, black limousine.

"One for each city," Ivy said briskly. "How nice to
be a potentate."

Damian looked at her as if she'd lost her mind.
Perhaps she had, she thought, as the limo sped away.

That time in Athens, doing a spread for *In Vogue*, Ivy
had spent hours, exhausting hours, in Kolonaki Square.

The photographer had shot her against the famous
column that stood in the square. Against the well-
dressed crowd. Against the charming cafés and shops.
The stylist had dressed her in haute couture from Dolce
& Gabbana and Armani and elegant boutiques in this
upscale neighborhood.

Now, Damian took her into those same boutiques to
buy her clothes.

"I don't need anything," she told him coldly.

"Of course you do. That's why I brought you here."

"I have my own things, thank you very much."

"Is that why your trousers don't close?"

She blushed, looked down and saw only the

slightly rounded contours of her gauzy shirt. Damian laughed softly.

"A good guess, *neh?*"

A clerk glided toward them. Damian took Ivy's hand and explained they needed garments that were loose-fitting. Ivy said nothing. This was his show; she'd be damned if she'd help. So he cleared his throat, let go of her hand and, instead, curved his arm around her and drew her close.

"My lady is pregnant."

There was an unmistakable ring of masculine pride in his voice. Ivy flashed him a cool look and wondered what would happen to all that macho arrogance if she added that she was pregnant, courtesy of a syringe.

"She carries my child," he said softly, and placed his hand over her rounded belly as if they were alone.

And that touch of his hand, not proprietary but tender, changed everything.

For the first time, Ivy let the picture she'd refused to envision fill her mind.

Damian, holding her in his arms. Undressing her. Carrying her to his bed, kissing her breasts, her belly. Parting her thighs, kneeling between them, his eyes dark with passion as he entered her and planted his seed in her womb.

"My child, *glyka mou,*" he whispered and this time, when he bent to her, Ivy rose on her toes, put her hand on the back of his head and brought his lips to hers.

The clerk in a tiny boutique on Voukourestiou Street said there was a little shop that specialized in maternity clothes only a few doors away.

Ivy said they didn't need anything else. A dozen

boxes and packages were already on their way by messenger to the limousine that waited on a quiet, shady street near the square.

To her amazement, Damian agreed.

"What we need is lunch." He smiled, tilted her face up to his and gave her a light kiss. "My son must be hungry by now."

Ivy laughed. "Using a baby as an excuse to fill your own belly is pathetic."

"But effective," he said, laughing with her.

They ate in a small café. The owner greeted Damian with a bear hug and the cook—his wife—hurried out from the kitchen, kissed Damian on both cheeks, kissed Ivy after introductions were made, then beamed and said something to Damian, who laughed and said *neh*, she was right.

"Right about what?" Ivy said, when they were alone.

Damian took her hand and brought it to his mouth. "She says you are carrying a strong, beautiful boy."

Ivy blushed. "Do I look that pregnant?"

His eyes darkened. "You look happy," he said softly. "Are you? Happy, today, with me?"

He had phrased the question carefully. She could answer it the same way. Or she could just say that she *was* happy, that when she didn't stop to think about why they were together, about how he'd come into her life, about what would happen next, she was incredibly happy. She was—she was—

"Lemonade," the café's owner said, setting two tall glasses in front of them. "For the proud papa—and the beautiful mama."

Ivy grabbed the glass as if it were a life preserver.

After a moment, Damian did, too.

* * *

She should have known Damian wouldn't leave without stopping at the maternity boutique.

They went there after lunch and found the jewel-like shop filled with exquisite, handmade clothes that could make even a woman whose belly was ballooning feel beautiful.

Desirable.

Ivy caught her breath. Damian heard her whisper of distress and brought her close against his side.

"Forgive me," he said softly. "I have exhausted you."

"No. I mean—I mean, I guess I am a little tired."

He smiled into her eyes. Pressed a kiss to her forehead.

"What is your favorite color, *glyka mou?*"

"My favorite color?"

"Green, to match your eyes? Gold, to suit your hair?" Instead of waiting for her answer, he turned to the hovering clerk. "We want everything you have in those colors."

"Damian!"

"Please, do not argue! You are tired. We are done shopping for the day."

His tone was imperious. Arrogant. Ivy knew she ought to tell him so…

Instead she buried her face against his shoulder and thought, *Just for today, just for now, let this all be a dream.*

Not the beautiful clothes, the elegant shops. They didn't matter.

Damian did.

She could pretend, couldn't she? Pretend he was her wonderful, incredible lover? Pretend they were together because they wanted to be? Pretend they had planned this baby, longed for it together?

What harm could it possibly do?

They flew home in the gathering twilight, trading the lights of the city for those of ships, of islands, of stars.

This time, Ivy went willingly into Damian's arms when he insisted on carrying her from the helicopter to the Jeep he'd left beside the airstrip hours before.

He put her into the passenger seat, then got behind the wheel and started the engine, let it idle as he stared out the windshield.

"Ivy. I have waited all day to tell you this." He cleared his throat. "I was very angry this morning."

Ivy sighed. So much for dreams. The day was over. Back to reality.

"I'm sure you were," she said quietly, "but—"

"Angry is too mild a word, *glyka mou*. I was furious."

"Damian. You have to understand that—"

"I have done a terrible thing."

"You *must* understand that…" She swung toward him. "What?"

"I brought you to my island so I could take care of you. Instead I've terrified you."

The soft night breeze tossed Ivy's hair over her cheek. She swept it back as she stared at the man seated beside her.

"I—I behaved badly that first night." He took a deep, deep breath, then expelled it. "And then, this morning… I had no right to turn my anger on you but I did and because of that, you walked a steep, long road under the hot sun."

Say something, Ivy told herself, for heaven's sake, say something!

"Walking is—walking is good for me."

"Ivy." His voice was rough. "I'm trying to apologize and—" He looked at her and smiled. "And it's not something I'm very good at."

Something in her softened. "Maybe because you don't do it very often," she said, smiling a little, too.

He grinned. "There are many people who would agree with you." He cleared his throat, engaged the gears and the Jeep moved forward. "So we will start over. I will take care of you."

"Damian. I don't need you to take care of me. I've been taking care of myself for a very long time."

"It's what I want."

Ivy hesitated. "Because of—because of the baby."

"That is part of it, of course. But I want—I want—"

He hesitated, too. What *did* he want? Things had seemed so clear this morning. He'd made Ivy his responsibility; that meant buying her whatever she needed.

But somewhere during the course of the day, that had changed. She'd gone from being his responsibility to being his pleasure and joy.

"I want to do the right thing," he said, hurrying the words because that was safer than trying to figure out where in hell this line of thought might lead. "I should have done that from the start instead of rushing off like a frustrated schoolboy the night I brought you here."

"You don't have to apologize," Ivy said quickly. This wasn't a topic she wanted to discuss. "I understood."

They had reached the palace. He pulled up in front of it, killed the engine and took her hands in his.

"I know it's no excuse but I've never lost control as

I did that night, *kardia mou*. I've never wanted a woman as I wanted you."

He spoke in the past tense. She understood that, too. He'd gone to Athens. Satisfied his—his needs.

"It was just as well that call came from my office. If I'd remained here, I don't know—I don't know what would have happened."

She stared at him. "You mean, you went to Athens on business?"

"What else would have taken me from you that night?" He gave a halfhearted laugh. "If anyone had ever suggested I would be grateful one of my tankers hit a reef…"

He hadn't left her for another woman's bed. Why did that mean so much?

"As for this child… No, don't look away from me." He cupped her chin and turned her face toward his. "How can we start over if we keep hiding things from each other? I did not know anything about a child. Do you really think, had I known, I would have abandoned it?"

Ivy shook her head. "Kay said—"

"Kay lied," he said sharply. "And that is the truth. I may not be a saint but I swear to you, I did not do these things. I did not ask Kay to become pregnant, and I certainly did not ask her to have a stranger become pregnant in her place."

"Me," Ivy said in a small, shaky voice.

"You," Damian said, bringing her hands to his lips. "But you are not a stranger any longer. You are a woman I know and admire."

"How can you admire me when you think—you think I did this for money? I didn't, Damian, I swear it. I didn't want to do it at all but—"

"But?"

But, I owed my stepsister more than I could ever repay.

She couldn't tell him that. The enormity of her debt. What would become of his admiration if she did? Only Kay knew her secret, and Kay had made her see that she must never tell anyone else.

"But," she whispered, "Kay took care of me after I—after I left foster care. I would have done anything to make her happy and so I said I'd do this…" Ivy bowed her head. "But I lied to myself. How could I have thought I'd be able to give up my—give up this baby?" Her voice broke. "Even the thought of it tears out my heart."

Damian took her in his arms, rocked her against him while she wept.

"Don't cry," he murmured. "You won't have to give up the baby, I promise." He pressed a kiss to her hair. "I am proud you carry my child, Ivy."

She looked up, eyes bright with tears. "Are you?"

"I only wish—I wish that I had put my seed deep in your womb as I made love to you." He kissed her; she clung to his shoulders as she kissed him back. "What I said in New York has not changed. I want to marry you."

"No. I know you want to do the right thing but—" She swallowed. "But I wouldn't be a good wife."

He smiled. "Have you been married before?" When she shook her head, his smile broadened. "Then, how can you know that?"

"I just do."

"We would start out together, *kardia mou*, I learning to be a good husband, you learning to be a good wife."

Ivy shook her head. "It would never work."

"Of course it would." Impatience roughened his voice. "Look at what we already have in common. A child we both love." His hands tightened on her shoulders. "I want my son," he said bluntly. "And I intend to have him. You can become my wife and his mother—or I'll take him from you. I don't want to hurt you but if I must, I will."

He was right, never mind all her pie-in-the-sky scheming this morning. Damian would win in a custody battle, even if she told the court her secret. He was the prince of a respected royal house. She was nobody.

Worse than nobody.

"What will it be? A courtroom? Or marriage?"

Ivy bowed her head, took a steadying breath, then looked up and met Damian's eyes.

"I can't marry you, Damian, even if—even if I wanted to. The thing is—the thing is—"

"For God's sake, what?"

"I don't like…" Her voice fell to a shaky whisper. "I don't like sex."

She didn't know what reaction she'd expected. Laughter? Anger? Disbelief? Surely not his sudden stillness. The muscle, knotting in his jaw. The way he looked at her, as if he were seeing her for the first time.

"You don't like—"

"No."

"Is that why you stopped me the other night?"

Ivy nodded. She would never tell him everything but he was entitled, at least, to know this.

He nodded, too. Then he got out of the Jeep, opened her door, drew her gently to her feet and into his arms.

"It's late," he said gruffly. "Much too late an hour of

the night for truths and secrets like this. I'm going to take you to your room and put you to bed."

He believed her. She was stunned. Men who came on to her, who called her frigid when she turned them away, never did.

He lifted her into his arms and she let him do it, loving the strength of his embrace, the warmth of his body, wishing with all her heart that things were different. That she was different.

And realized, too late, that the door he shouldered open, the bed he brought her to, was not hers.

It was his.

She began to protest. He silenced her with a kiss that left her breathless.

CHAPTER NINE

MOONLIGHT washed through the French doors and lit Ivy in its creamy spill.

Damian wanted to see her face but when he tried to lift her chin, she shook her head.

Was it true? Did this stunning, sensual woman dislike sex?

Earlier in the day, sitting on a too-small sofa in one of the boutiques, trying not to look as conspicuous as he felt, trying, as well, to figure out how in hell he'd gotten himself into this because he'd never, not once in his life, gone shopping with a woman—sitting there, arms folded, while Ivy changed into a dress in the fitting room, the salesclerk had bent down and whispered how flattered the shop was to have Ivy Madison as a customer.

Damian had frowned. How did the clerk know Ivy? Then he'd happened to glance at a glossy magazine on a table beside him and there was Ivy, smiling seductively from the cover.

In the days since she'd walked into his life, he'd thought of her as a lot of different things, all the way from scam artist to mother of his child. And, yes, gorgeous, too.

What man wouldn't notice that?

But he'd never thought of her as a woman whose face was known around the world.

He'd picked up the magazine, opened to a spread of Ivy modeling beachwear. She stood facing the camera in a white halter gown that clung to her body. In a crimson bikini that paid homage to her breasts and long legs. In a butter-yellow robe that hung open just enough to make his pulse accelerate.

He thought of other men, faceless strangers looking at those same photos, feeling what he felt, and he wanted to hunt the bastards down and make sure they understood they were wasting their time dreaming about her because she belonged solely to him.

Crazy, he'd told himself.

And then Ivy, his Ivy, had walked out of the dressing room, stepped onto a little platform in a gown he supposed was attractive—except, he hadn't really noticed.

All he'd noticed was her.

She was beautiful. Not in the way she was in the magazine, gazing in sultry splendor at the camera but as she was right then, a flesh and blood woman looking questioningly at him.

"What do you think?" she'd said.

What he'd thought was that she was so beautiful she stole his breath away.

"Very nice," he'd said.

The understatement of the year, but how did you tell a woman you were a heartbeat away from taking her in your arms, carrying her into the dressing room, kicking the damned door closed and making love to her? Doing it again and again until she was trembling with passion, until she admitted that she wanted him, that she would always want him.

Now she'd told him she didn't like sex.

It could be another bit of deceit to tempt him further into her web.

Damian's jaw tightened.

It could be...but it wasn't. He remembered what had happened in this same room, three nights ago. How she'd responded to him with dizzying abandon until he'd tried to take things further.

Without question, she'd told him the truth.

"Ivy?"

She didn't answer. He brushed the knuckles of his hand lightly against her cheek.

"Is that what happened the other night? Is that the reason you stopped me?"

"Yes."

The word was a sigh. He had to bend his head to hear it.

"You should have told me," he said softly.

"Tell you something like that?" She gave a forlorn little laugh. "When a man's about to—about to—to try to—" A deep breath. "I don't want to talk about it. I just thought you should know why I could never—I mean, the idea of marriage is out of the question anyway but—but if—if there were even the most remote possibility—"

"You're wrong, *agapi mou*. About everything."

His voice was so sure. God, he was so arrogant! And yet, right now, that arrogance made her smile. Despite herself, Ivy turned and lifted her eyes to his.

"Doesn't it ever occur to you," she said softly, "that there are times it's you who's wrong?"

"But you see, sweetheart, I wasn't going to have sex with you. I was going to make love to you."

"It's the same—"

He kissed her. Kissed her without demanding anything but her compliance, his mouth warm and tender against hers. Kissed her until he felt her tremble, though not with fear.

"You don't like sex," he said softly. "But you like my kisses."

"Damian. I can't. Really, I just—"

He kissed her again, just as gently, and felt a fierce rush of pleasure when her mouth softened under his.

"Damian." Her voice shook. "I don't think—"

"Shh." His hands spread across her back, applying just a little pressure when he kissed her again, enough to part her lips and touch the tip of her tongue with his.

A whisper of sound rose in her throat. Did she move closer or did he? It took all his self-control not to pull her into his arms.

"Sex is a physical act, *glyka mou*. It's part of making love but it's hardly all of it."

"I don't see—"

"No. You don't. Let me show you, then. Just another kiss," he added, when she began to shake her head. "I only want to taste you. Will you permit me to do that?"

He didn't wait for her answer. Instead he put his mouth against hers.

"Open to me," he said thickly. A second slipped by. Then she moaned, rose on her toes, tipped her head back and let him take the kiss deeper.

Damian kissed her over and over, his tongue in her mouth, his hands buried in the chestnut and gold spill of her hair.

He told himself he would keep his promise. That he would only taste her. But as her skin heated, as she sighed with pleasure, he put his lips against her throat, slipped her blouse from her shoulders, kissed his way to the vee of her silk T-shirt.

"Ivy," he whispered, his hands spreading over her midriff, the tips of his fingers brushing the undersides of her breasts. "Ivy, *kardia mou…*"

Her hands lifted, knotted in his shirt. His name sighed from her lips.

The room began to blur.

He told himself to go slowly. To do no more than he'd said he would. But she was leaning into him now, her hands were cool on his nape and he bent his head to her breasts, kissed them through the silky fabric of her shirt.

She made a broken little sound deep in her throat and arched her back. The simple motion made an offering of her beaded nipples, taut and visible beneath her T-shirt.

It would have taken a saint to refuse such a gift.

Damian was no saint.

He kissed the delicate beads of silk-covered flesh. Drew them into his mouth, first one and then the other. Ivy's cries grew sharper. Hungrier.

So did his need.

He dropped to his knees. Lifted her shirt and found he'd been right about the half-closed zipper.

Slowly he eased the trousers down her hips and legs.

"Damian," she said unsteadily.

He looked up at her. "I'm just going to undress you," he whispered. "Then I'll put you to bed and if you want me to leave, I will. I promise."

She hesitated. Then she stepped out of the trousers and when he saw her like that, wearing the silk T-shirt, her long legs bare, her feet encased in foolishly high heels, he wondered why in hell he'd made such a promise.

But he would keep it.

He would keep it by stopping now. By standing up. By—all right, by reaching under the T, undoing her bra, only because she wouldn't want to sleep with it on…

Ivy stumbled back. "Don't! Please, don't."

Her voice was high; her eyes were wide with fear and, in a heartbeat, Damian understood.

She'd said she didn't like sex. He'd foolishly, arrogantly assumed she was simply a woman unawakened.

He knew better now.

Ivy, his Ivy, didn't like sex because she was terrified of it. A man had hurt her. Taught her that sex was painful or evil or ugly.

Damian spat out a sharp, four-letter word. Ivy began to weep.

"I told you," she sobbed, "I told you how it would be—"

"Who did this to you?"

She didn't answer. He cursed again, took her in his arms, ignored her attempts to free herself and wrapped her in his embrace.

"Ivy. *Agapi mou. Kardia mou.* Do not cry. Ivy, my Ivy…"

He'd lost his accent his second year at Yale but it was back now, roughening his words and then he was talking in Greek, not the modern language he'd grown up speaking but the ancient one he'd studied in prep school.

The Greek of the Spartans and Athenians. His warrior ancestors.

He knew what they would have done. It was what he longed to do. Find the man who'd done this to Ivy and kill him.

Her soft, desperate sobs broke his heart.

He held her against him, rocking her, whispering to her, soft, sweet words he had never said to a woman before, never wanted to say and, at last, her tears stopped.

Gently he scooped her into his arms and put her in the center of his bed, stroked her tousled hair back from her damp cheeks.

"It's all right," he murmured. "It's all right, sweetheart. Go to sleep, *agapimeni*. I'll stay here and keep you safe."

He drew the comforter over her. She clutched at it and rolled onto her side, turning her back to him. He wanted to reach for her again, to lie down and hold her, but instinct warned him not to. She was too fragile right now; God only knew what might push her over the edge.

So he sat beside her, watching until her breathing slowed and her lashes drooped against her cheeks.

"Ivy?" he said softly.

She was asleep.

Damian dropped a light kiss on her hair. Then he went into his dressing room, took off his clothes and put on an old, soft pair of Yale sweats. He padded back into the bedroom, drew an armchair next to the bed, sat down, stretched out his long legs and considered all the creative ways a man could deal with a son of a bitch who'd taught his Ivy that sex, the most intimate act a man and woman could share, was a thing to be feared.

He'd go from A to Z, he thought grimly. But "Assault" was too general. "Beating" was too simple.

"Castration" was a lot better. He stayed with that scenario until sleep finally dragged him under.

Something woke him.

The moon had disappeared, chased into hiding by wind and rain. The room was as black and frigid as Hecate's heart.

Damian padded quickly to the French doors and closed them. Damn, it was cold! Was Ivy warm enough under the comforter? It was too dark to see anything but the outline of the big bed.

He turned on a lamp, adjusting the switch until the light was only a soft glow. Ivy lay as he'd left her but the covers had dropped from her shoulder.

He shut off the light. Carefully leaned over the bed, began drawing up the comforter...

Zzzzt!

A streak of blinding light, then the roar of thunder rolling across the sea.

Ivy sprang up in bed, saw him leaning over her... and screamed.

"Ivy! Sweetheart. Don't be afraid. It's me. It's only me."

He caught her in his arms, ignored the jab that caught him in the eye and held her against him, stroking her, whispering to her. An eternity seemed to pass until, finally, she shuddered and went still.

"Damian?"

Her voice was thready. He drew her even closer, willing his strength into her.

"Yes, *agapimeni*. It's me."

Another shudder went through her. "I thought—I thought—"

He could only imagine what she'd thought. Rage, deep and ugly as a flood tide, filled him, left him struggling to keep his composure.

"You thought it was old Hephaestus, playing games with lightning bolts on Mount Olympus," he said with forced cheerfulness.

Was that tiny sound a laugh?

"Storms here can be pretty fierce during the summer. They scared the heck out of me when I was little, and it didn't help that my nanny would glare at me and say, 'You see, Your Highness? That's what happens when little boys don't listen to their nannies.'"

He'd dropped his voice to a husky growl that was less his long-ago nanny's and more a really bad Count Dracula, but it worked. His Ivy laughed. A definite laugh, this time, one that made him offer a silent word of thanks just in case old Hephaestus happened to be within earshot.

"That wasn't very nice of her."

"No, but it was effective. For the next few days, I'd be the model of princely decorum."

"And then?"

Lightning, followed by the crash of thunder, rolled across the sky again. Ivy trembled and Damian tightened his arms around her. "And then," he said, "I'd revert to the catch-me-if-you-can little devil I actually was." His smile faded. "You'll be fine, *glyka mou*. I won't let anything happen to you, I promise."

She leaned back in his embrace and looked up at him, her face a pale, lovely oval.

"Thank you," she whispered.

"For what?"

"For—" She hesitated. "For being so—so... For being so nice."

Nice? He'd bullied her, berated her, accused her of being a cheat and a liar. He'd forced her to come with him to Greece, told her he owned her...

"I haven't been nice," he said brusquely. "I've been impatient and arrogant. It is I who should thank you for tolerating me."

That rated a smile. "We're even, then. I'll forgive you and you'll forgive me."

He smiled back at her. A moment slipped by and his smile faded. "Ivy? Are you all right?"

"I'm fine."

"Good." God, how he wanted to kiss her. Just one kiss to tell her he would keep her safe from lightning and thunder and, most of all, safe from whatever terrible thing had once happened to her. "Good," he said briskly, and cleared his throat. "So. Let me tuck you in and—"

"Where are you sleeping? If I'm taking up your bed—"

"Don't worry about me."

"But where..."

"Right in that chair. I, ah, I thought it would be a good idea to be here in case, you know, in case you needed me."

"You? In that little chair? Where do you put your legs?"

He grinned. "They say a little suffering is good for the soul."

"It looks like a lot of suffering to me."

"Easy," he said lightly. "First you tell me I'm nice. Then you say I'm a candidate for sainthood. If you aren't careful—"

"Sleep with me."

Her voice was low, the words rushed. He told himself he'd misunderstood her but he hadn't, otherwise why would a pink stain be creeping into her cheeks?

"Just—just share the bed with me, Damian. Nothing else. I just—I don't want to think of you, all cramped up in that chair." She licked her lips. "If you won't share it, I'll have to sleep in the guest room. Alone. And—and I really don't want to. Be alone, I mean. Unless—unless you don't want—"

"Move over," he said, his voice gruff, his heart racing.

Ivy scooted away. He climbed onto the bed, slid under the covers, held his breath and then thought, to hell with it, and he put his arm around her waist and drew her into the curve of his body.

"Good night, *agapi mou*," he murmured.

"Good night, Damian."

He closed his eyes. Time passed. The storm moved off. Ivy lay unmoving in his embrace, so still that she had to be asleep and he—he was going to lose his mind. He *would* be a candidate for sainthood, by morning.

"Damian?"

He swallowed hard. "Yes, sweetheart?"

Slowly she turned toward him. He could feel her breath on his face.

Her hand touched his stubbled jaw; her fingers drifted like feathers over his mouth.

"Ivy…"

Her hand cupped the back of his head and she brought his lips down to hers.

His heart turned over.

"Ivy," he whispered again but she shook her head, kissed him and drew even closer.

One of them had to be dreaming.

Her lips parted. The tip of her tongue touched the seam of his mouth. He wanted to roll her on her back, open her mouth to his, savage her mouth with kisses.

But he wouldn't.

He wouldn't.

He would do only what she asked of him. He was not a saint but neither was he a beast.

Ivy whispered his name. Lay her thigh over his.

Damian groaned, caught her hands and held them against his chest.

"Sweetheart," he said raggedly, "*glyka mou*. I can't—" He cleared his throat. "Let's—let's sit up. In the chair. I'll hold you and—and when sunrise comes, we can watch it together and—and—"

She silenced him with a kiss that told him everything a man could hope to hear. Still, he held back and she took the initiative, rolling onto her back, holding him close, arching her body against his.

"Ivy," he whispered, and let himself tumble into the hot abyss with her.

He kissed her mouth. Her eyes. Her throat. She gave soft little cries of pleasure and each cry filled his soul.

He kissed her breasts through the thin silk T-shirt, sucked her nipples into his mouth and she went crazy beneath him, sobbing his name, clutching his shoulders, and he thought, *Slow down, slow down, God, slow down or this will end much too fast.*

But he was lost.

Lost in Ivy's scent, in her taste, in the silk of her hair and the heat of her skin.

He pushed up her shirt. Bared her breasts. Kissed the creamy slopes, teased the pale pink nipples, her sweet cries urging him on.

He sat her up. Pulled the shirt over her head. Unhooked her bra and her breasts, like the most precious fruit, tumbled into his hands.

He kissed them, kissed her belly, round and taut with his child and thought, as he had before, how perfect it would be if he and she had made this child together.

Then he stopped thinking because she was tugging at his sweatshirt.

He reared back and tugged it off. She arched against him, her breasts hot against his chest, and her moans of ecstasy almost unmanned him.

Her panties were the merest whisper of silk. He drew them down her legs and she arched again so that he sank into the spread of her thighs.

"Ivy," he said thickly.

"Yes," she whispered. "Please, yes."

She lifted her face and he kissed her, tasting her tears, tasting her sweetness, and something stirred deep, deep inside him, something stirred within his heart.

And then he was inside her. Inside her and she was so tight. So tight…

"Damian," she sighed, and put her hand between them.

The world spun away.

He groaned, thrust forward and Ivy cried out and came apart in his arms.

He held on as long as he could. Sheathing himself within her. Pulling back until it was torture, then sinking deep, feeling her come again and again until, finally, he let himself go with her. Fly into the night, into the sky, into the universe.

And knew, as he collapsed against her, that sex was, indeed, only sex. Making love was what really mattered.

And though he'd been with many women, he had never really made love until tonight.

CHAPTER TEN

DAMIAN was asleep.

Ivy had slept, too. For a little while, anyway, safe and warm in his embrace.

Then she'd awakened.

And, just that quickly, the memories came rushing back.

She'd lain beside him for another few minutes, telling herself not to let this happen. Not to spoil the wonder of Damian's lovemaking with the ugliness of those memories.

It hadn't worked.

Finally, carefully, she'd slipped from under the curve of her lover's arm and risen from the bed.

A soft cashmere throw lay at its foot. She'd wrapped herself in it, held her breath while she opened the French doors and stepped out on the terrace.

When would she finally be able to forget?

A little while ago, when the fury of the storm had invaded her dreams, it spun her back in time to another night a long, long time ago.

No, she'd whimpered, deep in the dream, *no!*

It hadn't mattered.

She'd come awake in terror. And when she saw the figure bending over her, that terror had wrapped its bony hands around her throat.

"No," she'd screamed—and then Damian had spoken her name.

He was the man leaning over her bed, not a fat monster who stunk of beer and sweat.

He hadn't grabbed her breast, squeezed it, laughed as he ripped her nightgown open.

He hadn't clamped a sweaty palm over her mouth as she tried to fight him off, her fifteen-year-old self no match for a man who earned his living swinging a pick ax.

Not a sound, he'd said, his stinking breath washing over her. *You make one noise, just one, I'll tell the social worker you stole money outta my wallet and you'll be back in Juvie Placement so fast it'll make your head spin.*

She hadn't stolen anything. Ever. The first time, in a different foster home, they'd said she'd taken a hundred dollars. She hadn't—but Kay said she had to be lying because the only other person who could have done it was her. Kay. Was Ivy accusing her of theft?

Kay stayed in that home. Ivy was sent back to the Placement facility. Eventually they'd put her in another foster home.

Kay turned eighteen and left the system.

"See you," she said.

And Ivy was alone.

Six months in one place. Three in another. Bad places. Dirty places. And then, finally, a place where the woman just looked right through her and the man smiled and said, *Call me Daddy.*

Ivy had felt her heart lift.

Daddy, she'd said, and even though he wasn't like her real daddy—whom she barely remembered—or her stepfather, Kay's father, whom she'd loved with all her heart—even though he wasn't, he was nice.

At least, that was what she thought.

He bought her a doll. Some books. And when he began coming into her room at night, to tuck her in, she'd felt a little funny because he also took to kissing her on the cheek but if he was her daddy, her real daddy, that was okay, wasn't it?

A light wind blowing in over the sea raised goose bumps on her skin. Ivy shuddered and drew the cashmere blanket more closely around her.

And then it all changed. One night, a storm was roaring outside. Lightning. Thunder. Rain. It scared her but she finally fell asleep—and woke to see the man she called Daddy standing over her bed.

Even now, all these years later, the memory was sheer agony.

He'd hurt her. Hurt her bad. He came to her each night, night after night, and when she finally tried to tell the woman, she'd slapped her in the face, called her a slut…

And Kay had come.

Ivy had flown to embrace her but Kay had pushed her away.

"What'd you do, huh?" she'd said coldly. "Don't give me that innocent look. Did you play games with this man like you did with my father?"

"What games?" Ivy had said in bewilderment. "I loved your father. He treated me as if I were his own daughter."

The look on her stepsister's face had been as frigid as her voice. "Only one problem, Little Miss Innocent. He already had a daughter. Me."

She'd lived with Kay for a few months but she knew she was in the way. And then, a couple of weeks after she turned seventeen, a man walked up to her on Madison Avenue, handed her his card and said, "Give me a call and we'll see if you have what it takes to become a model."

Kay had said yes, fine, do whatever you want. Just remember, never tell anybody what you did because they'll tell you how disgusting you really are.

Ivy moved out, the agency sent her to Milan, moved her into an apartment with five other girls. She sent Kay cards and letters that all went unanswered until she made the cover of *Glamour Girl* and Kay called to say she was so sorry they'd lost touch and how proud she was to be her sister...

"Glyka mou?"

Ivy spun around as Damian walked out onto the balcony. He'd pulled on his sweatpants. They hung low on his hips, accentuating his naked chest, muscled shoulders and arms, the abs most male models worked like machines to develop.

Beautiful. He was so beautiful. And so good and decent and kind...

"Sweetheart." He gathered her into his arms. "What's the matter?"

She shook her head, not trusting herself to speak, afraid that if she did, the lump that had suddenly risen in her throat would give way and she'd burst into tears of joy.

"Agapimeni." He tilted her face to his and brushed his lips gently over hers. "Tell me what's happened. Why did you leave me?"

I'll never leave you, she thought. *Never, not as long as you want me!*

"I just—" She swallowed, blinked away the silly burn of tears. "I woke up and—and I could still hear the storm, way off in the distance, and I wanted to—I wanted to see…"

Smiling, he cupped her face and threaded his fingers into her hair.

"A little while ago, you were afraid of the storm."

"That was before you made me see I had nothing to be afraid of."

Something dark flickered in his eyes. "Never," he said fiercely. "Not as long as I'm here to protect you."

Her heart lifted. How wrong she'd been about this man. Arrogant? Overpowering? Never. He was simply sure of himself, and strong.

And tender. And caring. And she felt—she felt—

"It was more than the storm you feared." His arms tightened around her. "Do you want to tell me about it?"

Yes. God yes, she did! But not yet. Not now. Not when her feelings were so new, so confused.

"It's all right." He kissed her. "You don't have to tell me anything you don't want to tell me."

"It isn't that. It's just…" She hesitated. "What's happened. This. It's all so—so new…"

"You mean, us," he said. When she nodded, he lifted her in his arms and carried her through the French doors. Gently he lay her on the bed and came down beside her.

"Are you happy?"

She smiled. "I'm very happy."

Slowly he eased the cashmere blanket from her shoulders, revealing her breasts, her belly, her body to his eyes.

"You're the most beautiful woman in the world," he whispered. "And I'm the luckiest man."

He dipped his head. Kissed her throat. Bent lower and circled a nipple with the tip of his tongue.

Ivy trembled. "Oh. Oh God, that feels—it feels—"

He licked the nipple. Sucked it into his mouth. She wound her arms around his neck, stunned at the sudden sharp longing low in her belly.

"How does it feel?" he said gruffly. "Tell me."

"Wonderful. Damian. It feels—"

His hand slipped down her belly, into the curls between her thighs, into the heat between her thighs, and found her clitoris.

Ivy moaned with pleasure and arched against his fingers.

"Please," she whispered. "Please."

"Please, what?" he said, and the thickness in his voice added to her excitement.

"Please," she sighed, "make love to me again."

He kissed her mouth. Kissed her belly. Parted her thighs and put his mouth to her and the first touch of his tongue sent her flying.

And then he was inside her, deep inside her, and she was lost. He said her name and she disintegrated into a million, billion pieces that flew to the far ends of the universe…

And knew the truth.

She had fallen in love with the complicated, impossible, wonderful man in her arms.

She lay beneath him, arms wrapped around him, his weight bearing her down into the mattress, his heart racing against hers, his skin damp from their lovemaking.

Until this moment even thinking about those things—
a man's body on hers, the thud of his heart, the scent of
his sweat… Just imagining those things, remembering
them, was enough to bring a dizzying wave of nausea.

But this was Damian.

And this was, as he'd promised, the difference
between having sex and making love.

I love you, she thought, *Damian, I love you…*

Had she said the words? Was that why he was
rolling away?

"Don't go," she said, before she could stop herself.

Damian's arms closed around her. He drew her close
to him, their faces inches apart.

"I'm not going anywhere, *glyka mou,*" he whispered.
"I'm just too heavy to lie on top of you."

"You're not."

He kissed her, his lips warm against hers.

"My sweet fraud," he said softly.

It was a soft, teasing endearment. She knew that.
Still, it hurt because she *was* a fraud.

She hadn't told him about her past.

Hadn't told him about his baby.

And she had to tell him. He had to know. But
when? When?

"You're trembling." Damian drew the comforter over
them both. "Better?"

"Yes. Fine."

"Mmm." He grinned. "Indeed you were." He gave
her a long, tender kiss. "I was afraid I might hurt you,
sweetheart. You were so tight."

His voice was low and filled with concern. This was
either the exact moment to tell him everything—or the
exact moment not to.

How could she admit to her ugly past?

How could she admit to the lie she'd told him?

"Sweetheart? Did I hurt you? God, if I did…"

"No! Oh, no, Damian, you didn't hurt me." Ivy took his hand, brought it to her mouth and kissed it. "What we did—"

"Making love."

"Yes. It was wonderful."

He held her against him for a long moment. Then he cupped her face and tilted it to his.

"I'm sorry I frightened you before."

"It wasn't your fault. I was—I was dreaming. And then I heard the thunder and I saw the lightning and—"

"And, you thought I was someone else. Someone who'd hurt you."

She couldn't lie, not when his arms were around her. "Yes."

Rage swept over him. Her whisper only confirmed what he'd already suspected.

"A man."

Ivy buried her face against his throat.

"Who?"

She shook her head. "I don't want to talk about it."

Yes, but he did. He wanted a name. He wanted to find this faceless son of a bitch and kill him.

Ah, God, Ivy was trembling and he knew damned well it had nothing to do with the temperature of the room. Damian cursed himself for being an ass.

"Forgive me, sweetheart." He kissed her hair, her temple, her mouth. "I'm a fool to talk about these things at a time like this."

"You're not a fool," she said fiercely, looking into his eyes. "You're a good, kind, wonderful man."

He forced a smile to his face. "That's quite an improvement over being—let's see. An SOB, an arrogant bastard, a son of—"

She laughed, as he'd hoped she would. "Well, sometimes... No. Seriously you're not any of those things I called you."

His hand moved slowly down her spine, cupped her bottom, drew her more closely against him.

"We didn't know each other," he said softly. "And it's my fault. I stormed into your life—"

"Seems to me I was the one who did the storming."

Good. She was smiling. He hadn't spoiled this amazing night for her after all.

No more questions...for now. But he would ask them again. A monster had done something terrible to Ivy.

Something sexual. Something violent.

Had he been caught? Had he paid for what he'd done? Not that it mattered. He would find the man and deal with him in his own way...

"Damian?"

He blinked. "Yes?"

"I'm glad we stormed into each other's lives."

He smiled and lifted her face to his so he could kiss her again. How had he lived his life without this woman?

"So am I. And now we have all the time in the world to get to know each other."

Ivy put her hand against his jaw. "Being with you tonight has been—has been—"

"Making love, you mean."

Her heart lifted. "Making love with you, yes. It was—it was so wonderful..."

How he loved the sound of her voice. The feel of her in his arms. How he loved—how he loved—

"For me, too," he said huskily. "I've never—I mean, you and I…" He cleared his throat, amazed at how difficult it was to say the next words but then, they were a kind of commitment, given all the women in his past. "What happened between us is… It was very special, *glyka mou.* I've never experienced anything like it before."

Ivy's face was solemn. "I'm glad because…" She touched the tip of her tongue to her lips. "Because this was—this is—it's the very first time I ever—I ever—"

She was blushing. Amazing, that this beautiful, sophisticated woman would blush when she talked about having an orgasm.

Amazing, too, that his damnable ego took pleasure in the thought that he had done for her what no other lover had done.

"Your first orgasm," he said softly, and smiled. "Part of me is sorry that's been denied you but I have to admit, part of me is… What?"

"I'm not talking about having an orgasm." Her voice was so soft he had to strain to hear it. "I'm talking about…" She swallowed. "You're right," she said, rushing the words together. "Something did happen to me, a long time ago. And because it did, I never took a lover until—until—"

The hurried words trailed off. Ivy tried to look away but Damian wouldn't let her. He cupped her face, kissed her mouth, told her what honor she had brought him, by letting him be her first lover.

Then he rolled her gently on her back.

"And your only lover, for the rest of our lives."

He kissed her. Caressed her. Touched her as if she were as fragile as a cobweb until she sobbed his name

and showed him with her mouth, her hands, her body
that she would not break…

Showed him, without words, what was in her heart.

Showed him that she had fallen deeply, forever in love.

They flew to Athens the next morning to see an obstetrician, who examined Ivy, looked over the records that
Damian, ever in command, had somehow had trans-
ferred from her New York OB-GYN, smiled and said,
neh, everything was fine.

Was she certain? asked Damian.

The doctor said she was.

Because, Damian said, he'd noticed things.

The doctor and Ivy both looked at him. "What
things?" they said in unison.

Well, his Ivy didn't eat as much as she should.

His Ivy? The phrase went straight to Ivy's heart. She
smiled and put her hand in his.

"My appetite's just fine."

"Yes, *glyka mou,* but you are eating for two."

"Ms. Madison's weight is right on target."

Damian didn't look convinced but he had another
question. What about exercise? He had walked her all
around Kolonaki Square only yesterday. Was it too
much? Should he have permitted—

"Permitted?" Ivy said, her eyebrows rising again.

Should he have let her do that? Damian asked

"Ms. Madison is in excellent health, Your Highness.
And," the doctor added gently, "she is hardly the first
woman to have a baby."

Damian's authoritative air vanished. "I know that," he
said, "but I am the first man to have one." A beat of silence;
the doctor smiled but not Ivy. "I mean, I mean—"

"You mean this is your first child," the doctor said. "Of course, Your Highness. And I promise you, everything is fine."

Outside, on the street, Ivy turned to Damian. "I understand why you're so concerned. You—you lost a baby, with my sister."

"I *thought* I lost a baby," Damian said carefully. "But it was a lie."

"Yes." Her eyes clouded. "A terrible lie. But believing you'd really lost a baby must have been almost as bad as having it happen."

Damian wanted to take her in his arms and kiss her, but they were on a crowded street. He made do with taking her hand, bringing it to his lips and pressing a kiss into the palm.

"I'm concerned because of you," he said. "If anything happened to you…" He took a deep breath. "Ivy. You are—you are—"

My love.

The words were right there, on the tip of his tongue, but that was crazy. He hardly knew this woman. And there were still so many unanswered questions…

Besides, a man didn't fall in love after, what, a week? There was no reason to be impulsive. To make a move he might regret.

"You are important to me." He brought her hand to his mouth, kissed the palm and folded her fingers over the kiss. "Very important."

Ivy nodded. They weren't the words she yearned to hear, but they were close.

"I'm glad, because—because you're very important to me, too."

A smile lit his face. "Words meant to feed a man's ego," he said teasingly.

"Words that are true. Being with you, carrying your baby..." She hesitated, afraid she would blurt out too much. "I've never been this happy. And I want you to know that—that no matter what happens, you will always be—you will always be—"

She fell silent as their eyes met.

Damian's heart turned over at what he saw in her face.

Years ago, he, Lucas and Nicolo had celebrated surviving finals week at Yale by driving to an airport in a little town called Danielson.

They'd taken a couple of hours of instruction, strapped on parachutes and boarded a plane after drawing slips of paper to decide which of them would go first.

He'd won.

"Or lost," Nicolo had said, grinning.

It came back to him now, the way he'd felt standing in the plane's open door, the wind trying to pluck him out, the ground beckoning from a million miles below.

What in hell am I doing? he'd thought.

"Jump," his instructor had yelled.

And he had.

God, it had been incredible. Stepping into space. Soaring above the earth, then falling toward it.

Incredible.

He'd jumped for years after that but as much as he'd loved skydiving, he'd never quite felt the excitement, the sheer wonder of that first time.

Until now.

Until he saw the smile in Ivy's eyes. Felt his heart thump as she lay her palms against his chest.

He reminded himself that he really knew nothing about her.

Reminded himself that she hadn't given a reasonable answer as to why she'd agreed to Kay's incredible request.

And now there were more questions. Who had hurt her? Why wouldn't she talk about it?

One call to a private investigator and he'd have the answers he needed in, what, a week?

That was what he had to do. He was a logical man. He always had been. That was how he'd saved Aristedes Shipping. With logic. Common sense. By taking one step at a time.

By *not* jumping into space.

Skydiving, skiing down a glacier… A man could run risks in such things but not in those that were life-changing.

Damian took Ivy's hands in his. They were icy-cold, despite the heat of the day. She had opened her heart to him and now she was waiting for him to say something.

And he would.

Something logical. Something sensible. Something that would not put him at risk…

"Ivy," he said, "my beautiful Ivy. I love you. I adore you. Will you be my wife?"

She stared at him as if he'd lost his mind. Well, maybe he had. But when she smiled, and her eyes filled with tears, and she said she loved him with all her heart and yes, she would be his wife, yes, yes, yes…

It wasn't anything like that first jump.

It was ten thousand times better.

CHAPTER ELEVEN

Ivy stood ankle-deep in the surf, her face turned up to the hot kiss of the sun.

A month ago, Minos had been a forbidding chunk of rock rearing up from a depressingly dark sea.

Now, it was paradise.

White sand beaches. Towering volcanic rock. Firs, pines, poplars that climbed its slopes, anemones and violets that poked slyly from the deep green grass.

And around it all, the Aegean, wine-dark and magnificent, just as the poet, Homer, had described it centuries before.

Could a place look so different just because you were happy?

Yes. Oh, yes, it could.

Not just a place. The world. The universe. And happy wasn't the right word to describe how she felt.

She was—she was complete.

Being with Damian, being part of his life, having him a part of hers, was wonderful.

He was everything. The sun, the moon, the stars… She laughed out loud, threw up her arms and did a little dance right there, as the wavelets foamed around her ankles.

Surely nobody had ever been this much in love. It just wasn't possible.

Ivy eased down to the sand, legs outstretched in the warm surf, arms back, basking in the glorious warmth of the Greek sun.

The only thing warmer was Damian's love.

That so much joy had come from something that had started so badly... Not the baby, she thought quickly, putting a protective hand over her belly. Never that. She'd wanted the baby almost the moment she'd missed her first period and known, for sure, she was pregnant.

Known she wanted the baby—and that she'd made a terrible mistake, agreeing to Kay's awful plan.

That was the bad start. The plan. Not the original one, which had been hard enough to say "yes" to, but the one Kay had dropped on her at the last possible second.

How could she have agreed to it?

Ivy shut her eyes. The truth was, she'd never agreed to it in her heart.

The joy of the sunny morning fell away.

In the end, Kay had asked too much of her. She'd owed her so much, yes, so much, but giving up the baby?

She knew now that she could not, would not have done it.

Wasn't it time to explain that, to explain everything, to Damian?

Slowly Ivy rose to her feet, tucked her hands into the back pockets of her white shorts and began walking along the sand.

Of course it was.

At the beginning, Damian had assumed she'd made

a devil's bargain. He knew better, now, that she'd never do something like this for money.

And because he loved her, he'd stopped asking.

That didn't mean he wasn't entitled to the truth.

It was just that telling him meant telling him everything, starting with what had occurred when she was fifteen and ending with the day a doctor was to implant Kay's eggs, mixed with Damian's sperm, in her womb.

Except—except, it hadn't happened that way.

Ivy swung blindly toward the sea, remembering her stepsister's face that day.

Kay had shown up at Ivy's apartment hours ahead of their scheduled appointment at the fertility clinic.

"Everything's changed," she'd said desperately. "My doctor says my eggs are no good. There's no point in implanting them inside you."

Ivy had taken Kay in her arms, patted her back, said she was sorry even as a mean little voice inside her whispered *You know you're not really sorry, you're relieved. Carrying a baby, even one that wasn't actually yours, would have been agony to give up.*

"Oh, Ivy," Kay had sobbed, "what am I going to do? You have to help me!"

"I wish I could but—"

Kay had raised her face. Amazingly her tears had not spoiled her makeup.

"Do you?" she'd said. "Do you really wish you could help me?"

And she'd laid out a plan so detailed, so complete, only a fool—a fool like Ivy—would have believed she'd just come up with it.

Ivy had listened. Halfway through, she'd raised her hands in horror.

"No! Kay, I can't do that! You can't really ask me to—"

Kay's eyes had darkened. "So much for all these years you've told me how grateful you were I took you out of that foster home."

"Of course I'm grateful! But—"

"Out of a situation you'd created."

"I didn't. I didn't!"

"Of course you did," Kay had said coldly. "Flirting with that man. Hanging all over him."

"I never did! I was just a kid. He—he hurt me, Kay!"

"Spare me the sob story," Kay had snapped. "What counts is that I was your lifeline and now, when I ask you to be mine, you look at me as if I'm the devil incarnate and you whimper 'no, I can't!' Is that your idea of how to repay a debt?"

"Kay. Please. Listen to me. What you're asking—"

"What I'm asking for is what you owe me, Ivy. You're always saying I saved your life. Well, now you owe me mine."

It had gone on for hours, Kay talking about what she'd done for Ivy, how Ivy owed her everything, Ivy saying no, no—

In the end, she'd finally given in even though she knew it was wrong, knew she was taking the first step toward breaking her own heart, knew she could not imagine how she would ever give up a baby conceived with a sperm-filled condom, with a syringe, both conveniently tucked inside a little box her stepsister had produced…

"Glyka mou?"

Ivy looked up. Damian smiled as he walked toward her. He was shirtless, barefoot; he wore only denim shorts. His jaw was stubbled because today was Saturday and he hadn't shaved…

Her heart rose into her throat.

How she loved him!

And how cruelly she was deceiving him.

She wore his ring now—a diamond so magnificent it made her breath catch just to look at it. A tiny gold shield that bore his family crest—a lance, a shield and, she now knew, an ancient Minoan bull—dangled from a delicate chain around her neck. Their wedding day was only a week away—and she was still living a lie.

Tears welled in her eyes just as Damian reached her.

"Hey," he said, taking her in his arms, "sweetheart, what's wrong?"

Everything, she thought, everything was wrong! What would he think of her when he knew exactly why she'd been afraid of sex? When he knew the truth about the baby?

"Ivy? *Kardia mou,* tell me what makes you weep."

She couldn't do it. Not yet.

"I'm just—I'm happy, that's all," she whispered, burying her face against his shoulder.

Damian held her close, kissing her hair, her temple, rocking her gently against him…

Aware, in every fiber of his being, she was not telling him the truth.

Yes, his Ivy was happy. He knew it because he was happy, too, though "happy" was far too small a word for what he felt.

He was ecstatic.

Love, commitment, the Big M word had always seemed meant for others. He was not ready to settle down and have children, or even tie himself to one woman.

Then Ivy came along, and all of that changed.

He loved looking up on a Sunday morning to see her biting her lip as she worked a crossword puzzle. Loved the sound of her laughter when a wave caught him and soaked him from head to toe.

Loved the way she fit into his arms when he took her dancing at the little jazz club on the seedy edge of Piraeus, the way she closed her eyes and let the music wash over her.

He loved waking with her in his arms and falling asleep with her in them at night.

That his child was in her womb was icing on the cake.

It wasn't her child, not biologically, and yes, he wished it were, but the other day, when a tiny foot or maybe an elbow had jabbed against his palm, he'd suddenly thought, *Ivy is the reason this precious life exists.*

And he'd imagined his son slipping from her womb, feeding greedily from her breast, and his heart had filled with almost unimaginable joy.

"*Glyka mou,*" he'd whispered, "I am so very happy."

And his Ivy had smiled, brought his mouth down to hers, shown him with her lips, her body, that she was happy, too.

Did she really think he would believe she was weeping in his arms now only because she was happy?

Something was troubling her. Something she'd been keeping from him far too long.

Gently he lifted her in his arms and carried her up the beach, to the dark blue awning of the sprawling cabana he'd had built after he'd inherited Minos and started spending most of his time on the island. He sat her in a lounge chair, went inside the cabana, brought out a box of tissues and blotted her eyes, held one to her nose.

"Blow."

She did. He almost laughed that his elegant Ivy could sound like a honking goose but a man who laughed when his woman wept deserved whatever punishment he got in return.

After a while, her tears stopped.

"Better?"

She nodded.

"Good." Damian squatted in front of her and took her hands in his. "Now, tell me why you weep." He brushed her mouth with his. "The truth, sweetheart. It is time."

Ivy raised her head. "You're right," she said. "It is." She paused. "I—I haven't been honest with you."

Damian nodded. "Go on."

Her face was so pale. He kissed her again, putting his love, his heart, into the kiss.

"Whatever it is," he said softly, "I will still love you."

Would he? She took a steadying breath.

"I've let you think a man—a man hurt me and—and that's the reason I was afraid of sex."

Her words came out in a rush. Damian's smile tilted. "But?"

"But—but it was my fault," she said, her voice so soft it was barely a whisper. "I mean, he did hurt me, but—"

"If someone hurt you, how could it possibly be your fault?"

She told him.

She started at the beginning. The death of her own father. Her mother marrying Kay's widowed father a couple of years later.

"I loved him almost as much as I'd loved my real father," she said. Her voice trembled. "So when he died—when they both died, my mom and my stepfather—"

"Ah, sweetheart. Stop if it hurts you to talk about it."

"You need to know, Damian. I—I need to tell you."

He nodded. "I'm listening."

"It was almost unbearable. Thank God I had—I had Kay."

"Kay." His mouth twisted.

"I was ten. She was fourteen. We'd never been close—the age difference, I guess—but when our parents died…" Ivy swallowed hard. "They put us into foster care. Together. And Kay was—she was—"

"Your lifeline?"

There it was. That same word Kay had used. Ivy nodded. "Yes."

"And?"

"And—and we were in one place that was okay. In another that wasn't. And—and I was accused of—of taking money—"

Damian tugged Ivy from the chaise into his lap. "You don't have to tell me any of this," he said, trying not to let her hear the anger in his voice, the anger of a man imagining a child dropped into a state system, alone, unwanted—

"I hadn't stolen the money, Damian. I don't know who did, but they—they put me back in the Placement center for a while."

God, his heart was going to break. And he knew, without question, who had stolen the money and let Ivy take the blame.

"And then they placed me with—with a man and a

woman. Not Kay. She'd turned eighteen. She left foster care."

"*Ivy.* I love you. There's no need to—"

"I have to tell you so you'll understand why I—why I agreed to carry Kay's baby."

"And mine," he said softly.

Ivy nodded. "Yes. You have to know, Damian."

"I don't," he said gently, and meant it. "But I can see that you have to tell me."

She nodded again, thankful that he understood.

"So," he said, cupping her face, "tell me, and we can put the past behind us."

Could they? When he knew everything? Ivy prayed he was right.

"They placed me with this couple. She didn't pay any attention to me. Well, she did, but—but he—he was kind to me. He said he'd always wanted a daughter. A little girl of his own. He bought me things. A doll. I was old for dolls but nobody had given me anything since—since our parents' deaths and—"

"And you were grateful," Damian said, and wondered at the coldness stealing into his heart.

"Grateful. And happy, even though I didn't see Kay anymore. I understood," she said quickly, seeing the lift of Damian's eyebrows. "I mean, she was busy. Working. She had friends. She was grown up and I..." Her voice trailed away and then she cleared her throat. "My foster father said he knew I was lonely. He began coming into my room to tuck me in. To kiss me good-night. I thought—I thought he was—he was—"

"What did the bastard do to you?"

She stared at Damian. She had seen him angry, even furious, but she had never seen him like this, his eyes black, his mouth thinned, his hands so tight on her shoulders that she knew his fingers must be leaving bruises on her skin.

"He…" *Oh God. Oh God…* "He raped me."

Damian hit the little table where he'd put the tissue box so hard it almost shattered. His arms went around her; he held her tight against him.

"And—and it was all my fault."

"What?"

"My fault, Damian. I didn't realize it until—until I finally found Kay's phone number and called her, and she came to the house where I lived and I told her what had happened and she made me see that I'd provoked it, that I should never have let him tuck me in or kiss me or even buy me that doll and I *knew* that, all along, I knew it was strange but I just thought—I just thought he liked me. Loved me. That he really wanted to be my father, and—"

Damian kissed her.

There was no other way to stop the racing river of pain-filled words except to cover Ivy's mouth with his and kiss her and kiss her and kiss her until, at last, she began to cry, her tears hot and salty against his lips.

"Ivy," he whispered, *"agapimeni,* my darling, my heart, none of it was your fault. Damn Kay for telling you that it was!"

"It was. I should have known—"

"What? That a monster would take a little girl's grief and use it to slake his sick desires?" Damian rocked her in his arms. "Ivy, sweetheart, no one would ever think what happened was your fault. Surely when you reported it—"

"I didn't."

"What?"

"He said—he said, if I told anyone, he'd deny it. And if—if a doctor examined me, he'd say—he'd say he'd caught me with boys in the neighborhood. And since I'd—I'd already been accused of stealing money, they'd believe him, not me. And I—I knew he was right, that nobody would listen to me—"

Damian pounded his fist against the table again. This time, it shattered and collapsed on the sand.

"Who is this man? Tell me his name. I will kill him!"

"Kay took me to live with her. Do you see? She saved me, Damian. She saved me! If she hadn't taken me from him—"

"She did not save you," he said viciously, his accent thickening, his thoughts coming in Greek instead of English. "She used you, *glyka mou*. She told you— you, a child—that you had caused your own rape."

"She made me see my foolishness, Damian."

"And she waited and waited, your bitch of a stepsister, waited until a time came when she could demand repayment," he said through his teeth because now, finally, he understood why Ivy had agreed to bear his child.

"No." Ivy's voice was a broken whisper. "You don't understand. I owed her for saving me."

Damian fought for control when what he really wanted to do was find the beast who'd done this and kill him. And, *Thee mou*, if Kay were alive...

"Ivy," he said, "listen to me. You saved yourself."

"I didn't. If I'd saved myself, I'd never have let what happened happen."

"Sweetheart. You thought this man loved you as a father. Why would you have ever imagined otherwise?

You were a child. Innocent. Lonely. Alone." He paused, framed her face with his hands, made her meet his gaze. "Kay lied to you. It was never, not even remotely, your fault."

Ivy stared at him. "No?" she whispered.

"No. Absolutely not." He drew a breath. "But she'd planted the seed, and she knew it. So, years later, when she wanted something she knew you would not wish to do—"

"Bearing a baby for her," Ivy said, as the tears flowed down her cheeks. "Oh, Damian, I didn't want to! I said no, I couldn't, I couldn't have a child in my womb, feel it kick, see it born and—and give it up—"

"And she said…" He struggled to keep his tone even. "She said, you owed it to her."

"She said she'd saved me once and now—now I had to save her."

Ivy began to sob. Damian folded her into his arms. There was nothing more to say except one phrase, and he repeated it over and over and over, until, finally, her weeping stopped.

"I love you, Ivy," he repeated. "I love you with all my heart."

She drew back and looked at him. "Even after this?"

"Especially after this," he said softly. "Because now I know what true goodness is in your heart, that you would agree to make such a sacrifice for someone you loved."

"Damian. There's—there's more."

His mouth was gentle on hers.

"Later."

"No. No, now. I have to tell you now."

"Later," he said, and kissed her again, and then he

lay her back against the warm sand, under the warm sun, and when he made love to her this time, Ivy wept again.

With happiness.

CHAPTER TWELVE

THEY spent the afternoon on the beach.

Damian had arranged everything. The picnic lunch brought them by Esias. The chilled champagne.

When the sun began its soft pink, purple and violet drop into the sea, Ivy smiled and asked if Damian had arranged for that, too.

"Because the sunset is perfect," she said softly, resting her head on his shoulder as she stood in the curve of his arm, "just like this entire day's been perfect. It's beautiful enough to put a lump in my throat."

"You are what is beautiful, *kardia mou*," he said, drawing her closer. "And I love you with all my heart."

She hesitated. "Even after what I told you?"

"*Neh.* Yes. I told you, especially after that. I only wish it had never happened to you, sweetheart. The ugliness of it. The pain—"

"You took it all away, that first time we made love."

Damian turned her toward him. "Ivy. I want you to promise something to me."

She smiled. "Just ask."

"Never be afraid to share anything with me, *glyka mou*. Your hopes, your dreams…" He ran his thumb lightly over her mouth. "Your darkest secrets," he said quietly. "I will love you, always. Do you understand?"

And, just that quickly, she remembered what she had tried to forget during the long, glorious afternoon.

The final truth.

The last secret.

How would he deal with it? He'd understood why she'd agreed to carry a child of Kay's, but could he understand this?

Not even she understood it. Yes, Kay had been frantic. Yes, there'd been no time to think. And, yes, considering her own plans for the future, her conviction she would never want to make love with a man, that she'd surely never, ever marry, it had made a crazy kind of sense…

"Ivy. Why such a sad look in your beautiful eyes?"

Ivy ran the tip of her tongue over her lips. "There's one last thing I have to tell you, Damian. I tried, hours ago, but—"

"But," he said huskily, "I was more interested in making love than listening."

He smiled. She did, too. Then she rose on her toes and pressed her lips to his.

"Let's go back to our bedroom."

"A fine idea."

"I'll shower, and then—"

"*We'll* shower," he said, with the kind of sexy look that always turned her inside out. "And then we'll have dinner on the terrace in the garden." He took her hands and raised them to his lips. "And you can tell me this last secret so I can kiss you and tell you that whatever it is, it changes nothing."

"I love you so much," Ivy said, her voice breaking. "So much…"

One last, deep kiss. Then they walked to the road, where Damian had parked the Jeep, and drove to what had now become home.

They showered together, and made love, and dried each other off and, inevitably, made love again.

Then they dressed.

Ivy put on a classically long, slender black gown with thin straps. "Look at how my belly shows," she said, laughing, and Damian quickly knelt and put his lips to the bump.

Maybe, she thought, holding her breath as she looked down at him, maybe what she had to tell him would go well.

He rose to his feet and took her hand. "You are so beautiful," he said softly.

She smiled and looked at him in his white jacket and black trousers. "So are you."

He laughed, even blushed. "Men can't be beautiful."

He was wrong. Her Damian *was* beautiful. In face and body. In heart and soul. And yes, he *would* understand this, her last secret.

He had to.

Damian led her down the wide marble stairs, through the oldest part of the palace to a columned terrace in a garden that overlooked the sea.

The table was lit by tall tapers in silver holders. Flowers—white orchids, crimson roses, pale pink tulips—overflowed from a magnificent urn. Champagne stood chilling in a silver bucket and a fat ivory moon sailed over the Aegean…

And standing beside the table, smiling, looking even more stunning than in the past, stood Kay.

Ivy cried out in shock. Damian said a single sharp word. Kay's smile grew brighter.

"Isn't anyone going to say hello?"

"Your Highness." Esias, standing near Kay, all but wrung his hands. "I could not keep the lady out, sir. I am sorry. So sorry—"

Damian dismissed his houseman with a curt nod. His hand tightened on Ivy's but, after a shocked couple of seconds, she tore free of his grasp and ran to her step-sister.

"Ohmygod, Kay! Kay, you're alive!"

"Bright as always, Ivy. That, at least, hasn't changed."

Ivy reached out to hug her but Kay sidestepped, her eyes locked to Damian's.

"And you," she said, "were always a fast worker. I see you didn't waste any time, replacing me."

"Obviously," Damian said, his voice cold, "you didn't die in that car crash."

Kay laughed. "Obviously not."

"Did you have amnesia?" Ivy said. "You must have, otherwise—"

"People have amnesia in soap operas," Kay said. "Not in real life. I went off a cliff into Long Island Sound. Everyone thought I'd drowned."

"They declared you dead," Damian said in that same icy voice.

"Well, I wasn't. I washed ashore a couple of miles away. Carlos's uncle—he's with the government—and a discreet doctor kept the story out of the papers." Her hand went to her face. "I had some bad cuts—it took a lot of plastic surgery—but I'm all healed now." She tilted her head to catch the candlelight. "What do you think, Damian darling? As good as new, or even better?"

"What do you want, Kay?"

"What do I want?" Her smile hardened as she moved slowly across the terrace to where he stood. "Why, I want my life back, of course." She stopped in front of him and lay a hand on his chest. "I want you, darling. A wedding ring. And that delightful little lump I see in my dear sister's belly, as soon as it's born."

Damian caught her wrist and drew her hand to her side.

"Sorry, but you're not getting any of those things." He stepped past her and put his arm around Ivy, who was trembling. "Ivy and I are getting married."

"Ah. You're angry about Carlos. It didn't mean a thing, darling. You're the only one I ever loved."

"You've never loved anyone in your life," he said coldly.

Kay's eyes narrowed. "You don't understand, Damian. I'm back. Whatever little trap my dear sister sprang on you has no meaning now."

Ivy stiffened. "I didn't—"

"Hush, *glyka mou*. There's no need to explain. Kay and I never had marriage plans."

"We certainly did!"

"We did not. *You* had plans, Kay, the first time you told me you were pregnant." Damian's voice turned even more frigid. "It was a lie."

"It wasn't. My doctor—"

"I've seen your doctor. You were never pregnant. And you and I never discussed artificial insemination."

"That's all in the past. I'm pregnant now. I mean, Ivy is. With..." Her eyes flashed to Ivy. "With your child and mine. She did tell you that, Damian, didn't she? That she's carrying your baby? My baby?"

Damian's jaw tightened. "Ivy carries my son." He put his hand on Ivy's round belly. "*Our* son. Hers and mine."

Kay's face paled. "What do you mean? Ivy? What did you—"

"Nothing," Ivy said desperately. "But I will. I will! Kay, you can't just come back after all this time and—and—"

"I can," Kay said fiercely. "I have. And I want what's mine."

"Biology doesn't make for motherhood," Damian snapped. "You were alive, yet you didn't see fit to tell me that you were. You didn't see fit to tell Ivy, even though you knew she was pregnant." His mouth twisted. "You have given up any right to this child."

"I've given up nothing! Not you. Not the baby. And nothing you say or do will change that."

Damian touched Ivy's cheek with a gentle hand. Then he stepped away from her and walked slowly toward Kay.

"I am not a fifteen-year-old girl," he said softly. "I am not a frightened child who will bend to your will. Your lies cannot make me think you are anything more than you are. An evil, selfish woman."

"Ah." Kay laughed. "So, she told you her sad story, hmm? About how the big, bad man molested her?" Her smile vanished; she shot Ivy a look of pure evil. "Liar! Why not tell him the truth? That you were a seductive little bitch—"

"Watch your mouth," Damian snarled.

"A seductive little piece of tail." She whirled toward

Damian. "It's the truth and she knows it. First she seduced my father—"

"No!" Ivy shook her head. "Kay. You know I never—"

"Seduced him. Batted her lashes. Crept into his lap. Told him how much she loved him—"

"I did love him! I was a little girl—"

"And then he died. Her mother died. They put us in foster care and she stole money."

"I didn't steal anything! Kay, I beg you, don't do this!"

"I got out as soon as I hit eighteen. And my dear stepsister lucked out. They put her in another home with a man like my father. And when the poor bastard finally took what she'd been waving under his nose—"

"Paliogyneko!" Damian grabbed Kay's arm and jerked her forward. "Get out! Get the hell out of my home. If I ever see you again, I'll—"

"My God, you bought her story! She told you he raped her. And you believed it!"

"Kay," Ivy pleaded, "stop! We're sisters. I always loved you—"

"Stepsisters. And your supposed love doesn't mean a thing to me." Kay spun toward Damian. "What else did she tell you? That she's been scared of sex ever since?" She threw back her head and laughed. "Look at her, Damian. Think about the life she's led. She moves in a world where people trade in flesh. Where women sell cars by making men get hard-ons. Do you really think my dear stepsister is a sweet portrait of virtue?"

Ivy shook her head. "Damian. Don't listen to her. I've never—"

"You want to know what a good, kind little innocent

my stepsister is?" Kay flashed a vicious smile. "That baby in her belly?"

"Kay. Oh, please, please, please, Kay, don't do this!"

"You remember that charge at Tiffany? That I let you think was mine? It wasn't. I spent it on her. On Ivy. She wanted a necklace. Diamonds. Rubies. I bought it for her."

"Damian. God, she's lying!"

"It was the price for the baby." Kay paused, threw a triumphant look at Ivy, then turned back to Damian. "Because, you see, she's right. I *did* lie, darling. That baby inside her? It's yours, all right…but it's yours and Ivy's."

Ivy swung toward Damian, saw the color leach from his face.

"What?" he said, his voice a husky rasp.

"I found out I couldn't use my own eggs. So I said, Ivy, let me use yours. And she said—"

"Damian. Listen to me. It wasn't like that. It wasn't—"

"I said, how about letting me put my lover's sperm inside you? How about conceiving a baby for me? And she said, is he rich? And I said, yes, he's a royal. And she said, how much can you get out of him? And I said, well, I couldn't come right out and ask for money but I could buy her something she wanted, and she said, how about this necklace at Tiffany? And that was enough until she thought I was dead and she figured, hey, no more middleman. I can collect all the bucks, marry Kay's prince and live the life I've always wanted."

Ivy saw the horror in Damian's face. She turned and ran.

No footsteps came after her.

No footsteps. No Damian. Kay's story was a hideous blend of truth and lies and he'd believed it.

She raced through the vast rooms of the ancient palace, through the entry hall. Esias called to her but she ran past him, out the door, down the steps, along the road that led to the airstrip, her breath sobbing in her throat.

"Ivy!"

She heard the footsteps now. Heard Damian's voice and knew she could not face him. She hadn't told him the final truth for just this reason, because she'd feared what she'd see in his eyes, a look that asked how a woman could agree to conceive a baby and give it up.

"Ivy!"

Weeping, she ran faster. A high-heeled sandal fell off and she kicked away the other one, felt the gravel cutting her flesh and knew the pain of that was nothing compared to the pain in her heart.

"Ivy, damn it…"

Hard arms closed around her.

"No," she shouted. "No, Damian, don't—"

He swung her toward her, his face harsh and angular in the moonlight.

"Ivy," he said—and kissed her.

Kissed her and kissed her, and at first she fought him and then, oh then, she sobbed his name and leaned into him, wound her arms around his neck and kissed him with all the love in her heart.

"*Glyka mou,*" he said, his voice shaky, "where were you going?"

"Away. From here. From you. From all the lies—"

He caught her face in his hands, kissed her again and again.

"I love you," he said, "and you love me. Those are not lies."

"How can you love me now that you know—"

"Don't you remember what I said this afternoon? That you would tell me your last secret and I would tell you I loved you? That I would love you forever?"

"But the baby—"

"Our baby," he said, a smile lighting his face. "Truly our baby, sweetheart, *neh?*"

"Yes. Oh, yes. Our baby, Damian. It's always been ours."

"You did it out of love for Kay."

She nodded. "Yes. No. I thought I did it for her—but I did it for me, too. I was sure I would never marry. Never have sex. Never have children. And I thought, if I do this, if I have this baby, I'll be its aunt. And its mother. In my heart, I'll always be its mother, even if the baby never knows."

"Sweetheart. You're trembling." Damian stripped off his jacket and wrapped her in it. "Come back to the palace."

"No. Not until I've told you everything." Ivy took a deep breath. "So—so I let Kay—I let her do the procedure. And it took. I missed my very next period—" Her voice broke. "And that was when I knew I'd made a terrible mistake, that I would never be able to give away the baby." Her hand went to her belly. "My baby."

"And mine," Damian said softly.

Ivy nodded. "My baby, and yours. I called Kay. I told her. I said she had to tell you the truth. She said it was too late, that we'd made a bargain. I said I would never give up the baby. And then—and then—"

"And then," he said gently, "you thought she'd died."

"Yes."

"So, you waited for me to contact you because you thought I knew all about the baby."

"Not all. I mean, I thought you knew I was carrying your baby but Kay had made it clear she didn't want you to know it was my egg, not hers, that had been fertilized."

"But I didn't contact you."

"No. I assumed it was because you were devastated, losing Kay. That you'd adored her, just the way she'd said you did. And I thought—I thought I owed it to you to let you know the baby was fine, that you were going to be a father, and—and—"

"And?" he said softly.

Ivy shuddered. "And, I hadn't figured out the rest. How to tell you I was the baby's real mother. When to tell you. And then you said you didn't know anything about a baby, that I was up to some kind of awful scam, and I didn't know what to do—"

"Come here," Damian said gruffly, and he gathered her into his arms and kissed her. "Ivy," he whispered, when finally he raised his head, "*glyka mou,* I am so sorry."

"For what?"

"For all you've been through. I love you, *agapimeni.* I love you with all my heart, and I promise to spend the rest of my life making sure you know it. Will you let me?"

Ivy laughed. Or maybe she wept. She couldn't tell anymore because her joy was so complete.

"Only if you let me do the same thing for you," she said, and kissed him.

They made their way back to the palace, arms around each other. At the front steps, Ivy paused.

"Kay?" she said questioningly.

"Gone," Damian said flatly. "She came by boat, or maybe by broom, for all I know, and she's gone back the same way."

"It breaks my heart," Ivy whispered. "To think she hates me enough to have told such lies…" She took a deep breath. "She's still my stepsister. I can't help but hope that someday—"

Damian drew her close. "Anything is possible."

But he knew, even as he said it, that of all the things that had been said on this night, that was the biggest lie of all.

The wedding was on Damian's yacht, anchored just off Minos.

The sun was bright, the sea was wine-dark and the bride, of course, was beautiful.

Some of the models Ivy had worked with for years were there, as was her agent.

There were two best men instead of one. Nicolo Barbieri—Prince Nicolo Barbieri—and Prince Lucas Reyes.

Nicolo was there with his beautiful wife, Aimee, and their adorable baby.

Lucas was alone, by choice.

"Bring a date," Damian had told his pal but Lucas knew better. A man took a woman to a wedding, she got ideas.

Useless ideas, he thought firmly, because as happy as Nicolo was, as happy as Damian was, they could keep the marriage thing for themselves.

Not me, he told himself as he watched Damian kiss his glowing bride, never me.

But never, as everyone knows, is a very, very long time…

BILL✦NAIRES' BRIDES

by Sandra Marton

Pregnant by their princes...

Take three incredibly wealthy European princes
and match them with three beautiful, spirited women.
Add large helpings of intense emotion and passionate attraction.
Result: three unexpected pregnancies...and
three possible princesses—if those princes have their way....

THE ITALIAN PRINCE'S PREGNANT BRIDE
August 2007

THE GREEK PRINCE'S CHOSEN WIFE
September 2007

THE SPANISH PRINCE'S VIRGIN BRIDE

Prince Lucas Reyes believes Alyssa is trying to pretend
she's untouched by any man. Lucas's fiery royal blood is roused!
He'd swear she's pure uninhibited mistress material,
and never a virgin bride!

Available October wherever you buy books.

Look for more great Harlequin authors every month!

REQUEST YOUR FREE BOOKS!

2 FREE NOVELS PLUS 2 FREE GIFTS!

PASSION GUARANTEED SEDUCTION

YES! Please send me 2 FREE Harlequin Presents® novels and my 2 FREE gifts. After receiving them, if I don't wish to receive any more books, I can return the shipping statement marked "cancel." If I don't cancel, I will receive 6 brand-new novels every month and be billed just $3.80 per book in the U.S., or $4.47 per book in Canada, plus 25¢ shipping and handling per book and applicable taxes, if any*. That's a savings of close to 15% off the cover price! I understand that accepting the 2 free books and gifts places me under no obligation to buy anything. I can always return a shipment and cancel at any time. Even if I never buy another book from Harlequin, the two free books and gifts are mine to keep forever.

106 HDN EEXK   306 HDN EEXV

Name _____ (PLEASE PRINT) _____

Address _____ Apt. # _____

City _____ State/Prov. _____ Zip/Postal Code _____

Signature (if under 18, a parent or guardian must sign) _____

Mail to the **Harlequin Reader Service®:**
IN U.S.A.: P.O. Box 1867, Buffalo, NY 14240-1867
IN CANADA: P.O. Box 609, Fort Erie, Ontario L2A 5X3

Not valid to current Harlequin Presents subscribers.

Want to try two free books from another line?
Call 1-800-873-8635 or visit www.morefreebooks.com.

* Terms and prices subject to change without notice. NY residents add applicable sales tax. Canadian residents will be charged applicable provincial taxes and GST. This offer is limited to one order per household. All orders subject to approval. Credit or debit balances in a customer's account(s) may be offset by any other outstanding balance owed by or to the customer. Please allow 4 to 6 weeks for delivery.

Your Privacy: Harlequin is committed to protecting your privacy. Our Privacy Policy is available online at www.eHarlequin.com or upon request from the Reader Service. From time to time we make our lists of customers available to reputable firms who may have a product or service of interest to you. If you would prefer we not share your name and address, please check here. ☐

HP07

Men who can't be tamed...or so they think!

If you love strong, commanding men,
you'll love this brand-new miniseries.

Meet the guy who breaks the rules to get exactly
what he wants, because he is...

HARD-EDGED & HANDSOME

He's the man who's impossible to resist....

RICH & RAKISH

He's got everything—and needs nobody...
until he meets one woman....

He's RUTHLESS!

In his pursuit of passion; in his world the winner takes all!

Laine knew her marriage was a sham. So she fled—still a
virgin! Now she must face Daniel again—and he wants to
claim the wedding night that should have been his....

Look for

INNOCENT ON HER WEDDING NIGHT

by Sara Craven,

the first book in this new miniseries, available in October
wherever you buy books.

Brought to you by your favorite Harlequin Presents authors!

Look out for more Ruthless men, coming soon in Harlequin Presents!

www.eHarlequin.com

HP12670

HARLEQUIN® *Presents*®

NAME: _____

ADDRESS: _____

_____

_____

TELEPHONE: _____

E-MAIL: _____

_____ I want to pay by credit card.

__ Visa   __ MasterCard   __ Discover

Account Number: _____

Expiration date: _____

SIGNATURE: _____

Send this form, along with $2.00 shipping and handling for your FREE books, to:

Historical Romance Book Club
20 Academy Street
Norwalk, CT 06850-4032

Or fax (must include credit card information!) to: 610.995.9274.
You can also sign up on the Web at www.dorchesterpub.com.

Offer open to residents of the U.S. and Canada only. Canadian residents, please call 1.800.481.9191 for pricing information.

She laid her hand along his jaw, his square, bristled, unyielding jaw, and said, "I always wanted you. I still do."

He managed a low ironic snort. "A dreamer and a drifter then, and now a failure as a father and a washed-up rake."

She didn't care if he saw the tears of frustration that burned down her cheeks. "Next time make love to me properly. You haven't done that yet."

His knuckle wiped away a tear. "There is nothing proper about what I want to do with you."

A thrill ran through her belly. "Is that a promise? Because I want you do to improper things to me."

"Good Lord, Sophie, I left you a virgin."

Impossible man. "I did not thank you for that then. I do not thank you now."

She wheeled toward Simon's room. Lionel's large hand, so tender moments earlier, caught her in a vise. "Where do you think you're going?"

"I still work for you, my lord, and no half-satisfactory dalliance in the hallway is going to distract me from my duty."

At Simon's room, she closed the door behind her and collapsed against it, her face in her trembling hands. What had she done?

She had almost made love with Lionel Westfall, earl of Wraxham, in the hallway at the door of his sons' bedroom. A small smile started, then spread across her face.

Her blood pulsed through her body, and she felt more alive than she had felt in years. He'd bruised her mouth and pinched her nipples tender, and her mound still throbbed with a delicious ache.

She had loved it. He had too.

Not that what they'd done was love, or anything close to that exalted, honorable estate. No, he'd called her love as she imagined most rakes addressed their many conquests, and even that had pleased her. For she and Lionel just acted on their lust, a state her bawdy books described as *Lechery, Distemper, transcendent Pleasure and Delight.*

She wrapped her arms around herself and padded softly across the floor to Simon's cot. He was sleeping lightly, one matchstick arm flung restlessly over his head, the other clutching his covers. She tested his forehead. It was cool, but her touch roused him.

"Story, if you please, ma'am," he murmured drowsily.

So she sat at the head of Simon's bed, snuggled him to her ribs, and recounted one of Aesop's fables as if it were a lullaby. When his breathing deepened, she tucked him in, kissed him, and stood as any mother would.

Motherhood had never been a hope for her, not even to so sweet a child.

Your father, she whispered to herself so he could not possibly hear, *was my first love, and will be my first lover.*

Lionel had protested that he'd reformed, but his eyes, hands, mouth, and manhood all said, as far as she could tell, that he was still a rake. The rake who could deliver her—splendidly, ecstatically—into all the pleasures she had missed.

But could she, spinster, bluestocking, country lass, measure up to the worldly women of his London experience? Her bawdy books had taught her how to make love to a man.

If only they could teach her how to seduce him.

Chapter Fifteen

Dear Ned, I cannot but thy Fate deplore,
In Love! In Bedlam *would have pleas'd me more,*
Should such a Serious Oversight commit?
Can'st thou so well with misery dispence?
That 'gainst thy Self thou do'st a War commence.
—A Disswasion from Love and Matrimony (1702)

Lionel sat up, feeling ridiculous.

He was on the rack, or the next worse thing, on a thin carpet atop a marble floor in front of the twins' door. In maneuvers in the West Indies, he'd slept under wagons, in barns, on sand. But sentry duty in his own hallway had to be the most absurd, demeaning mission of his career.

His sons could not have sneaked out. Would that they had, anything for action. For his neck felt permanently tilted left, his knee had locked half cocked, and his groin throbbed with a painful need for Sophie. Under his rumpled breeches his smallclothes were still sticky with the price of his restraint.

The next time Sophie sprawled across his lap, all lusty will-

169

ing female, he'd sink into her hot, wet welcome to the hilt.

Not that he could have her, next week, next month, next year. He didn't have the time, money, or energy to have any woman in his life, or the naïveté to take on a new wife.

His rampant lust mocked every reservation, claiming him at the merest thought of Sophie's full breasts and wet, clumsy kisses. Had he ever been that young, that innocent?

He dug his fingers into his aching knee and straightened it. Plague take it, in London women sought him out because they'd heard from lady so-and-so about the feathers, or rumors from the duchess of his midnight games with cravats and oil.

Sophie hadn't sought him out.

But sex—a game with other women—with her was dangerously in earnest.

She'd stumbled into his arms and crashed his jaded defenses, reducing him to the grateful, lusting schoolboy who'd read poetry to her when he'd wanted to devour her. Even now, her ivory skin, her innocent lustiness made him as randy as his eighteen-year-old self.

Randier. He knew so much more what to do with her. To her. For her. To the devil with feathers, cravats, and exotic oils. Sophie's innocent lustiness—Sophie's quest—could inspire him to new heights.

The moon set hours ago, and Wraxham House was waking. He stretched, and his neck and knees and shoulders popped, cracked, creaked. From belowstairs, coal clinked into buckets, and cook pots clanged on stoves. An aroma of frying sausages seeped up through Wraxham's antique halls.

He had few morning memories of the house in Mayfair. After Simon's birth, he'd rarely spent the night there. And that had pleased his wife, his dear departed distant wife.

He stood in the last darkness before dawn, rumpled and scruffy, and adjusted his rising arousal inside his breeches.

On the rack.

He wanted more.

He wanted Sophie's hot mouth, round buttocks, dark-fleeced mound. He wanted the bud of her womanhood.

Damn. He could not afford the luxury of a liaison.

And Sophie, God help her, could not afford him, a burnt-out rake who could neither love nor marry her, who came burdened with one son courting nightmares and three sons courting jail.

For he was at the mercy of Simon's next episode and the twins' next escapade.

And what *could* he do to intervene in Graeme's hazardous situation?

Something. Something soon.

He let out a gust of breath and strode down the hallway to his suite. At least Marcus and James, second and third oldest, were in the best of hands. Lionel's old schoolmasters at Abercairn made men of boys. They wouldn't tolerate the kind of nonsense that faced him here.

A brisk walk across the sheep pasture cleared Lionel's head and brought him to the rector's doorstep at the unfashionable hour of seven-thirty in the morning.

The Right Reverend Adolphus Bowerbank, Oxonian and rector of Wraxham, Finglenook, and Brookings Green, must have thought it early too. Peering at Lionel through thick spectacles, his eyes goggled. Lionel had not met him privately in twenty years.

"Heavenly days, my good Lord Wraxham!" he blurted, hurrying to take Lionel's cape and walking stick. "Do come in. Whatever can I do for—" He peered up worriedly. "Oh, my word! Is my daughter quite all right?"

Possibly not, Lionel thought, remembering what he'd done to her mouth and breasts and buttocks. A better man than he would have blushed in shame to face the rector after last night's tryst with his spinster daughter.

But Lionel was not a good man, and a habit of indifference to the world's opinion stood him in good stead. "She was in excellent spirits when I saw her last, and my sons are thriving under her instruction."

"Ah, are they indeed?" The rector clapped his hands together in innocent glee. "I *knew* my daughter would be an asset to your household. And you?" He scowled with ministerial intuition. "You haven't come calling so early in the day to compliment my daughter."

Lionel smiled wryly. "Regrettably, no. Although I will not retract my praise of her good work."

"Then pray come in, my lord, and have a seat." Sophie's father bustled about to clear a jumble of papers and antique tomes from a wobbly chair. "I keep a pot of water on for tea. May I offer you a cup, and perhaps a scone? Miss Gatewood brought a batch of scones the other day."

"Most kind, Bowerbank, yes, of course," Lionel said, skeptically observing his own reactions. He hadn't expected Sophie's father to receive him with courtesy, and he found it dislocating to be in Sophie's home. Worse yet, he didn't like asking for help from the man who'd driven him from Wraxham House so many years ago.

But annulments and special licenses were Bowerbank's domain, not Lionel's province as a magistrate. The elderly Oxonian might also have an inkling of how the university dealt with a tangle such as Graeme's.

The rector returned carrying three meager scones and a mismatched silver tea service on a tatty bamboo tray. His poverty was worse than Sophie had admitted, and Lionel could see yet another instance of his father's slack hand in estate affairs. The good reverend didn't even have a scullery maid this early in the day. Did he have any help? He'd had Sophie, Lionel realized to his chagrin.

And Sophie had had no help at all.

Bowerbank poured and served, and then sat with an air of spiritual authority. "May I take it that this matter is of a personal nature, my lord?" His tone was remote but not unkind.

"Family," Lionel said lamely. No longer nineteen and not

172

personally in the wrong, he felt culpable for everything.

"Ah. Then let me assure you of my discretion, both as Wraxham's rector and your servant."

"Thank you, Bowerbank. And yes, the situation calls for it." Lionel related what he knew of Graeme's predicament.

"Dear, dear me. In love, you say?" The rector clucked with unfeigned sympathy. "That will be the sticking point. Always is with these young men."

Lionel could not detect an allusion to his affair with Sophie. "Evidently she will seek an annulment," he said. "If she succeeds, he cannot get a special license without my knowledge or consent, am I correct?"

"You are right, up until he is of age, but the north road to Scotland, ah"—Bowerbank made a helpless gesture with his hand—"that will tempt them and should worry you."

"True enough. Everything hangs on the annulment then."

"Which you wouldn't want to stand in the way of. It could be a mercy for the girl, if what she claims is true. Any doctor can confirm her innocence, even if her husband corrupted her with base acts. As for charges, a professor hasn't a great deal of money to bring a civil suit."

"My thought exactly," Lionel said. But he had not expected Sophie's father to be so conversant with the ways of the world. "I will of course take care of the girl."

"Naturally, my lord. It wouldn't do to free her of an onerous marriage and then throw her upon the world."

"That would only strengthen my son's plan to marry her."

"Dear me, he has a plan. That is worse than I thought. You know nothing of her?"

Lionel broke a cold scone in two. "Nothing. I confess I hope your Oxford connections might shed some light."

Bowerbank nodded. He had matriculated with the dean of Graeme's college, as a matter of fact, and could write to him. "Do you have the names of the tutor and his wife?"

Lionel jotted them down.

Bowerbank read them, clucking absently as he tapped the

paper in his hand. "Never heard of the man. He must be since my time. I should like to make inquiries about the girl's claims. She could be innocent indeed. Or . . ." He shook his snow-white head in sympathy. "Can you have the letter delivered?"

"Yes." Carter would do it. He was a far better horseman than Tims and would welcome a break from duty as well as a bracing ride. While Tims . . . It was becoming more evident every day that Tims belonged in London, in someone else's service. "My man can get it there today. And I can do no more," Lionel said and stood to leave.

The rector showed Lionel to the door. "Always a difficult matter, my lord, young love," he said kindly. "Painful for the lovers, but agonizing for the father. One must act. One can never sit by idly when a child is bent on error."

If error it had been, Lionel thought as he strode home across the sheep pasture, remembering Bowerbank's reaction those many years ago. Until this moment it had not occurred to him that anyone other than him and Sophie had suffered when their fathers ended their affair.

Bowerbank must have been beside himself. He'd kept his daughter home and bound to him for life.

The kissing gate creaked as Lionel passed through it. It had always creaked. With Sophie that summer he had been rash and reckless, but—he knew this now, he who had sought to forget her under half the skirts in London—he had once loved her truly.

Loving Sophie had not been wrong. It had been the one bright shining moment of his wasted life.

As a rule, Lionel preferred engaging in duels and combat on a good night's sleep. Failing that, he downed a third cup of the stoutest tea Laframboise's kitchen could brew, ordered a fresh pot for his office, and sent for Carter to attend him. It was barely nine o'clock.

Lionel's desk would be piled high with petitions to review for this afternoon's assizes, and Tims always left a stack of letters, assiduously copied by candlelight, no doubt, for him to sign.

But when he got to his office, his estate agent was already there, along with his secretary and his son, the latter looking gaunt and wary and put out.

Let it not be said, Lionel thought wryly, that he'd learned nothing during his years of military service. Officers were well served by making subordinates wait.

Carter glowered, Tims shifted, and Graeme started to stand.

"Sit, son, sit," Lionel said and busied himself at his desk. "I will just look over these papers and deal with these two gentlemen before you and I get down to business."

Said gentlemen's attention homed in on his son. No doubt Lionel's staff were ears to the doors over Graeme's untimely homecoming. Who was more likely than trusted agents and secretaries to keep abreast of the latest developments?

A passion to protect his son from household gossip seized Lionel.

Tims sidled forward, curiosity leaking from his pores.

"Begging your pardon"—Tims bowed at Graeme—"Lord Cordrey"—and at Lionel—"my lord." Then he said in an unctuous undertone, "The mortgage deeds are returned with corrections and amendments needing your immediate attention."

Carter raised a brow. "Mine is the more urgent matter, my lord."

Tims held his ground. "If I could just put them before you, my lord—"

Lionel held up both hands. "Gentlemen. I can attend to two things in one morning. As to the deeds, Mr. Tims, I will see to them as I can."

Lionel flipped through the waiting correspondence, chafing. Surely the man could see there wasn't a chance in hell he would tip his hand about his son.

"These will be read and signed by noon, and the deeds. You may go, and I will hear Carter."

Carter gave a smug smile at his triumph, and the secretary's face blackened. "Go, Tims," Lionel snapped.

For an instant, Tims's weak chin lifted in mutiny, but he regained control and blinked submissively. "Of course, my lord, as you say. Anything else, my lord?"

"That will be all," he said, and turned to Carter as Tims backed toward the door. "A task for you, Carter."

"And a problem for you, my lord," Carter said, asserting his business without flinching.

Lionel gestured him to go on, keenly aware that his heir was taking lessons in how an earl handled his men.

"In front of him, my lord?" Carter asked, with an arrogant nod at Graeme, who'd claimed a chair opposite the desk.

Carter often tested protocol. Lionel preferred his nerve to Tims's deference. But not today, in front of his defiant son.

"Naturally, any estate concerns are his."

"It's about the family," Carter cautioned.

"Even more so," Lionel said. He could see Graeme's tension rise.

"As you wish, my lord," Carter said, but grudgingly. "The village is rumbling against the twins. A petition will be presented at your next session, and Owen Hill plans to bring a charge of malicious mischief against them at that time."

Sophie was right. Paying the man had been taken as an admission of guilt. "We can only step up our search for the real criminals. Have you any fresh clues?"

"None, my lord," Carter said. "I questioned Hill's neighbors and Grimsby's handlers at the kennel. Wraxham's inhabitants had the universal good fortune of a sound night's sleep. No one saw a thing."

Lionel swore softly. "Worse luck."

"I thought so. Grimsby, as you may know, is a keen tracker. Yesterday he walked the squire's grounds and the town with me in search of clues. We found nothing to confirm or contradict the unfortunate evidence of the marbles."

Lionel stood and took a few frustrated strides around his

office. "Who would set them up? And why? They're just boys."

Graeme shifted in his chair, looking more and more perplexed.

Carter ignored him. "If I may venture a suggestion, my lord, I am afraid the only safe course is to lock up the boys against future mischief."

Lionel stopped pacing. "That presumes my sons are guilty."

"It need not. If they were locked up safe and another, um, event occurs, there would be your proof."

"I won't jail them, not even in their rooms, as long as they deny the deeds."

Carter's curt nod bespoke his disagreement. "As you wish, my lord."

"They are supervised, Carter, day and night. That must suffice. Now, as to your task. The Reverend Adolphus Bowerbank is preparing a letter for you to deliver."

Carter snorted. "A letter, my lord? Surely a footman—"

"A confidential letter, Carter, sealed, to the dean of Graeme's college. You are to wait for his reply."

"My day is full, my—"

"Cancel everything," Lionel snapped, then added, "As matters now stand I must stay with my sons."

Carter blew out a breath. "How long do I wait for the reply, my lord?"

"As long as it takes. But press for a prompt reply. I expect you back tomorrow."

"Yes, my lord," Carter said, and stalked from the room.

Lionel returned to his desk, but Graeme challenged him. "If this letter is a move to discredit her, sir, I won't stand for it."

Lionel gave his severest military scowl. "Only she can discredit herself, with your help."

"What are you planning, sir?"

"That will depend on what I find out."

Graeme hovered stubbornly over the desk. "I fail to see how you can help, a man of your reputation."

Lionel arched a brow, letting silence speak.

Graeme swallowed hard. "You must admit, sir, you haven't been a sterling model of an upright life."

Lionel leaned back in his chair. "Which puts me in an excellent position to advise you when I see you making the mistake of your young life."

"Glencora isn't a mistake," Graeme said with desperate conviction.

"Glencora is married," Lionel ground out. But he wondered if being a father would be this hard if he had gone about it differently. If he had gone about it right.

His strong, wrong son was fighting tears. Tears no one could understand better than Lionel could. He stood up, crossed his arms, and looked out the window in respect for his son's privacy. Wraxham's sheep dotted Wraxham's fields, bright white patches on a quilt of emerald grass and flowering hedgerows, the natural world and its denizens blissfully unaware of the storm within.

"We won't abandon her, son," he said roughly. "If your story is true and your young woman's marriage can be annulled, we will offer her protection, a safe, discreet place to live, a new life."

"But, sir, if you could just meet her," Graeme said.

"No doubt I will," Lionel said grimly. "Meantime, I will handle this in your best interest. As I am handling the accusations against your brothers. Yours is not the only problem our family has brought to Wraxham, son."

Lionel proceeded to lay the charges against the twins before their older brother.

Graeme's frown deepened. "Max and Alex would never be so malicious."

"That is my hope," Lionel said.

"Your hope, sir?" Graeme asked. "Can you not see what happened? The villagers would not think so ill of us if they thought better of you."

Lionel set his jaw. This was the ultimate consequence of his neglect of his sons, his estrangement from his wife, his exile from the estate. If he'd raised his sons here, the town would regard them with tolerance and pride. "I can't change my past, son. And you can't use it to justify sacrificing your future for a married woman."

Graeme's youthful anger pulsed between them. "Are we finished, sir? I should like to be excused."

Lionel let him go, feeling his failure as a father in his bones. He hadn't berated Graeme for a fool as his father had berated him. He wouldn't banish Graeme to the military at the risk of his sanity and his life or push him into a mercenary marriage in order to save an estate in arrears. But neither would he stand idly by while his son threw everything away on an affair with a married woman.

Lionel slammed his fist onto his desk, welcoming the spike of pain. He'd come home to Wraxham with the dream of redeeming the years he'd lost with his sons. He'd wanted to get to know them. He'd meant to help them grow into better men than he'd become.

But he didn't have the damnedest idea how to counsel his heir or spare him the pain of a disastrous love affair.

Chapter Sixteen

Great was the din, and loud the roar,
When Jealousy, with fury tore,
Provoked the hideous fray . . .
—The Temple of Prostitution (1779?)

Sophie could simply take no more.

"Boys! Turn to your history lesson. Now," she ordered, and in the schoolroom, the twins resumed their seats but not before they fanned the window curtains, finger-drew stick figures on the dusty chalkboard, and set her father's antique globe a-spinning.

For now, Troy was over and done with, and it was on to Athens's glory days. However would she top the Trojan horse in their imaginations? If they lived in London, she could have taken them to Lord Elgin's little exhibit of friezes from the Parthenon.

But they were not in London.

They were in the dreary rainy countryside, and they were cranky, bored, and hollow-eyed as if from lack of sleep.

Elbows bumping, they dragged out their Gibbons and bent their tousled brown heads over a chapter on Greece, knees jiggling, feet tapping. If the rain would ever stop, she would order them to take their pent-up energy out of doors.

She rubbed her aching temples with her fingertips. A long morning of the twins' capers had given her an unremitting migraine. Although it seemed more likely that her migraine was brought on by blasted hopes and frustrating dreams.

Where *was* Lionel? she wondered, fidgeting. Up till now, he'd dropped in on the schoolroom every day. Could he be avoiding her after last night's accidental tryst? Not only had she thrown herself on his body, she'd also vowed to do so again, and not stop until he'd given her full satisfaction. Perhaps he'd seen her boldness for the last gasp of a pathetic spinster that it was.

More likely her inexperience was laughable to a man who had, so Celia said, his choice of London ladies and not-so-ladies, women expert in the ways of love.

Sophie put the chalk away, dusted her hands, and checked the boys' Latin exercises with half a heart. Max's grammar was improving, although he lagged behind his twin, and his youngest brother was fast catching up to him.

All day long, the image, taste, and touch of Lionel had disrupted her. She couldn't take back anything she'd said or done with him. She didn't want to. She closed her eyes against the throbbing at her temples and saw his rugged profile in the moonlight, strained with pleasure stolen off her body.

And felt his big warm hands cupping her buttocks, pushing her belly onto his thick hot arousal . . . Ah, another thrill coursed between her legs, and spread across her mound.

Mercy. She was becoming the bawd of her erotic fantasies, consumed with the father even while she was in the schoolroom with his sons, but she couldn't stop herself. She didn't want to. Living so near Lionel day in and day out, she breathed his scent, tasted his kiss, felt him in her imagination, in her blood, vivid, powerful, glorious.

She marked the last of the boys' Latin, and looked out. The rain had stopped. Through clouds a weak sun dappled the sheep-shorn lawn. "Put your books away neatly, boys. We're going out for air," she announced.

Max and Alex leapt for joy, and even Simon whooped. Then they busied themselves storing their things, and she breathed out in relief. She should have let them loose hours ago, and would have but for the lowering clouds and intermittent rain. She too welcomed a stroll, even if the day had turned cool and windy. She drew her stole around her shoulders and closed the schoolroom door.

Downstairs the twins tumbled onto the brilliant green east lawn, their sturdy legs pumping. Simon hurried to keep up.

In a snap, the twins produced cricket paraphernalia and enlisted her and Simon to play in a far corner of the field. Sophie teamed with Max against Alex and Simon.

Across the way, Celia strolled onto the terrace, a blond slash of sunlight in an elegant citron-colored frock.

"Hallo, Miss Upton," Max shouted across the sloping lawn.

Alex gestured for her to come. "We could use another player."

Celia waved a queenly negative from the terrace and took a place at a polished table of wrought iron, a determined spectator with a book tucked under her arm. Some chaperone, some friend! Sophie thought, but good-naturedly. Celia saved herself for dances.

Sophie rarely danced and never had played cricket. Too bad the boys' eldest brother wasn't here to fill her role. She'd not seen a sign of him during this long, long day. She shoved up her sleeves and swung at her first ball.

"Gads, Miss Bowerbank," Max said, but not in awe. Her terrible aim put Max at a disadvantage. Screwing up his face with the difficulty of his task, he undertook to teach her how to swing the bat, his manner exacting and his instructions surprisingly clear.

To Sophie's surprise, not only did she take to his direction, but she also took great pleasure in hitting the luckless ball with her wooden bat.

Thwack! into the beech hedge that divided lawn from field. "Oh no!" Max groaned. "Brava, Miss Bowerbank," Alex said, applauding, and sent Simon running to retrieve the ball. Alex cocked his arm, and Sophie set her bat.

Thwack! through the ornate iron railings that bordered the path to the pleasure garden. Alex bounded over them into the greenery to search. "Lost," he cried, triumphant. "Irretrievably lost." And prepared to throw.

Sophie set her feet and squinted.

Thwack! out of bounds and out of sight onto the south drive. Max covered his face with his hands, Sophie threw down her bat in distress, and Simon yielded to a fit of giggles.

"Bravo, Alex!" Celia cried, and set down her book to applaud. "Splendid toss."

Side out, and it was Simon's turn at bat, Max pitching.

Sophie's teammate motioned her to take up a position near the terrace and Celia. "You cannot expect me to defend the entire east lawn," she shouted.

"Yes, ma'am, all of it," he yelled back.

She didn't have the heart to tell him that mistakes in Latin were the only things she had experience catching.

Simon's bat dwarfed him, but he took it up with a fierce scowl of determination. He swung and missed and swung and missed again. He adjusted his stance, face puckering with frustration.

Poor little tyke, trying to keep up with his older brothers, Sophie was thinking when a brisk clop, clop, clop of horses trotted up the graveled drive.

She turned to look, heard Simon's bat crack into the ball, and felt something crash into her jaw. She reeled and crumpled to her knees, aware of spiking pain, alarmed shrieks and shouts, the sounds of horses trotting, people running, and a snowfall of tiny lights behind her eyes.

The trotting stopped, footfalls neared, and she heard Lionel's dark rumble, in command and furious. "Make way!"

He reached her first, one hand beneath her shoulders gently straightening her legs and skirts, arranging her across his lap. His warm fingers pressed her throat to find a pulse, and he was murmuring with reassuring calm, "Sophie, I've got you, can you hear me? Can you open your eyes? No? Relax and breathe, love, breathe. I'll take care of you."

But chaos broke out around them, voices on top of frightened voices, boys in more distress than she. "Miss Bowerbank, are you hurt?" "Wake up, Miss Bowerbank. Oh, please, Miss Bowerbank, wake up!" the twins cried, their voices indistinguishable to her.

And Simon wailed in horror, "I didn't mean to."

And Celia said in a trembly whisper, "Good heavens, my lord. She can't be dead?"

No, not dead, Sophie thought, but she felt very far away. Her eyes were too heavy to open, and her mouth would not form words.

"No, Miss Upton, she's not dead," Lionel said. "But she took a nasty blow. Graeme, come!" he ordered his son, like an officer in battle. But this was not battle, this was just an accident. She struggled to tell Lionel not to worry, but her jaw throbbed so.

"Get Beane and go for a doctor," Lionel instructed. "And send Nesbit down with blankets."

"Oh, those boys, those cruel, cruel boys. I saw everything, my lord." Celia drew near, distress in her usual whisper.

Her distinctive floral scent wafted over Sophie.

Its sweetness made Sophie queasy. Queasier.

"She looks an awful fright," Celia went on.

Someone's hand—Lionel's hand? It had to be—cupped the back of Sophie's head and gently, slightly tipped her head from side to side. "She's been hit upside the head with a cricket ball, Miss Upton. Of course she looks injured."

"We should take her inside. She'll catch her death of a chill in this miserable weather."

"I'll move her after the doctor sees her, Miss Upton, and not a moment before."

Celia sniffed at his rebuttal, but asked prettily, "What can I do to help?"

"A handkerchief, if you can spare one," Lionel said gruffly.

There must be blood, its coppery taste was on her tongue.

Sophie felt Lionel shift beneath her, as if reaching for something, and then his hand dabbed gingerly at the corner of her mouth.

"Thank you," she croaked.

"Oh, she can't even speak, my lord, she *is* dying," Celia whispered dramatically. "Can we not do anything to save her?"

But Sophie's head was clearing, and she struggled to sit up.

Lionel instantly cupped her closer to him, and spoke softly, his breath warm at her ear. "Shh, Sophie, don't force yourself. The doctor's coming, you take your time."

Her eyes cracked open, and there was Lionel, his bright white shirt open at the neck, his tawny hair damp, his steely eyes dark with worry. Handsome, she thought woozily, even more than when they were young, even more than in the moonlight.

His harsh features softened with relief. "There you are, Sophie, love. There, you're going to be fine."

Behind her she heard a faint shriek and a delicate thud upon the ground, and Lionel grimaced. "Miss Upton? Miss Upton!"

There was a moment of shocked silence. Then the boys burst into chatter.

"Boys, take off your jackets," Lionel ordered, "and cover Miss Upton. The doctor will be here soon."

"What happened? What's wrong with Celia?" Sophie asked.

A muscle in Lionel's jaw jumped. "Your Miss Upton has just had herself a little faint."

Sophie furrowed her brows. It was so confusing. "How odd," she said, and surrendered herself to the solid warmth of Lionel's arms.

185

*   *   *

Odd indeed, Lionel thought, enjoying the feel of Sophie in his arms rather more than he believed he ought, given that one of his sons had nearly killed her. He corrected himself with stern military precision: not killed, not grievously injured.

But when he'd seen Sophie collapse in a heap and not get up, not even raise her head, he panicked and his imagination ran wild with fear and horror.

Was a wild imagination Celia Upton's problem too?

He couldn't have imagined anyone more in the pink of health than the carefully coifed, beautifully adorned Miss Upton until she just up and swooned.

Or had she? Almost two weeks of her company had shown him she had an uncanny ability to make herself the center of every conversation and any situation.

Sophie, all kindness and gratitude, deferred as if her inconvenienced friend were doing her the greatest favor.

Not this time, by damn. This time Sophie's needs came first, and he would see to it. Nesbit crossed the lawn laden with thick plaid blankets, and the wheels of a light carriage churned up gravel in the driveway. He glanced over his shoulder to be sure.

A tall, thin crowlike creature cloaked in black lunged out of a dashing carriage and sprinted across the lawn, a great black satchel flapping at his side. Graeme ran beside him. In seconds, the doctor knelt at Sophie's side, not even breathing hard. Nor did he take the time to properly bow, as Fotherington might have done. That suited Lionel fine.

"Maitland Maddox, Your Lordship," the doctor said, even as he gently inspected Sophie's purpling bruise with lean, skilled fingers. "Honored to make your acquaintance."

Then he said with practiced medical cheer, "I say, Miss Bowerbank, haven't I warned you about standing in the way of flying objects?"

Sophie smiled. "Oooh, ouch!" She raised her hand to her injury.

"No smiling for at least a week, Miss Bowerbank," Maddox said with brisk sympathy.

"That was Miss Gatewood's young rooster, my good sir. Very unpredictable birds, young cocks," Sophie mumbled, her lips barely moving.

Maddox hummed and continued gently probing Sophie's jaw. "Can we hope your teeth escaped assault?"

"They'd better not have knocked her teeth out too," Lionel said to Maddox.

"Not their fault," Sophie said, then tested with her tongue.

"How not?" Lionel asked. "I saw their ball strike you down. You could have been killed."

"I looked away."

"What the devil distracted you from boys and balls flying all around you?"

Her green eyes blinked up at him, as if he were a nodcock. "You, my lord."

Damnation. That devil, him, he thought, annoyed and far more pleased than a man should be when the upshot of her interest in him had been injury. To cover his emotion, he called for blankets. Nesbit handed them over, and Maddox swaddled Sophie in them, holding out only one for her still unconscious friend.

Shifting to Celia, the doctor extracted strong smelling salts from his medical supplies and held them under her nose. She sat up, coughing violently, and a runnel of spit trickled down her chin.

Maddox retrieved a cloth from his layers of black clothing and handed it to her.

Celia furtively wiped away her little faux pas, sputtering, "Really, Maddox. Must your wretched remedies be so harsh?"

"There, there, Miss Upton. Those of us with delicate constitutions must make great sacrifices to be well. Can you stand? Lord Cordrey, if you will assist her."

She cast a pout at Lionel as if he should have leaped to help her too.

Graeme gallantly jumped to Celia's aid. Lionel had been burning angry at his son all day, keeping him forcibly in his office in the morning and at his side throughout an afternoon of cases at the grange. The lad's present fervor—and Lionel's memory of his own past intentions—had set him worrying that Graeme would flee back to his one and only love at the first opportunity. Much as Lionel regretted Sophie's injury, he could hope it and Miss Upton's fainting spell might divert his chivalric son from his romantic entanglement.

Meanwhile Maddox was asking Sophie to open and close her mouth and move her jaw from side to side.

She did so, wincing.

"Well done, Miss B.," he said with continued cheer. "Nothing a nice fresh slab of raw liver won't take care of. Shall we adjourn inside to a tidy fire, and I will give you your instructions . . . by your leave, that is, my lord," he added, in an afterthought.

Lionel was not offended. He'd not seen such medical candor and efficiency since the war, and he was damned glad to have it here on behalf of Sophie.

When everyone was gathered in the drawing room—Celia, Max, Alex, Simon, Graeme, Sophie, and himself—Maddox gave Sophie final instructions on how and how long to apply the liver to her jaw and advised her to limit talking.

"I will have dinner sent up to her," Lionel said, determined to give her the most assiduous care now that his sons had failed to do so.

"No, no," Maddox said. "You go right down to dinner, Miss B. You stay awake, and I'm sure His Lordship can appoint someone to waken you a time or two during the night."

"Whatever for, Dr. Maddox?" Sophie asked.

"Merely a precaution in the event that you also hit your head too hard upon falling. But I do believe the damage is confined to your pretty face."

Sophie blushed a healthy red, and Lionel bridled. The good

doctor wasn't above a bit of flirtation with Sophie, which struck Lionel as wildly inappropriate.

Maddox drew himself up to his immense gangly height. "Do call upon me at any time, my lord," he said with a twinkle. "Ladies in distress are so much more diverting than cranky cows in calving season!"

"Maddox, you insufferable toad, go home," Celia chided him, obviously annoyed to be linked to breeding bovines.

Maddox gave Celia a deferential bow that somehow showed no deference at all. Lionel walked him to the door and thanked him, then returned to attend Sophie. He sat silent and useless, waiting in a fog for Mrs. Plumridge to announce dinner, unable to erase the sheer horror that had shot through him when he'd seen the ball strike Sophie and she fell.

Chapter Seventeen

Pox take the thing Folks call a Maiden-head,
For soon as e'er I'm sleeping in my Bed,
I dream I'm mingling with some Man my Thigh,
Till something more than ord'nary does rise;
But when I wake and find my Dream's in vain,
I turn to Sleep only to Dream again . . .
—The Fifteen Plagues of a Maiden-Head (1707)

"His Lordship should protect you from his wicked sons and their horrid tricks!" Celia announced as she closed the door to Sophie's room behind her. She'd come to help Sophie put herself back together for dinner.

Sophie's poor dress was ruined, as she saw when Celia helped her strip it off, and her frizzed hair tousled beyond repair. Celia's dress was fine, however, Celia having conveniently swooned onto the full-length stole she'd wrapped around her shoulders.

"For pity's sake, Celia, it was just an accident. Wraxham doesn't have the power to prevent an honest mistake."

"Nevertheless, you should speak to His Lordship about it. In fact I shall complain to him myself," Celia went on.

"You'll do no such thing!" Sophie said, horrified. "His Lordship could not have been more concerned, or kind."

"I'm not sure my heart can take any more violence at their hands."

"I was the one injured," Sophie said, pulling a long face, then grimacing in pain. Any expression whatsoever only set everything to throbbing all over again. "And I have nothing further to say to His Lordship about it."

"But you know how sensitive I am."

"Whereas I'm as sensitive as a rock," she said ironically.

"Don't despair," Celia said. She fluffed a dry frock over Sophie's head and held out its sleeves for her arms. "A dab of powder here, a little sartorial magic there, and I'll have you looking your old self in no time—" She broke off to inspect Sophie's bruise with icy fingertips. Sophie flinched and Celia furrowed her brows in sympathy. "Except for this unfortunate disfigurement. Poor dear Sophie. I'm sure, as His Lordship says, that it will heal in no time. If I were a bruise, I would heal on the spot if Lord Wraxham ordered me to do so," Celia added brightly.

Sophie was not amused.

"Cheer up, Sophie dearest," Celia said, pinching Sophie's unhurt cheek. "I'm trying to make you laugh."

"Dr. Maddox forbids me to laugh for at least a week. Can you please do something with my hair?"

Celia's fingers went to work, evidently taming the frizzles into curls. She was expert at fashionable coiffures. Her own blond curls glittered, as perfectly in order as when she'd first left her room this morning. Finally she twisted a lock of hair in front of Sophie's ear and stepped back to admire her handiwork.

A little scowl marked her pretty brow. "Tch, tch. Pity. We used to be in bloom."

Sophie cringed inwardly. "Blooming isn't seemly for women of our advanced ages."

"A lady of any age can bloom when opportunity is afoot."

Perhaps, Sophie thought, but how could she know that opportunity was hers?

Sophie's bruise, the good doctor had said, would take a month to heal. Could her plan to seduce Lionel survive her convalescence?

A bracing cup of hot beef tea cleared Sophie's head and gave her strength to sit through the evening meal, if not actually eat any of M. Laframboise's elaborate entrees. The twins would have reviewed every instant of her dreadful accident—the blow, the fall, the blood, the rescue, and the ensuing bruise—and relived them with relish if Lionel had not ruled the subject off-limits at the dinner table.

Celia brought matters round to the poet Byron, her favorite for his daring in word and deed and love, and the more so, Sophie thought, since she'd come to Wraxham House.

Could she be trying to impress His Lordship, as she unfailingly referred to him? Sophie squelched the thought. Celia was her friend, so alarmed after the accident by the sight of Sophie's blood that she'd actually fainted.

Graeme held forth for Mr. Blake, arguing for the purity and originality of his childlike verses and the vision of his remarkable engravings.

Celia thought Mr. Blake's ditties pretentious, unsophisticated, and unfashionable. Her set-down of his otherworldly engravings nearly brought her and Graeme to blows. For Graeme was quite as committed to his poetic ideals as his father had ever been, Sophie noted wistfully, and yet he could not hide a depression of his spirits . . . or was it an underlying restlessness?

She sighed. It was hard to keep pace with the ups and downs of young hearts.

It was hard to keep pace with her own.

Dinner ended happily with a remarkable almond custard, a sweet mild dish exactly tailored to Sophie's queasy appetite.

When everyone was done, Nurse Nesbit swept the boys upstairs to their rooms. Lionel turned to Sophie, and Graeme stood gloomily beside him.

"Miss Bowerbank, if you feel up to it, kindly join my son and me in the library," Lionel said formally, as if he hadn't held her in his arms and tenderly touched her battered face just this afternoon on the rain-dampened east lawn.

Celia almost squirmed with curiosity but said with exact propriety, "Sophie, I should be happy to accompany you—"

"Thank you, Miss Upton." Lionel stopped her smoothly. "But if you will excuse the three of us for a few moments, we won't be long."

Despite the many pleasurable and enlightening hours Sophie had spent in the library, she had never seen its vast space so lit up at night. She was at home here, with the blazing candles glinting off the gilt-edged spines of hundreds upon hundreds of leather volumes that lined shelves stretching up to the richly carved and painted ceiling. She was at home with books, even with, she thought with secret pleasure, those hidden bawdy ones.

Lionel ushered her to a massive brocaded chair, and fluffed a pillow behind her back as if she were an invalid. "My son wishes to have a word with you," he said less smoothly than in the dining room. "We—he would have done so earlier but for your accident."

Graeme stepped forward, grimly determined, obviously rehearsed. "Last night I jumped to unflattering assumptions about you, madam."

Sophie was astonished. After the afternoon's confusion, last night's unpleasantness seemed ages ago. But Graeme's accusations and her mortification came back quickly enough.

"I apologize most sincerely," he went on, his face bleached with shame, "for any discomfort I may have caused a woman of your character."

Character? Sophie thought, mortified by the memory of torrid hallway embraces with Graeme's father. She could not be sorry for what she'd done, but she wanted more than anything to ease Graeme's pain.

She offered him her hand, and said gently, "I should much prefer for us to be friends, Lord Cordrey."

Shock played across his face. Then he bowed over her hand with a guarded smile. "I should like that above everything, Miss Bowerbank," he said, his earnestness so like the younger Lionel's that Sophie blinked. She was suddenly aware that Lionel was watching, keenly, and that he might disapprove of her offer of friendship to his son.

Too bad. She'd had an orderly life. A rich, useful, productive life where she had earned the respect of others and herself. Lionel had disrupted that life, thrusting her into his family's difficulties for his convenience and distracting her with his masculine sensuality to boot.

Kindness to others came naturally to her, and he would have to learn to live with that.

"Are you home long?" she asked. Graeme gave a puzzled nod, and she mentioned her and Celia's poetry nights.

"Do you write, Miss Bowerbank?" he asked, his passion for poetry shining through.

She warmed to him even more. "We only read, I'm afraid, but we read widely. Perhaps you would like to join us."

"I'd be pleased to, madam. If you would tell me what to read first."

The group had not yet decided. Under Lionel's interested gaze, she and his heir settled on Walter Scott's "Lay of the Last Minstrel" for Thursday evening rather than risk another fracas over Lord Byron and Mr. Blake.

Lionel dismissed Graeme with a command to attend to Celia in the drawing room, and the young man left, his shoulders sinking again with his misery unresolved.

Sophie pulled her stole around her, alone with Lionel at last, her fantasy of seducing him dashed. She was too sore, weary, and disfigured to mount the campaign she'd planned, and he was too remote to respond to her if she did.

Besides, the way he treated Graeme puzzled her. "I'm sorry, my lord, but what in the world are you doing to your son? He looks more miserable by the hour."

Lionel stiffened in his black evening wear, every inch the unapproachable earl. "He has earned his misery," he said grimly, and related a somber story of Graeme's expulsion from Oxford over an affair with his tutor's wife.

Different though it was, Graeme's plight took her back to the painful intensity of her and Lionel's parting. Misery for the father and the son stole over her. "If he was wrenched away with everything unsettled, forced to leave her behind, no wonder he's so . . ."

"Moody, dark, unreachable? Feeling betrayed by his elders, and murderous?" Lionel bit off the words, a dangerous edge to his voice. "I remember those feelings too well."

So did she. Losing Lionel had felt like dying. "The more reason to afford him sympathy," she said firmly.

"Sympathy, codswallop. The wench is married. *Married.* And he—he has everything before him. She is older, more experienced. She must have seduced him." He paced, swearing softly. "And a dreamy romantic chap like Graeme must have been damnably easy prey."

"That is a decidedly uncharitable view of women, my lord, and an unflattering perspective on your son."

But even as she chided him, their conversation astonished her. Last night she'd all but seduced her onetime lover, this afternoon he'd tenderly held her in his arms, and tonight she was arguing with him as if she were his wife.

What could it mean? And where did she now stand with Lionel and his family? Was she the boys' tutor? The father's friend? The earl—the man's lover?

Oh, how she wished for the experience of a worldly woman. Or an insight into Lionel's closed heart.

"It's worse than that," he said, pacing still. "I cannot speak to him without recrimination, nor he to me, except in anger."

She was not Lionel's wife. She wasn't Graeme's mother. So she weighed her words. "The situation is at fault, not you, my lord. It is impossible for both of you."

He stopped pacing and pulled a chair up to her, a new-fashioned one with spindly legs. It looked like it would break beneath a man of his stature. "Truth is, I can't let him out of my sight," he confided, sitting at an angle to her, but very near.

"My father was like that with me after you . . ." She trailed off, uncomfortably thrust back to that wretched time. "But then, we'd always been close."

He covered her hand with his. "I envied you that."

"You envied me?" She was shocked to think that the privileged young viscount had envied her anything.

"My father and I shared nothing," Lionel said. "How was I to know how a man raised sons? I thought boys raised themselves. Boys, and tutors."

How awful for him. She'd had no idea he felt like that about his childhood, but he looked ready to throttle the hounds of hell. She turned up her hand beneath his and laced her fingers into his.

"It was different for me, my lord," she said. "After my mother died, my father tutored me himself. Then after you left that summer, he put me to work on his commentaries. It was important, mentally taxing work, and it took my mind off you. Perhaps you can find something similarly important for Graeme?"

Lionel thought a moment, then shook his head. "Between Tims and Carter, the estate is taken care of."

"He seems very good with Simon," she suggested.

"Does he? I had not noticed."

He had not been looking. Or, given his admission, had he not known what to look for? She could nudge him a little. "He could help me in the schoolroom."

"You want help? When I'm paying you sixty pounds?" Lionel scowled, but did not remove his hand.

"Now that I've seen the scope of my duties and your sons' mischief, sixty pounds doesn't begin to cover my labors," she said, trying for lightness.

His scowl deepened.

"I only meant that helping with Simon would give Graeme a worthy task," she went on. "A worthwhile duty to occupy his hours and his mind."

Lionel looked at the walls of books, his profile somehow savage against the golden candlelight. "Very well then, I'll send him to the schoolroom in the morning. We'll see if you are right," he said gruffly, and released her hand, stood, turned on his booted heel.

"Thank you, my lord," she said, after him, her defenses going up as he disappeared into Wraxham House's corridors. It was a good idea. She needed help, and poor Graeme—who was grieving his mother and had only just lost the love of his life—obviously adored his little brothers. He could be the key to her plan of reconciling Lionel with his sons.

So why was Lionel being so stiff-necked about it?

Graeme didn't show up until almost noon, but Sophie determined not to breathe a word of his lateness to his disapproving father. Although still as gloomy as dark clouds before a summer storm, Graeme had a bent for tutoring. He was gentle with Simon and firm with the twins, defusing their mischievousness by challenging them with harder and harder lessons based on his own studies. They buckled down, and flourished.

She embraced this glimpse of learning as young men experienced it. It crossed her mind that she might soon be ancillary to the boys' needs, a stopgap measure to be dismissed the minute a suitable man was found.

All the more reason to get serious about seducing Lionel. Given the latest signs of his displeasure with her, she'd better be quick and clever about it.

Last night, awake with aches and pain, she'd checked on

Simon late, fretting over what to do if Lionel was in the hall-way.

He'd not been at his post.

Perhaps she'd gone too early, and he would have been there later.

Perhaps, and more likely, for she feared the worst, her in-experience had put him off.

She tucked Simon in and skulked back to her room alone.

The next night, she crept out again, steeling herself for the disappointment of not finding Lionel along the way.

"Miss Bowerbank?" came a whisper from the dark floor. She was still two doors away from Simon's room.

She startled, then said hopefully, "My lord?"

"No. It's Graeme, ma'am," the hushed voice said. His long lanky body unfolded, and he stood respectfully before her. "Forgive me. I didn't mean to alarm you."

"I didn't expect you. What are you doing here?"

"Guarding the twins' door. My father told me about the ac-cusations against them, and the measures he was taking, so I offered"—Graeme ducked his head as he put himself for-ward—"to stand in for him."

It was a noble offer on Graeme's part . . . and a neat solution on Lionel's to ward off another hallway debauch.

Disappointment trickled through her. "Your nights will be rather long," she said.

"It isn't as though I can sleep," Graeme said fatally. Which spoke volumes of his passion, more than anything she'd heard him say in the schoolroom and the drawing room.

"Ah, your . . . friend."

"Glencora," he said miserably. Sophie would have thought he was overacting, but she'd felt that selfsame misery over Lionel.

"Do you have news of her, Lord Cordrey?" she asked, whether from a Celia-like curiosity or rectorlike concern for a member of his flock she could not be sure.

"Not a word," he said, his voice harsh with frustration. "My father cannot disinherit me, so he cuts me out of this. If you'll pardon my saying so, Miss Bowerbank," he added with an edge of anger, "your father has cut me out as well."

"My father?"

"He wrote to the dean of my college, and Carter brought back an answer. *They* know something. They're *doing* something. Everyone knows but me."

"I'm very sorry." But she could say no more, for she too had been left out.

"Not half as sorry as—" he began angrily, then stopped. "Forgive me, I forget myself. It's just that no one believes me. And I had only her word for the horrors and humiliations the old man heaped upon her."

"I suppose I daren't ask," Sophie ventured as tactfully as she could. But she wanted him to talk. She feared he would explode without some outlet for his outrage.

"And I daren't say, not to a lady of your reputation. But he made her do things for him no decent man should ask a wife, or even ask, pardon me, a bawd."

"Was she . . . harmed?"

"Only in spirit, and yet she feared that he was going to require more and more scurrilous acts of her to satisfy him. Oh, I shouldn't speak of this to you."

He probably should not. Because she'd read of scurrilous acts that shocked her to the core, so she could imagine whips and bonds, deprivation and humiliation.

She patted the back of his hand, a scant reassurance. "I truly believe, Lord Cordrey, that your father will help Glencora and act in your best interest, just as he does your brothers'."

For she had to give Lionel credit, she thought as she slipped into Simon's room. By letting Graeme take his place at the twins' room, Lionel was bringing his eldest son into the family fold, just as she'd recommended. It pleased her that Lionel had heeded her advice.

Given the affection she'd seen between Graeme and his brothers, perhaps she could push her advice one step further and get Graeme out of the hallway and into a proper bed. What did she have to lose? Lionel had already removed himself from her path.

Still, his attention to his son had to be the most important thing, she told herself, no matter what came of her futile attraction and pathetic fantasies.

A week passed, and Sophie's unsightly bruise turned a sickly yellow green, which mattered less the less she saw of Lionel. He showed up only for evening meals. Unfortunately.

Because the less she saw of him, the more she obsessed about him.

Sophie came to quite like Graeme, despite his unpredictable but daily descent into the mopes. Between the schoolroom and his nightly vigils, he was practically underfoot. More and more she saw traces of the sensitive lad she'd loved in the unhappy son. Which left her in sympathy with Graeme and mystified by her growing obsession with his father.

But she couldn't have him if she saw him only at dinner, sitting at the far end of the table, chatting idly with Celia while guarding his sons.

The twins, though they looked more and more tired, grew steadily more restless. If Graeme hadn't been there in the daytime to help with lessons and supervise their play, she could not have controlled them.

In the afternoons, Celia took to joining Sophie on the terrace to read her books and watch while Graeme taught his brothers a ferociously fast game from the university called hockey. Max, Alex, and even Simon thought the game was all the crack. Sophie didn't know whether to rejoice at their distraction or worry for their safety.

"Don't fret, Miss Bowerbank," Graeme reassured her. "They're not good enough, fast enough, or strong enough to do each other serious damage."

She tried not to fret as she watched them streak across the

lawn. Vigorous sport had to divert their energies from mischief. And yet exertion added to their fatigue.

After a while, Celia closed her book. "I agree, Sophie dearest. The twins have the most dreadful great black circles under their eyes. They must never sleep. You don't suppose they're getting out despite His Lordship's precautions?"

Sophie didn't want to think so. And yet the entire southern elevation of Wraxham House was windowed, and its old central buildings must have secret passageways galore. They could have discovered a way out. She could not bring herself to share those fears with Celia.

"It's probably growing pains, Celie. Nurse Nesbit says they're growing so fast it takes a team of seamstresses to keep them in clothes. And Laframboise complains that they wolf down his removes with no appreciation of his talents."

Celia huffed. "Nevertheless, we should tell His Lordship, and sooner rather than later. Anything could happen any time."

"True enough."

Despite their eldest brother's presence, their schoolroom hijinks did not stop. Though fewer, they were diabolically more clever. Cornstarch in the ink forced Sophie back to the dusty chalkboard. A plugged-up flue smoked up the classroom and sent everyone outside coughing.

"You wouldn't want to look as if you'd been caught off guard," Celia pointed out.

Sophie sighed. "No, I just can't do it, Celie. Not until they do something dire, something that doesn't make me laugh."

Moments later, Lionel strolled out onto the terrace wearing a tweed jacket and well-worn riding boots. A slight smile relaxed the sharp planes of his face, and his tawny mane was in sporting disarray. Sophie's insides churned. He'd let his hair grow longer and looked vital and alive, so like the lad who'd stolen her heart that she could hardly bear to sit beside him, a confirmed spinster, failed seductress, frumpy dowd.

"Miss Upton, Miss Bowerbank," he said, properly acknowledging them by rank. He pulled up a wrought-iron chair nearest Celia, stretched out his long legs, and watched his sons gallop about his lawn. Once he cupped his hands around his mouth and yelled, "Alex! Guard your right!"

Then he explained, "Graeme knows Alex is left-handed, and he's exploiting that."

"I don't understand, my lord," Celia said.

Lionel enthusiastically explained the game's fine points to Celia. Her face scrunched prettily as she struggled to get its rules and regulations straight.

To Sophie, the rules were less important than the result: Lionel was mesmerized by his sons' every move. She should give herself credit for helping restore his sons to him, and to the devil with her fantasies.

Shortly Celia prodded in a whisper, "I do think you should tell him, Sophie."

Sophie pressed her finger to her lips. "No, shush."

"He has a right to know," Celia insisted, a little louder.

Lionel's gaze stayed fixed on the field. "Know what, Miss Bowerbank? After everything we've been through, I can manage it."

Sophie sighed. Blast Celia, just when things were going so much better between the father and the sons. "It's just that the twins look tired, my lord."

"What do you mean, tired?" he asked, then shouted, "Eyes on the ball, Simon!"

"They look as if they are losing sleep, my lord."

Lionel turned a steely gaze to her. "Explain."

Sophie cleared her throat, dreading his reaction. "During lessons, they are by turns restless and . . . I don't know how to describe it . . . sometimes irritable, sometimes inattentive. As if they weren't sleeping."

She stopped, and Lionel waited.

Celia leaned forward helpfully. "What Sophie is trying to say, my lord, is this: As if they were not in their room at night. As if they were getting past yours and Lord Cordrey's guard."

Sophie bit her lip in consternation. That was her worry exactly. But she had been hoping against hope that she was wrong. And she hadn't been ready to present her suspicion to Lionel, not when she had no evidence.

"Miss Bowerbank, do you concur?" Lionel said, the relaxed country earl snapping into the keen, questioning magistrate.

"They do not seem well rested, my lord, it is true. And yet, Lord Cordrey, I know, is guarding the door in the night, and he tells me you are there before dawn."

Lionel went silent, and Sophie felt his tension, not the alertness of watching his sons at play, but the strain of doubt.

What did they do at night? Didn't all grand houses have secret passages?

"They must be sneaking out the windows," he said grimly.

"How terrifying," Sophie blurted.

"Terrifying? They only need a rope tied to a bedstead. The high bushes on the ground would catch them if they fell. It's a Wraxham family tradition."

She knew nothing of boys, but an image of a young Lionel and his younger brothers routinely descending the walls of Wraxham House did nothing to reassure her. "You do not sound concerned, my lord."

"Oh, I'm concerned, Miss Bowerbank," he said ironically. "If Max or Alex hurts himself I'll kill him. But under these clouds of suspicion, I cannot let them run free."

"They aren't running free," she insisted. "One of us is with them every hour of the day. I wouldn't believe it without proof."

"I'll get you your proof then. Come," he said, and rose and practically lifted her out her chair. "Excuse us, Miss Upton. We will leave you with your book."

Sophie stretched her stride to keep up with Lionel's angry pace. The family's rooms faced north, Sophie's and Celia's guest rooms too. It took a few minutes to walk a flagstone path around the east wing to the handsome Palladian design of the north elevation. He knew exactly which of the high-sashed

203

windows belonged to Max and Alex's room. His gaze traveled up the golden stonework to the sill.

"The little devils!" he ground out.

Sophie's heart sank. Scuff marks, dozens of scuff marks, faint but undeniable, tracked up and down the wall.

"I can't tell if they were using ropes or sheets," he said, his fine mouth a straight line of vexation. "That settles it. No fishing, no hunting, and pony rides and games only when one of us can supervise. As for the windows, I'll have them nailed shut. That should clip their wings."

"My lord! You might as well send them to bed with bread and water. Talk to them, at least," she advised.

"Oh, I will talk to them. I will talk to them."

Just before dinner, Sophie recognized Celia's quiet rapping at the inner door to her chamber. She was so disheartened that she didn't want to go down to dinner, let alone report on the scalding scolding Lionel had given his sons, her protests before and after notwithstanding.

But her friend and chaperone deserved forewarning of how low things had sunk, and so she let her in and explained what happened.

Celia's eyes glistened with concern. "You had to tell him, Sophie. He's been shirking his responsibilities to his sons."

"No, he has responsibilities to everyone, but I'm the one responsible only for them." Sophie shook her head, mad at the situation and furious with herself. "I should have handled it on my own. I let him down."

"I think it's the boys you should worry about."

"I am worried about them too. I, for one, believe them."

"You believe that they were out tracking down the real culprits? Balderdash!"

"Indeed I do. Celie, they were *crying*. Not from shame that they'd done wrong, but from hurt that they were being wronged. First by your father, then by the butcher, and now by their father. But most of all by me."

"If not them," Celia asked, "then who? Gypsies and vagrants have been in short supply this month. Or has His Lordship given up the search?"

"I'm not privy to his suspicions, but Wraxham House teems with malcontents. It would take a month to rule everyone out."

Celia brightened with her usual lust for gossip. "Such as?"

"Nurse Nesbit grumbles, fearing she will lose her job to me. Laframboise clearly feels his talents wasted in the country. Mr. Tims, if I understand it right, is unhappy that Mr. Carter was advanced before him."

"And as for Mr. Carter, a more arrogant man I have not met." Celia put a beringed finger to her cheek. "Do you suppose anyone has thought of Beane?"

"Beane?" said Sophie. "There you are then. His Lordship has a great deal of work before him."

Celia clucked. "I fear a disaster."

Sophie rolled her eyes. "It's already a disaster, Celie."

For the boys, and for their father. How could Sophie hope to help repair their relationship when everything kept going wrong?

Chapter Eighteen

Of late I wonder what's with me the Matter,
For I look like Death, and am as weak as Water,
For several Days I loath the sight of Meat,
And every Night I chew the upper Sheet . . .
—The Fifteen Plagues of a Maiden-Head (1707)

Sophie flung off her fine linen sheet in a welter of confusion and desire.

Should she ditch her plan to take Lionel as a lover?

Should she pledge herself, nunlike, to a life of purity and sacrifice for the benefit of Lionel's much maligned and misunderstood sons?

Or should she return to her father's house where she read good books and did good deeds and had good friends?

If only she could quell her attraction to Lionel. If only she could rein in her desire.

But no, like the plagues released upon the world when Pandora opened that forbidden box, Sophie's lust for Lionel—arrogant, intransigent, unfeeling man that he'd turned out to be—swirled through her, strengthening by the day.

And night. How could a woman be such a ninnyhammer as to entertain lustful, erotic thoughts for a man who held her opinions—and therefore, *her*—in such low regard? How?

Because at heart, she'd believed she could change his mind.

She sank beneath the linen sheets on her bed in his guest chamber and wallowed around in misery for a few more moments. Weeping actually, and dreading the break of day.

She'd signed on to tutor Lionel's sons, flattered that he'd acknowledged her learning and ability.

And flooded with memories of that too-brief summer interlude they'd shared.

Would that memories flooded him too.

She poked her bare feet out from under the sheets and sought the plush pile of the Aubusson carpet with her toes. A Wedgwood pitcher and basin awaited her in a corner of the room. She padded over, weary from her restless night, and blinked at her ravaged image in a mirror with a carved, gilded frame.

Pity. We used to be in bloom.

She *was* pitiable, worse off in every way than when she'd undertaken the noble task of rescuing Lionel's sons and restoring them to their father.

Her bruise had gone sickly yellow and made a perfect circle at the left corner of her mouth. She tested it with her fingertips and found a hard lump in its center. In the depths of her dark night, she'd discovered that the bruise made crying hurt as much as laughing.

The gray smudges under her eyes looked like yesterday's ashes from the grate in the dining room at home. Worrying that yesterday's disaster would trigger Simon's terrors, she'd checked on him last night nearly every hour. At least Lionel had taken her advice and moved the twins into Graeme's chamber. And then nailed those windows shut.

On her long trips down the hallway to Simon's room, she no longer had to face Graeme's distant courtesy and decided chill. Evidently he felt she'd betrayed his brothers to their father. She could not help that.

Back in her room, she slipped out of her night rail, dampened an embroidered cloth, and washed her body and her breasts, underneath them too, where they'd begun to sag. Her neglected nipples puckered in the early morning chill. How she longed for Lionel to kiss her breasts again. She hungered to feel the sweet tug of desire coil into her womb.

She hungered for him to kiss her as he used to do.

Early one summer morning all those years ago, she'd dared to meet him in the pleasure garden, her slippers and the hem of her skirts drenched with dew. The bosom of her sprig muslin frock laced in front, and he'd untied it with his beautiful square hands. He'd pulled the fabric back and her breasts sprang free, his breath quick and his clear handsome features rapt with awe and admiration.

He'd made her feel beautiful.

He'd lifted her breasts with his hands, tested their weight, and explored their shape. The look of yearning on his face made her think of heaven. Then he'd begun to kiss her, circles of kisses around first one breast and then the other until tears of pleasure sprang into her eyes.

"Don't cry, love," he'd said when her tears dropped onto his face. And he'd taken one nipple in his mouth and gently suckled until her throat tingled, her breasts ached, and her legs tightened, and pleasure like a pure white light shot between her legs.

She touched herself now, standing naked and alone before the ornate mirror in a chamber Lionel reserved for guests. But she was his employee. An empty hollow ache settled between her legs.

She was a silly tearful spinster too, hoping hopes and dreaming dreams long put aside.

She put them aside again and dried her tears, gently dabbing the bruise beside her mouth.

It was time to open the schoolroom, time to return to Lionel's sons and duty. She picked out her plainest dress, once ruby, faded into rose, as she was fading into middle age, a barren spinster, knowing only the shadow pleasure she could give herself.

She should get there early to set up her lessons and steel herself to confront three unhappy boys and one miserable young man. No, two unhappy boys, she thought, for Simon was not accused of anything, and he'd slept well. She'd seen to that.

In the hall, her feet sped over the plush carpet, taking her past antique tapestries, marble-topped pier tables and chests along the way, up granite stairs, their treads worn from centuries of Westfalls in the Wraxham line, from boys going upstairs for their lessons.

For now, she was part of that.

She paused before the carved schoolroom door, less elaborate but no less rich than the renowned wooden carvings in the public rooms downstairs.

She opened the door and went inside. It was still early so the boys weren't late, and yet something seemed out of place. A book? A chair? A table? No, everything was present and accounted for, just subtly askew. She checked her desk. It was as she'd left it when the boys had gone out to play, her three books stacked neatly to her left and her quill pen brandishing its plume to the right where she could reach it easily. She scanned the room, cataloging desks, chalkboard, chalk, books, everything in order.

Except . . . where was her father's antique globe?

A chill snaked down her spine. She whirled around.

The globe was not in its usual spot by the window, where daylight made it easier to see its fading demarcations of empires and barbarian regions of the ancient world.

She looked behind the screen and gasped in horror.

Garish paints splattered her father's antique globe. She came closer, inspecting it in disbelief.

It had not been so much painted as . . . defaced.

Ruined. Its venerable leather, faded shades of brown and yellow, was lost, lost forever. Washes of watercolor coated Russia and the polar regions, and drizzled over the Mediterranean down the Sahara to the equator.

Tulip red, iris blue, leaf green—all tacky to her touch.

Worse. Each was a hue the boys had used in yesterday's art lesson, the one lesson of the day that had riveted their attention.

She'd told them she treasured her father's globe.

They wouldn't have done it, would they?

She twirled the ruined globe and held back a sob. Her father had taught her Homer on this globe.

Oh dear, oh no. Its ruin looked like retribution.

Yesterday, she'd told Lionel that the twins looked tired. She'd gone with him to check the wall outside their chamber's windows, to see if they were sneaking out at night. They had been, and he'd punished them, too severely, to her way of thinking.

They'd protested vehemently. "*We're innocent. You have no proof.*" He'd taken away the few rights and privileges they enjoyed in their new country life.

It was so unfair.

Unfair enough to lead them to do this?

Yes. This time, Sophie was convinced.

Graeme arrived first with Simon.

"What happened? Who did that?" Simon asked, his chocolate-brown eyes wide with dismay.

She couldn't tell him her suspicions.

Graeme saw her hesitation. "You blame my brothers," he said fiercely. "They could not have. They were with me through the night."

"They could have slipped out while you were dressing," Sophie said.

Graeme sat down and picked up a book.

Moments later, Max and Alex dragged in, their faces dark with resentment over yesterday's injustice. They goggled at the

210

globe, as if surprised—a clever touch! she thought, and turned on them.

"You boys may think I deserve this for betraying you to your father. But my father did not deserve it. This was one of his most prized possessions, generously lent to add interest to your lessons."

They looked like rabbits caught in a snare, hunched and frozen, powerless to escape.

"You think we did it!" Max said, as if stunned.

"We would never do a thing like that, Miss Bowerbank," Alex said urgently. "It isn't even funny."

"Your father will see no humor in it either," she said.

"You can't tell him," Alex burst out. "He'll believe we did it. He already thinks that we're . . . that we . . ." Manfully he choked back tears.

Sophie was almost touched. But she'd had her fill of hijinks and tomfoolery and ever-escalating pranks, followed by pleas of innocence. This was personal, this was . . . mean.

Up till now, they may have been truly innocent, but they'd wreaked their revenge on her because of her role in their latest punishment.

And yet, even now, she couldn't bear to make them stand in corners or spank their hands with rulers, and she would never cane a soul. She found a Bible verse—*do unto others*—and made them write essays imagining every good deed they'd ever left undone.

It did not seem enough. Neither did staying on at Wraxham House. This morning she would fulfill her obligation. This afternoon she would pack up her foolish hopes for the boys and her dreams of their father and go home where she could be of use.

After the midday meal, Sophie put Graeme in charge and banished the four boys to cricket on the lawn, the only play not ruled off-limits. She'd postponed leaving past the point of pain, waiting to consult with Lionel. He hadn't stopped by once.

211

She retreated to her room, arguing with herself all the way. Halfway there a sunny Celia caught up to her. "Lessons done early, Sophie dear?"

"No earlier than usual," she mumbled painfully. "I sent Graeme outside with the boys to play."

Celia clasped her arm, pulled her to a stop, and studied her face. "Why so glum, dearest?"

Tears threatened to spill over. Sophie stifled them and made herself say as if it were a matter of no import, "We had another incident."

"Those horrid little monsters!"

Guilty as charged, it seemed. But Sophie forced a smile. She absolutely refused to admit her hurt and disillusionment to someone who thought she was past her bloom. "They protest their innocence, of course."

"But what did they do?"

Sophie gave a brief account, and her friend's sunny face turned stormy. "And after that, you spent the entire morning with them? And they still deny it? You must be furious."

No, she was disheartened by the act, disillusioned with the boys, and disappointed that her efforts had seemed to come to naught. "No, not furious, not anymore."

Celia huffed. "They should be tarred and feathered, burned at the stake. Or at least transported."

Sophie could not feel so vengeful. And she wouldn't prosecute the twins to anyone but their father. "I blame myself for putting my father's globe in harm's way."

"Stuff and nonsense. The schoolroom should not have been in harm's way. But it was, and you may be. You cannot stay here in jeopardy. I think you should resign."

Resign. Sophie had planned to do just that, but in defeat, not fear. She couldn't resign from fear. "I can't leave the boys in the lurch with everything up in the air."

Celia's blond curls bounced as she shook her head. "Sophie, Sophie. Think of everything those wretched little hellions have done."

"They're *boys,* Celie, bright, bored, spoiled boys. I have to believe I can help bring them closer to their father."

Celia patted her hand. "A noble but futile endeavor, dearest. Things went wrong with them a long, long time ago. No one can expect you to fix it. Certainly not His Lordship. He's an earl, just like any other earl: He snaps his fingers, and everybody jumps."

Sophie squeezed her eyes shut. He had snapped his fingers, and she had jumped, but not in any way Celia imagined. "He needed my help," she said stubbornly.

"Bah! He took advantage of your convenience."

"Without me, poor Simon has no one."

Celia sniffed. "He has that nurse, and a nurse should suffice. His Lordship is using you, Sophie, asking you to do more than any one person could, far more than any woman should, and asking you to do things he should have done himself years ago."

Put that way, Sophie had to reevaluate. She'd had far too many of the exact same thoughts. Though convinced she was not in danger, she was in over her head. With the possible exception of Simon, she was doing no one any good.

So she should just pack her things and leave.

Leave Lionel.

A sob caught in her throat.

So there it was. The truth of why she'd come, why she'd put up with the boys' worst tricks, why she didn't want to leave.

She was in love with Lionel, still earnest and passionate behind his urbane facade. She'd always been in love with him.

So Celia was right that Sophie had to leave, but not for the reasons she named.

Because Sophie realized that satisfying her erotic yearnings would never be enough. And physical love was all he had to spare.

Chapter Nineteen

So bright the tear in Beauty's eye
Love half regrets to kiss it dry.
—*Byron,* The Bride of Abydos

Lionel could stand it now.

A week had passed since Simon's ball struck Sophie, and Lionel braved the east lawn in the afternoon to see by the light of day how her bruise had healed.

On the lawn Graeme was drilling his brothers at hockey, keeping them under control, settling into the household's routine.

Lionel fingered a note inside his waistcoat pocket with anticipation. It was from Abercairn, the usual middle-of-term report on James and Marcus. It would be good: They were sterling students. For the first time since his wife's death, he could sit back and feel that his family was all in order.

Lionel crossed the lawn to the terrace and took a seat beside Miss Celia Upton, heiress of Upton Grange, a bouquet of blue from the satin ribbons in her hair to the silk slippers on her little feet.

She discreetly closed a slender volume in dark blue calf with gilt rules and lettering, and batted her azure eyes. His stomach clenched. She couldn't possibly think her spinster's stratagems would work on a cynic like himself.

Thank God, Sophie batted at his ideas and opinions.

Almost instinctively he took out his snuffbox—neglected but not yet abandoned—and nodded at the slender volume. "Poetry again, Miss Upton?"

"You must know Lord Byron, my lord."

"Distantly," he said. He had passed the man in dark, smoky places, but never, at his wildest, stooped to the baron's decadence.

She inclined her head as if sharing a secret. "Word is, he's a scandal."

A confirmed sybarite, the poetical peer dined on women like her for breakfast. But if the woman was after a morsel of juicy gossip, Lionel could oblige.

"I never credited the rumor that he entertained two hundred different women in as many nights," Lionel offered, like a forbidden candy. "The logistics are lunacy."

"La, my lord, you make me blush."

Which she then did on cue.

He was not impressed. Ariadne had explained that trick, along with many others in her repertoire. Ah, Ariadne. He fingered his snuffbox and thought of her plumy curves, and remembered urban artifices. At this wearying moment, he'd pay solid sterling for the purity of an honest monetary contract between a willing woman and a man of means.

"Byron would make you blush, madam, not I."

"Do you really think so, my lord?" she asked in that patently false breathlessness that annoyed him so.

"If nothing else, his supposed liaison with his half sister— ah, but such details are not for the ears of a lady like yourself."

Her eyes goggled. That ought to sell a few more copies of the chap's scribblings for him.

He nodded at her little leather volume. "Which piece do you read?"

"*The Bride of Abydos*," Celia said. Her lips curved to attract him. "Although, after what you say, it disappoints me. I should have expected something more carnal and more daring."

Plague take the woman, and her transparent attempt to lure him. She didn't. She bored him to his toes. She was every greedy, grasping woman that had plagued his London days.

He stifled a yawn and said, "Trust me, madam, if the man told all, you would require smelling salts."

She didn't have a comeback. Yet. The expression on her face said she was groping for a retort, and a suggestive one at that. Up till now, Sophie's presence had shielded him from her presuming, but not tempting, chaperone, but . . . Where the hell was Sophie?

He turned his attention to his sons, shouting instructions through a few more kicks and falls and fumbles. Then he re-marked, "Miss Bowerbank does not attend her duty this after-noon."

Celia Upton looked grave. "If you can find her, I fear you will find her crying."

He curbed every instinctive impulse to pummel an answer out Sophie's friend, but scowled instead. "My tutor could bet-ter supervise my sons if she cried here. What the devil is it now?"

"I'm sure I don't know, my lord, what her thoughts are after this latest incident."

He pinned her with a wrathful glare. "Do not say, Miss Up-ton, that you kept me here gossiping about that insufferable philanderer while there has been another incident."

Celia Upton's icy facade of perfect sociability cracked. "I—the—but it's over and done with now, my lord."

"I will be the judge of that, Miss Upton," he said through

gritted teeth, "if you will tell me what transpired while I was unavoidably away today."

Her mouth primmed, not prettily, for once. "This morning in the schoolroom, Sophie discovered her father's antique globe had been . . . well, ahem, quite frankly, my lord, violated."

"What do you mean, *violated?*" he grated.

She lifted her chin. "Covered with paint, my lord. Someone slathered watercolors on it from the boys' art lesson yesterday."

Someone indeed. Rage wracked him. Images of medieval tortures flashed before him, iron cuffs and clanking chains, but he said with bare control, "So where do you think she is?"

"I honestly don't know."

Honesty, he thought grimly, might well be a virtue she was unacquainted with. But what did he know of her? She was Sophie's longtime friend, here on his account and at her own inconvenience in the requisite role of chaperone. Sophie needed her, and he would put up with that.

"Thank you, Miss Upton. If you will excuse me," he said with barest civility, and strode onto the lawn to interrogate his sons about the latest Wraxham family disaster.

Red-faced from exertion, the twins denied they'd ever touched the globe in question when Lionel confronted them on the lawn. He'd hated every minute of the interview, lie piled onto lie. They feigned hurt and astonishment when Lionel banished them from the playing field and to their room without supper. Come to think of it, why hadn't Sophie lashed them to their quarters?

And why was she crying?

And why had she disappeared?

Worry mixed with anger as he stalked into the house.

Sophie wasn't in the schoolroom or the drawing room. Lionel knocked at her chamber door, but she did not answer. Blast. She would have if she'd been inside. He paced the hallway, agitation growing. Where could she have gone? Where should he go next?

For damned and certain, he'd be drawn and quartered before he would yell up and down the hallways and embarrass her before the staff.

He checked the kitchen. No, Laframboise barred all but the kitchen help.

The stillroom, no. Mrs. Plumridge shooed out all trespassers.

His office, not likely. He kept it locked. He checked the latch. Still locked. Now the library . . . that seemed a possibility.

So he stalked off, but found it empty, an echo, a mockery. He descended the central marble staircase that led from the family quarters upstairs to the public rooms below, his anger and his bemusement growing.

Nothing to do but look behind every door. He heard her first, sniffling quietly, in the cool wooden depths of the private family chapel. He peered into the darkness, and slowly her shape emerged from the enveloping shadows. He wasn't used to thinking of her as beautiful—bold and brilliant, yes, compassionate and kind, and stubborn, too. But standing before the altar, hugging herself in misery, arms crossed over her breasts and hands gripping her shoulders, she was a picture of beauty in distress.

His heart, what there was left of it, reached out to her, and he strode across the room, the heels of his riding boots clicking on the uneven stone pavings.

She wheeled in shock, and he took her in his arms, pulling her firm ample body to his. There was an instant of resistance, and then a tide of yielding. He snugged her closer to him, murmuring into her ear, "God, Sophie, I am so sorry they destroyed your father's globe. I couldn't find you, I thought you'd left."

"I *am* leaving, my lord," she muttered, her mouth against the lapels of his jacket.

"Of course, you want to tell your father," he said with perfect understanding, enjoying the perfect rightness of her in his arms. He should have held her earlier, and often. He could make things right. "But that's my responsibility, and I'll do it with the twins in tow. They will maintain his yard and gardens for the rest of their natural lives. Or any other arduous chore of his devising."

He lifted her chin and gazed down at eyes glistening with tears. They tracked down her rosy cheeks. His sons had done this to her. *He* had, and he regretted it in a shut-off chamber of his heart that hadn't felt such pained compassion for another being since he'd come back to London from his fated tour of duty in the West Indies. He bent his head and kissed the salt tears off her face.

She braced her arms against him and pushed away just enough to leave a yawning gap between her breasts and his chest, between his groin and her belly.

"I am *leaving,* my lord," she repeated, word by carefully articulated word.

He kissed the other cheek, feeling the sudden lack of her soft warm belly against his urgent heat.

"I will find your father another globe, Sophie," he promised. For this, for her, he would promise anything.

"If you must," she said. But she was subdued and distant, not at all her usual brisk way of standing up to him.

"I must. I will. As for the boys, I sent them to their room. And I'm not finished with them."

She turned, teardrops on wet lashes, and a defeated but determined look in her eyes. "You do what you must, and I will too."

"Of course," he said soothingly, not sure what she meant.

"You see, I thought we were making progress."

"You *are* making progress. They are," he said impatiently, caught off guard by her disconnected observations. "I haven't sat in on their lessons for nothing. You've done well. Their improvements are obvious."

"No, I mean I thought they were coming to feel the same

affection for me that I feel for them. But obviously not."

Your work here is not about their affection, he started to say. *It's about mine.*

But the thought was so staggeringly out of character for him that he shoved it to the backmost reaches of his mind.

"Rubbish," he said instead. "Simon thinks you walk on water, the twins vie for your approval, and Graeme shows you his poems."

She blinked. "You know about the poems?"

"It doesn't take a genius to guess what's on the foolscap he passes to you in the drawing room."

She smiled faintly. "His are rather better than yours were at his age, my lord."

Lionel, he thought, angry, possessive, and wishful all at once. Would he never be able to restore that easy conversation they'd once had? But she had stubbornly set herself against that friendly intimacy. "It would not be difficult to best my youthful excesses," he snorted.

She gave an impatient push with the heel of her hand. "I must return home, my lord," she said.

He agreed. "Your father must be told. But I'd prefer to tell him myself."

She backed away, engaging his gaze. "Listen to my words, my lord. I am moving back home. I am going to live with my father," she said, enunciating as if he were dull-witted or deaf. "I will not return to Wraxham House."

He opened his mouth to object.

"No, my lord. I must have been daft to take on the boys. I came to help, and have not."

He thought for a moment. After such a blow as the damage to the globe, a crisis in confidence was understandable. She just needed bolstering. "You have no idea how much my spoiled brats' manners have improved under your tutelage. Even Simon has a shy new smile."

She reminded him of the twins' schoolroom hijinks, adding

several he'd not heard. "They're getting worse, and I may even be the reason for it."

"That's not remotely possible. Graeme is right. They aren't mean."

"Their tricks are," she said, and dried her tears. "It isn't as if they didn't have ample reason: They never wanted a woman as a tutor. I embarrass them."

She had extracted herself from Lionel's arms and walked across the chapel floor. He followed, searching for a way to persuade her to stay. Money, conscience, pleas, seduction.

At the door she stopped. "I'm going to pack my things. Will you kindly send Beane up to fetch them home?"

Disbelief and a dozen protests lodged in his throat. *It's not your fault. They'll do better. I'll do better. They still need you. I still need your help. I'm bloody sorry for everything. Everything.*

But he let her go. She wasn't going to change her mind. He couldn't talk her into seeing things his way, he couldn't kiss her into staying, and he couldn't well take her prisoner and lock her in her room.

Because being an effective tutor depended on her being free and willing to continue with his troubled sons.

Afterward, Lionel retreated to his office. An extended stint with tedious estate papers would cool his temper and his overwrought anatomy.

Tims was bent over papers. "Stack of correspondence for you on your desk, my lord."

Lionel walked over and shuffled through the rigidly straight pile. Sign, sign, sign, consider, reject. They were routine requests—for His Lordship's aid for an ailing tenant, His Lordship's patronage for a needy painter, His Lordship's attention to a debt of his father's, a bill being framed for the House of Lords, an estimate for renovations to His Lordship's hunting box in Devon.

"There was a letter from Abercairn, my lord." Tims's pen scrabbled noisily across a page. "But I can't seem to find it."

Lionel patted the front of his jacket. "The term report. Yes, I'll get around to it."

"Odd time for a term report, my lord. A week early, if I reckon right."

Was it? Lionel checked the postmark. So it was. Beset with duties, sons, and Sophie, he'd lost track of time. Term reports came in the middle of the month. He broke the seal and unfolded the fine linen paper.

My lord, it began,
With regret, we must request that you come to Abercairn posthaste to reclaim your sons . . .

Reclaim James and Marcus? His second and third sons, sterling lads, earnest students—they were in trouble too? Anger blurred his vision, anger where there had been pride and confidence. And distance, his original sin come home again to roost. His eyes scanned the page. *Rebellion. Expulsion. Permanent.* He crumpled the damning letter in his fist and almost threw it in the grate. But Tims hadn't asked for a fire—it was May, after all—and he didn't want his secretary or some scullery maid privy to any details having to do with the downfall of these last of his six sons.

Anyone, that is, but Sophie.

Because he would have to go to Abercairn, which would take most of a week up and back. Which meant Sophie could not leave Wraxham House as she planned. She had to stay to maintain a semblance of order and respectability, to say nothing of safety and security for his most vulnerable link, Simon.

And if she wouldn't stay on as the boys' tutors, he didn't know what in bloody hell to do.

He didn't bother knocking at the door to Sophie's chamber, where she had gone to pack.

She didn't bother looking up. "My mind's made up, Celie," she said over her shoulder, evidently recovered from her tearful interlude in his family's private chapel. "You were right. It isn't safe. We're packing, and we're going home. I told Lionel a little while ago."

He twirled her around into his arms.

"*Lionel*," he said grimly, "has decided, Miss Bowerbank, that you must stay."

She didn't even blink. She twisted from his grasp and pointed to the door. "Out!" she ordered, obviously surprised into more than her usual boldness. "I am packing, my lord, and I am leaving. If you are a gentleman, you will remove yourself from my bedchamber until I have vacated it."

"If I were a gentleman, Miss Bowerbank, you would have no reason to leave."

He would empty out her luggage by force if he had to.

He stalked over to her bed. Her one trunk sat on it, squat and battered. He looked in.

"This is full of books," he said in disbelief.

"It takes more books than frocks to tutor children, even the sons of a noble lord."

"It takes more stamina than you evidently have to stay a full course," he heard himself snap back. Inexcusable of him, but all the Wraxham males were blundering through this miserable month of May.

"You don't have to insult me, my lord. I admit I failed."

"Not only do I not agree, I need you to stay and keep on doing what you've been doing very well."

Her chin jutted up. "All evidence to the contrary."

"No evidence to the contrary," he countered instantly. "Whose side are you on, Sophie?"

She gathered an armload of books to her breasts and dumped them in the trunk. Even under duress, he couldn't stop his gaze from fixing on the generous fullness of her bosom.

"Theirs, my lord," she said in a more reasoned tone. "They never wanted a woman as a tutor. And they're right. A female tutor cannot guide them as a man would."

"If you are truly on their side, you can guide them now," he said, his tone more reasoned than his distracted attention. He took the crumpled letter from his pocket and smoothed its wrinkles. "Read this."

She scanned it, her anger changing instantly to sympathy. "I am sorry to hear of it, my lord. I don't know James or Marcus, but you must be surprised."

"Yes, in a word." He'd been stunned actually, but her concern took the edge off his shock and anger. A slight edge.

She stubbornly fitted another three-volume set of books in amidst her hoard of texts. "I do not see how I can be of service."

"I cannot leave them in the care of Mrs. Plumridge and Nurse Nesbit, with the occasional oversight of Mr. Tims. His and Carter's duties will double with me away. No one but you can properly oversee the boys."

"Properly? It's been mayhem with you here. With you away I foresee anarchy."

"Worse, without you," he said, frustration clawing at him. "Graeme cannot be expected to forestall anarchy, given his romantic preoccupations."

"My father could forestall it, my lord. Ask him," she said with the fervor of a prisoner who'd found her cell door open. "He's quite imposing when wronged. All those years of communing with a wrathful God, I think."

Lionel didn't find that in the least amusing. The Right Reverend Adolphus Bowerbank was old, and had only ever taught one dreamy bookish girl. A tiger when called upon, but still.

"I wouldn't dream of tearing him away from his parishioners or his commentaries. But he could reinstate the boys' morning prayers and evening vespers."

She blew out a gust of dissent. "You are being impossible, you know."

"How so?"

"Without you here to back me up, I have no authority with your sons beyond good will. And we both know that is spent."

"Very well then, let me put it this way. I will do what I must to entice you to stay."

"Bah. You don't want to pay me that much money."

He pressed his lips together. He didn't want to pay her any money. He wanted her—her boldness, her intelligence, her patience with the twins, her kindness to Simon, her sympathy for Graeme—he wanted all that here for them now and for him when he got back.

All that, and the hot response she gave him every time he touched her.

"There's another way to do this," he said.

Her eyes glinted with acid humor. "Indeed. Hire a man from London. Hire a team of tutors. Hire a faculty."

"That's not what I have in mind."

She glared at him. "I am not privy to the workings of your mind."

It should be obvious. Did she not have a clue?

"Bloody hell, Sophie, all you have to do is marry me. As my wife, you would have full authority over the boys, over everyone."

The color leached from her face.

Ah, progress. "You would have your good name and my consequence as well. In return my sons would have your supervision and your guidance."

She crossed her arms and took a shocked step back. "And you would have a lowly rector's daughter as your bride. You cannot overlook my station."

"To the devil with your station," he said.

"That, my lord, was the most unsatisfactory marriage proposal I have ever read of or imagined," she said. "As a matter of fact, I'm not even remotely tempted to consider it."

Damnation. In his haste, he had been churlish and dictatorial. He humbled himself. "My sincere apologies, madam," he said, then added, desperate to win her over, "I've only proposed once in my life, Sophie, and I did that with a gun to my head."

Her eyes went keen again. "You've a gun to your head now, my lord. I can tell you, being on the receiving end, those desperate volleys aren't very flattering."

"How not flattering? There isn't another person in the world I would even begin to consider asking for her hand in marriage."

She laid her hand across her chest, just at the point, he could not help noticing, where the upper slope of her still sumptuous breast began to rise. "It is customary, my lord, to profess undying love, even where there is no affection."

Bugger all, the vixen wanted love. Bloody bad break for her. His jaded heart was all out of that ephemeral commodity. Had been since the day their fathers had driven him off the property. But to hesitate before her now could only make matters worse. He felt like a bumbling schoolboy, and then it struck him.

"You want me on my knees."

She went all serious, her brown eyes warm and sad. "No, my lord. I only ever wanted to marry a man who loved me. A man I loved equally in return. But after you and I . . . did what we did, I could not offer myself to any decent man."

Did what we did?

"But we never—"

"If I held to my standards once and refused a perfectly respectable marriage offer from a thoroughly decent man, why would I compromise myself now?"

The truth lanced like a spear. "You mean that, after I left that summer, someone offered marriage and you refused him?"

She shrugged sadly. "That was a long time ago, my lord."

"Did you love him?"

She lifted her chin. "I could have done."

"But you were—you are—unsullied."

"Not in my heart, my lord. Not in my heart."

Damn his rotten luck. She had wanted him then, as much as he had wanted her. Had she loved him too?

226

His chest tightened, and he could not catch a breath.

For he, jaded rake, cynical spouse, failed father, had been loved.

By the first and only woman who had touched his heart.

"We could try for love," he said with an unexpected, unwelcome flare of hope.

He saw the lameness of his effort in her solemn face.

"Too late, my lord." She smiled sadly . . . or wistfully, he could not be sure. "That time came, and passed."

She made a little show of returning to her half-packed trunk.

He had one last argument. He intercepted her, claimed her in a hot embrace, and breathed into the delicate curved shell of her ear, "We still have this to recommend the match."

To his surprise, she yielded as she had before, with a tiny whimper in her throat. Her pliant body pulsed against him, fearlessly, unlike the virgin she still must surely be. He opened his mouth and deepened the kiss, keen to heighten the hum of arousal between them.

With a moan she opened for him, instantly as responsive as the most accomplished courtesan. His pulse pounded in his rock-hard manhood, and he clasped her bum and pulled her to him.

"Lionel, let's not—" she began to protest, but her words made a feeble fight against her body's invitation.

Currents of hot yearning coiled from her belly to his shaft, and he ground against her, saying in a rhythm with his futile thrusts, "Sophie, Sophie, don't deny us this."

He wanted to be in her. He only had to tear her clothes off, rip to shreds the modest muslin frock that she so vainly clung to as a mark of her low station, and tup her till she screamed.

Then, to the degree that he could summon reason, he thought better of adding rape to his already clumsy proposal.

He settled for a torrid clench. Which she accepted with an avid, desperate grasping that he recognized as a woman's quest for her ultimate in pleasure. She was rocking in his arms, shuddering against him. He pushed a thigh between her legs, and she threw back her head and rode him to her satisfaction. Glorious. There was nothing he liked better than a woman finding her own pleasure. Still clad in his confining breeches, he spurted to an end himself, jerking against her hot mound with an arching ache of half completion.

For long moments the only sounds in the room were their mutual gasps. She clung to him like a life raft, and he allowed himself a moment of hope. He raised his head, admired a fine sheen of perspiration on her upper lip, and allowed himself a further moment of congratulation.

She had given herself into his hands, and he had broken through her reservations and brought her pleasure.

But she stiffened in his arms. "Very clever, my lord, to play upon my weakness."

"Physical love is not a weakness, Sophie. It's a stroke of great good fortune, rare and wonderful, and a strength."

She pulled away from him and stood like a tutor delivering a lecture. "But still not fair of you, my lord, knowing how I have yielded to you before. So let me remind you of the reasons we ought not to marry. First, it cannot be wise to saddle your sons with a stepmother so soon after their loss. Second, like your first wife, I'm of a different class, and have only known you briefly."

Anger leaked through his sensual stupor. "You are not at all like—"

"Shh," she whispered, her fingers on his mouth. "Unlike your first wife, I bring nothing."

"You bring—"

"We have only this inconvenient physical attraction to recommend a match."

He wrapped his hand around her fingers, and said, "You may think it inconvenient, but I swear you cannot know how rare."

"Not your best argument, my lord, to remind me of your other women."

Perverse wench. Didn't she see, there was no one but her?

Didn't she see, he'd swived his way through London looking for her? "There are no other women anymore," he growled, frustration mounting.

"Your son Graeme, for one, assumes there are."

Lionel swore a vulgar oath.

"Marriage lasts forever, my lord, and a bad one even longer than that."

"You assume our marriage would be bad."

"There will not be a marriage, my lord. Our fathers once thought it expedient for us not to marry. I won't marry you now for expediency."

He pulled the trump card from his sleeve. "My sons need you, Sophie."

"And I can still help. I will stay as we originally agreed. If Graeme can continue as he is doing, I will enlist my father for morning prayers and vespers. It will do the twins good to face the man whose globe they destroyed."

Lionel had the familiar, confusing sense that he had won, and that he had lost. "Consider this. You would be a countess."

She gave him a sad, enigmatic smile. "Consider this, my lord. If we don't marry, you don't have to wait three days for a special license. You can leave for Abercairn tonight, and bring the boys back three days sooner."

He didn't like for a woman to have the last word, but he allowed it. He'd insulted her enough for one day, and still she'd acceded to almost everything he'd asked.

Everything but the one thing he wanted most.

Chapter Twenty

Marriage is Bondage, but where Cupid *Reigns,*
The Yoke is easie; glorious are the Chains . . .
— The Ladies Choice (1702)

Not all battles are fought on battlefields, Lionel groused to himself, two days, four hundred fifty miles, thirty-seven changes of teams, a dozen river crossings, and one carriage breakdown later. He'd made the journey to Abercairn School in good but far from his record time—one day on a relay of horses—which he'd set on a dare when he was seventeen.

This trip, the faster he went, the harder he pushed his teams, the farther he got from Sophie's perverse refusal to marry him. He'd almost scourged her words from his mind, but not her embrace. So he drove harder, faster, until weariness dulled his senses. And still he wanted her, her laughter and her learning, her boldness and her beauty.

And he wanted to prove his sons innocent. James and Marcus were soberer lads than Max and Alex, and he had every reason to believe their headmaster had exaggerated some breech of protocol into rebellion. To believe he could be persuaded to let the boys stay on.

He was not without concerns. Their mother had died two months ago and their grandfather a few weeks later, for God's sake. The distance had been far too great for them to travel from Abercairn to Wraxham in time for either funeral, but letters had flown back and forth, announcing, grieving, consoling. Manly souls, they'd insisted that they had each other. He had only himself to blame if letting them face their mother's loss alone had led them to go astray.

At last, Abercairn presented its dour stone face, the mists of Scotland rising around its buildings. Lionel got out and stretched his aching knee. Inside, a short fat factotum conducted him into the headmaster's suite. The parlor was smaller than he remembered, colder, and shabbier. But its threadbare upholstery and faded rugs had been disciplined into spotlessness.

In the inner office, Headmaster Cullen MacEnery sat behind a bulky desk, as forbidding as the crags that barricaded Abercairn from the world outside.

Lionel's second and third sons stood before him at attention as he had used to stand when called upon the carpet. They'd each added a good two inches in height since last summer.

Fifteen-year-old Marcus, leader of the schoolboy rebellion, was the taller of the two and more nearly blond. His jaw jutted in defiance.

James, at fourteen, betrayed apprehension: His blue gaze would not meet Lionel's.

"Good afternoon, my lord," MacEnery droned with dictatorial control. Lionel's spine bristled with memories. "I would bid you welcome but for the gravity of the occasion. Your sons, as I informed you by the post, are charged with—"

"I wish to speak with them alone." Lionel cut him off. He would hear their version of events first, or they'd all three walk out of here with never a backward glance.

"The charges are incontrovertible, my lord."

"And a private interview between a father and his sons is the merest courtesy."

MacEnery thumped his desk in irritation. "Their mutiny turned our staff upside down. Unarmed, my men were terrified. We had to call in troops."

"Nevertheless, Headmaster," Lionel said, forcing calm after the jolt of that new bit of information.

MacEnery waved them off. "The parlor is not in use, my lord."

Lionel clasped each boy's shoulder and pushed them out. Despite their height and broadening shoulders, they felt so young and vulnerable he wanted to hold them as he'd only recently held Simon, for the first time ever.

But fathers didn't fuss over sons or coddle rebels.

"Troops?" he managed not to roar, the moment they were alone. "Headmaster's letter said only that you armed yourselves against the staff and mounted a siege. That was bloody damn well enough."

"We didn't force them to bring in troops, sir," Marcus said, soldier-straight.

"They seem to think you made it necessary."

Marcus didn't deny it, but said, "There was never a shot fired, sir."

There could have been. Lionel's heart catapulted to his throat at the very thought, and outrage swiftly followed. "And you launched this campaign in the first place because . . ."

"They caught Andrew Budd cheating. We wouldn't confirm that he did it. We wouldn't confess that we were involved. We weren't, but we could never betray our friend. So they cut off our privileges," Marcus said.

"Hockey, sir, and cricket," James explained indignantly. "Which they had promised they wouldn't do."

Lionel crossed his arms over his chest. Their version did not square with the headmaster's letter. He'd suspected, hell, he'd hoped, it wouldn't. "Go on."

"Marcus and I seized the keys to the college, sir, and we

232

took swords, guns, and bludgeons from the munitions room, and provisions from the shops."

"How the devil did you get the keys?"

James puffed up. "It wasn't so very difficult for us to entice the night warden from his post. He's partial to his port, you see. When he stepped out, we sneaked in and nicked 'em."

Lionel scowled. But it sounded like a perfect lark, worthy of himself and his brothers at their wildest. "They should expel you on the theft alone."

"We returned 'em quick enough. Besides, none of the Old Boys would be such weasels as to tell on us, not after this."

"So you mounted a siege."

"Like yours, sir, on St. Lucia. Once it was clear we wouldn't stand down, they had to negotiate with us."

Lionel arched a brow. "Negotiate as to what?"

"The food is rather bad, sir, and some of the younger boys need more than they're allotted, and thicker blankets, too," Marcus said.

"But not you?" Lionel asked. He remembered thin hot gruel and long cold nights in this stern, forbidding place, and for the first time entertained serious doubts about the wisdom of expecting his sons to uphold the family tradition.

"No, sir," James said stoutly. "We eat what they put before us. As for the cold, if you could take it, and Graeme and our uncles and Grandfather, so can we."

"But we thought they should be fair and keep their word, not only this time but also in future. We would have stood down if they hadn't kept on persecuting Andrew."

"Persecuting, how?"

Marcus's eyes blazed with indignation. "They'd already caned him. One punishment of one person for one crime is enough."

James just wanted his father to understand. "But they made Andrew choose between resigning or turning himself in for more punishment. He resigned, and we did too, and everyone else followed."

"The letter says that they expelled you," Lionel said.

Marcus's brow knotted, and then he said fiercely, "They didn't have to expel us. We could not, in honor, stay."

Lionel swallowed against a surge of pride over the stand his sons had made. He'd stormed up here, sure he could patch things up with MacEnery so that his sons could stay.

The hell with that. "We're going home. Go to your rooms and collect your things." They didn't have much. Abercairn didn't allow it. "I'll settle up with MacEnery."

Which he did in short order, and left the headmaster's quarters swept by relief and pride, and an unfamiliar sensation very like descriptions he had read of love.

His sons were coming home with him today. All of his sons would be at home, all in one place, all his at last.

And then he had the oddest thought, clear as stars above a summer meadow: If Sophie stood beside him as his countess and their mother, his family would be complete. Because he didn't know how to handle six strapping sons at once, but with her help he could.

And yet how to bring a reluctant woman round to marriage? He wouldn't pretend to romantic feelings he had never had, and neither his worldly goods nor his promises of pleasure had swayed her. But he couldn't take no for an answer. Not that he had wooed her, or knew how. No, he knew everything about seduction, and nothing about courtship.

Which he could set about to learn, as soon as he got his sons home.

Three interminable days had passed since Lionel had left, Sophie thought, finishing tomorrow's lessons and putting away her book. With him away, there was much to do, even though Mrs. Plumridge and Thomas Beane oversaw daily household matters and Carter and Tims handled estate affairs.

Simon grew lonelier and more troubled each day of his father's absence. She could see it in his silence and his drawn pale face. So she shrugged into her nightgown and slipped out into the hall.

Nurse Nesbit met her when she opened Simon's door, as she'd done the previous two nights. "What you're doin' is not what Doctor recommended, miss, and it's not what his mother wanted neither," she chided her, apparently assuming she knew his father's will.

But Penelope was gone, God rest her soul, and the good doctor was in London. "Until and unless Simon's terrors strike again, Nesbit, you will best please me by supporting my work. I am going to read to him now as I did last night."

Nesbit clucked her tongue in warning. "I will report this to His Lordship, ma'am."

"By all means, do. Just don't omit that Simon has been sleeping through the night, and without the terrors."

Older women of a certain girth could not be said to flounce out of a room, but Nesbit approximated it.

At tea, Sophie shared her spat with Celia.

"Just don't you come to me, Sophie, when Simon has another fit. I've heard him shrieking from my chamber, and that's as close to madness as I want to get."

"He's not mad, Celia."

"So you say."

Sophie warned Graeme that another nightmare could occur at any time, and told him how to handle it.

"I doubt I would hear, now that I'm back in my old bedroom with the twins. But I will call you, Miss Bowerbank, if I hear the slightest noise."

No nightmares came. No untoward incidents occurred, no accidents, no injuries, no malicious mischief in Wraxham House or in the world beyond. Simon slept through the night. Graeme helped her teach his little brothers. The twins began to look more rested. An uneasy peace reigned.

Only Lionel was missing.

She tried not to think of how she'd turned down his proposal, of how she'd flung herself at him anyway, of how she'd thrilled to the quick soaring pleasure he had given her.

She really tried, but late at night, after she'd readied the next day's lessons and tucked Simon in, she retreated to the library to her bawdy books, which had added intrigue and secret pleasures to her spinsterhood.

The poems and stories in her bawdy books no longer distracted her. Worse, they deepened her sense of loss. What had those poems and stories and her steamy imaginings to do with the intricate entanglements of marriage?

Lionel Westfall, earl of Wraxham, had actually asked her to marry him. Never mind that he had bungled his proposal by offering a hodgepodge of every reason but the right one.

She had bungled her response.

Even now she could be his. And she, smart, proud spinster bluestocking that she was, had had every reason to accept him. Marriage would give comfort to her and security to her father. Marriage would give her the sensual fulfillment that she knew now without a doubt she'd find with Lionel. Marriage would give her children, would give her a boisterous, all-consuming family. Marriage would give her a life with the only man she'd ever loved, days, nights, weeks, years.

Would give her love.

No. That was the sticking point. Lionel, Lord Wraxham, did not love her.

Did not love her.

Marriage would not give her love.

She was not going to throw away her independence for a loveless marriage, not for his sons, not for her safety, and not for hot erotic liaisons in the night. And she wasn't going to place herself in the humiliating position of asking Lionel again if he loved her.

Because he didn't. He *liked* her, enjoyed their mental skirmishes, and appreciated her interventions with his sons. He also *lusted* after her. Which was flattering and deeply gratifying, coming from a gazetted rake. And unflattering, for the selfsame reason. He'd lusted after a lot of women in his lifetime. She probably hadn't been his first, and likely wouldn't be his last.

But *like* was a tame emotion, and *lust* an unreliable one.

Like might last forever, and *lust* fade overnight . . . or find another object.

She deserved love. She required love. She'd waited for it all her life.

Lionel's carriage lurched and swayed under a gibbous moon. They'd crossed the border into England, and had three long days to go. James had nodded off, but Lionel felt Marcus watching him. Studying him.

"Wasn't the moon like this, sir, that night you fought on St. Lucia?"

Whatever he'd expected, he hadn't expected this. "Yes, enough to see by."

"Enough to kill by?"

Lionel's gut clutched, to remember that exact night, that exact fatal moon. "Or be killed."

His second eldest watched this English moon until the carriage road went into a wood. "I did lead the siege, sir. I barely slept, the way you said you hardly ever slept."

The confession startled him. "Are you thinking you to be a soldier, son?"

"I liked it, sir."

Lionel choked up. "There's honor in it, but I wouldn't want you killed. Or even injured."

That night at an inn in Yorkshire, Lionel finished a last porter at the bar and returned to their rooms. Marcus was quietly sobbing while his brother slept. Lionel put an awkward palm on the boy's wiry back.

"Son . . ." he said, utterly at a loss.

How to comfort a bereft boy when he'd never known comfort himself?

"I didn't mean to disgrace our name, Papa. Next year, I would have been dux. But the dominie was going to cane

237

Andrew a second time." Dux, head boy. Dominie, headmaster.

He wrapped his arm around his son's shoulder, as he had done with raw recruits. "You did right, son," Lionel answered, and his throat closed on a swell of pride and tenderness.

Papa. He was Papa.

Sophie marked off the sixth day like an inmate in a dungeon awaiting her release. Lionel had said the trip would take about a week, two days north at speed, then four days back returning the boys at a reasonable pace if he had to bring them home.

He was bringing them home. She realized it, and the brothers must too. They'd been giddy today, almost silly. Even the usually dreamy Graeme had been restless. As soon as Max and Alex returned from their now weekly stint with Mr. Eliot in Squire Upton's garden, she'd turned the four Westfall scions out of the schoolroom to burn off their energy in games on the lawn.

She stayed behind to straighten up and start tomorrow's lessons. Soon she lost herself in the Caesars and the geography of Rome.

First she heard a whisper. Something bumped outside the schoolroom door. "Shhh" and "Don't drop it." Graeme's long arm pushed the door and held it open. Max and Alex, grunting under the weight and size of a rugged wooden box, ducked under his arm.

Sophie knotted her brow. They wouldn't play a trick on her in daylight, would they? she worried. And felt terrible to have such doubt.

But no, they wouldn't play a trick on her, not with those earnest, expectant faces. And not with Simon along. He was bringing up the rear, bearing a hammer and a pry bar.

The twins heaved the box upon the table that had borne the model of Troy. Simon handed them his tools. Max and Alex worked the pry bar under the box's lid. Nails shrieked against wood as they prized off the top and propped it against a table leg.

Graeme, the tallest, reached in and pulled out . . . a great round globe.

They'd brought her a globe? Sophie blinked back tears.

Graeme put it in the twins' arms. They walked it to where she stood behind her desk and gently set down a ratty old leather globe.

She gawked, she knew she gawked.

Max and Alex ducked their heads and ventured grins.

"It's just that you've been so sad, Miss Bowerbank," said Alex.

"And we know how important that globe was to you because it was your father's."

"But how . . . ?" she asked. And when? And why?

Graeme stepped up. "We pooled our resources, ma'am. Your father gave me the name of an antiquarian in Reading when he came for prayers."

She touched the globe. They held their breaths.

It wasn't even close to the globe she'd lost. Its leather was pocked and foxed and stiff. Its seams were frayed. Its boundaries of Greece and Thrace were inaccurate.

It was the dearest, sweetest gift she'd ever gotten in her life.

Alex cleared his throat. "We're so awfully sorry your globe was ruined, Miss Bowerbank."

She could hold on to her doubts or believe these earnest children and accept their gift.

"We're looking out to catch the bugger who did it," Max said fiercely. Loyally.

She melted into tears. She'd been right and she'd been wrong. They were rascals. They weren't vandals. They were boys, and innocent.

One of them tugged the sleeve of her old muslin dress.

"Don't cry, Miss Bowerbank." It was Alex.

"You're prettier when you smile." It was Max.

She looked through wet lashes across the room to Graeme. He shrugged, not a shrug of insolence or indifference.

A shrug that said *we're trying*.

They were. She opened her arms to the twins. "Thank you, loves," she said to Alex on her left and Max on her right. Their clean boy smells tugged at her senses, and then she felt their awkward hands, pat, pat on her right shoulder, pat, pat, pat on her left.

She watched them pour out the door to go back to batting balls across the lawn, hot sweet tears trickling down her cheeks.

That night, Sophie hoped the last night before Lionel returned, she retreated to the library. An ormolu clock ticked the early morning minutes slowly by. She selected another forbidden book from an obscure shelf, and sighed. They hadn't returned today, so it must be tomorrow. She curled up on a deeply upholstered sofa with a book she'd chosen from the shelf, her legs tucked beneath her, and flipped to an earnest ode on what a woman should look for, and avoid, in marriage.

She'd hoped it would be an antidote to her ravaging desire.

"Miss Bowerbank?" a man's voice said from right behind her.

Startled, she snapped her book shut and shoved it out of sight between the velvet cushions. They were green, and it was green, and so perhaps she would escape discovery. Graeme, tall and gaunt in the shadows her candles cast, had sneaked in on her.

"What's wrong?" she asked, untangling her legs. "Oh dear, it's Simon, isn't it?"

"No, madam, Simon is well. Please, stay," he said. He gently touched her forearm to keep her in her chair. "He was sleeping soundly as I walked by. But if I may presume, I have wanted to, ah . . . confide in you for some days."

"You have word of Glencora?"

He puffed out a breath. "None yet."

Then what? Sophie frowned, and waited.

"I, ah . . ." His complexion darkened in the amber light, and he gave a crooked smile. "This is even more awkward than I imagined."

Sophie smiled back. Since his apology, their relationship had only gotten better. She would welcome a confidence. "Will it help if I promise not to breathe a word of this to your father?"

The flush darkened. He was a shockingly handsome young man, every feature crisp and classic. The unfortunate Glencora had to have fallen head over ears in love with him on looks alone.

As Sophie had with Lionel.

"It's about my father, actually. And you."

"Oh." Oh dear. It was hard to keep a pleasant expression on her face, or even a neutral one. Graeme probably wanted her to leave his father's house. Which was understandable, given his first impressions.

"I overheard him . . . ah, propose to you, ma'am," Graeme said, hesitating, then sped up. "I came upon the two of you by accident. I shouldn't have listened, but I heard you, and there's no pretending I don't know."

"Then you know I refused him," she said calmly. But her face burned. Good God, had Graeme seen their torrid embrace? She wished she was a worldly woman. She wished she could disappear.

Graeme took a footstool and sat on it before her. His position was as touching as it was unexpected. "Which is precisely the point I wanted to address, if you will bear with me."

Her throat closed with mortification, but she lifted her chin. "Of course, Graeme. Do go on."

He put his fist to his mouth; he took it down; he shifted his legs. "This is none of my affair. But you see, I think you're wrong."

Of course he thought her wrong. "Ah," she said, struggling to sound attentive but unconcerned.

"Yes, ma'am, wrong to refuse him. And more than that, wrong *about* him."

She blinked, baffled.

"I mean, it was arguably the least appealing, most insufferably arrogant offer a man could make. And I quite agree with you that a man should not propose to a woman he does not love, but just because he didn't *profess* his love doesn't mean he doesn't love you."

"I'm not sure I follow . . ."

Graeme braced himself and blurted, "My father's in love with you, ma'am, and I want to urge you to reconsider his proposal."

"Oh dear, Graeme, oh no," she said, as gently as she could. "First, he would have to ask again, which I don't think he'll do. He hardly seemed upset when I turned him down."

"I am willing to play the go-between."

She was touched, but tried to make light of the whole ridiculous idea. "I'm afraid people in love see love all around them, even where it isn't likely, or advisable."

Graeme's face fell. "I may be young, Miss Bowerbank, and unversed in the ways of the world, but I'm not blind. You should see how he looks at you."

She'd seen how Lionel looked at her: with the ravaging eyes of a gazetted rake. She could not tell his son that. "Any man living alone for the first time in twenty years notices every woman who comes near him. He's just missing—" She stopped herself. She could not well tell his son that he was missing the London women he'd had at his beck and call. "Your mother," she concluded.

Graeme's brow knotted. "Do you not know about them?"

She shook her head. She knew as much as she could bear and more than she would admit to.

"My parents' marriage was not a love match. My grandfathers arranged it, one to save our estate and the other to gain a title for his daughter. Once married, my parents barely saw each other, let alone spoke."

She'd known that, even hoped it in a jealous, petty corner

of her mind, but to hear it put so bluntly pierced her heart for Lionel's sake.

Which was worse? Her twenty years living without love, or his, living with disdain and distance?

"There was a rumor," Graeme went on, "that he had loved someone before her, a girl of no means, too young and too poor for him to 'waste himself on,' I believe the phrase goes."

Sophie prayed the low light hid the blush that burned her face. "Sounds like romantic nonsense, frankly. Whoever would promote a rumor like that?"

"My aunt Julia, actually, one intolerably boring summer down here when I was railing against my father for fobbing me off on Grandfather. She dearly loves her brother and was urging me to understand him. She told me about the girl, how my grandfather banished my father into the army and broke his heart."

Sophie's heart raced. Had it hurt Lionel to leave her? He'd married another soon enough.

"Yet he and your mother had all six of you," she pointed out.

"Love is not duty, and duty is not love," Graeme said, sounding suddenly wise. "Please, Miss Bowerbank, give me some credit. I may be young, but as a man in love, I think I know love when I see it."

She had been thinking about love longer than he'd been alive, and she had an idea or two. "Love and lust, passion and infatuation have much in common. Wise men confuse them all the time. Wise women too. They can be hard to tell apart."

His mouth twisted in dissent. "Be that as it may, I have never seen my father look at another woman as he looks at you. I wish you would reconsider, Miss Bowerbank. He truly needs a wife. He deserves to be loved."

She folded her hands in her lap, her lonely, empty hands. She didn't even have a book to clutch for comfort. "Graeme, I—" she began.

243

He held up a hand. "No, please, hear me out. My brothers need a loving, unselfish mother."

"Graeme, it's not that simple."

"But what if it were?" he asked, leaning toward her, eager to press his point, and earnest too. "What if love is the one pure true emotion that cuts through rank and manners and joy and pain—that cuts through everything to unite us in some transcendent union, in a loving family, in shared happiness, truth?"

His voice quavered with his intensity.

He was going to be so hurt.

"That sounds lovely, Graeme, poetic almost, even ideal. But life is not a dream. It comes with limits and constraints," she said, feeling the sadness in her bones, the dullness life had brought her to. "We just don't get what we hope for and dream of."

He stood abruptly. "Then what's the point of hopes and dreams? To torment us, to send us to hell? Because I have hopes and dreams, and I'm not going to turn my back on them. On her." He slapped a hand against his leg in disgust. "Perhaps you can. Perhaps my father can. But I see what I see, and I know what I know. My father is in love with you, and I think you're in love with him, and if the two of you want to live your lives apart, and die before your time, proud and lonely and alone, you can never, ever say I didn't try to warn you."

"You sound as if you think it's easy. Trust me, nothing is harder," she said, reeling inside from his astonishing assertion.

For Lionel could not say he loved her.

He had talked and acted like the man he was, a rake, a consummate lover, and she had every reason to keep her true feelings to herself. "There are other people, other concerns. There are consequences."

"I didn't say it's easy. It hasn't been for Glencora and me. It's been painful, scary, risky. But I can live with that pain, I will face those fears, and I will take those risks."

"You are young."

"You're not old. So why not take a chance? What have you got to lose?"

The last shreds of dignity, the self-respect of believing herself worthy of love, the self-worth of holding out for it—she could lose all that. But it was far too private, too tender, to admit to a young man she'd barely met.

So she stood, aware of the betraying book she'd shoved beneath the cushions. She floated her skirts over to conceal the little bump it made.

"Thank you, Graeme, for your concern. You're a good son," she said, and she meant it.

"You'll think about it," he persisted.

"Oh yes." She barely thought of anything else.

Chapter Twenty-one

A Married Life was first contriv'd above,
To be an Emblem of Eternal Love;
And after by Divine indulgence sent,
To be the Crown of Man, and Wife's content . . .
—An Answer to the Pleasures of a Single Life:
or, the Comforts of Marriage Confirm'd and
Vindicated (1701)

He'd quit taking risks a long, long time ago, Lionel thought, as his carriage swayed down the road toward home under a rising moon. On the cushioned seat facing forward, James and Marcus slept. A tangle of gangly young male arms and legs sprawled into the well, invading Lionel's space. He planned to stop the coach at Reading and take one more night at an inn before making a last push for home.

A week ago, he'd astonished himself. It wasn't like him to risk his pride and newfound freedom by proposing marriage. It must have been a sign of the desperation his sons had driven him to, to ask any woman for her hand, even Sophie. Because he'd told her the truth. There wasn't another woman in the world he'd have asked to take on the burden of his enormous family's escalating problems.

Once he bollixed that proposal, it had been too late to go back and avow love, even for form's sake. She would have seen it for the hollow expediency that it was, coming from his jaded heart.

But as the coach jounced over another rut, it struck him as sad that he and Sophie hadn't come to some agreement. If he had to marry again, he didn't want to start fresh, searching among strangers for a bride. Sophie fit Wraxham. She fit his sons. He lusted after her body, and he admired her mind. As for her principles—well, she'd have to forgive him if he wasn't as honorable as she was.

He would have been a good husband to her.

And to her alone.

Because if he married her, that was an end to all other alliances. A life of debauchery had not been his dream when he'd fallen for Sophie at nineteen. But Sophie was probably right. The time for them to love had come, and passed.

Odd, he'd never have taken her for a reader of those romantic novels. She'd seemed a reasonable woman. He wished she hadn't pinned so much importance on *love*. Despite his experience with Penelope, he'd seen a few happy alliances based on trust, intelligence, a commonality of ideas, and straightforward healthy lust. He saw nothing wrong that. A marriage based on those things was preferable to one grounded in the whirlwind of emotions that infatuation provoked.

Good God, look at what romantic love was doing to his eldest. No, Lionel and Sophie would be better off without that, even if it meant they never married.

But how the devil was he to manage six sons at home?

Because he'd never thought of risk in the same breath as fatherhood. But on the long hours of this journey, his family's prospects scrabbled about in his head like wharf rats on a sinking ship: An angry husband could drag his eldest into court. Irate schoolmasters had almost opened fire upon his rebels. Townspeople held vendettas against his miscreants. And monsters, evil, slimy, hulking monsters stalked his youngest in his sleep.

He knew now, as he had not known in Penelope's lifetime, that he would give his life to protect each and every son. Yet every time they'd needed him, he had not been there to safeguard them. Somehow Sophie would have helped. As tutor, she'd helped already. As wife and stepmother, she would help even more.

And afraid to risk his heart, he'd bollixed winning her.

Some hero, some man of affairs, some peer of the realm he'd turned out to be.

He rapped his cane against the carriage overhead, signaling his coachman to look out for the next stop.

Marcus was startled wide-awake, so rapidly on his guard that Lionel winced. "How much longer, Papa?"

"Not long. A few more minutes."

"I mean to home," he graveled in his new deep voice.

"Ah. Tomorrow, late," Lionel said, glad to share a simple answer with this stranger, with this son.

James stirred, sat up, and rubbed his eyes. "Are we there yet?"

"You're not complaining, are you?" Marcus asked.

"It's taking us forever," James said, voice breaking with weariness and a boy's change into manhood.

Marcus cuffed his younger brother's shoulder. "Westfalls don't complain, Jem, and Westfalls don't give up."

God, how long since Lionel's father had passed the family motto on to him? How long since Lionel had badgered his brothers to do the same?

So long he'd almost forgotten it.

Westfalls don't complain, and Westfalls don't give up—the words had mocked him down the years.

Because he'd changed it to *Westfalls don't take chances.*
Westfalls don't take risks.

And look where that had gotten him.

Where it had gotten them.

It had brought them, each and every one, to the brink of
ruin.

"Perhaps I should take the risk, and marry His Lordship for the
boys' sake," Sophie said, still agonizing over her decision not
to marry Lionel a week after he had left.

She and Celia were sitting on the terrace by the east lawn,
warmed by a mild sun on a late May afternoon. Max and Alex,
Simon and Graeme were charging across the field in pursuit
of a ball and each other. It was the only time of day Graeme
cast off his mopes. Evidently Lionel, working with her father,
had persuaded Graeme that they were doing everything they
could on Glencora's behalf, and his meddling in her marriage
would only make matters worse.

Sophie had broken down and confided to Celia that Lionel
had proposed to her seven days ago. Seven long days ago. But
she left out both his unromantic words and his passionate
embrace. But in the aftermath of that latter pleasure, she'd
spent the week imagining more embraces. Wild, mad wants,
sure to end her up in bedlam or a house of ill repute.

"Perhaps," said Celia caustically, "you should cut off your
head and have it served to him on a platter." Celia, glittering
in creams and golden silks, had dressed rather more elabo-
rately today than any day this week. Sophie forgave her that.
She had managed a new ribbon for her least-worn day dress,
anticipating Lionel's overdue return.

But she couldn't forgive Celia's severity. "Celie! You should
be ashamed to think such thoughts."

"On the contrary, dearest, His Lordship should be ashamed.
What's more brazen than his effrontery, his disregard of every
propriety?" Celia sniffed in disgust, but it came out like chok-
ing. "As your chaperone, I must remind you that nothing—but

249

nothing—about that proposal does honor to you or justice to your virtue."

Thank the good Lord, Sophie had not breathed a word to Celia about her increasingly slippery claim to virtue.

"But he has compelling reasons, pressing problems, vast responsibilities," Sophie said, rushing to Lionel's defense. "He's right to want a helpmate."

"A helpmate! How can you be so naive?"

"It isn't as though either of us were young and unversed in the ways of the world."

"Bah! Everything you say shows your naïveté, dearest. He should have apprised me of his intentions. He should have spoken to your father. And he should have met you in the drawing room with me in attendance or just outside the door. He didn't meet you there that evening because that's where I . . ." She trailed off, brilliant blue eyes narrowing with suspicion. "So where exactly did this proposal take place?"

Sophie wasn't about to volunteer that information.

"You were packing your trunk to go. You were . . . ," Celia went on, realization dawning, ". . . in your chamber. Oh, Sophie, oh no. He proposed to you in your bedchamber. What an out-and-out bounder he is. Servants could have seen him come out. I could have caught you in that compromising situation. And his poor sons! What if they'd stumbled upon the two of you together, alone? Such an immodest, immoral example for him to set before young minds. How could you allow it? How could he?"

Allow it? Sophie hadn't given appearances a thought, so consumed she'd been with having Lionel to herself.

The boys swerved dangerously near in hot pursuit of a ball kicked out of bounds. Since Sophie had accepted their globe, they played with new exuberance. She watched them with new trust and tenderness.

Graeme scooped up the ball and directed his brothers down the field. "So sorry to disturb, Miss Bowerbank. Miss Upton," he said, breathing hard, his usually pale face flushed with healthy exertion.

Sophie waved him back into play and turned to Celia.

"How could I prevent it, Celie? It is his house."

"The house of a confirmed rake," Celia whispered, her gaze on Graeme's retreating back.

"For the sake of his motherless sons, he says he has vowed reform."

"And tigers changes their stripes. Sophie, you must evacuate this wicked den of masculine retirements and amusements. The minute he steps foot inside this door."

"You exaggerate the danger," Sophie said.

But Celia had no idea of Sophie's danger or her willingness to embrace it.

"Besides, my refusal of his proposal doesn't release me from my agreement to tutor his sons."

"Very well then, I will tell your father. He will see to it that His Lordship sets you free."

"My father supports my presence here, or have you forgotten?"

"Sophie, dearest, think. Reputation is the only thing we women have. We are what we appear to be."

Sophie glared at Celia's inconsistency. "Whatever happened to *anyone can get away with anything in these great country houses?*"

"That's different. That applies to worldly people like myself. You are an upstanding rector's daughter, a model to everyone, until you admitted one of London's most storied rakes into your boudoir."

"*Formerly* one of London's most storied rakes. He means to reform, and I for one believe him."

"He has mistresses," Celia whispered.

Sophie grew indignant. "We've seen no sign of mistresses."

"Whom do you think Graeme mistook us for, some long-lost aunts?"

Oh. "Oh." Of course Lionel had women. *Had* had women.

251

He'd put them behind him. Or so he'd said. "We've seen no sign of untoward women."

"Precisely, dearest, don't you see? That's how men of rank and privilege manage it. He installs you here, competent and trustworthy person that you've proven yourself to be, and then he's haring off to London."

Sophie had not thought of that. But a lack of lovers could more than account for his ever-ready passion in her presence, and a cold, hard heart—unreformed—could explain his lack of love.

"If he gets a few extra gropes and kisses off you whilst he is at home, well . . . no rake would be averse to that."

"You have a dark, dark view of mankind, my friend," Sophie ventured, her own hope waning.

"And you are perpetually the most innocent of romantics, dearest. Too bad." Celia squeezed her hand in sympathy. "Any liaison with the earl of Wraxham is bound to break you of that."

And bound to break her heart, Sophie thought with a wrenching insight. Because Celia's protests had the ring of truth. Tigers don't change their stripes. And rakes don't give up their pleasures.

So Sophie would have to leave.

But not before she could be sure that Simon was safe, Graeme was settled, and Max and Alex were exonerated.

Exhausted from the drive, the distance, and the endless demands of boys, Lionel wheeled his brougham onto the great circular drive and threaded his team up under the portico at Wraxham House's front doors. If he could spend four days and nights cooped up with two of his sons in a carriage and a mix of inns and hostels—and no one that much the worse for wear—he could handle all of them, on his own, with no help from anyone.

Even if it meant occasionally imposing military rule.

It was late afternoon, the sun on a slant through steely

clouds that had massed to the south throughout the day. The golden stones of Wraxham House had gone gray beneath the lowering sky. His home had never looked so austere, so unwelcoming. Except for four boys and a pack of dogs racing in circles on the east lawn.

"May we join them, sir?" Marcus asked, his hand eager above the latch.

"Go. Beane will unload your trunks."

Marcus snapped the latch down, and he and James tumbled out of the cab. Boys shrieked and whooped in welcome, and in moments Lionel's six sons thundered up and down the lawn. He hadn't had them together at Wraxham House since, Lord, when? Since his sister's wedding to Harry Pelham four years ago.

Lionel stood for a moment by his brougham, his hand on the black door above the ornate family crest. Pride filled him, and regret. He'd sired them, and relinquished them to Penelope's tender mercies. Never again would he hand over his responsibilities for them to another person. Share them, yes, but only with Sophie. He ordered his coachman to put the team away, and Beane to unload their little trunks.

Then he strolled over to the terrace, sighting gold- and rose-clad ladies, bright as the blooms of summer flowers, out of the corner of his eye. But he fixed on his sons, on the rumble, the swirl, the strength, the strain, the future of the line.

The ball popped out of the huddle, and Simon—Simon?—grabbed it and ran.

Fabric whispered near him. And a familiar voice.

"Simon grows bolder and better, my lord. Welcome home."

Lionel turned, and it was Sophie, studying him with her solemn green eyes and wholesome face. She looked delicious, poised, determined. Determined to leave or determined to stay? Determined to marry him or not?

It was all he could do not to reach out and touch her.

It was all he could do not to ask.

"Yes, my lord, welcome home." Celia Upton, a golden reed

253

in shimmering silk, vied for his attention. "We barely managed without you."

Sophie shaded her brow with her hand and watched the field. "James and Marcus look no worse for wear."

"They won't be going back to Abercairn," he rasped, jolted by the pain of admitting that out loud. Jolted that he wanted Sophie to know. That he could use her counsel.

"Ah," she said, accepting and commiserating in a single syllable. "You will have to start your own school, my lord. Perhaps I can help you round up tutors."

For the first time in a week, no, months, no, years, he threw back his head and laughed. He envisioned long lines of men in sober black trooping in for interviews with the indomitable Miss Bowerbank, meeting his squadron of hellions, and tearing back to London as if the hounds of hell were on their heels.

Then it struck him.

After she helped find new tutors, she would leave.

"I expect you to stay, Miss Bowerbank. We wouldn't know what to do without you."

Celia Upton's polished face pruned. "Miss Bowerbank cannot stay, my lord, under the circumstances."

Another incident? He knotted his brow at Sophie. "Circumstances, my lo—Miss Bowerbank." He caught himself. He was so relieved to see Sophie, so happy to be wrangling with her, he'd almost said *my love*.

Sophie's lips, her kissable lips, pressed in chagrin. "Miss Upton must be referring to your kind offer, my lord. The one before you left. I told her, strictly as my chaperone, that you had . . . rather in haste . . . proposed marriage."

Ah, damn. "Ah, that," he managed casually.

Sophie met his gaze. "Yes, that."

"Even if you should retract your ill-considered offer, my lord—" Celia began.

"Miss Bowerbank," Lionel said, cutting Celia Upton off and demanding Sophie's gaze. She looked up, her green eyes guarded. "Sophie. I don't retract my offer. I am happy to repeat it, as I have not changed my mind. But whether you accept me, I trust you will stay until suitable arrangements are made for my sons."

"I have decided, my lord—"

"Sophie! No—" Celia Upton broke in vehemently.

"Let her speak, Miss Upton," Lionel said, giving Sophie's friend his haughtiest glare. "You can have no possible objection to her speaking, here, before you."

Celia Upton's face flushed red, a natural flush this time, a disapproving anger such as any vigilant chaperone might display on being overruled on a point of propriety. But he was her superior. "I have decided, my lord," Sophie began again, "to stay, as you request, until the boys are properly settled, and Simon most especially sleeps reliably in peace."

"Humph," Lionel said, but hope kindled in chest. "That could take forever."

"I think not, my lord," Sophie said crisply. "I don't plan to stay forever, and despite your absence, he slept like a lamb. Something—his oldest brother's presence, I believe—has had a palliative effect. As to your other offer—"

"Sophie, I defy you to go on!" Celia Upton blurted, cross as a mother goose. "With regard to that other offer, my lord, you must take it up with me, who am Miss Bowerbank's chaperone. Then you may be sure, I will insist that you consult her father."

Talk to Bowerbank, Lionel mused wryly. A novel thought to a man of his age and position. Both women shifted uncomfortably. The old man could have no objections. Marriage was legal, marriage was moral. And the good reverend owed him a kind turn.

"A cracking good idea, Miss Upton. Surprised I hadn't thought of him. Even he must see marriage as the best refuge for a reforming rake. I shall speak to Sophie's father first thing tomorrow morning."

Sophie's brow knotted in consternation. He'd been right. She'd been going to refuse him a second time. Ha! All was fair in war and marriage proposals. Tomorrow he would see what her father had to say about her refusal.

The boys roared up and down the lawn, and Celia Upton sat down more properly than he had ever seen her do, her fan, her reticule, her beringed fingers picture perfect, but a perfect picture of what?

Success? Or failure?

He'd been right about her too: She'd been angling for him for herself.

Lionel held a chair for Sophie. She sat stiff and blushing, and he sat beside her. By old habit in the awkward moment, he took out his enameled snuffbox to celebrate his little domestic victory.

"Oh, for pity's sake, my lord, would you put that nasty foppish affectation out of my sight?" Sophie exploded.

Interesting, he thought, smothering a grin. Already his Sophie was ordering him about as if she were his wife.

Chapter Twenty-two

Can you resist the potent pow'r,
That leads us to the dusky bow'r,
In melting, tim'rous mood;
That cherishes the fond desire,
And makes each bosom feed its fire,
And wish to be subdued.
—The Temple of Prostitution (1779?)

Lionel tossed aside another ruined cravat, frustrated with his clumsy fingers, or the excessive starch. He could tie the buggers in the dark, in strange places, on the run. But a simply tied cravat, like a simply lived life, was turning out to be deceptively hard.

He had to make it work before going down to dinner. The cravat was part of his new plan to seduce his reluctant bride. When he next got her alone, it would be easier to rip off. As would his shirt. As would his country breeches.

He should have seduced her when they were young. Seduced her, and gotten her with child. No matter what her objection to his suit—which, damn it to hell, seemed to be based on the most romantic notions of ephemeral love garnered from overindulgence in poetry and novels—she would marry him for the child.

There were better reasons to marry him than that.

She should marry him for what he did best—late nights, long waits, lavish caresses, lush kisses, luxurious ecstasies, lingering aftermaths of pleasure.

He'd not yet put his proposal before Bowerbank, his last ally against her stubbornness. According to Tims, the ever-dutiful rector had spent his day attending ailing parishioners.

Except for the minor matter of Lionel's upcoming marriage, things were looking up. Tonight he was going down to a second dinner with all six of his sons under his roof, gathered round one table. He swallowed against a choke of pride. Two days and a night had passed with no untoward events, no unexpected arrivals, no letters bearing unanticipated news. And that—on top of his week away without a single incident—boded well for their new life.

A few more days of this, and he could cashier the old Lionel, debauchee and cynic, and install the earl of Wraxham, confirmed optimist, benevolent country peer, beloved paterfamilias.

Bloody hell, he could end up happier than his old friend Harry.

It was time for dinner. He shrugged into an evening coat of midnight superfine and crossed his bedchamber. It had been his father's bedchamber, his grandfather's bedchamber, and so on back to the War of the Roses. He wanted a better life than theirs, a happier life, a decent life. He wanted to care for his wife. For his children. For the children he and Sophie would have. As he had at last begun to do for his sons. He opened his door.

And there was Sophie, her face pale and drawn.

"Something awful," she said. "And you are needed."

That kind of need he didn't want. But he followed her, demanding an explanation.

"Another incident, but worse," was all she would say, and she pressed him down the hall. The late afternoon sun slanted through the tall windows, casting a peaceful golden glow. Muffled shrieks came from a few doors down.

Muffled, feminine shrieks.

"I'm afraid the culprits have had a go at Celia," Sophie explained.

"Bloody Chr—" He broke off in front of Sophie. And noted she had not leapt to the conclusion that the culprits were his sons. "Tell me she's not hurt."

"She is in a state," Sophie said, stopping before the door to his late wife's suite. Before weeping and wailing and gnashing of teeth.

His gut clenched, and his mind boggled for an instant. Penelope had had fits like the one erupting from within. Penelope was dead. Somehow Celia had ended up in Penelope's suite, Lionel realized, and she was distressed. Moments ago, his world, his and Sophie's world, had looked so calm.

"What in bloody hell has happened, Sophie?" he almost roared.

"It's her dresses, my lord."

Lionel, damn it. "What about her bloody dresses?"

Sophie reached for the latch. "You have to see this for yourself."

"No." He closed his hand over hers and said deliberately, "I'm done with surprises."

She let out a puff of exasperation. "They've been ruined. With knives, scissors, we don't know how. But . . ."

The shrieks gave way to sobs, and Lionel clicked the latch and strode in. Penelope's old bed was a memorial to feminine extravagance set in a sea of Chinese fabric covering the walls and draping the tall windows that overlooked the north lawn and Wraxham's fields beyond. He'd always hated her decor.

Celia Upton, in sumptuous silk, wept over a pile of shredded

259

fancy dresses on the lavish counterpane. A needle of distaste pricked Lionel.

"Thank heavens, you're here, my lord. I returned from shopping in the village"—she draped one ruined dress over her forearms and held it out for him to see—"to this."

She'd worn that golden gown for guests. On the counterpane lay a yellow, a blue, and a figured silk, sleeves ripped from armholes, skirts slashed in ribbons up to bodices.

"My good Miss Upton," he said, trying to offer comfort. But anger tore him. Celia Upton might be the most affected woman in all England, but the damage to her clothing was malicious. "My sincere apologies that your lovely gowns should come to such a sorry end at Wraxham House. I will see to it that they are replaced."

Celia's face glistened with tears. "I'm afraid I am a troublesome guest, my lord."

"Not at all, madam." Even fashionable ladies, he reminded himself, suffered pain. He touched a consoling hand to her fashionably sloped but shuddering shoulder.

Celia dabbed her tears with a sodden handkerchief of fine French lace. "It isn't your fault, my lord. After everything that has gone wrong, I should have locked my door against them when I went out."

Against *them?* He didn't want to ask. "You suspect . . ."

Her blue eyes widened in dismay. "The twins, my lord. Of course, I don't want to, but one's thoughts turn naturally to . . ."

"Naturally," he repeated, hanging on to civility by his fingernails, "I will investigate. But my sons would have been playing on the lawn while you were out."

Celia's face pinched. "Not all of them, my lord. James and Marcus—"

"James and Marcus are no vandals," he said, cutting her off. "They disobeyed their masters at Abercairn on a point of honor." He gestured to the tattered dresses in disgust. "There's no honor here."

Sophie spoke up. "I believe James and Marcus were keen

to see the horses and had excused themselves to go to the stables."

"That is easy enough to verify," he said. "My sons don't go about despoiling ladies' dresses, Miss Upton. But we will find who did. No one wants you to be inconvenienced or insulted."

Celia descended into a fresh volley of tears. "So very sorry to appear ungrateful, my lord. It's a natural conclusion for one to reach after everything that has gone before."

"None of it confirmed," he reminded her.

He reminded himself.

Because none of it had been disproved. He'd been able to disprove nothing or to find anyone other than his sons to pin things on. But this, like Bowerbank's antique globe, had to be someone on the inside.

"Nor would you want it confirmed," Celia said with delicate sympathy. "I can understand that, a man's own sons." But her insinuation was clear. She blamed his sons, and she pitied him.

"Truly, Celie." Sophie inserted herself firmly into the conversation. "It could be anyone. Someone in the household, getting into the schoolroom, my room, your room."

"But who? And why?" Celia sniffed. "Next you will say Nurse Nesbit, who disagrees with Simon's treatment. Or Mrs. Plumridge, who complains that her house has been taken over by a band of savages."

Does she indeed? Lionel thought. The old battle-ax. "In fact, Mrs. Plumridge commands the keys to every room and closet in the house. As to Nesbit, an unhappier nurse could not be found," he said gravely. "There are other suspects. As magistrate in your father's stead, I am committed to prosecute offenders, whoever they may be."

"I meant nothing by it, my lord," Celia said, retreating.

But he was quite enjoying this line of thought, the first in a while to amuse him, outside of thoughts of Sophie. "As well to suspect Laframboise, who complains that our inferior palates destroy his talent."

"Or Thomas Beane," Sophie chimed in, apparently buoyed by suggestions that might exonerate her students, "who skulks about in that tall, lanky frame of his. Frightening, really."

Celia dabbed stray tears. "It isn't kind to mock me, Sophie."

"It isn't pleasant to suspect everyone in the household either," Lionel said. But like Sophie, expanding the slate of suspects cheered him up. "Come to think of it," he added, "my money is on Mr. Tims. He creeps so much more convincingly than Beane skulks."

"And has done so longer, has he not?" Sophie put in, growing almost cheerful.

"Be that as it may, you must see, my lord, that Miss Bowerbank cannot safely stay." Celia's voice rose, Lionel noted, as she used Sophie's formal name. "I have been wrong to support her staying here and exposing herself, exposing both of us, to insult and to danger."

"Insult, true, but the danger has not yet been personal," Lionel pointed out.

"The boys would never do that," Sophie said.

Celia ignored her friend. "Surely, my lord, you can find a team of qualified men to handle your sons. Two women of learning and refinement cannot be expected to, not for one more day."

"No, Celie, that won't do," Sophie said. "I promised Lord Wraxham, come what may, to stand by his sons until suitable replacements can be found. It's the least I can do for Simon."

"Come what may? Oh, Sophie dearest. You're making an awful mistake." Celia slumped on the edge of her bed, dissolving into another flood of tears, a delicate picture of a damsel in distress. "Then I too must stay, whatever the risk."

Bugger all, Lionel thought. For he was weary of Miss Upton's poses and proprieties, suspicious of her purpose, put out with her professions of friendship and loyalty. He couldn't abide her likeness to grasping London ladies and worse, now, to his late wife. He didn't like snares laid to entrap him into marriage, and he despised the way she treated Sophie.

From belowstairs, the bell gonged for dinner. Reluctantly he put on the mantle of the helpful host. "Are you enough recovered, Miss Upton, to join my sons and me for dinner?"

She gave a pretty scowl. "But yes, if you will excuse me that I cannot change into proper dress."

"No matter, Miss Upton. You look fine," he said. He adjusted his cravat, and offered each lady an arm. Celia clung to him, rather like an anchor. Sophie's lighter touch, however, shored him up. "Tonight we are on country manners."

And on edge. For Celia Upton dominated dinners with her literary London chatter, and he had had enough of her today, worrying that her expensive day dress would not suit for dinner. Devil take it, she was better fitted out than his modest Sophie in her old battered silk, a genteel poverty he could not wait to remedy. Sophie surpassed her in every other way, in wit and sense and loyalty.

And he wanted nothing more than to toss out everyone and have a private evening with the incomparable Miss Bowerbank.

Sophie sat by Simon's bed and watched his gentle, peaceful breathing, trying to soothe her jangled nerves. She and Lionel had made sure that he heard nothing of this latest crime and felt no more disruption in his life than the return of his remaining brothers home.

That disruption, like Graeme's return, had left him even more settled, more content.

Sophie brushed back a lock of Simon's hair, worrying. They'd kept the affair of Celia's dresses from the other children too. Lionel adamantly opposed accusing them; as father he knew nothing, and as magistrate he had everything to investigate.

Celia, the victim, had taken exception to their approach.

Speaking privately to Sophie after dinner, she'd not minced words. "Of course I blame the boys, dearest. Clearly, the only question is whether to blame the twins or newcomers James and Marcus."

Sophie's temper flared. She worried about the newcomers herself, who were even more put out at the thought of a woman tutor than the twins had been. But that had no connection to Celia's clothes.

"Bah! The boys would not harm anyone who applauds when they play ball. You've done nothing to, for, or with them."

"Neither had my mother, or Owen Hill, or the Misses Gatewood." Celia laughed, a forced, sarcastic little laugh that spoke volumes to Sophie of how deeply the destruction of her precious wardrobe had offended her. "Honestly, Sophie, you're the only one they have reason to resent."

Sophie resented Celia's comment. But Sophie was certain that the twins had no reason to have hard feelings about her. They'd made their peace with the gift of that old battered globe, and Sophie had worked hard to make amends for her brief loss of faith in them. She'd even defended them to their father.

Not that they knew that.

She wouldn't have to defend them anymore.

He defended them himself now, and Sophie respected that. In fact, she was overjoyed that Lionel stood by his sons in these latest incidents. In time, backing them would stand him in good stead with them. It stood him in good stead with her. Aroused as she was by Lionel the rake, it was the loyal father who touched her heart.

Whereas Celia touched her nerves. What was she playing at, apologizing and flattering Lionel one moment, accusing his sons the next? Of course Sophie felt dreadful about the dresses, and not a little worried. Sleep would be no friend to her tonight.

What would be next? Or who? Though on a smaller scale than the topiary gardens and the butcher shop, the latest violations were personal, vindictive, and violent. At least Lionel had a whole new raft of people to consider as criminals.

After dinner, he'd set off to question them.

For his and the boys' sake, and for Simon's peace of mind, he couldn't find the perpetrators a moment too soon.

Chapter Twenty-three

TULLIA: Just before them, towards the upper Part of the C—t, is a Thing they call Clitoris, which, is a little like a Man's P—k, for it will swell and stand like his; and being rubbed gently by his Member, will, with excessive Pleasure, send forth a Liquor, which when it comes away, leaves us in a Trance, as if we were dying, all our Senses being lost, and as it were summed up in that one Place, and our Eyes shut, our Hearts languishing on one Side, our Limbs extended, and, in a word, there follows a dissolving of our whole Person, and melting in such inexpressible Joys, as none but those who feel them can express or comprehend.

—A Dialogue between a Married Lady
and a Maid (1740)

Lionel pushed back from his favorite table at the Wraxham Arms and spoke to half a dozen townsmen and tenants on his way out. It crossed his mind, as he crossed his lawn, simply to storm Sophie's room and seduce her.

To settle *something* in his and his sons' unsettled world.

But the idea that Celia Upton could be listening at the adjoining door of the two women's rooms withered any impulse for that false expediency.

After dinner, he'd interviewed everyone he and Sophie had facetiously put forward as suspects in the destruction of Celia Upton's fancy dresses. All had alibis, all airtight, all publicly witnessed. He was relieved that his own staff were in the clear. That, however, left him with no suspects but his sons.

Mrs. Plumridge and Laframboise had spent the afternoon belowstairs in the kitchens, provisioning the house for June amidst reported tirades and flying pots and pans. The Frenchman, Lionel thought privately, was not long for his current post, innocent or not.

Nurse Nesbit, who ordinarily spent afternoons alone tidying the nursery while Simon was occupied at school or play, had enlisted Thomas Beane to rearrange the boys' sleeping quarters now that James and Marcus had come home. Two birds were exonerated with that stone too.

Even the fastidious Tims, whose name Lionel had tossed into the ring as a preposterous absurdity, had spent the afternoon harassing Carter over some agricultural accounts. Which ruled out Carter too, whom Lionel hadn't even planned to investigate.

This latest mystery did not bode well for sleep—or for his wrapping up his tenure as magistrate with anything like success.

He strolled past the drawing room, the dining room, and turned to the private stairs to his suite.

A ribbon of light glowed beneath the threshold of the library door. It had better not be Graeme, no matter his lust for poetry and whatever that wench's name was. He should be in his rooms safeguarding the twins.

Lionel cracked the door and looked in.

Lounging on the sofa in a pool of light was Sophie, her eyes closed, her dress in disarray, a book open in her hand.

What in Hades was she doing here, well after midnight?

Had she learned nothing from the latest attack?

Sudden fear choked him. Was she a victim of the next one?

He charged across the room, assessing her as he drew near. Her heavy woolen nightgown gaped open. Her night rail parted at the throat, showing the rise of her ample breasts. Its hem was drawn up wantonly above her knees. One hand rested on her belly, palm up in a kind of languor. He crossed between her and the candles burning on the mantel, his shadow falling on her face.

She shifted, and the book tumbled to the floor.

She was ravishing. Or had been ravished. His pulse pounded in his throat. He forced calm. No, he was panicking, off his form as a soldier and besieged by scenes from battle-fields, when he should be calling up erotic scenes from count-less boudoirs. Because he looked more closely at her. Her thinly covered breasts rose and fell, pulling the worn fabric across her nipples, shadowed points of chill. Or arousal.

What had happened here?

She was alive, he was sure of that. But how the devil had she come to be so disheveled? He knelt beside her, barely noticing the creak of his bad knee. The book she'd held lay on the carpet, spine up, half open, like a tent. He picked it up, a thin, used volume cheaply bound in boards. Sophie was reading poetry? Indeed, he opened it to . . . It looked like an ode, not one he recognized.

He skimmed stanza after stanza, his loins firing to its lusty meter.

Prostrate I traverse o'er her Form Divine,
Embracing ev'ry Part where nameless Graces shine.

Legs in Cupid's Fetters locked
. . . sweet binding Chains,
The heat of fervent Love diffuse through all our Veins
. . . her Thighs I freely trace . . .

Bugger all. Sophie had found his father's erotic books.

Thumbing through the one she'd dropped, Lionel found a sensuous engraving of a sylvan scene. He scowled, amazement rising, arousal stirring. A man and woman sat surrounded by cupids, draped erotically in scanty sheets, their legs, breasts, bellies, chests visible, everything exposed except their most private parts. And all entwined.

The book was worn. The book was used.

The book was bawdy.

Sophie had been reading this book.

His Sophie read bawdy books.

He read the title: *The Pleasures of Coition, or the Nightly Sports of Venus, A Poem.*

Disbelief, then astonishment stole across him. Lust thudded through his loins.

Gently he touched her forearm. "Sophie, love," he whispered, "do not be alarmed."

Her eyes blinked open, and she gave him a sweet smile of recognition. It turned to horror.

"Oh, dear Lord!" she cried. She started up, and her mouth settled in a pout of surprise. Her night rail gaped open at the neck, uncovering full breasts. She splayed a hand across one luscious breast, too large to cover fully. The other breast was free, pale white, delicately veined, and tipped with deepest coral. Scrambling to cover herself, she twisted on the couch, tangling her legs in the hem of her night rail and exposing creamy thighs.

The other hand splayed lower, over the dark and secret curls at the join of her legs. His shaft, already on alert, hardened and saluted her raw beauty with drops of desire.

"I should like nothing better than to be your dear lord,

Sophie," he said, with effort suppressing a grin of anticipation that lit him from the inside out. "Your décolletage suggests you are not innocent of what that might entail."

Her green eyes widened with guilt. "I fell asleep, my lord."

"Nights are wasted in indulging sleep."

She patted the dark brocaded cushions anxiously. "I had a book."

He held its spine up, so she could read the title and see that he knew. "This book?"

"Heaven help me." She covered her face with her hands, leaving both her breasts above and her dark curls below bare to his appreciation.

"Heaven will not help in this, my love," he rasped, savagely repressing a grin of triumph—and the urge to jump upon her. But no, no rush. He had her where he wanted her.

Where he'd wanted her since the day he'd been forced from home.

She drew up her knees and wrapped her arms around them, concealing everything except her bare slender feet and succulent toes.

"But I should be delighted," he went on as if it were conversation over tea, to put her more at ease, "no, deeply gratified to provide the help you seek."

Her chest, her throat and then her face darkened in a blush of misery. "Don't mock me, my lord."

Lionel, he thought but did not want to divert her from the subject of the bawdy books.

"I was never more serious in my life. Perhaps you would explain what you are doing with this little volume."

She drew herself up, Athena arming herself for battle. "It's not the only one."

He arched his brow in inquiry. "Indeed."

"There's quite a collection, as you must know, my lord."

"Yes," he said gravely, struggling not to betray how very amused, how very interested he was in her knowledge of it. "I just didn't know you'd found it."

"Inevitably, given my work cataloguing the family books and papers."

"Ah, yes. They were still behind the treatises on breeding sheep, I suppose. My brothers and I dipped into them from time to time."

"Ha!" she said, her spirits recovering. "I'll bet you'd read them before when we—"

He shrugged, admitting it. "The question is, however, what are you doing with it now?"

She sat up, tried to hide inside her dressing gown.

He gripped its lapels in his hands, smoothed them back, opening her breasts back to his view. "Don't. Don't cover yourself from me. Do tell me about the books."

Her eyes darted to the door, but she forced them back to engage his gaze. "If you must know, I am embarked on a study of pleasure." It was as pure an act of courage as he'd seen on the battlefield. His brain saluted that. But his heart tripped like a schoolboy's. Amazing. With other women, any other women, he was practiced at calculation and refinement. Only Sophie had ever reduced him to this adolescent state of eagerness and lust.

"Pleasure," he repeated, almost licking his lips, a fox savoring the hapless hen. "Do go on."

She swallowed, and sailed forth clearly into uncharted waters. "Pleasure between men and women."

"I can show you everything you need to know about pleasure between men and women. Between one man and one woman."

She lifted her chin, and said, "And about pleasuring myself."

That set him back. It did him in. He froze in a rage of lust and blaze of understanding. That explained the randy wench who'd met him at the kissing gate and waylaid him in the hall.

But just how far would Sophie dare to go? How far, given she had been this forward, did she want to go?

"Show me," he said hoarsely.

She glanced at the door again. "I cannot."

"Wait. Don't move." He pressed her to the sofa, only to realize that his hands were trembling. He squeezed hers, to reassure her and to hide his rapidly eroding control. "I'll be right back."

He limped across the room and drew the lock across the door. It clanked into place, loud as the pulse drumming in his ears. It occurred to him that he could block the door with a chair, or bookstand, or desk.

But that would take time, and he had waited for this moment for twenty years. Returning, he arranged candles on the mantel opposite the couch.

She had not moved. His mouth went dry. His throat closed. His arousal strained against his breeches. He tore off his cravat, a single simple movement. That much went as he'd planned. He shucked his coat, opened the placket of his shirt, and paused in bemusement.

She was watching him with academic interest, studying his neck, his half-bared chest, and then—her gaze sliding downward—his breeches, still buttoned, tenting over his erection.

To be gazed on, consumed, by a virgin with knowledge.

He had never felt so urgent. So raw.

"My lord?" She licked her lips, coral lips, her pink tongue peeking out, testing the air, teasing him.

"Plague take it, Sophie. Call me by my name, as you used to do," he said, his voice scraping against that fervent wish and making it a demand.

But she did not, would not say his name. She'd conscientiously maintained this sign of their difference. Her face scrunched against crossing this first, great barrier between them and his position.

"Please, Sophie," he said more harshly still.

"Lionel," she whispered finally in a dear sweet voice, an echo from the summer they had lost.

"Good. That is a good start."

"My lord—Lionel, I like it that we should be equal. Equal in—"

He felt her gather her resolve.

"—in nakedness."

Nakedness. His heart hammered in his chest. What he would have given as a young man ever to have been naked for her, to have seen her naked. Never mind that the word must be hard for her to say.

She'd said it.

So it was a simple matter to strip off his shirt, kick off his boots, unbutton his fall. She waited, watching his every move with that academic interest. That intelligence that first drew him to her.

Had he ever loved a woman with his mind?

He took the hand that rested on her breast, kissed it, and replaced it. He lifted the other hand that half concealed the dark delta of her charms, kissed that hand, and returned it too, pressing it back gently with his own hand to assure her of the rightness of what she was doing. Of what they were doing.

"Show me how you pleasure yourself, love."

She swallowed hard. And closed her eyes, not a no but not a yes.

The burn of her self-consciousness shimmered between them.

"Don't be afraid, love. Don't be afraid of anything with me," he said, rising to his knees and leaning in to kiss her face. "You know how to do this, don't you?"

It seemed she could only nod. But she did, and her eyelids, damped by tears of emotion, fluttered against his mouth. He kissed her forehead, kissed the apples of her cheeks, the determination of her nose, the stubbornness of her chin, and then he brushed his lips over the tenderness of her mouth. Her lips parted, and her sigh feathered across his face, so he kissed her for a moment in good earnest before pulling away. Then he reminded her.

"Show me, love. It will pleasure me."

Eyes still shut, she yielded with a whimper in her throat. He watched her ease her fingertips into her curls, midnight in the candlelight. He watched her fingers seek the divide her curls concealed. Tentative at first, her fingers made small rhythmic circles of discovery. Of arousal. With difficulty he restrained himself from touching her and taking over, his loins afire at her voluptuous innocence. At her courage.

Her head lolled back, as if she was nearing ecstasy, and the marble column of her throat tempted him for kisses. But kissing her there would disturb her progress and disrupt his view.

Instead he put a hand to her free breast and tweaked its nipple tenderly, then tightly. She moaned, and her body spasmed.

"So beautiful in love, my love, don't stop." His heart pounded; his shaft jerked in lust and sympathy.

For Sophie's seeking her own fulfillment for his pleasure shook him to his core. She was wanton, she was generous, and he wanted to tup her till he hurt.

But suddenly her hand, pearly white in candlelight and glistening with the dew of her own desire, stopped. Simply stopped. "Don't make me do it alone again, my lor—my Lionel," she bit off in an anguished whisper. "I always wanted only you."

With a growl of acquiescence, he leaned over her, capturing her mouth and plunging his tongue in it as desperately as he wanted to sink himself into her quim.

But he still had a particle of reason, that fragment of cognizance all rakes reserve to themselves.

Sophie was a virgin. The first time he pleasured her, by God, he would not cause her pain. Pleasure, pleasure. He'd failed as a soldier and a husband, and he might be a failure still as father, earl, and magistrate. But pleasure, he did pleasure best.

He rained kisses down her body, suckling one nipple gently, taking the other hard. She moaned. His arousal twitched in anticipation.

He probed at her navel, wanting her to know that he could bring her pleasure there, there where her skin was pearly white, where her flesh was round and promising, there above the contrast with her beautiful dark curls.

They hid her secrets.

They hid her delights.

Bracing her hips with his hands, he touched her nub with the tip of his tongue, blowing his hot breath to test her readiness. She squirmed beneath him, lifting restless hips to meet his mouth.

"Lionel, please," she insisted, moaning.

But it occurred to him that she did not know exactly what she asked for, how much better it could be.

He knew. And he wanted to possess her, all of her, even as he brought her to her peak. He released her hips, slid one hand up her body to her mouth, and bade her take his fingers into that hot private secret part of who she was. He groaned with pleasure at the slippery slide of her tongue against the stiffness of his fingers, so like the hot channel below. He probed there roughly with his other hand. She was ready, astonishingly ready for one so innocent. Her sheath was creamy wet, and he slid his fingers in up to her maiden barrier, teasing her. Tormenting her. Pleasuring her. She cried out as he insisted, and rocked against his fingers with unfulfilled desire.

She was ready for his mouth. He moved downward. He circled her nub with his tongue again, but that was not quite what she wanted. Digging her fingers into his hair, she pressed his head tighter to the center of her passion.

He absolutely loved the taste and smell of women. Washed, recently washed, even sometimes not quite washed at all.

Sophie smelled of soap and tasted of salt and yesterday. Yesterday unfilled. The nub that was the center of her passion was swollen with desire. He loved the shape of it, the heat of it, the privacy of it, and he loved *it*, her body, her, with the first and only gentle reverence he had given to a woman in his wasted, wastrel life.

She began to quake beneath him. He moved back up her

body, her belly, hips, quim, shaking beneath him, his hands replacing his mouth. She let out an anguished cry. She surged up to him, and her wet hot sheath contracted and released around his fingers, contracted and released, and broke. She was spent. He'd watched her there, helped her there, brought her there. His manhood thickened. Throbbed. Flared.

He was next. He would bring her back.

But she was *here. Now.*

"Oh no," she moaned, "this isn't what I wanted. I didn't know it could happen so fast." She was crying, gulping sobs, and she pounded his chest with violent conviction. "You leave me a virgin."

He had violent feelings too. If she'd had clothes on, he would have ripped them off. If she refused him, he would pin her to the floor.

"What must I do for you to rid me of my troublesome virginity!" she cried.

Damn. He'd wanted her to have satisfaction, but he'd missed what she needed most.

He tipped her chin with his fingers. "I wanted you to feel pleasure, not pain."

"Pain? Virginity is the curse of my life, my lord. If you would free me, do not leave me a virgin."

He inclined his head, astonished by her fervent plea. "You are quite sure."

"I abhor ignorance of any kind, my lord."

"*Lionel,*" he insisted.

Unexpectedly, she touched his face with the back of her hand, rubbing it against the scrape of a day's growth of beard. "Lionel," she said firmly and with purpose. "If you have any mercy, you will release me."

Release Sophie.

He'd turned his back on London. He would probably save his estate. He would stand by his sons through thick and thin.

But nothing, *nothing,* would satisfy him more than to relieve the surprising Miss Sophie Bowerbank of her troublesome virginity.

Chapter Twenty-four

At first I Hand in Hand engag'd;
Then at a Distance threw a Dart;
Last a full Push I made, enrag'd,
Which pleasing, pierc'd her vital Part.
Each answers ev'ry Stroke, their Part each play,
We boldly act, and all Love's Duties bravely pay.
—The Pleasures of Coition (1702)

Sophie dried her eyes, the better to see him. Lionel, the long-time object of her torrid fantasies and heated longings, in the flesh. For years, she'd pored over etchings in the old earl's books, wondering if men's bodies really looked like that—so unlike her own, and not what she'd imagined from her inno-cent explorations with Lionel that fated summer.

Naked, Lionel Westfall, earl of Wraxham, was magnificent. Candles from behind him on the mantel put his torso in shadow, but she could make out a sprinkling of tawny hair swirling across his chest and arrowing down his belly, which was flat and ridged with muscle. He turned nearer to her, can-

277

dlelight striking his body full on. He looked stronger, more muscled, more male.

More scarred.

She clapped her hand to her mouth, muffling a gasp of horror.

For Lionel had been stabbed. She saw inch-long scars, white on white, much too near his heart. Vicious slashes zigzagged across his torso as if someone had tried to sever his head, cut out his heart, disembowel him.

"Dear God," she said, voice breaking. "Lionel. Dear God." Hot tears burned her eyes. Ages ago she'd heard he'd almost died, an event so unthinkable that she'd imagined dramatic, heroic narrow escapes. A bullet had grazed his head perhaps, or he'd taken an improbable fall from a horse and gotten up and walked away. Nothing like this gory devastation. He'd been run through with a lance, a sword, a bayonet, she had no idea which. How had he survived?

"Ancient history, love," he tossed off. But his body went rigid as she traced the stab wounds near his heart.

"You could have died."

His gray eyes were bleak. "Most of my men did," he said brutally.

Had her father known of Lionel's near death and not told her? She'd been sitting safe at home, reading books, jealous of Lionel's adventurous life. Her heart had been bruised; his had been slashed at, his body run through with intent to kill. She shuddered at the thought. Perhaps those scars explained his irony, his distance, even the loveless marriage.

"If I could only heal you . . ." she offered.

"No, love. Love me," he said roughly. Refusing sympathy or comfort, he pried her hands from off his scars and moved them down his heated flesh. "And look at me," he ordered. "I like it when you look at me."

Not at his scars, she understood. For him, his scars marked failures. His arousal marked success, his refusal to die, to quit, to despair, his grab at life.

278

So she obliged him, her gaze skimming the breadth of his chest and the light swirl of tawny hair that stretched from nipple to nipple. She thought those private, graphic words, vowing not to falter when she had a chance to say them, or any others. She refused to act the shy, ignorant virgin anymore. It felt as though she'd been educating herself for this moment forever.

A wry smile crooked a corner of his mouth, as if her hesitation pleased and amused him. As if he read her thoughts. She shivered, she felt so exposed. Boldly she looked lower. A rich, dark spread of manly hair, lighter than her own, covered his loins. Rising from there, hard and savage, stood the instrument of his passion. *Think the words you learned for it,* she told herself.

His *Thing,* his *Member,* his *Erection.*

"Touch me, Sophie. If you want me, touch me."

She pushed down anxiety, summoned courage and desire. This was what she'd wanted, waited for, and so why hesitate? Because . . . because. She wanted their coming together to be perfect, like the stories in her books.

She reached to touch him, her hand small and white against the bloodred thrust of his . . . *shaft* . . . *spear.* Bawdier words from bawdier books streamed through her mind, warlike and brutal.

The head of his shaft spasmed at her touch, and she closed her fingers round it. It was hard as the iron rods of the kissing gate where he'd held her in thrall, but hot. His eyes closed, his expression metamorphosed from the guarded, cynical face he showed the world, to something private, rapt, and luminous.

In the most shocking book, a woman kissed a man as Lionel had just kissed her, her mouth to his member. She slid off the sofa and knelt before him, her bare breasts free between her arms, her unruly hair spilling over her shoulders onto the tops of his thighs. Shameless, daring, free.

She kissed the head of his amazing shaft—it was ten thumb

breadths long and four thumbs thick, and it thickened as she rubbed it. He gave a groan of satisfaction. A thrill of power pumped through her veins: She'd pleasured him so easily. She ran her tongue around its hood, and drops of passion welled up. She licked them off, tentative at first, then with conviction. Lionel tasted of sea salt and smelled of manly musk and earthy secrets, and she wanted to devour him, drive him to distraction as he had driven her.

But he cupped her face with warm strong hands and kissed her mouth, her cheeks, her eyelids as if in apology.

"I won't last another minute, love," he grated, straining against something she did not quite understand.

Her face heated in consternation. This was so much more intimate and intimidating than in books. "Oh, I didn't know—"

"Shh, love. You've done no wrong. You could do no wrong."

His corded arms lifted her and laid her on the sofa, her back and buttocks exquisitely alive to the plush velvet and rough weft of its brocade cushions, her bare breasts and belly open to his view. His lustful scrutiny.

In an attack of self-consciousness, she drew up her hands to screen herself. She was slack and frumpy, her breasts too large, her hips too wide to bear up under close inspection of a man like him, fit and hard and feral, the toast of London ladies. "I should be younger, thinner," she choked out, sure her old body would disappoint him.

His eyes danced with lust, and he gently pulled her hands away. "You're ripe, womanly and luscious, everything a man could want." Then almost reverently, he kissed her nipples, her belly, her private curls, and looked up, and smiled a smile she recognized from years ago, boyish and earnest and sincere.

Suddenly, she felt beautiful and powerful, young again, almost loved.

He stretched his long, muscled body alongside her, naked, and as comfortable in his skin as any man could be. "Now, my dear Miss Bowerbank. There's the matter of your virginity to be gotten rid of. If your mind's made up."

Her heart turned over in her chest. *Yes, please.* "I've waited long enough."

He gave her a quizzical look, his gray eyes dark as the evening sky. "I suppose you know that this will hurt."

"I understand it only hurts a woman once, some more than most. More rarely, some are not hurt at all," she said, and grimaced. She must sound prim and bookish.

"Ah, you did read all my father's tracts," he said, giving her a wry, approving grin. His fingers dug into her curls, found her swollen nub, and began that rhythmic gentle pinching that he did so well.

"Why are you doing that?" she asked, puzzled. "I already reached my . . ." She broke off, not yet bold enough to keep her vow and say words she'd only read.

". . . Your pleasure? transport? orgasm?" he finished for her, his fingers unrelenting.

"Yes, all of that," she bit off in frustration. She'd vowed to say those words, real words, and she was stuttering over them like a ninny.

"And so you think it's my turn?" He added a nipple to his assault. It puckered beneath his tongue and tingled between his teeth.

"Isn't it?" she asked, growing miffed and flustered. "Don't tease me, Lionel. I despise being ignorant."

The corners of his eyes crinkled with sympathy. "Ignorant? On the contrary, love, you seem . . ." He blew on her breast, and her nipple puckered obediently. ". . . ready. I don't normally bed virgins, Sophie. But I thought with your knowledge of lovemaking, we might be able to help you find pleasure too with your deflowering."

She was suspicious of his mood and skeptical of his plan. "None of the books I read described anything like that. On the contrary, they make it perfectly clear that a woman's first time is always a trial, even an ordeal."

He arched a brow. He was even more savagely handsome by candlelight, his tawny hair tousled, his nose a sharp blade, his jaw square. "And in your experience these books are always right."

"They have been so far," she said, relieved. He seemed to accept that she had some knowledge of her own, that she wasn't a complete and utter ninny about the art of love. "They were right about what you might do, and how I would feel during and afterward, and how you would look"—she gazed down at his shaft, quite directly, she thought with pride at her growing ease in this new uncharted realm of sensual delight—"there because—"

"Sophie, love—" He stopped her, puffing out a breath of exasperation. An arousing breath, warming her other nipple. It puckered tighter for him.

She gasped. Her books had been silent on this particularly thrilling tactic of Lionel's. It always worked. It always sent a sliver of sensation coiling through her. Which always settled, throbbing, between her legs.

Lionel was watching her intently. "It's time for you to stop, and let me do what I do best."

With that, Lionel Westfall, Sophie's first and only love, proceeded to show her with his hands and mouth and teeth and tongue exactly what it was that he did best and, when she was gasping with desire, with the full length and breadth of his accomplished manhood. *Member, shaft,* she thought to herself. He slid it in and probed at her last barrier. He stroked, but it hurt, and she couldn't help wincing.

"Be sure, love," he said.

"Take me, Lionel, please," she begged. "Love me."

He was whispering hot, dark words, some she'd read and others new to her, shockingly vulgar and astonishingly arousing, all meaning *come for me. Come hard, come now.* She lifted her hips to meet his final, piercing stroke, no pain so great as loneliness, and with a final jutting drive, he stabbed her, tore her.

Freed her.

She bit down on her pain, and he spasmed, spurting into her depths. Between them, it grew wet and hot and sticky. He was growling his passion, tupping her, swiving her, possessing her, his face dark and abandoned to the joy and the fury. He pushed more deeply into her. The head of his shaft bumped her womb, past the pain, and his fingers pinched her nub. Astounded, she felt her sheath contract around him, and then she was shuddering beneath him in a shaking, quaking release.

Relieved, she clung to him, her arms and legs boneless with pleasure and release. His shaft stayed deep inside her and hard, not flagging or drooping as her books said men's organs did. Gradually his breathing eased, and hers. Gradually their damp skins dried. A candle guttered and went out.

"You really do do this best," she whispered with a sigh of blissful contentment.

"God, Sophie, you are a randy little wench," he said, his growl low and approving at her ear. "Now you'll have to marry me."

Marry him. She struggled to sit up.

He pinned her with his strength. "Yes. Marry me, Sophie. You know it's the thing to do."

Anger overcame her lassitude. "I wouldn't mark the boys' Latin exercises in my present state," she said crisply. "I certainly won't agree to anything as complicated as marriage when I can barely walk."

He groaned. "What's so complicated about marriage? You say yes. I say I do. And everything I own is yours."

"You have a charming manner, my lord," she said ironically.

He glowered. "Of course I have a charming manner. I'm a bloody rake."

"Precisely my point."

He lifted his hand. "Bloodier than usual." It was covered with her virgin blood. He grinned with pure male pride of possession, scooped up his abandoned cravat, and wiped himself clean.

"Don't try to distract me, my lord."

"*Lion*—"

"Lionel," she said, exasperated. "And what are your reasons for proposing marriage this time, Lionel?"

"They're the same as they were before I left for Scotland."

"That's not good enough."

"Oh yes, and then there's this tupping business, which you seem to have quite an appetite and aptitude for."

Yesterday she would have blushed; tonight she swelled with satisfaction. "You are quite accomplished too."

He let her go to spread his hands. "Then marry me."

Regret twisted through her. She couldn't change her terms. He seemed incapable of meeting them. "We needn't marry to continue this."

"Bloody hell, Sophie. You'd be a mistress, a kept woman, no better than a common bawd. I think more highly of you than that."

"Just not enough to love me."

The glower was back, the growl. "Is that what this is about? Love? Romantic, ephemeral, circulating-library, trumpery-novel *love?*"

Her heart sank. She'd been right. He truly, simply did not understand. "Not exactly."

He prowled over to the fireplace, naked, his beautiful shaft still jutting in arousal, his temper flaring too. "Bloody hairsplitting, logic-chopping, bullheaded woman."

"You may think it's bullheaded of me to wait nineteen years for the love of my life to come home. But it's not splitting hairs if I refuse to marry a man who cannot say he loves me."

But his manhood loved her. It saluted her, dark and thick by candlelight and firelight, and that would do her wondrously well for now. She joined him by the fire, naked as the day she was born for the first time ever in the presence of a man, circled her fingers around his tireless shaft, and said, "Which shouldn't interfere with lovemaking. I believe we have some unfinished business. Although I might need some instruction."

With that, she dropped to her knees and took his shaft into her mouth. And with that daring and forbidden kiss, she enticed the earl of Wraxham to continue with her education.

The old earl's bawdy books had left much unexplained, Sophie thought euphorically the next evening after dinner. She slipped out of her old silk dress, more than ready to retire to bed. She'd barely slept last night. She'd drifted, once or twice, in Lionel's arms, but she couldn't call it sleeping, not with her heightened sense of his male skin and muscles and his long, strong bones, his deep, lazy breathing, the steady beat of his heart. And the readiness of his amazing manhood.

No, the books hadn't told her she would have such a sense of freedom, the way she'd floated through her day, filled with joy and energy, undaunted by the demands of boys, the distraction of meals, the mood of Celia. Who must have caught a case of the mopes from Graeme, Sophie thought, impervious to anyone else's unhappiness, in fact, slyly amused by everything in her day. In her life. Poor Celia, still a virgin, still untried, still unfulfilled. Of course she had the mopes. Perhaps, Sophie thought playfully, she could set her up with Lord Deveraux, or failing him, the handsome Mr. Carter.

The books hadn't described the delicious soreness, inside and out, that had followed Sophie through her day, reminding her at odd moments of the pleasures she had shared with Lionel, of pleasures she hoped would come. The skin of one elbow was abraded where he'd introduced her to an exotic, scandalous position on the rug in front of the library's fireplace with its little fire. That had been the third time. Or had it been the fourth? No matter.

She couldn't put *that* elbow on the table for a while.

Muscles she had never known existed ached, but the ache was deeply satisfying, reminding her that she was now a woman, no longer a maid, an old maid, a spinster.

She was freed into a new tyranny.

One night would never be enough.

She stretched her arms and slid off her tatty old silk dress, its still luxurious folds caressing her newly sensitive breasts and hips and belly like so many fingers. Lionel's fingers. Her fingers had caressed him too. While exploring his body, she'd discovered a patch of skin high inside his thigh behind the sacks that held his seed. There, the skin was silken, tender, secret.

No, her books hadn't come close to telling her everything, most especially this. Alone together, naked together, making love together, she and Lionel had become a world unto themselves, a private, intimate, revealing world known only to themselves.

She should sleep. She pulled on her night rail and her dressing gown, worrying. Should she go to his room? Would he come to hers? Did he expect to find her in the library? Oh, but, she thought, with that delirious inner smile that had followed her through the day, she couldn't wait for them to do it in a bed. Her bed, his bed, any bed in Wraxham House, that would suit just fine. *Every* bed in Wraxham House.

She giggled, feeling young and loved. Or rather lusted over. Lust was nice. Lust was wonderful, she thought with a pang. Lust was better than nothing.

But it still wasn't love.

She yawned. She was oh, so tired. Unwilling to crawl between the sheets—he might yet come!—she belted her dressing gown, curled up on the counterpane, and fell into the deepest sleep of her life.

She dreamed of Lionel, a long luxurious dream in which they were young again, sneaking out to meet in the fields between the rectory and Wraxham House. No one knew. They were secret lovers. He was not yet quite so tall as now. They lingered in the sun, dipped their toes into the waters of the millpond, sat by the riverbank, arguing over poetry. He was slimmer, fairer, sweeter. He lay beside her on its mossy bank, and told her that he loved her. He drew her into his arms, kissing her, embracing her, touching her in daring places he had never touched, holding her, and loving her until the sun began to set.

Sunset! Heaven help her, she was late! Her father would be frantic. Furious. She shot up and began to run for home, panicky dream-running, breathless and futile. Lionel pursued her to the kissing gate and trapped her there, pinning her in its iron fingers, her arms behind her back. She struggled to free herself from his cruel grasp, to slap his face for ruining her tender, erotic dream.

She couldn't move her hands. "Let go my hands," she screamed, but he had bound her mouth. She tried to kick, but he had bound her feet.

And then a muffled voice, not his, not one she could make out, muttered, "Up, up, Miss Bowerbank, get up. We're going on a little walk."

Chapter Twenty-five

But lo!—there's mischief in the wind . . .
—The Temple of Prostitution (1779?)

"M'lord?" asked a deep male voice.

Who? What? Lionel felt a heavy hand shake his shoulder rather harder than anyone ought to shake the shoulder of a former soldier and a peer of the realm.

"Beg pardon, m'lord, but you fell asleep. Hours ago."

Lionel opened an eye, annoyed and addled. And too groggy to move. He hadn't been this drunk in months. And where in hell had he gone drinking? And why? His head rested on his arms, which were folded on a crude stained table. Smoke veiled the room. A few men's voices droned. A woman laughed, the loose laugh of an easy virtue.

He pushed back from the table, and the room spun.

"M'lord, d'ye want a room upstairs? It's late."

How late, he didn't even want to know. He craned his head, neck creaking. Tobias Jolly, tavern keeper at the Wraxham Arms, peered down on him with a worried frown.

"Needed at home," Lionel muttered, his lips strangely uncooperative.

"Yes, m'lord, sorry to bother you, m'lord. But when Hill and Blevins fall out over the price of mutton, I always called Squire Upton. They've torn the place to flinders more than once."

"Not a problem," Lionel said. Had it been a problem? No, Jolly's call for help had come right after dinner. "Did they leave peaceably?"

"Hill and Blevins?" A smile split Jolly's broad face. "No harm done."

So why was Lionel still here? Why wasn't he at home, with Sophie in his arms?

No, no, Jolly had insisted. Stay, and have a beer.

Blast, he must have fallen asleep.

"I have to get back," Lionel said.

And urgently, he thought. His rusty warrior's instincts told him something was not right.

He crossed the tavern's worn board floor, carefully placing one unsteady foot before the other.

Something was not right with him.

He'd admit that he was tired. His amazing sleepless night with Sophie had given way to a relentlessly busy day. But still, nothing he hadn't done a hundred times. Except that he'd never had a night with Sophie. And spending that night, sensual, consuming, tender, with her changed everything . . . not that he was in any condition right now to examine what or how or why.

"D'ye want me to fetch a horse then, m'lord?" Jolly asked, following him to the door and down the steps.

"No, Jolly. Thank you." It wasn't a quarter mile to home, and his knee didn't hurt.

His knee didn't hurt? His knee always hurt.

He shook his head to clear his muddled brain, and started walking. A half moon and a spangle of stars gave an old soldier enough light to make his way.

Fiona Carr

Wraxham was a cozy, if not yet prosperous, village. Leaving the tavern, Lionel passed tidy cottages, the rectory, and the church, which faced the market square. The square had shops for cloth and trinkets, lace and meat, bread and sweets, tinware, saddlery, not that he patronized the local merchants. That would have to change. He made a mental note: All things are not made best in London. He could support his people here.

Market day had come and gone this week, so the square was empty save for its ancient cross, clock tower, and town stocks, unused in his brief term as magistrate.

He cut across the square. A muffled cry, high-pitched like a cat on the prowl, broke the late night silence. He looked around, dragging a hand across his face to clear his muzzy head.

Not a soul in sight. Not a creature. A night bird sang.

Then came another cry, lower than the first, but from the same direction, the moan of a creature in distress. A human creature.

What the devil? He focused on the sound. Twenty paces ahead, he could just make out the ancient stone uprights of the town stocks.

The uprights, and a figure doubled over between them.

Blast those idiots. Hill and Blevins must have taken their fight into the streets. The winner had clapped the loser in the stocks.

Lionel stalked across the cobbled surface of the square, blistering reprimands at the ready.

It wasn't Hill or Blevins. Dark thick hair streamed over a woman's shoulders and spilled forward over the stocks.

A woman. Young like Sophie. Dark like Sophie. In the stocks?

God have mercy, it was Sophie.

Head clearing, stomach churning, he broke into a run. He sank beside her, his heart hammering against his ribs.

Sophie—his lover, his mate, her arms lashed behind her back and her ankles shackled in the stocks.

Her body angled forward, pitching her forehead onto the upper yoke of the stocks. A blindfold and a gag flattened her hair to her skull. In the moonlight, her cruel bonds were white and luminous. Below them, her thick dark hair fanned her shoulders, limp in the damp night air. He could see her breathing, painfully.

Someone would pay for this, he vowed. Or die.

"Sophie, love, it's Lionel," he murmured and gently lifted up her bent body. She flopped back into his chest, her wrists bound behind her back. He pulled her shoulders to him, willing his body's heat to ease her pain and his strength soothe her fear. She smelled of lavender and the damp wool of her nightgown. Beneath the gag she moaned, a wrenching inarticulate sound, not a Sophie sound of reason and intelligence.

"Steady, love." He searched her body with his hands. Was she wounded too? "I'll have you free in moments."

But his fingers fumbled at the knot, a maliciously tight knot that added injury to insult. He'd have cut it with a knife, but he had only a watch and his bloody useless snuffbox.

Finally it yielded, and the gag swung free. The fabric was fine, like a lady's sash. Or a gentleman's neckcloth.

One of his neckcloths.

He couldn't be sure until he saw it in the light. But if it was his neckcloth, that ruled out outsiders and narrowed the perpetrators to only the thirty-seven people on his staff.

Or to his sons.

They couldn't. They wouldn't. No, someone else was after her. And if things had gone this far, not even his sons were safe. He jammed the neckcloth in a pocket, vowing not to say a word to Sophie in her present state. Or to anyone until he had some proof.

"Lionel? Where are . . . ?" She was sobbing, slurring her words. She couldn't complete her thought.

"Safe, love. Safe with me," he whispered.

But was she safe? And was she safe with him?

He wrapped an arm around her body, a hand around the crown of her head. She nestled into him, shuddering with cold. "But where . . . ?"

"In the village square, love."

Brought here by God knew who for God knew what purpose under heaven. He wanted to howl. He forced a calming tone.

"Someone locked you in the stocks. I found you as I was walking home." He kept talking, nonsense words, trying to reassure her, trying to break through her lethargy, still suspecting injury. "Hold on, Sophie. Blindfold next," he said, turning to the second knot. But it was hard to focus. It was hard to see. A tree blocked the bright moonlight, and just before the dawn the night had grown cold.

He picked at the cloth, his fingers slow and stupid. When its knot finally yielded, he pocketed the blindfold too. And turned to her.

Her eyes were half open, and her mouth half closed. The gag had been tied tight, as if she were a man, a criminal, a danger. "Sophie, love, I'm so sorry." He kissed her forehead, eyelids, and the corners of her wounded mouth gently, for she'd been hurt. Violated.

"Hmmm," she mumbled—*home*—but thickly, the way his mouth felt, the way his tongue felt. Dull. Drunk. Was Sophie drunk? Not off the wine he'd seen her drink at dinner. Her usual one glass—

Bloody hell. His blood chilled. "That's it," he said.

She craned her head at him. "That's what?"

What? She'd been drugged. He'd been drugged. He never fell asleep at tavern tables, not after only a couple of glasses of wine and an unfinished brandy. Jolly had had to wake him like a common drunkard.

He steadied her with both hands to her shoulders. "How do you feel, love? Can you tell me?"

"Strange . . . thick."

She sounded strange and thick, far away and inarticulate.

The way he felt. Bugger all. They had both been drugged.

"Let's get you up, and you'll feel better." But he hadn't freed her wrists.

The moon shed no light on the double knot that bound them. His fingers felt along the rough hemp rope. It had been wrapped around and around her wrists in a figure eight. He worked the double knot, trying not to tug too hard and do more damage to her wrists.

So much for speed, so much for his vaunted military experience. He was slower than a slug in a winter garden.

He winced. Every time he tugged the knot she moaned. He bit his lip, concentrating not to hurt her. Finally the knot loosened, and he unwound the rope.

Her arms flopped to her sides, limp, and she groaned in pain.

His heart twisted. She could have been here for hours, abducted from his home, stolen out from under his protection. Some protection. A rage he'd only known in battle swamped him. Tamping it back, he forced himself to massage her shoulders, checking them for injury. "Does this help?"

Her head bumped his chest in acknowledgment. He worked down her arms but she pulled away. "Wrists hurt."

Under the silver moonlight, they were splotched with blood and bruises. He bandaged each wrist with the neckcloths used to gag and blindfold her. Then he continued down her arm, massaging her fingers. "And this?"

"Fingers numb, they tied them too tight," she said, her voice gaining strength as she sat up and moved.

"Who tied them, love? Who brought you here?"

She shook her head against his chest. She didn't know.

"How many of them, do you think?"

She gave a shaky sigh. "Two, I think. Perhaps three."

Blackguards. Monsters. To do this to his Sophie.

The one person in his life who had never let him down.

For aching long moments, he rocked her to his body, her head resting in the bend of his neck. If Jolly hadn't summoned him for help, he'd have been sleeping soundly in his bed, oblivious of her peril.

"Can you sit now on your own?"

She nodded beneath his chin.

"That's my brave love," he said, his throat closing with pride. She had courage, she had heart. "I'll get those stocks off. Hold on."

The stocks backed up to a stone wall. He went round the front to remove the wooden pin from the hasp. It was jammed into the staple, stuck fast. Whoever brought her here meant for her to be here when the village woke. Neighbors would have found her. Friends. Or gossips. Or vagrants.

Outrage pumped through him. He clawed at the stone wall behind her, barking his knuckles against jagged flint. A stone came loose. He knelt before the stocks and hammered at the wooden pin. The old iron hinge clanged beneath his blows, at odds with the early morning strains of countless birds. His Sophie had been abducted from under his own roof.

He had not been there for her.

The pin popped free. The rusty hinge squeaked as he lifted the top yoke of the weather-beaten old oak stock. Grunting, he hoisted it and set it aside.

"Sophie, you're free," he said softly.

She didn't move her legs.

She had shapely legs, trim ankles. Last night they'd aroused him. Everything about her had aroused him. Tonight he could only rage at the sight of her lovely limbs restrained, at her brutal treatment.

"Let me help you." Carefully he freed her legs and helped her flex her knees.

She groaned. He felt her pain in his bones.

"We need to get you home," he said hoarsely, putting his arms around her body to help her up.

"I can stand," she protested, but crumpled with a cry, grabbing him for balance. "Legs numb, sorry," she gasped.

His gut clenched. He should have taken Jolly's horse, but

no. With his wretched knee, it would be harder to manage both the horse and Sophie. He slid his arms under hers and lifted her, aware as he stood of a lavender ribbon of daylight marking the eastern sky. He could see her face now, strained with pain and dull with, what? Fatigue? Fear? The lateness of the hour?

It must be almost four. Birds sang in cheerful earnest from treetops, meadows, and rooftops of the town. Villagers would soon be up and about their morning business. He could best shield her from their sight if he took her home by the footpath between the rectory and Wraxham House.

He swept her into his arms. He wanted to carry her, marry her, protect her with his power, his name, his life.

"Your knee," Sophie murmured, twisting from him.

He set her down. She bent over, her hands on her knees, and then stretched up, groaning and shivering.

Her groan did him in. Her shiver made him strip off his coat and drape it over her shoulders. "To the devil with my knee," he grated. "I'm carrying you home."

"No, the walk will do me good," she insisted, her spirit returning but her words still slurred. They must have drunk the same drugged wine at dinner. But he was larger and more used to spirits, if not to . . . what? Laudanum, he guessed. Mrs. Plumridge kept the household medicines under lock and key. But it was no secret where the keys were kept.

Slowly, arm in arm, they started down the cobbled street of town, him limping, her wobbly but determined under the gradually lightening sky.

The last stars winked out of sight, and the flat white plate of a moon was setting. It was a new day, and the most troubling set of questions yet.

Lionel had rescued her. He'd come out of the night, and found her, and rescued her from pain and public humiliation. Sophie wrapped her arm around Lionel's waist for balance and security. His waistcoat warmed her and its smell of scented soap

295

and Lionel comforted her. The sun was rising and birds were singing and her head was clearing and she was walking through the morning damps alone with Lionel, the only man she'd ever loved, her lover.

Sweet summer fragrances wafted over the gentle downs. The footpath wound across the sheep pasture toward the kissing gate. A lamb bleated for its mother, and a ewe baaed back. Lionel opened the gate, and she stepped into its ensnaring fingers, overcome to be here with him again now that they were lovers. Truly lovers. Twenty years had passed, and not a day. Nothing had changed of her feelings for him, and everything. He folded her in his embrace, and she felt that she'd come home.

He kissed her mouth tenderly, as if she might break. She cupped his face, his beloved face, his real face a hand's breadth away, not the face she'd imagined in her fantasies. She loved the manly feel of his square bristled jaw beneath her palms. She loved his chiseled features shadowed in the pearly morning light. She loved him. And in this moment, it didn't matter that he had never said that he loved her.

"You are still so beautiful to me," she murmured, her words coming easier.

His face softened in surprise. "Ah, Sophie," he said.

"We never met at dawn." Speaking was getting easier, but her thoughts jumped about.

"We would have, if I could have found a way," he said.

"I was so astonished that you noticed me."

"How could I not notice you? You were—"

"Awkward, bookish."

He brushed hair from her brow. "You were beautiful and smart."

"You'd been away to school, to the university, to London."

"I was happier here."

"I was a green girl, the rector's daughter, who just loved books. And you. I loved you. I still do."

He looked at her in the dawn light, his gray eyes warm.

"God, Sophie. You make me so happy. If only I had—"

"No *if onlys.*" She put cold clumsy fingers to his mouth. "We were foolish."

"You may have been foolish. I was a bloody reprobate."

"A bloody thief. Thief of my heart," she said, with no reproach. But there was something she had to tell him, something nagging at the edge of her mind.

"Then marry me, Sophie," he said, brushing her lips with all the respect and tenderness any woman could hope for from a lover. From a husband.

But still. "You don't have to offer because we're lovers now," she said.

"This isn't about last night. I can best protect you as my wife with the weight of my name, the resources of my estate, and my own vigilance behind you."

Her head spun. Could that be true? "I was safe before," she argued, but she couldn't have been or else she wouldn't have been abducted. Oh, her head was still so muddled.

"You were alone and vulnerable. Don't refuse me, Sophie. Don't deny yourself. You have such passion to share. Share it with me." He was golden in the early light, and as earnest as the boy she'd loved, no sign of the London rake or the cynical lord.

And she was tempted, tempted.

Why had she been so stubborn?

Ah, love. She'd wanted him to love her. Which was better? Love or lust? Safety or risk? But hadn't she thought it a risk to live without his love? Or a risk to live without him? She shook her head. Logic failed her. It was all too complicated.

"Mrs. Plumridge can move your clothes into my chamber," he went on. "Your father can arrange for a special license. And I will find the villains who did this to you and put *them* in the stocks—for a week, a month, a year."

She didn't care about the men who'd taken her. She only cared for him. What if she'd been wrong?

After all, her bawdy books had told only partial truths about the art of making love. What if all the other books had misled her about love?

"I need your love," he pressed on. "My children need you. Sophie." He kissed her brow, her cheeks, her chin. "Sophie. Think about it."

And she—she could give him that love, him and his sons and the children that would surely come.

"I'm thinking about it."

Chapter Twenty-six

Teach me at once to Love, and Guard my Heart.
        —The Ladies Choice (1702)

Dong. Dong. Da-dong, dong, dong. The bells of St. Philips pealed, and Sophie moaned and stirred beneath her covers.

Was it Sunday already?

Heavens, she had to get up and fix her father's breakfast before church services. But her head pounded, and her stomach roiled, and she was oh, so tired.

She opened bleary eyes to a palette of rich dark colors.

Colors? Her bedchamber in the rectory was sunny, cramped but white. These walls were covered in forest-green silk. An oil painting of horses ready for a hunt hung opposite her bed. Sporting horses, in her room? Oh yes, the Stubbs.

She was in Lionel's guest room, her chamber at Wraxham House. She drew up her hands to throw off her covers, and pain seared her. She held up her arms, the loose sleeves of her night rail sliding to her elbows. Bruises and abrasions circled both wrists.

Last night came shuddering back. She'd awakened in the stocks, bent and bound and abandoned. Lionel had freed her and helped her home in a slow, painful walk. For safety he'd insisted on her sleeping in his suite.

She wasn't sure she'd ever feel safe again.

But for the boys' sake, she'd refused to stay with Lionel. She'd slept alone. She must have dropped off from the drug and slept into midmorning. The sun was climbing in the sky. St. Philips's bells pealed on, her head throbbing as they clanged.

She dragged herself to her ewer and basin to wash up. The ewer sat on a spindly-legged table by the window. Her books still lined its sill where she'd unpacked them, hoping to make a difference here.

Crumpled beside the basin lay long narrow neckcloths, starched and splotched with rusty bloodstains. Her blood. She shivered. After Lionel had untied her, he'd bandaged her bleeding wrists with the selfsame cloths that had gagged and blindfolded her.

She shook them out in the quiet morning light, and they unfurled like banners. They were as fine as the linen neckcloths Lionel had shed for her in the library the other night. She ran her fingers along the length of the cloths.

One end bore the Wraxham crest, discreetly embroidered in white.

Her hands started to shake.

What were her abductors doing with Lionel's neckcloths?

Steadying herself, she poured water into the basin, wet a muslin washcloth, and scrubbed the touch of strangers from her body. She put on the dress with the longest sleeves to cover her battered wrists and went downstairs, too sick to be hungry, too weak not to eat.

In the breakfast room, Laframboise had provided enough food for a houseful of weekend guests. Lionel's sons, handsomely turned out for Sunday services, hovered over it.

"Good morning, Miss Bowerbank," Simon chirped. His scarlet velveteen stretcher deepened his rosy cheeks and set off his chocolate eyes.

"My, you're handsome this morning," she said, past her aches and pains.

"Are you coming with us to chapel?" asked Max.

"Yes, of course, dear, just like last week, and the week before," she said with a smile. But the corners of her mouth cracked where the gag had chafed the skin, and Max's platter of sausages and eggs made her stomach queasy.

Tea and toast might help. She looked about for some. But she really wanted to go back to bed and press cool cloths to her spinning head.

What had they done to her last night?

And who were *they*?

Alex's towhead hovered over a tray of hot-cross buns and pastries dripping with sugary icings. She should insist that he eat hearty food, but her head ached too much to make the effort. She poured a cup of tea, put two dried crusts on her saucer, and sat at the long mahogany dining table.

Graeme angled up alongside her, gaunt and haggard. "Miss Bowerbank?" he said, his tone as gentle as his father's at the stocks last night. "Are you quite all right?"

No, her mouth was dry, her wrists burned, and every muscle in her body ached.

"I'll be fine, thank you, Graeme," she said.

Last night she and Lionel had disagreed on major matters—whether she should stay in his rooms, whether they should marry. But they'd agreed not to disturb the boys with word of her abduction.

"Good then," Graeme said. "Father had a bit of business with Carter, but I'll escort you to services if you'd like. We have . . ." He glanced at the clock on the mantle. ". . . Only a quarter hour—"

In swept James and Marcus, bumping shoulders and wrangling.

"I didn't ruin the last one, you did," Marcus said.

"If you hadn't tried the hardest styles, you wouldn't have had to tie so many knots, and you wouldn't have ruined the others," James said, heading for the sausages.

Sophie blinked. What knots? What others?

Graeme walked up with eldest brother authority and inspected the white cravats tangled around their necks. "You're a little young for Mailcoaches and Mathematicals, Marc, whichever one this wretched mishmash is supposed to be," he said.

"We're just practicing," Marcus protested, snagging two plump hot-cross buns and a couple of bursting sausages.

"And, Jem," Graeme went on, "that Ballroom knot has no place on a boy in St. Philips on a Sunday morning."

Sophie's hand began to tremble, her fine china cup rattling on its fine china saucer. Neckcloths, cruel, awful neckcloths. Her tongue could almost taste the starched flax that had gagged her last night. Her eyes almost itched from the stiff linen blindfold. Not even Lionel's gentle touch had banished her horror, waking in the dark, unable to see or speak or move.

She set down her cup and saucer and forced herself to take a last bite of crust and a sip of tea.

She must collect herself. She was just overwrought. A nice quiet ride to the church followed by her father's droning sermon had to help her put last night's misery behind her.

"Wait for Papa," Simon cried when the Wraxham family carriage pulled up under the portico.

Graeme handed Sophie in to the massive black-crested coach. "Father will meet us at the chapel, Simon. No pushing, Jem," he cautioned as his brothers clambered in behind them, rowdy as a litter of pups. Large and rowdy pups, tumbling over one another, yet carefully managing not to bumble into her. Still, Sophie groaned.

Her hope for a nice quiet outing was dashed.

"Here, Max and Alex, sit by me," she said, patting the padded velvet bench for the twins to take places next to her.

Graeme swung a wriggling Simon up and held him on his lap. James and Marcus, all knees, elbows, and large feet, settled beside Graeme, large and awkward under Sophie's regard.

The coach lurched off, six matched blacks drawing six Wraxham scions at a stately trot past the sheep pasture. Sophie squinted. In the distance, the kissing gate tucked into a dip in the downs. Last night the footpath leading to it had been dark, damp, and narrow. Last night within the gate, addled from the drug, she'd told Lionel she loved him.

The twins crowded their heads out the window opposite to count black sheep.

"I got the first one," cried Alex.

"That one's not black. He's gray," Max said.

"Gray *is* black, you nodcock, and *he's* probably a *she*," Alex argued.

Graeme rolled his eyes at Sophie, then said, "No bickering, lads. We're off to chapel, and you will be on your best behavior, with Father here or not."

Simon poked his big brother. "They'd get a lot more sheep if they counted white ones."

Max and Alex hooted, and Graeme laughed.

Across from her, James and Marcus whispered, plotting or sharing secrets or planning an afternoon of games on the east lawn—who knew?

When James noticed she was watching, his gaze slid away.

The coach jounced over ruts in the lane and cobbles in the village square. It rumbled past the stocks. They looked large and cold and cruel. Sophie dug her fingers into the upholstered cushions and closed her eyes. Dizziness returned. She looked up at the lads to steady herself and pressed her head against the velvet squab. She would not give in to fear. She would fight her wooziness from last night's drugs.

When the carriage drew up at St. Philips, the boys put on their dignity and moved with her into the sanctuary like a well-shepherded flock of lambs. They filed into the family pew at the front of the sanctuary, Graeme first and Marcus last, the

303

two eldest flanking their younger brothers. They scooted close together to make room for Sophie and their missing father.

She heard Lionel's confident, quick stride behind her. He slid in beside her, smelling of expensive soap and country air, as he'd smelled last night when he'd rescued her, and the night before when he'd freed her from that older burden, her virginity.

Her stomach dipped. His large body swamped her senses, and his energy charged the air around her. But his chiseled profile stared straight ahead. For a moment she was crushed, but he was keeping a proper distance in a public venue. She had to approve.

In the pulpit, her father opened his psalter and began. She knelt when everyone else did, repeated prayers with the congregation, and tried to sing. But the gag had hurt her mouth, and it was so sweet to hear the younger boys' alto and soprano voices, the older boys' harmonious new ranges, and their father's rich baritone.

So sweet to be surrounded by so much maleness, by so many reflections of Lionel. For the boys were awfully like their father, each in his different way. Graeme had Lionel's earnest idealism that had first stolen Sophie's heart. James and Marcus had his fire that had captured her imagination. The twins had his sense of mischief that once made her laugh, and Simon had . . . There might be something dark in Simon, but Simon had his father's gentleness that had tended to her wounds.

Goodness. She'd fallen in love with them, each and every one, hadn't she?

Even James's and Marcus's clumsily retied neckcloths tugged at her heart. James had gone for a simple Napoleon that crisscrossed his neck without a knot. Marcus had tied a jaunty bow, at odds with his military bearing, but in line with his high spirits. Its ends spilled over the lapels of his dark blue coat.

Heavens, she thought as the hymn ended, she was immersed in the Westfall men, and loving it. Absentmindedly she returned her hymnal to its rack but fumbled. It dropped to the floor. Oooh, she was such a ninny. She'd pick it up next time she knelt.

"Marcus, see to that book," Lionel whispered above her head.

With a grimace, Marcus swooped it up and turned to her, his white bow flashing in her face.

The crest on his white bow flashing in her face.

Sophie's father began the homily, and she sat, her heart thudding. She'd never noticed crests on Graeme's neckcloths, so why did Marcus's neckcloth have them? Could he have been involved last night?

Perhaps. The strapping lad beside her sat rigid and apart as if to touch her would be poison.

Her mind raced. Marcus already had his father's height, and was as strong as a man, he and his brothers galloping tirelessly up and down the east lawn for hours at a time. Did that make him strong enough to drag a drugged woman a quarter of a mile?

Her stomach roiled. And James, was he involved? Fresh from leading a revolt at school, the two boys had the will, and they had reasons. They hadn't taken to her. They'd whispered in her presence and averted their eyes when she looked their way, a replacement they didn't want for the mother they still missed.

Up in the pulpit, her father droned on in his reassuring way. She was not reassured. It wouldn't have taken them much planning. A little laudanum from Mrs. Plumridge's medicine chest, a few neckcloths from their father's wardrobe, and the odd piece of rope from Wraxham's stables—that would have done the trick. Amassing that paraphernalia of crime would have been a drop in the bucket for two lads who'd stolen keys, commandeered weapons from their school's armory, and besieged its entire faculty. And yet . . .

Frantic, she sorted through the familiar speculations: Tims, Beane, Carter, Nesbit, even Laframboise. Tims and Beane,

Beane and Carter, but she couldn't imagine a partner for the sullen cook, and it was impossible to imagine a woman having any part of this.

Still this time, it had to be someone—some ones—from the staff, and she couldn't rule out the boys.

Lionel would be crushed. She loved him for his dream of uniting his sons behind him. She'd had high hopes of helping him realize his admirable goal. To her dismay, she'd become the stimulus for mayhem that threatened to tear his family apart. It was bad enough if James and Marcus had turned against her. It would be hard to turn away from the younger boys. It was terrible to ruin Lionel's dream of bonding with his sons.

Her feelings for him, even her feelings for the boys, didn't mean a thing: His sons' abhorrence was a dire prelude for marriage, a disastrous start for a new family.

Her heart twisted in her chest. Sharing her suspicions with Lionel wouldn't fix a thing, either way. What if she was wrong? And if she was right . . . what could she do, but leave?

Pews creaked, boots clicked, and fabric rustled. Her father gave the benediction, and his parishioners rose. Tall and elegant beside her, Lionel touched her elbow before he turned away to answer a tenant's petition. She blinked back bitter tears. She would go home now, make a quick, clean break, give no excuses, offer no explanations, allow no recriminations.

The Misses Gatewood were overjoyed to see her, slowing her progress down the aisle. At the church steps, she caught up to Lionel speaking to Lady Upton in soft, considerate tones. Squire Upton was doing better, would resume his post as magistrate in a few short weeks. Casting a disapproving look at Sophie, Lady Upton marshaled her daughters, save the eldest, into a ladylike landau.

Lionel gave Sophie with a private smile, the smile that had first won her in the kissing gate. Her heart shifted in her chest, and broke. But she lifted her chin and said firmly, "I find I must return to my father, my lord."

A shadow of confusion crossed his face. But because they were in public, surrounded by his staff, her neighbors, and her father's parishioners, he said formally as she had done, "Of course, Miss Bowerbank. I'm sure you have arrangements to make."

She swallowed hard. "I'll send a note for Celia to pack my things and send them on."

"That's just as well," he said, as determinedly as she. "You will be getting a new wardrobe."

No, she wouldn't be getting anything, not a new wardrobe, not a new family, not a marriage to the love of her life. But her courage, which had shored her up for weeks of tests and trials and challenges, failed, and she could only say, "Good-bye, my lord," and quickly leave before her resolve crumbled.

"Beg pardon, my lord," said Tims from behind his desk when Lionel entered the office. "I was just copying correspondence into my letterbook."

Lionel sharpened the nib of his hawk's-feather quill, worrying.

Tims scribbled furiously. "Don't let me stop you, my lord."

"No," Lionel said.

Tims couldn't stop him but Sophie had. She may have faced last night's ordeal with a courage that touched his heart and made him proud. But during her father's homily this morning, her demeanor had changed from exhausted to stricken. He hadn't wanted to let her out of his sight, but perhaps a visit with her father would do her good.

She must need time for rest and for reflection.

From his own battles, he understood aftermath.

He planned a visit too.

"I thought I saw Carter leave this morning, my lord," Tims added.

"He did."

"Anything I need to take care of in his absence, my lord?"

"No, Tims, nothing," he said, scrabbling about for a note.

For Lionel was putting things in order. Bowerbank's inquiries about Graeme's Glencora had verified everything his son had said, and more. The lass was orphaned and needed a respectable asylum, which the Misses Gatewood were delighted to provide. She was also bright and needed a position, just as Bowerbank needed someone in Sophie's place. Lionel had just this morning resolved both matters, and sent Carter with Mrs. Plumridge to bring Glencora to the rectory.

"Lord Cordrey seems to have settled in, my lord. Masters James and Marcus are quite well, I trust."

"All well, Tims. All well."

He'd shanghaied one of his brothers into taking Graeme under his wing as an aide in the Home Office in London. Lionel had hopes of placing James and Marcus at Winchester School near home for Michaelmas term in the fall. And he'd conferred with Maitland Maddox on Simon's condition. Maddox had given Sophie's commonsense handling of Simon's terrors a ringing endorsement.

With his sons taken care of, Lionel had only to secure Bowerbank's permission—and a special license—to marry Sophie.

All well, all well.

He smoothed the sheet of paper, dipped his pen in ink, and wrote.

Sophie's heart was broken. No, it was breaking over and over again. Else why would leaving Lionel hurt so much?

She was sitting with her father after dinner in his book-lined parlor in the rectory. It was a mild June evening, and a mild June breeze whispered through the open window, making the lace curtains flutter like lazy butterflies.

Her life was back to where it had always been. Almost.

"I must respond to His Lordship's request, Sophia," her father said, tapping a folded letter of finest linen stock on his desk.

Sophie had been in an exhausted, miserable sleep when Lionel had dropped off a note in the afternoon.

Her father flipped it open now and handed it to her. On its top margin was the Wraxham crest, the crest embroidered on his neckerchiefs, here engraved in burnished gold.

Lionel's tall scrawl covered the entire sheet.

My good sir, At your earliest convenience, kindly arrange a special license for me to marry your daughter.

W.

We have every reason for haste.

Sophie's face flamed. Lionel had as much as told her father that he'd breached her. She'd told her father she'd come home to stay.

"Burn it," she said, flinging her hand toward the little grate. Her eyes stung with tears of misery and vexation. She'd left Lionel, and couldn't tell her father why.

Her father peered over his spectacles, his pale blue eyes solemn. "You might not be so fortunate this time, my dear."

"I was not fortunate then," she said. "I could not possibly have been with child that summer."

"Could you now?"

Yes. No. "I am no longer young."

"Sophia," her father said gently, "women of your age quite often have children."

"Not their first," she said desperately.

"I have seen such come to pass," he said. "So . . . what am I to do with Lord Wraxham's request?"

"Burn it. He is not in his right mind."

Her father chuckled. "No indeed, he is not. The man who brought this request had the resolve and urgency one expects of a besotted youth."

Besotted? Her breath hitched in her throat. Graeme had said so too, and he knew his father better. But no, she must think of those boys. Think how much they needed him. Think how much damage she had done with James and Marcus.

She must think for Lionel as well.

"His Lordship may appear besotted, but he denies that he loves me."

"Ah, love." Her father paused in philosophical mode. "Life's great mystery, without which we are as sounding brass of a tinkling cymbal."

She braced for a sermon. "I came home to stay. Don't you want me here?"

"Sophia, darling, you have been the light of my life, and more so, since your mother died. You're respected in the village, endlessly helpful to me, and indispensable to my parishioners. I couldn't be more proud. With me, you live a good and useful life. But you could have more."

"Everything I need is here."

"But my passions are not yours, daughter. If they were, I would welcome you back with open arms. But when Lord Cordrey left years ago—I see this now—your passion left, so you adopted mine. But, tell me, are my passions truly yours?"

"Papa, your work engages me."

He sat beside her on the worn couch where he had counseled so many over the years and took her hand in his ink-stained, bony one. "I was wrong. But you were so young, I didn't realize that he would be the only one for you."

"Which cannot matter, Papa, as he no longer believes in love."

"Sophia, the man offers you status, security, luxury, and the respect of everyone."

And erotic pleasures beyond her wildest fantasies, she added secretly. But she put those behind her now. Again.

"Haven't your weeks in that house given you a sense of everything you would gain?"

Or everything she might lose. For she couldn't imagine that Lionel's lust for her would grow into love. He'd lived a London life. He'd known peeresses, literary ladies, diamonds of the first water, actresses of renown, even apparently the most desirable ladies of the night. If he didn't start their marriage in love with the woman Sophie had become—bold, bookish, and argumentative—what would the years bring?

Indifference at best, and infidelity. And no fantasies in her books or her imagination could protect her from that.

And what good would she be then to his sons—if she could overcome their antipathy for her—or the children she and Lionel would surely have?

Darkness had settled on the downs, and her father started closing up the house as he'd done every night of every year of her long-drawn-out spinsterhood. He shut windows with satisfying thunks, banked the fire and made the embers crackle, snuffed out candles with a puff of breath.

Her simple life with him was rich with domestic pleasures and timeless ideas. Before Lionel Westfall had come back home, she'd been happy with that. She could be happy again. She had willpower and resources. She had good friends, good books to read, good deeds to do, and a dear, kind father to take care of.

Alone in her room, she gave way to silent racking sobs, tears burning down her cheeks. Long days and lonely nights of fantasies came down to this. Her father would always need her dutiful presence.

Lionel could replace her, and he should.

But it was so quiet here. How had she not noticed the dull silence of the rectory? No shrieks and whoops and galloping feet racing up and down the lawns. No riotous laughter to join in on. No heartbroken tears to wipe away. Not only would she never be with Lionel, she'd never be with the boys, never be able to comfort or console them or congratulate them or watch them grow into fine upstanding men.

She changed into her nightclothes and crawled into bed. Her back ached. Her blistered feet stung. Her wrists and ankles hurt from last night's misadventure.

But the gaping hole in her heart was not from her aches and injuries. Nor was it about losing Lionel, her lover. Loving him

311

had opened her body and her soul to ecstasy, but loving his sons had opened her heart to joy, to a new world of great risk and great fulfillment.

That was the love that she'd been seeking, the love she had to give.

She had had no choice but to walk away.

Sleep would not come easily if it came at all.

Little wonder that some hours later she sat up with a jolt when a carriage clattered to a halt outside the rectory. She drew the curtain back to look, and her stomach dropped.

It was Lionel's coach, come to fetch her in the dark.

Something must be terribly wrong for him to come for her at night. Should she go?

No, she'd barely decided to leave, barely dried her tears.

But what if it was Simon or the twins?

She could not turn her back on them. She threw on an old day dress and raced down the stairs, heart in her throat. *Hurry, hurry, hurry.* If he knocked before she got there, it would wake her father.

Chapter Twenty-seven

'Tis lovly Woman makes the Souldier fight . . .
—An Answer to The Pleasures of a Single Life (1701)

Lionel swirled brandy in a snifter by the low glow of a dying fire. Not that the weather called for it, but the warmth in his life had just gone out. After Bowerbank's homily, he'd found Celia Upton packing Sophie's battered trunk. She'd quickly informed him that Sophie had no plans of coming back.

He'd been stunned. What had gone wrong? Only last night in the kissing gate, Sophie had all but said she'd marry him. This morning in the chapel, desire had pulsed between them. Her leaving made no sense. Sophie wasn't like other women, fickle and capricious.

Tomorrow he would go to her, and they would have it out.

He flipped another page in one of Sophie's erotic books, trying to fathom her. Voracious scholar that she was, he'd bet she'd read every line—from *twining arms*, to *limbs by grateful Venus yoak'd*, to *panting breasts* and *gentle bites* and *thousand wanton Kisses sporting*. Tantalizing thoughts. He wanted that

313

Sophie back, in his arms and in his bed. And she had wanted him. Damn it, what had gone wrong?

A delicate rapping at the library's door should have warned him: No such luck tonight. Celia Upton streamed in, in dishabille of whispery tulle and expensive lace. Her dressing gown was yards above her station, but her flutter of distress seemed real enough. Ha, he thought, who would chaperone the chaperone until her charge returned?

"My lord, your son has taken one of his fits. The smelling salts aren't working."

"Salts!" Lionel exploded. He'd put the child to bed and left him drifting peacefully. "Who in hell ordered salts? We're trying to calm the child, not make him worse."

Celia frowned. "Of course, my lord."

He plunged into the unlit hall. The old pendulum clock chimed the hour. Midnight. Simon's terrors were right on time.

And Sophie was not here.

Simon's room was in chaos. Candles glared from every sconce and chamberstick, footmen splashed buckets of cold water into Simon's copper tub, and Nesbit pinned him down.

Simon thrashed and moaned, besieged by monsters in his head and on his bed.

Celia Upton watched and wrung her hands.

Lionel fought his old urge to run, to cover his ears, to strap down his son and muffle cries as awful as the cries of men in battle, as horrifying as the screams from the surgeon's tent.

Lionel charged the nurse and lifted her bodily off his son.

Blood spurted in his face. "What the devil!" He staggered back, stripped the cravat from his neck and wiped his eyes, and stepped up to see. A quill stent stuck out of the large purple vein at Simon's elbow. A small bowl of his son's blood spilled onto the sheets.

Rage streaked down Lionel's back. He towered over Simon's nurse. "No one gave you leave to bleed my son. Ever."

Scarlet-faced, Nesbit blubbered. "I—she—we tried the salts, my lord, but they—"

314

"We *never* use salts, and as to bleeding— By heaven, woman, he's just a little boy. You are dismissed," Lionel spat out, turning to his writhing son.

God. Blood oozed down his thin arm.

Lionel stripped off his neckcloth and made a hasty tourniquet above the puncture in the vein. His mind just registered that the old nurse fled, the floorboards shaking from her weight.

In moments, he staunched the flow of blood and turned on the dumbstruck footmen. "Get out. Take those buckets with that cold water, and get out."

They bowed and ran, water splashing, doors slamming.

For a moment, everything was quiet, except for Simon's tortured writhing. "What can I do to help, my lord?" a chastened Celia Upton asked.

"Fetch Graeme," Lionel said, not bothering with courtesy. "His room is two doors down. Take a taper. Do not wake the twins."

Graeme burst in in his nightshirt, sank to his knees beside the bed, and gasped at his brother's blood. "What the—"

"Bring me pen and paper, son."

He was back in seconds. Lionel scribbled two quick notes.

"Go to the stables, get yourself a horse, and have them harness a coach. On your way out, rouse Carter to take the coach to the rectory with this note for Miss Bowerbank. You deliver the other note to Maddox, wherever he may be."

"Carter's gone to Oxford, sir," Graeme reminded him.

"Then summon Beane, or any able body who can drive a coach, for Miss Bowerbank."

Graeme left, and Celia Upton fluttered at the edges of Lionel's vision like an annoying midge. "Can I do anything else, my lord?"

He blew out a breath of exasperation. "Yes, Miss Upton, you can leave us to ourselves."

"But, my lord—" she protested.

"That will be all, Miss Upton," he said, not looking up.

Her slippers whispered across the floor, leaving him alone with Simon's broken sobs.

Lionel braced himself for a struggle, more with himself than Simon. This time he would stay with his son, no matter what the cost. Never again could he leave matters up to others. Never again would he hope someone else knew best and turn his head.

He loosened Simon's tourniquet. The bleeding had stopped, and he pulled his son onto his lap. Simon spasmed, and Lionel fought bitter bile rising in his gorge. For the boy's sobs drummed in his ears, his screams the cries of midnight battles, men with gaping injuries, dying agonizing deaths, dying in Lionel's arms. Cold sweat poured down his chest, pooled in the small of his back.

This was why he'd allowed Penelope's Draconian measures, why he'd tolerated Fotherington's regimen, why he needed Sophie so. Simon's little body pitched against him, his chest wracked with sobs and fiendish moans. Yet always afterward, Lionel told himself desperately, his son had been fine, pale, and hoarse, but a gentle little boy. And with Sophie's nurturing, a happy child had emerged.

Lionel held him through another struggle, absorbing its full force into his body. Simon hadn't had his terrors in weeks, a relief, a happenstance Lionel attributed fully to Sophie.

This attack could be attributed to her too, it struck him forcibly, because Simon had lost his trusted tutor.

And what the devil was taking Beane so long? It wasn't as if he'd had to harness the team himself. A quarter hour to the rectory, a quarter hour for Sophie to wake and dress, a quarter hour to drive her back.

She could have refused to come, and might have done, if Celia Upton told the truth. Not that he wanted to credit anything that woman had to say. But Beane, Beane was reliable. Beane would come back with a note.

From the hall, a clock chimed half after one. Sophie should have been here half an hour ago. If she was coming. He couldn't blame her if she stayed home after what she'd been through on his behalf. But would she have given up on Simon? No, the Sophie he loved would never have given up on the boy.

The Sophie he loved.

Bloody hell.

He loved Sophie.

The words burned his mind like warm brandy on the tongue.

Love. Not with that romantic, ephemeral, circulating-library, trumpery-novel kind of love. And not with his rakehell rutting obsession with her body either, although he couldn't help loving the body and the mind of a woman who read erotic books.

More than that, deeper than that, he loved the Sophie he'd found in this room, the Sophie whose arms had embraced his troubled son, the Sophie who'd taught his twins to build a city, the Sophie who thought his eldest wrote better poetry than he had written.

The Sophie who remembered his poetry, poetry written to her. When he'd been young and still had plans and dreams.

He stroked the crown of Simon's head as he'd seen her do in loving comfort. She'd taught him this, he realized as Simon's thrashing gradually eased, his cries turning into whimpers. And for the first time, Lionel held his son, the wrenching, gagging memories of war fading from his mind.

His own pulse slowed, and his heart squeezed with tenderness for Simon, and relief. He loved this child, his heart and flesh and bone. And to his amazement, he'd finally helped him, simply by holding him. He'd comforted and saved him.

He alone, Simon's father.

His exhausted brain registered a stir in the hall, and Maddox swooped in, crowlike and efficient, Graeme close behind. But not a sign of Sophie. So be it. She would come shortly, or he would deal with her recalcitrance tomorrow.

All business, no apologies, Maddox stepped up immediately

and scowled at the wound on Simon's arm. "I cannot recommend bleeding for a child, my lord."

"His nurse has been dismissed."

Maddox nodded a brief approval and put a hand to Simon's forehead, the other to his wrist. "Just as I thought. Miss B. was right about the lad. The simpler our response, the better."

Then he raised a winged black brow at Lionel. "Whereas you, my lord, look like a carriage wreck."

Lionel shrugged. He didn't remember when he'd closed his eyes. "Nothing a night's sleep won't cure."

"And a brandy? Lord Cordrey, how about a brandy for your father? Ah, and one for your amiable and ever-available country doctor. I shall sit awhile and observe our patients."

Later, after Maddox had finished his brandy and Graeme trudged back to bed, Lionel sat in silence. Sophie had never come, evidently thinking they had not needed her.

Which did not bode well for his proposal.

Or for his sons.

Or for his newly discovered love.

Sophie's arm went numb from rapping her shoe on the ceiling of the brougham, a sleek comfortable little coach that was now her prison. She dropped the shoe, massaged her arm back to life, and rapped the shoe again. Nothing, futile.

Fear trickled through her frustration, but what else could she do? Hours had passed since Barnaby Tims had pulled up to the rectory door and handed her Lionel's hasty note.

> Simon is worse than ever. Will you kindly come and comfort him? Yrs, W.

Yours, Wraxham?

Half tender, half remote. She pressed her lips together in vexation. But of course she'd come help Simon.

Innocently, stupidly she'd stepped into the brougham for Tims to drive her back to Lionel's. Except that they'd rolled past the golden pillars that marked the entrance to Wraxham House. She'd pulled down the window, and yelled up to the driver's box. There must be some mistake.

"You missed our turn! Our turn was just back there!"

Tims sped up, and she'd leaned out the window. Mercy, he was going fast. Too fast. She'd sat back on the posh leather cushions of Lionel's sporting little coach, incredulous.

She'd been abducted, good and properly. Tricked, hoodwinked, duped. She'd been a fool to blame James and Marcus, an idiot to leave the safety Lionel had offered her. And she'd failed them all, leaving Simon, and his father, in the lurch.

Simon was probably fine, she reasoned with herself. He hadn't had a relapse in weeks.

But was she safe? And what had she done to merit this?

Barnaby Tims was his personal secretary, for heaven's sake, a meek, unctuous man, a bit of a ferret, but still. Who'd have thought he had it in him? She thought of the gardens, the dogs, the globe, the shredded dresses, her night in the town stocks.

If Tims had done those things, what had he planned for her? Should she fear for her life, or her person? She wrapped her arms around herself and shuddered. He hadn't actually done anything violent yet.

She could leap to safety. Tims drove the brougham down a shaded lane, into a copse that offered a place to hide. She opened the door, gathering her skirts and her resolve to jump.

But the road whizzed by beneath her. Only a fool would risk life and limb and jump out at this speed.

She sat back. Tims would have to change horses eventually. And she'd be ready. In the dark, she searched the cab for an extra whip, a parasol, a pistol stored to fend off highwaymen. Nothing.

With no money, no defense, and no idea where she was or where Tims was taking her, she laid her head against the leather squabs and plotted her escape, worrying. How was poor little Simon? And what must Lionel think?

* * *

Birdsong, and a pale sun rising, and a fragrant, bony boy's body sprawled across him where he sat. Lionel smiled down on his son's tousled hair. Simon was at peace.

But Lionel was achy, exhausted, and uneasy. He flexed his stiff knee and looked around the room. No Miss Upton, thankfully. No Maddox. No Graeme.

But no Sophie either. She hadn't come. She hadn't sent a note. He didn't know whether to be insulted or alarmed. He thought of the ruined globes, shredded dresses, town stocks.

Alarmed. He was alarmed. His gut clenched. Anything could have happened. Lionel gathered up his sleeping son, tucked him into his cot, and set out to find out what had happened with Sophie, Beane first.

Beane was not yet at his post by the front door, not belowstairs at the servants' breakfast table, not upstairs in the servants' quarters. Lionel ignored his already throbbing knee and hobbled down the stairs to Graeme's chamber, and for the second time in as many days, jostled his heir awake.

Again, one eye squinted open. "Sir?"

"Did you send Beane for Miss Bowerbank last night?"

He sat bolt upright and rubbed his face. "Beane was, er, not available."

"Thomas Beane is paid to be available," Lionel grated.

Graeme gave a crooked smile. "He was, sir, to one of the chambermaids. But I ran into Tims on the stairwell."

"What was he doing up?"

"Couldn't sleep, he said. He was in his nightshirt, nightcap, carrying a warm cup of milk. I told him you needed Miss Bowerbank, and he offered to fetch her himself."

Tims? His dot-every-I, cross-every-T secretary who wrinkled his nose in disgust at the sight of a horse?

"Then he'll bloody well know why she never showed up," Lionel gritted, and headed for Tims's room, Graeme hopping into his pants one leg at a time as he hurried to keep up.

The spare room was cold and empty.

Graeme whistled in disbelief. "You don't suppose Tims is with a chambermaid?"

Lionel snorted. "Only if she looks like a ledger book."

"An accident then? I didn't even know he could drive a carriage."

"If there's been an accident," he said to Graeme, "we'll need more men, our men. Wake James and Marcus and bring them down to the stables. I'll have our horses saddled."

At the front door stood Adolphus Bowerbank, his snow-white hair sticking out in disarray.

"Thank heaven, my lord, you're up," he gasped as if he'd been running.

"Indeed, my good reverend," Lionel said mildly rather than alarm him. "I was just coming to see your daughter."

Bowerbank paled. "But she's not home. She did not come down for breakfast. I hoped she had returned to Wraxham House."

It would not be possible to spare Sophie's father pain. "I sent a carriage to fetch her for Simon, and it has not come back. I take it you saw no accidents along the way?"

"No, none."

A chill ran through Lionel. And a certainty. He didn't know why, but this time he knew who and how and when. "Tims has taken Sophie."

"Taken her, sir?" Graeme exclaimed. "Your secretary? To what end?"

Lionel's blood boiled. He did not know. "To what end was any of the mischief that has plagued us this spring? Tims did not want to be here." But if the man had been behind the worsening mayhem, he could only mean Sophie harm.

Bowerbank's jaw dropped. "Are you saying that Barnaby Tims abducted my Sophia?"

"Yes, apparently."

"Just bring her back. Sophia is my heart, my lord, and if you marry her, you had better give her yours."

It seemed he had, but he couldn't marry her if he couldn't

find her. And alive, or he'd tear Tims limb from limb. But he would shield Sophie's aging father from his fears.

"We have a great deal of work to do, Bowerbank. Tims has a three-hour start on us."

Bowerbank's bony hand reached for Lionel. "My lord, if I may . . ."

"Yes?"

"Your proposal to my daughter, I endorse it wholeheartedly. As best for her, and God willing, best for you."

"I trust this means you will set about obtaining the special license."

"If you will forgive my presumption, my lord, I have had it in hand these last several days."

Lionel swallowed against an upwelling of gratitude. "Thank you, Bowerbank. I'm grateful for your confidence."

Lionel ducked back inside to the gun room, picked up his favorite pistols, and headed out. At the carriage house, he confirmed a missing brougham and ordered his four fittest mounts saddled.

His three sons hit the stable yard at the dead run he'd seen them practice on the playing field.

But it was the edgy zeal of untried troops on the brink of battle that lit their faces. Shifting into his long-ago role as captain of raw recruits, he charged the boys—young *men*, strong, willing, and able—with the task of pounding on every door in town. Someone must have heard a carriage in the middle of the night. Graeme he sent to canvass homes to the less populous south and west, and James and Marcus to the east. He went north himself, vowing murder if Tims had set out for Gretna Green. If he had touched her.

"Be back before the town clock strikes half after five."

Lionel rode in half an hour later, cursing.

"Any word, my lord?" asked Bowerbank, his face lined with worry.

"No clues to the north, Bowerbank. I'm sorry."

And Lionel's knee had seized up after mounting his horse only a couple of times. Wherever they had to go, he couldn't ride there. A cripple would be no use to Sophie.

He ordered his best team hooked up to his racing phaeton. That would give him speed, and transport to bring Sophie home.

Stable boys rolled his sleek black phaeton from its bay. Grooms untangled well-oiled harnesses. His matched grays pawed and whuffled, eager for an early morning outing.

Lionel draped the elegant black-strapped harness on the first horse and buckled its breastplate into place, an ear out for his sons. Graeme galloped in with a face more dire than his worst mopes. "No luck, sir."

"Someone had to have seen something," Lionel growled.

"Not on the roads to Portsmouth or to Brighton. I asked at every house that looked awake, and woke the butcher."

Graeme was helping back the team between the traces when James and Marcus thundered up, faces aglow.

"We found them, Father," James cried, reining in his horse.

Marcus's mount pranced in place. "Miss Gatewood couldn't sleep. She swears she heard a coach after the clock struck one headed up the road to London."

Around them, morning chores had halted, and grooms and stable boys eavesdropped avidly. Lionel turned on them. "You lot, get back to work, and have this place shining when we return." Then he said gently to the snowy-haired gentleman who watched in despair, "Bowerbank, could you kindly stay with Simon and the twins?"

Tears of worry rimmed the reverend's eyes. "What should I tell them, my lord?"

Lionel checked the guns tucked into his breeches. Then he pulled himself into the phaeton's perch, relying on his arms to protect his throbbing knee.

"Tell them their father loves them, and will be back shortly with Miss Bowerbank."

Chapter Twenty-eight

Awake, my Fanny, leave all meaner things,
This morn shall prove what rapture swiving brings . . .
—An Essay on Woman (1763)

Would Barnaby Tims never stop this coach? Sophie worried. Panicking. She hadn't slept in days. She was so stiff and sore that every bump in the road felt as if it broke another bone. And it was dawn, at least two hours on the road, and no sign of rescue.

She fought back tears of fear and frustration. It struck her as the brougham barreled through yet another sleepy village that Lionel might have no idea she was even missing. Tims could have forged that note, and she would not have been the wiser. Lionel would not have been the wiser.

And her poor father must be getting up for breakfast only to find her gone, with no explanation. She couldn't bear to think what anxiety would do to his health.

She drew in a ragged breath. She would not give up. Farm wagons rolled onto the road. Mail coaches would be next. She

324

could signal a passerby for help. If, that is, Tims would slow the coach down enough for anyone to see her.

Suddenly he wheeled the brougham into an ill-kept inn and pulled abruptly to a halt, jouncing her into the seat opposite. Collecting her courage and her wits, Sophie threw open the offside door, jumped to the ground, and made a mad dash for the inn. There wasn't a soul in sight, not even a candle in the window. She could cry for help, but that would warn her captor she'd escaped.

In moments, he knew anyway. She heard footsteps, running up behind her. Just as she reached the safety of the inn, Tims grabbed her shoulders, ripping the worn fabric of her old muslin dress.

"Clever girl, our Miss Bowerbank," he panted, and clamped his wiry arms around her bosom and clutched her body to his tall thin frame.

Heaven help her, she thought, fear erupting in her. And revulsion at the touch of his creepy crawly hands. She closed her eyes and screamed.

"Now you can make this easy, or I will make it hard." Something poked her ribs. She opened her eyes, and he nudged her temple with a pearl-handed pistol.

"Coward," she said, and spat at it.

"A pleasing show of spirit, Miss Bowerbank. Where you are going, it should stand you in good stead," he said. He twisted her arm another notch and hauled her to her feet.

She screamed again in pain and helpless anger. To be so thin, he was awfully strong. To be so deferential, he was awfully mean. The inn's door opened, and a greasy, potbellied chap stuck out his head and raked her with a leering glance.

Hope sank. She saw what the man must see: a dapper gentleman battling a virago, her hair wild and tangled, her bodice ripped, her breasts half spilling out.

"Need help, guv'nor?" the innkeeper asked lazily.

Sophie shoved back at Tims, kicking and striking out with her free arm. Her captor tightened the arm he held, and said, grunting under her blows, "My sister—some bawds—aren't worth—saving."

Then he flung down some coins and turned her toward the brougham. "Just change out my team. And tell any quality that might come looking after her you didn't see a thing. He's the one that ruined her."

"He's lying," she called back. The innkeeper's laughter mocked her protest. Tims marched her across the courtyard and shoved her back inside the brougham, brandishing his pistol.

"Go ahead and murder me, you churl," she said, her arm aching.

"Never fear, my dear. You're worth nothing to us dead. However, you leave me no choice but this," he said. With a strength she hadn't imagined in him, he bound her legs and arms with leather reins and stripped a neckcloth from his throat to bind her mouth.

A crested neckcloth.

Dear God, she'd blamed Lionel's sons. How could she—who prided herself on learning, reason, and good deeds—have leapt to such a mistaken conclusion, she who had seen kindness and tenderness and merriment in all the other boys? James and Marcus had been shy around a stranger, embarrassed they'd been expelled from school, awkward about a woman tutor. Oh, she thought miserably, for all the faith she'd shown them, they were best served if their father kicked her out.

Tims pushed her into the well of the brougham, drew the curtains across the windows, and left her alone. The hostler switched the teams, bumping and rocking the brougham, as Sophie thought frantically in the dark. How could Barnaby Tims have turned abductor? How could she and Lionel not have guessed? How could he have plotted this, and everything that had gone before?

And what had he meant: worth nothing to *us* dead?

Us. He had not worked alone.

326

Whom could he have worked with? She'd crossed off everyone in the household a dozen different times. Not strong enough, not smart enough, too old, too fat. But still, as Celia had said, *Anyone can get away with anything.*

Anyone. Even Celia, Sophie's friend and confidante? Celia, who had recommended herself to be Sophie's chaperone. Ambitious Celia, who'd flirted with Lionel's city friends, and then with Lionel, who'd urged Sophie to leave. Wounded Celia, who'd never forgotten the loss of Ewan Ramsay, many, many years ago. Had she not forgiven too?

Celia and Tims.

Trembling with anger and betrayal, Sophie scrunched and twisted her battered body, but her hands couldn't reach the bonds that bit into her ankles. She was hungry and cold and exhausted, and she hurt so much she could barely see.

How much had Celia known about the various acts of vandalism? Could she have destroyed her mother's topiary and shredded her own dresses?

The first innkeeper Lionel and his sons talked to had not seen a brougham since yesterday morning, but he would be happy to change out Lionel's team.

No, they would soldier on with the grays. Racing fit, his pair could trot all day with a few breathers, and easily overtake the team his secretary had stolen and any livery hacks he switched to.

Lionel's sons mustered at his side, strong, confident, and able, his own private company of the keenest recruits who'd ever served with him. They followed him, dead set on catching Tims and rescuing their Miss Bowerbank.

It warmed his insides and gave him heart.

"Are you sure we're on the right road, Papa?"

No, he wasn't sure, for local gigs and wagons were already up and about, erasing any trail the brougham might have left. But it made sense that Tims would go to London, the city he knew best. It was large enough to get lost in, large enough to . . .

God help them. To dispose of Sophie in any manner whatsoever.

Lionel popped his whip over his team's heads, praying that everything he'd learned of racing in his wasted life would converge at his fingertips and speak to his best team. They'd had a breather at the inn. They could race to the next one.

The second inn was so ramshackle he was tempted to pass it by. But *Westfalls don't give up*, his sons had reminded him. So he pulled in, his sons lined up behind him like Wellington's most valued officers.

A unkempt innkeeper came out and admitted, after Lionel dropped a couple of guineas on the ground, that he'd changed out a team after dawn for a handsome brougham.

"Yes, a thin man was driving, well spoken."

"Passengers?"

"No, he was alone," the man said unconvincingly.

They watered their horses and sped off, Lionel grim with purpose. He'd killed men in his life, but never a man he'd sheltered in his home.

Thank heaven, Tims had not blindfolded her. Dawn's rosy glow had given way to the bright brass of early morning, and the sun's rays slanted through gaps around the curtains. She couldn't see her feet, or her shoes, or the ropes around her ankles, and she couldn't reach them with her hands tied behind her back. But she could gauge the hour.

And she could writhe and wriggle. She struggled for purchase on the slippery leather cushions. With effort she pushed herself upright.

The neckcloth Tims had cinched around her mouth reeked of his sour smell. Scooting over to the door, she hooked it over the door's latch and pulled it down around her neck. For a moment she felt freer, and thought of crying out to the coaches that thundered by. But Lionel's brougham bore the

Wraxham crest. Who would heed a woman's cries coming from a nobleman's coach?

She sobbed in her dark, rocking prison, but she couldn't even wipe her tears.

If Lionel had known, he would have come for her by now. But he hadn't, and she was on her own, desperate and desolate. Her richly appointed prison had only a little lantern on the wall beside a door.

A lantern of brass and glass, high up on the carriage wall.

One shard could set her free.

If only she could position herself to kick it. With her feet bound and hands tied behind her back, she lay on her side and kicked up but couldn't reach it. With effort, she lurched up, standing. She could hit it with her head. The brougham rocked and swayed. She closed her eyes, thankful her hair was thick, and butted at the lantern.

A sharp pain jabbed her scalp, and glass tinkled all around her. Slivers bit her naked shoulders. She drew in a breath and carefully scrabbled her fingers over shards and slivers she could not see. She only needed one cutting edge. A knife of glass. A blade of liberation.

There, that one, gingerly, and she had it. Hands behind her back, she sawed at the rope that bound her wrist, nicked herself, and concentrated harder.

The brougham jolted to a halt.

Baa, baa-ah, baa-ah, baa.

Goodness. The sweet bleating of a hundred sheep, the music of her life at the rectory, rose up all around her. A spring flock of ewes and lambs was crossing the road, and Barnaby Tims was stranded in an ocean of wool. She kept sawing at the rope, and she could hear Tims, cursing the shepherd and his sheep. But Tims was oblivious of her, thinking he'd secured her.

Baa-ah. Baa-ah-ah-ah. The rope fell away, and blood rushed to her fingers. She bent to cut the ropes around her ankles. Saw, saw, fast, fast. And her legs were free, and she was free.

This time, she would make a clean escape. She lifted the merest edge of curtain and peeked out the window. Tims was on the ground, crowded by a slow tide of sheep and arguing with their shepherd. Who shrugged his shoulders and pointed back to more sheep than she could count still pushing through a narrow gate to cross the road.

Baa-ah. Baa. Silently she slipped out through the door on the far side. Calming her breathing, she crouched among fresh white lambs and dingy poky ewes, then crawled toward the verge, away from the brougham, away from Barnaby Tims. Clear of the herd and paces away from him, she stood and ran toward home.

Lionel rounded a curve in the glare of morning sun and saw Sophie running toward him from afar, her rosy dress flying out, her nut-brown hair streaming past her shoulders. Beyond her, an ocean of foamy sheep flowed across the road, surging around Tims and the neat black brougham.

"Sophie!" Lionel called out, and cracked his whip over his team's heads, and galloped them to meet her.

His sons spurted ahead with whoops and cries of triumph, and the shepherd and his dog collected the bleating sheep. The boys reached Sophie before Lionel could, leapt off their mounts, and wrapped her in hugs of safety and celebration.

Lionel blinked back tears of relief and joy and . . . satisfaction. Standing black amidst the surging sheep, Tims flapped his arms and waved a beaver hat, swearing at the shepherd and his uncooperative flock.

Lionel swung down from his phaeton, waded through the phalanx his sons had formed around his bride-to-be, and took her in his arms for a hearty, lingering kiss.

Which she returned, throwing her arms around his neck and melding her body to his.

"Look out!" cried James. "There goes Mr. Tims!"

Tims climbed up onto his driver's seat and tried to whip his horses through the herd.

Graeme watched the progress of the sheep. "The road is clearing, Father."

"Just let us at the bastard," Marcus growled.

"We can take him, Papa," James said.

"No," Sophie cried, horrified. "He's armed."

"Armed," Lionel repeated grimly, and pulled two pistols from under his waistcoat. "James and Marcus, take my team and attend Miss Bowerbank, over behind those trees." He tossed Graeme a pistol. "Son, defend them. And if by any chance Tims makes it past me and comes back here, shoot him."

He swung up on one of the boys' horses and galloped off.

The boys encircled Sophie so she couldn't see, and all she heard were gunshots, each one piercing her heart.

"He can't be hit," cried James.

"Not Papa," Marcus said, but he did not sound convinced.

"Your father is a crack shot," Sophie reassured them.

But long agonizing moments passed before Lionel drove the brougham back to where they stood, the saddled horse tied behind the carriage. Tims slumped beside him, one hand holding a bloody shoulder.

Lionel help him down to face Sophie and his sons, and she could see the gun he held between the man's shoulder blades. His sons gathered round, bristling.

"Hanging's too good for him," said Marcus.

Bitterness stamped Tim's thin features. "I'm not the one that warrants hanging."

Because he had an accomplice inside Wraxham House. Sophie forced herself to face him. "You must mean Miss Upton," she said.

Tims thrust out his chin. "It was her idea, everything. The garden, the butcher—"

"And the marbles and the neckcloths," Lionel bit off. "Was framing my sons your idea, or hers?

Tims's face contorted. "Hers, it was all hers. She said Miss Bowerbank was planning to trap you into marrying her, to take your money, to lower your name. She said I was doing you a service."

Lionel snorted. "Do not delude yourself that you acted on my behalf, Mr. Tims. Miss Upton just found an apple ripe for picking, rotten at the core."

Sophie watched as he bound the man, pushed him inside the carriage, and shut the door. Then Lionel returned to her and said privately with soft wrath, "She was angling for me to marry her, and you were in her way."

"As I had been once before."

"Ah. The man you could have married. She'd set her sights on him too."

But that was not the half of it. Sophie braced herself to confront Lionel with the truth. "It's all my fault, my lord."

"You, least of anyone I know," he said, looping an arm around her waist.

Sophie allowed herself one last sweet moment in Lionel's arms, one last sweet kiss, and pulled away, looking from son to son to son and back to him, awash in love and tenderness for them all, and sorrow.

Because Lionel didn't want to hear the worst.

"What I'm saying is that I brought this on you and your sons by bringing my friend into your home."

"Rubbish, Sophie. I know where you're going with this, and it won't wash," Lionel said. He took a measure of the stubborn angle of her chin, the determined set of her jaw. "I stand by my offer."

"Offer? What offer?" asked Marcus.

"His offer to marry her," Graeme said solemnly. "Time to propose to Miss Bowerbank, Father."

It was past time, but Lionel waved them off and finished the kiss to his own gratification. And, it seemed, to hers. For she was as warm as the girl he'd fallen for, as willing as the woman he wanted, as true as the Sophie he loved with all his heart.

When he finally broke off the kiss, he asked her, so his sons could hear, "Miss Bowerbank. Sophie. Would you do me the great honor of marrying me?"

Clapping ensued before she could answer, and more filial intervention. "Are we going to get a special license, Papa?"

"Does this mean more brothers?"

"Can we be your best man?"

But Sophie was silent, her green eyes guarded.

Graeme cleared his throat. "Ahem, you're supposed to tell her that you love her, sir."

Lionel would tell her. He could tell her. Because he loved her, body and mind, heart and soul.

"No, it isn't necessary." Sophie said, a slight wobble in her chin.

"It is," he insisted, his voice clear and words unwavering. "I love you, Sophie Bowerbank."

"You mean for . . ." Her face flamed before his sons, and she whispered so they could not possibly hear, ". . . sex."

Ah, sex. He managed not to grin with pleasure at the thought. "And for who you are, a wise and smart and brave woman who puts up with us, who has brought us together."

"Bravo, Papa," Marcus cheered. "That should bring her round."

"A ripping good speech, sir," said James.

Graeme added, "You see, Miss Bowerbank, I told you he was in love with you."

Lionel looked daggers at his eldest son. "You told Miss Bowerbank I love her."

Graeme rolled his eyes, undaunted. "You were taking your time about it. Sir."

James and Marcus bumped shoulders of approval.

Lionel's cool gray eyes glittered with determination. And love. "I promise to make up for it, and marry her tomorrow." He glanced at his eldest sons. "Any objections, gentlemen?"

All three gaped. "Would it matter if we had any, sir?" Graeme asked earnestly.

"Yes," Lionel said. "You matter, all of you, the twins and Simon too. All my sons."

Graeme silently canvassed his brothers. They rolled their eyes, but gave awkward nods. Matters had gone altogether too treacly for boys of a certain age to tolerate.

"No objections, sir," Graeme said. "I can't speak for Max and Alex, or for Simon, but they'll approve. I'm sure of it."

Sophie's heart began to soar.

Lionel went on soberly. "I mean no disrespect to your mother's memory. Nor, I'm sure, does Miss Bowerbank. We must be clear on that."

"Yes, Father." Graeme again, speaking for everyone.

"So. Miss Bowerbank," Lionel said, looking tall and noble and quite pleased with himself. He was going to be a very fine father to his sons, and to the children she would surely give him. "There you are. Or rather, here we are. Will you have us? All of us, mind you. There are three more Westfall gentlemen at home."

It was too much to take in. Sophie's throat closed so tight she could not say the words that were on her heart.

That she loved them all.

That she'd loved Lionel all her life.

She hoped the tears trickling down her cheeks spoke for her.

"Ahem," Graeme said, as the silence drew out. "Father."

Lionel scowled.

"It is customary to kneel when proposing."

Sophie found her voice and Lionel's hand and clasped it. It was large and warm, and it steadied her. "Your father has a bad knee, Lord Cordrey, from injuries in the war."

Lionel turned her hand in his and bowed and brushed her knuckles with his mouth. "I have one good knee, love," he said, and knelt before her. "My dear Miss Bowerbank, Sophie, I beseech the honor of your hand in marriage."

"The honor, my lord," she managed, "will be entirely mine."

*   *   *

Lionel Westfall, fourteenth earl of Wraxham, was married to Miss Sophie Bowerbank by her father, the Reverend Adolphus Bowerbank, in St. Philips Chapel the very next morning, attended by Lionel's six sons. The noses of the youngest three were out of joint that they were made to dress up for a boring wedding, after missing out on a thrilling chase.

Other guests included the forgiving Misses Gatewoods and the marquis and marchioness of Rayne. Lionel's horse-mad sister, Julia, was not yet back in the saddle after delivering her third child, but she was hearty enough for a carriage ride. She and Harry arrived with Lionel's two nephews and his brand-new niece in tow.

Julia hoped, she said as she greeted her childhood friend, that Sophie would get right to work supplying the lack of daughters in her brother's family. He'd done a damn fine job on his first six sons, and she had every confidence he'd not lost his touch in bed.

Sophie blushed, for Julia had always been a little earthy.

Squire Upton, though invited, did not attend. He was spiriting his daughter away to Bristol to put her on a ship. His brother's Barbadian plantation would make a sweltering good exile for her for her sins. Barnaby Tims was locked up right and tight in the village jail awaiting trial for kidnapping.

Laframboise, after much blowing about and spouting off objections, prepared a luncheon fit for the Prince of Wales himself.

Everyone, sons and relatives and friends, feasted.

It was afternoon before Lionel and Sophie had a moment to themselves, and the bridegroom proposed they take a walk, his eyes dark with promise and desire.

In his chamber, which was now hers, he helped her change from slippers into serious walking shoes, planting teasing kisses way up past her knees.

"We could stay here, Lionel," she proposed, shivering with desire, and feeling brave and daring.

"We'll come back," he answered, "to this." He showed her

a locked, glass-fronted bookcase filled with the old earl's bawdy books. Lionel's bawdy books. Hers now too. Memories of a particularly racy scene of a wedding night made her face heat.

He kissed her burning cheek. "That's my love. Think about tonight. Let's go."

It was a short walk to the kissing gate, where she learned quickly that her cynical rake had expertise she'd barely begun to tap. Then he reached in a pocket and took out his snuffbox. "Another proposal, my love, for the best is yet to come."

She grimaced, disbelieving.

He grinned down at her bemusement, tawny under the afternoon sun, earnest and young again. He flipped open the enameled box and held it to her nose. She breathed in sweet country aromas of butter and honey and something fragrant—roses, perhaps, and lavender.

He dipped a finger in, touched it to her neck, and slowly kissed it all away. She sighed his name and shivered from the pleasure.

"I can think of other delicious places I would love to kiss," his voice rasped at her ear.

So could she. Think of them. Imagine them. Have them at long last.

"Sophie, love, will you be my bawd?"

"Night and day, my love," she whispered. "Night and day."

Historical Note

It was a silvery March afternoon in the Lake District, a magical rural fairyland so green and damp that moss covers mounds of stones and ferns sprout on every tree limb and all the dry-stack fences. My friend Loraine Fletcher and I were fell-walking around the Rydal Waters near Grasmere, where Wordsworth once lived at Dove Cottage.

Loraine and I crossed a rill and stepped into a round wrought-iron contraption, its four circular bars as large as the hoops beneath a lady's skirt.

"I'm a farm girl," I said, "but this is a new one on me."

"It's a kissing gate," Loraine said, consulting our trekker's map. A kissing gate is a type of stile, not unlike those glass revolving doors in big-city hotels and department stores. A farmer can push through the gate with his hands full and not have to open it or latch it back. But cattle, sheep or even goats can't bend their bodies enough to get through.

"Funny name, though," I said.

Supposedly, our guide book said, an enterprising suitor can trap the object of his affection in it and steal a kiss.

Or *kisses,* I thought. What if a young lord spied a lovely lady there and stole a kiss? Country neighbors, childhood sweethearts, perhaps, of similar mind and different stations ... And Lionel and Sophie's story was born.

Later, on a windy cliff overlooking a bay near Swansea, Carolyn Franklin showed me another version of a kissing gate. It was rectangular and made of wood. Too bad, I told her. In America such gates are prosaically called "walk-throughs."

As my story took shape, I discovered that Sophie was a rector's daughter, well-educated and well-regarded in the village. When the old earl, the hero's father, offered her work cataloguing his library, she had to come across his collection of racy books and drawings. I just knew we hadn't invented erotica in the twentieth century!

I was right. A little research turned up a remarkable new collection, *Eighteenth-Century Erotic Books* (Pickering &

Chatto, 2002, 5 vol.). It reprints dozens of texts dating from 1701 to 1791 and shows the variety of erotic materials Sophie might have found in the Wraxham House library. There were philosophical tracts, novellas, dialogues, and poetry, some of it quite good, much of it amusing, some shockingly explicit, some tame and almost wistful. A catalogue of Covent-Garden ladies describes dozens of bawds, their prices, and scandalous predilections.

But Sophie and I, and of course you, gentle reader, shun the low and vulgar tracts and indulge ourselves in the choicest clever, steamy extracts describing the delicious varieties of love between a lord and his lady.

Fiona Carr
April 2004